FIDDLER'S GREEN

OR

A Wedding, a Ball,
and
the Singular Adventure
of
Sundry Moss

#

##

 OR

A Wedding, a Ball,
and
the Singular Adventure
of
Sundry Moss

VAN REID

VIKING

VIKING
Published by the Penguin Group
Penguin Group (USA) Inc., 375 Hudson Street, New York, New York 10014, U.S.A.
Penguin Books Ltd, 80 Strand, London WC2R 0RL, England
Penguin Books Australia Ltd, 250 Camberwell Road, Camberwell, Victoria 3124, Australia
Penguin Books Canada Ltd, 10 Alcorn Avenue, Toronto, Ontario, Canada M4V 3B2
Penguin Books India (P) Ltd, 11 Community Centre, Panchsheel Park,
New Delhi – 110 017, India
Penguin Books (N.Z.) Ltd, Cnr Rosedale and Airborne Roads, Albany, Auckland, New Zealand
Penguin Books (South Africa) (Pty) Ltd, 24 Sturdee Avenue,
Rosebank, Johannesburg 2196, South Africa

Penguin Books Ltd, Registered Offices: 80 Strand, London WC2R 0RL, England

First published in 2004 by Viking Penguin, a member of Penguin Group (USA) Inc.

1   3   5   7   9   10   8   6   4   2

Copyright © Van Reid, 2004
All rights reserved

Map by James Sinclair

LIBRARY OF CONGRESS CATALOGING IN PUBLICATION DATA
Reid, Van.
Fiddler's green, or, A wedding, a ball, and the singular adventures of Sundry Moss / Van Reid.
p.   cm.
ISBN 0-670-03320-0 (alk. paper)
1. Moosepath League (Imaginary organization)—Fiction.   2. Men—Societies and clubs—
Fiction.   3. Portland (Maine)—Fiction.   I. Title: Fiddler's green.   II. Title: Wedding, a ball,
and the singular adventures of Sundry Moss.   III. Title.
PS3568.E47697F53   2004
813'.54—dc22   2003066557

This book is printed on acid-free paper. ∞

Printed in the United States of America
Designed by Nancy Resnick

To Maggie, Hunter, and Mary.

Contents

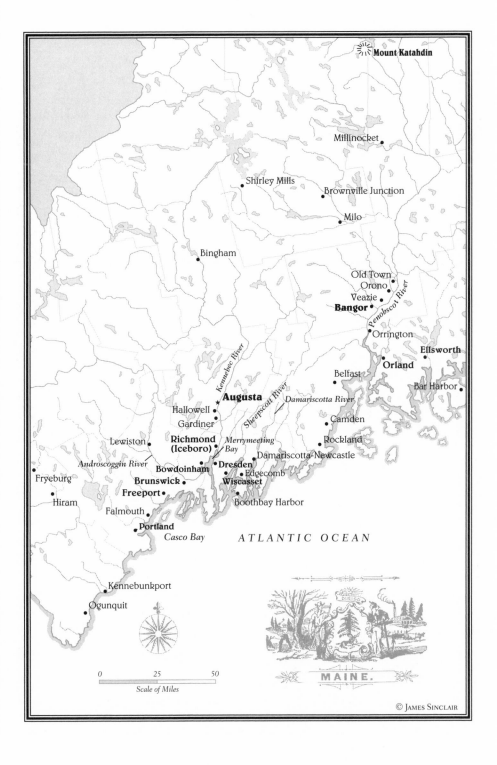

Mount Katahdin

Millinocket

Shirley Mills

Brownville Junction

Milo

Bingham

Old Town
Orono
Veazie
Bangor · *Penobscot River*

Orrington

Ellsworth

Orland

Belfast

Bar Harbor

Kennebec River

★ **Augusta**

Hallowell
Gardiner

Sheepscot River

Damariscotta River

Camden

Rockland

Lewiston

**Richmond
(Iceboro)**

*Merrymeeting
Bay*

Damariscotta-Newcastle

Androscoggin River

Bowdoinham

Dresden

Edgecomb

Brunswick

Wiscasset

Fryeburg

Freeport

Boothbay Harbor

Hiram

Falmouth

Portland

Casco Bay

ATLANTIC OCEAN

Kennebunkport

Ogunquit

DIRIGO

MAINE.

0   25   50
Scale of Miles

© James Sinclair

OR

A Wedding, a Ball,
and
the Singular Adventure
of
Sundry Moss

from the *Portland Daily Advertiser*
(Portland, Maine)
June 2, 1897

A QUESTION OF GENDER
NOT GRAMMATICAL!

Every month there seems to be a new inn or restaurant or combination thereof opening within city limits, and we are often
amused by the extremities to which proprietors will go for the
sake of drawing custom to their doors. Good food and a soft bed are
not the end of it; music and games and even the promise of intrigue
seem to wheedle the curiosity as much as the aroma of hearty cook-
ing apprehends the nose.

It is unexpected, then, when a tavern shuns unasked-for attention, which is exactly the case as of late with one such business
hard by the waterfront. The owners are closemouthed about an interesting matter that took place there on Saturday, despite which,
people have been dropping by, in hope of seeing the child who exchanged genders during the course of a single bath.

We are told that for months the child—a scrawny little waif, a
boy, whose parentage is either missing or suspect—has regularly
appeared at the tavern's back door and that the lady of the house,
just as regularly, took pity on the hungry face and fed it, never actually allowing the creature into her clean kitchen.

After involvement with a recent exploit of Portland's own
Moosepath League, reported in this journal last week, it was decided that the child should be taken in by the tavern owners, but
that he should first receive a good scrubbing, as this detail had
been avoided for six years or so—that is, the child's entire life.

What was the surprise of our Mrs. Taverner—whose real name we will not reveal—when she stripped off the little boy's garments and found a little girl hiding beneath! No one, including the proprietress—who has six children herself and is not easily fooled—had suspected that they were feeding a lass and not a lad, and even the child herself seemed unsure about it all. An explanation for the deception has not been entirely propounded, and much fanciful conjecture has been rife upon the street, though the tavern family discourages the same under their own roof.

We have visited the house ourselves, but the owners are keen to keep the business quiet, and we were impressed that the child's welfare (not to say, state of mind) would not benefit by further publicity and speculation, so the name of the business or its people will not be learned in this article.

It seemed too interesting, however, to let go altogether, and we put it before our readers, wondering if someone out there is privy to a proper explanation and promising that we will apprise the same with any forthcoming whys or wherefores.

from *Disguise, Dual Identity,*
and the Moosepath League
A Monograph
by Basil Penwall (1947)

There is no mention about the disclosure of Mailon/Melanie Ring's true gender in the private journals of the Moosepath League's charter members, and one writer, at least, has tried to make from this fact a case for Victorian prudishness. We are talking, however, about a six-year-old girl who had been directed by her father to "be a boy" since before she could remember, and there is, besides, evidence that Ephram, Eagleton, and Thump were simply never informed or that, having been informed, they either misconstrued the details or thought them immaterial. It is well to understand that what may seem prudery in our modern times was often simple *prudence,* a respect for privacy, and the sense that other people's affairs were not necessarily suitable for even the pages of a personal diary.

Years later Eagleton would write about Emma Craft, who traveled with the charter members for three days before her disguise as a young man was found out—by another party. (Several compilers have made note of how often events early and late in the league's history reflected one another, though those events more often than not came to very different ends.)

But for our present discussion it is enough to presume that among the members of the Moosepath League, Sundry Moss was probably the sole possessor of this knowledge concerning the "former Mailon Ring." At the time of the Dutten Pond incident, Ephram, Eagleton, and Thump still thought of Melanie Ring as the skinny little boy who had aided their escape from Danforth Street at the very beginning of their search for Mrs. Roberto. As for Mr. Moss, he would be heard to say (years later) that Melanie was "more niggle than inches," meaning, it has been supposed, that the room she occupied in his own heart and conscience was greater than her size might seem to warrant to the world at large.

PROLOGUE
THE DARK ROOM
June 3, 1897

ell, God bless the man!" said Mabel Spark when she heard that Mister Tobias Walton was to be married the next day. She had never met the chairman of the Moosepath League, but by his association with Messrs. Ephram, Eagleton, and Thump, she was sure she had every reason to think well of him. Standing at her kitchen counter in the back of the Faithful Mermaid (a respectable, if not entirely law-abiding, tavern on Brackett Street), she did not alter her rhythmic rolling of pie dough but cast a pleasant smile at the bearer of this news—Mister Walton's self-styled *gentleman's gentleman*, Sundry Moss.

"Hmmm!" said her husband, Thaddeus, who at that moment realized he had buttoned his shirt wrong. He lingered by the door to the tavern room, peering down at his substantial anterior.

"Your shirt's buttoned wrong, Thaddeus," said Mabel.

"Well, it is," he agreed. He couldn't see the better part of his buttons with that immense beard in the way, so he was left to pull out his shirttail to understand how he'd erred.

"And he can never get his undershirt on right side to," she informed their guest.

"Mom!" said their middle daughter, Annabelle, who was pouring Sundry a mug of coffee.

Their guest was not to be daunted by any reference to undershirts, however. "I had a great uncle," he informed them, "who rode his horse backward two and half miles on a bet."

Mabel laughed. She had plied him with a piece of apple pie and a slab of rat cheese, and he sat at the family table, offering this reminiscence between forkfuls.

"This is good pie!" said Sundry.

"It's the last of the apples from the cellar," she said. "But there's too much nutmeg."

"No, no," Thaddeus disagreed. "Never too much nutmeg."

Sundry thought about it. Long and lanky, with a square jaw and almost handsome features, he looked like a man—if still a young man (twenty-four, to be exact)—who knew a good piece of pie when he tasted it. The afternoon sun shone through the window over the dry sink and warmed his back, and he sat at the trencher as if he'd eaten there half his life, though he had visited the Faithful Mermaid only once before. He tasted the pie again. "I might have to have another piece before I can decide," he said with comic gravity, and it was clear from Mabel's smile that she would happily serve it to him.

"Was the horse backward, or your great-uncle?" wondered Annabelle, who was a bright girl of sixteen.

This question gave Sundry pause. "I'm not sure," he said. "I never thought to ask."

"Your Mister Walton and his lady must have wonderful plans for tomorrow," said Mabel. She was working the dough pretty hard, but there was a faraway look on her face. She had fond memories of her and Thaddeus's wedding, simple though it was.

"Not at all," said Sundry Moss. "They just announced it yesterday."

"Good heavens!" said Mabel.

"We were hoping you might be able to cook for the reception."

"Good heavens!" said the woman again.

"The Shipswood Restaurant is hosting the rehearsal dinner tonight," explained Sundry, "but they didn't think they could help out at the house tomorrow on such short notice."

Mabel exchanged looks with her husband. She had not gotten past the precipitate nature of the approaching nuptials. There was, in her experience, only one reason to rush a wedding, but she had understood that both groom and bride, in this instance, were well into their middle age. Thaddeus, too, seemed to have lost interest in his buttons.

Sundry knew what they were thinking. "There *is* a kid on the way," he offered, and they could not guess how wryly he spoke.

"Oh!" said Mrs. Spark. She glanced at Annabelle, who was old enough to understand this line of thought and young enough for Mabel to shoo from the room. Annabelle stood in the middle of the kitchen with Mr. Moss's coffee, looking as surprised as her mother.

"God bless the man, indeed," said Thaddeus quietly. He had met the portly, balding, and bespectacled Mister Walton and now thought him more enterprising than he would have credited.

The door to the tavern swung open, and Davey Spark tromped in with an armful of dishes. He paused long enough to take stock of people's faces; his father's was hard to read through that profusion of beard, but Annabelle's expression told her brother that there was something up.

"He's seven, I think," said Sundry.

"Seven?" said Mabel.

"The boy," Sundry explained.

"Seven?" said Thaddeus. *That* seemed like shutting the barn door after the horse was out.

"His sister's son." Sundry nodded seriously and did not let on that he understood where he had been leading them.

"Good heavens!" said Mabel a third time—though with a laugh in her voice. Her frown was replaced by the sort of look she employed when she caught her children at some minor sin. "Seven, indeed!" She blew a sigh of relief, but she might have swatted Sundry if he'd been any closer.

Thaddeus chuckled. Annabelle set the cup of coffee before their guest and rolled her eyes, which made Sundry smile.

He took a sip. "Thank you. The boy's mother sent him on his own from Africa. Mister Walton is supposed to meet him at Halifax, and he and Miss McCannon thought it well to make a family out of it."

"Don't we have some trade out there?" asked Mabel of her oldest son.

"In Halifax?" asked Davey.

"In the tavern."

Davey clattered the dishes into the dry sink at the back of the room and hurried back through the tavern-room door.

"We just birthed a half-grown child ourselves," said Thaddeus.

"Thaddeus!" said Mabel.

"I guess he knows about it."

"You did tell me," said Sundry.

"Might as *well* have been a birth," added the bearded fellow. "There was that much question as to what it'd be, in the end."

"Here she comes, by the sound," said Mabel, which was as much as saying, "Hush, now." Sundry did look interested. Mabel turned, her arms covered with flour, and watched two young children, both dressed as boys, charge in through the back door. "Wipe your feet!" said Mabel.

"We saw Mrs. Roberto!" said the taller child.

"Timothy, wipe your feet!"

"Pull it up, chief," said Thaddeus.

Sundry leaned back from his half-demolished pie to consider these kids. Tim was a wiry, yellow-haired seven-year-old with humor and awareness stamped all over him. Melanie Ring, who was, until recently, known as Mailon and thought a lad, was smaller and slightly darker, with pale blue eyes, and carried herself with a degree of gravity that seemed altogether out of step with the Spark household. No one quite grasped how much *she* grasped the discrepancy between the facts and the façade of her gender. Asked if she understood that she was a girl, she had said, "A little."

It was her father who had instigated the pretense, telling her that boys were not "hard put like girls." Burne Ring was a creature of the night and the bottle, and knowing that he would be of little use to her, he had put her in boy's clothes, told her to be a boy, and left her to her own devices. Even before the truth was generally discovered, the Sparks had decided to take the child in as one of their own, if her father would allow it. In the meantime, Thaddeus had decreed (against his wife's objections) that too much change all at once was unwarranted and that Melanie Ring should continue to dress as a boy until they had time to get used to the idea that she was not one.

"Now, what have you pair been up to?" asked Thaddeus indulgently, while the boy and the girl scraped their shoes at the threshold.

"We saw Mrs. Roberto!" said Timothy again.

"She's *some* pretty," said Melanie, with great feeling.

Tim might not have admitted as much himself, but he voiced no objection.

"Say hello to Mr. Moss," said Mabel.

"Are you in the Moosepath League?" asked Tim, who had seen Sundry with a member of the club the day before.

Sundry scratched his head, as if he weren't sure, but then nodded.

"How many are coming?" asked Mabel.

Sundry was up to this change in topic. "Oh, I'd say ten or twelve."

"Well, I'm making pies," she said, which may have meant she was too busy or that she was in the business and might as well make some more.

"Where did you see her?" Annabelle was asking Tim.

"Has Melanie spoken to her father yet?" said Thaddeus, and all other conversation came to a halt. He had forgotten that his shirt was half undone, its tails pulled out over his belt. "Have you spoken to your dad?" he asked the little girl.

Melanie seemed unsure.

"Have you told him that we'd like to take you in, dear?" said Mabel.

"He wasn't there yesterday," said Melanie.

"Where's that?" asked Thaddeus. The kid had been closemouthed about her father's whereabouts, and he half expected the man had run off.

"Down where he stays," said the child.

"She shouldn't be sent on her own," said Mabel.

Thaddeus nodded. "Why don't you take me there, fellow? I mean . . . why don't you take me there?"

"I'm not supposed to tell anyone," said the little girl.

"You wouldn't be telling me, you'd be *taking* me," said the broad and broad-bearded proprietor of the Faithful Mermaid.

Melanie was bright enough to understand what difference there was between *telling* and *taking* but might also have been uncertain enough about speaking to her father by herself to waver at the thought of having company on the errand.

"Let's do that," said Thaddeus as if she had already acquiesced.

The girl's expression revealed nothing. After a moment she said simply, "It's dark."

Thaddeus's brow furrowed. "We'll take a lamp."

"Shall I go with you?" volunteered Sundry Moss.

The gathered family considered the offer *and* its source carefully.

"*I'll* go!" said Tim.

"No, you won't," said his mother.

Thaddeus wondered where they *were* going. He liked this fellow Sundry Moss and was prepared to think highly of him. Moreover, any association with the Moosepath League was a mark of favor in the eyes of the Spark family; the charter members—Mr. Ephram, Mr. Eagleton, and Mr. Thump—had puzzled everyone at the tavern, but one could not fault their sincerity of purpose. Most important, Thaddeus didn't know *where* the little girl would lead them. "If you like," he said to Sundry. "Thanks."

Draped in his chair, arms folded and legs crossed at the ankles, Sundry looked as if he had just offered to go get the mail—sometime next week.

"Dark, you say?" said Thaddeus to the little girl.

"Oh, it will be."

There was a storm lantern by the back door, and Thaddeus shook it to judge how much oil was in it. Mabel wasn't very sure about this mission. There was no telling *what* hole Burne Ring, a notorious dipsomaniac, might have crawled into. "I want to know where you're going," she said.

Melanie's mouth formed a surprised O.

"She's not supposed to tell us," said Thaddeus.

Mabel chewed on this for a moment, then said, "You be careful. Tuck in your shirt and button up."

Thaddeus grunted and set down the lamp to tend to his apparel. When he began to fumble the buttons with his thick fingers, his daughter took over, and he lifted his chin so that she could reach under his great beard.

"It's no wonder you can't button your shirt right," said Annabelle. "You won't even look at what you're doing."

Thaddeus seemed amused. "I can't put my undershirt on right, either."

Mabel turned to Sundry Moss, who was standing, now, looking as ready as anyone could be. "Thank you," she said quietly, but he only pulled a bemused expression and shrugged. "What do you think he'll say?" she asked Melanie.

The little girl's eyes widened. "I don't know," she replied. "I haven't spoke with him for a while."

Mabel brushed the hair from Melanie's eyes. With her other hand, she snatched at Tim's collar. "You stay here!"

"Mommy!"

Mabel pulled the boy closer to her and said, "You be careful!" to her husband again.

"We're not going off to sea!" was all Thaddeus said as he disappeared through the back door. It was hard to imagine he could meet any danger, walking out into such a shining afternoon.

Sundry Moss put on his hat, gave a nod over his shoulder, and followed.

"I'll watch where they step," said Melanie.

When they were gone, Mabel said to Annabelle, "Go get Davey. I want him to follow them so that someone knows where they've gone."

Making their way down the busy sidewalks, Thaddeus and Sundry were surprised how quickly Melanie stopped, pointed, and said, "Over there."

Thaddeus looked across the street at the dilapidated building as if he'd never seen it before. The day was bright, and only a single billowed cloud was visible scudding east, but the decaying pile before them appeared to suffer under a lowering sky, as if shadowed by an accretion of soot and steam from the neighboring chimneys and stacks. More social distance than mileage lay between the Faithful Mermaid and Pearce Eddy's flophouse.

"You should have told us he was staying there," said Thaddeus to the little girl as they crossed the street. He wondered why he had been required to carry a lamp.

"Daylight not enough for you, Thad?" shouted some wag at the corner.

"Yes, it is, to be truthful," Thaddeus called back. "It's some of the people you meet that aren't so bright." This raised a laugh.

"He's not staying there anymore," said Melanie, scooting ahead of an oncoming wagon. "I'll show you." She led them by the dark doors to the cobbled alley alongside the flophouse. Thaddeus and Sundry hurried after. Halfway down the old way she paused to point out the tin lid of an old coal chute. "That's where I come up," she informed them.

"Come up?" said Thaddeus. "You mean, from where you and your dad stay?"

"It's down there," she said. "It was awfully cold this spring, but Dad says it'll be nice when the summer gets hot."

"Like a room at the Grand," said Thaddeus, but kindly. Melanie and her father were actually living *under* a flophouse, which seemed to him something symbolic and a picture of how far a body could fall.

Sundry was struck by the cool and dark of the alley. He gazed up at the sky, which had been pinched by the confines of the street. The air had lost its soft summer breath, and the sun its power to light the corners and hollows. Even the clamor of the busy street behind them had surrendered its vitality, stretching to a thin dissonance. A breeze met them from off the harbor and beyond the alley they could see the crowded precincts of Sturdivant's Wharf, where a great five-masted schooner, obstructing light from off the water, thrust its prow toward them—a giant peering into a cave.

When they emerged from the lower end of the alley, the harbor was more apparent and the bright fittings of a brig, anchored further out, seemed to wink at them. They were under the massive prow of the schooner when Melanie said with all due seriousness, "I didn't think you wanted to use the chute."

Thaddeus patted her head and said, "How does your father get there?"

She pointed at a crude ladder that dropped down the side of the wharf. Sundry peered over the edge and considered how cold the harbor water must be.

"Down there?" said Thaddeus.

"That's where Daddy goes."

The ladder was punky and weather-worn. Thaddeus gave it an experimental kick with the toe of his boot, and pieces of it squelched off. Sundry saw that a sailor on the deck of the schooner was gazing over the rail to watch them, and he gave the man a salute.

"Who would clamber down anything like that?" said Thaddeus.

"That's where Daddy goes," said the little girl. "I do sometimes."

"It's a way down," said Sundry. "It just may be *quicker* than a person intended."

"And a little farther," added Thaddeus.

"What is this place?" asked Sundry, indicating the building behind them.

"A flophouse," informed Thaddeus.

He might have said more, but Melanie Ring said, "We stayed there once." It might have been the City Hotel, from the look on her face.

"Let's take a look," said Sundry. From what he understood about the term *flophouse* he didn't know which would prove less pleasant—a plummet into the cold harbor or a tour of the city's dregs and near dregs.

With cracked pilasters ranked at either side of the wide front door, paintless walls and windows blinded with yellowed sailcloth, the looming building gave little evidence that it had once been the home of a prosperous business. There was only the faded sign of the Chalmers and Holde Shipping Firm still hanging beneath the cornice, which itself was chipped and splitting with exposure to the wind and damp air of the waterfront.

Sundry was a man of the countryside and a farmer by birth and upbringing. He was not unfamiliar with certain earthy verities of life, having mucked out stalls and held vigil with his parents over calvings and foalings. But farmers (or good farmers) take pride in the living quarters of their stock, and even in winter the barn doors are often thrown open to let in the sun and the air.

He had been, in recent months, exposed to some of the city's less reputable denizens—simply walking the streets, one saw the fierce and the destitute as well as the laboring and the prosperous—but he had never walked where the fierce and the destitute were the rule, though even in such a place it could never be said that they *ruled*.

Something more than a smell met them like a physical thing when they opened the door. A cacophony of snores and groans and coughing reached out, low and difficult to parse into separate elements. Thaddeus had had occasion to enter such a place in his lifetime, searching for a wandering relative or a delinquent customer, and he had experience enough to steel himself. Melanie walked in ahead of them as if there were nothing to separate the dank interior from broad daylight. But Sundry, who flinched at little, hesitated at the threshold like a suspicious cat. Suddenly the climb down the ladder at the edge of the wharf seemed less worrisome.

The light of day hardly entered with them, and when the door swung shut, there was only the occasional gas lamp, barely flickering, to give off a weak halo and mark the way. Sundry pressed a sleeve to his nose and mouth, hoping to stifle the fetor of unwashed bodies and stale liquor. A small way down the front hall was an old table with a leg at three corners and a stick propping up the fourth. Here sat a half-drowsing troll, grizzled and lank-haired, who *snapped to* at their approach and regarded them with instant suspicion.

"Where's Pearce?" asked Thaddeus.

The man squinted from Thaddeus to Sundry to Melanie and back to Thaddeus. "What time is it?" he returned, flashing toothless gums.

"Well, it must be three o'clock."

"He wouldn't be about," said the troll, hunched and gnarled over the table, himself like a piece of ancient furniture.

"We need to get down in your cellar," said Thaddeus straightforwardly.

"You can't do that," said the old man.

"Well, we need to."

"The stairs mightn't hold you, I daresay. Even Pearce won't go there. He says Darvey Bones is down there." The old man offered a grin and laughed. "It's haunted for sure, wouldn't you guess?" He looked down at his own knobby hands and muttered. "Those who were drowned over the years don't wander too far." There was an active quality to his use of the verb *drowned* in this sentence that caused a shiver. "I've heard them, even lately." The man looked up, delighted with this news.

"Where's the door?"

"To the cellar? You can't go there," said the old man, but he rose from his seat, which was in itself surprising, and hunchbacked and shuffling, led them past dark and doorless rooms. Sundry peered into one of these as they passed and was startled to see that ropes were draped four feet or so from the floor and that several men appeared to be sprawled on these— hanging by their armpits but sleeping. Others occupied the floor or something like great hammocks.

The halls grew dimmer as they went. The muddle of sound and the smells thickened about them, and Sundry was glad when the cellar door was forced open and something of the harbor air wafted up to mingle with the unhealthy atmosphere of the flophouse. "You can't go down there," said the old man again, even as the taverner tried the top steps.

"I'm not sure this is much refinement above the ladder," said Thaddeus.

Sundry thought he'd rather have chanced falling into the harbor than come through this place, but here they were.

"It doesn't creak too much," said Thaddeus, though the stair let out a painful groan when he put his entire weight on it.

Sundry was about to tell the little girl to stay where she was, but then he looked at the old man, who grinned with his toothless gums and repeated happily, "You can't go down there."

"Step lightly," said Sundry.

The ancient and long-unused coal room beneath Pearce Eddy's flophouse—toward the western end of the Portland waterfront—was not the darkest place Burne Ring had ever inhabited. That distinction must be reserved for his own self. Sometimes it seemed to him that wherever he went, he took with him a room even larger and darker than this black-walled chamber that shivered day and night with the footfalls and snores of the business above. In that larger, darker room Burne's head echoed with his own voice and the voices of others (if they really were voices) like sounds heard from across a vast floor. He rarely emerged from the coal room by day, and he never emerged, these days, from that darker place. The level of light in his memory had dimmed so that even his dreams were shadow upon shadow.

By the summer of 1897 Burne Ring was either drinking or starving for drink. To say that he had become a creature of the dark is not to suggest that he was wicked but only that flesh is weak. He sinned and repented and sinned again in rapid succession—sometimes in a matter of minutes. It was not a hard heart, besides, that brought him to these straits, but a broken one—a broken heart and the weakness flesh is heir to.

But weak flesh might amount to the same thing as wickedness. Burne's ability to settle his cravings by any legal means had greatly diminished; in fact, he hardly had the wits to sweep a doorstep these days, but he could filch from a backyard or pilfer from an unwary pocket without much planning. He stole and repented and stole again. He suffered for what he was compelled to do, and his suffering did not strengthen or enlarge him. What had not killed him made him weaker still.

Burne Ring and his lone child lived, after a fashion, in that coal black, coal-blackened room deep in the cellars of the old building. The room itself was only feet away from the edge of high tide, and when the wind came up at the full of the moon, the harbor was just another blind creature sniffing at the crumbling threshold. The man and the child were ghosts, hardly more than rumors along the waterfront, and if anyone knew or even suspected where they were living, nothing was ever said to Pearce Eddy, who ran the flophouse above them. Pearce thought the cellar haunted and stayed away.

There were piles of rags in one corner of the old coal room and planks that Burne had dragged from beneath the wharf and upon which they slept in the continual dark. Mailon could sense the dawn before the smallest hint of light (and never more than the smallest hint) found its way into the room. The child came and went without question. Sometimes *he* came back with food, and when he did, Burne judged his little son by his own downfall. In brief lucid moments when he could consider how that food must have been gained, a great anger offered to rise from within. What had Mailon done to come by food, or what had someone else done? But the thought and the anger were soon lost in the great black room that Burne inhabited. He could not stay angry at an echo. Sometimes he even ate what his little boy brought him.

Stretched in the corner of the room that once had held the fuel to feed the stoves and fireplaces of the Chalmers and Holde Shipping Firm before that company's decline and the present decline of the building itself into the waterfront silt, Burne Ring recalled the face of his son, but he had more or less forgotten his daughter, and it took him long, arduous moments to climb from his forgetfulness in the strange, dark hour when she returned.

Time grew and retracted without logic, and when he thought that he hadn't seen his son for a long while, he also knew that he could not trust his sense of hours passed. Something might have happened to Mailon, but how was the father to know? Then again, Mailon might have been at his side moments ago, those moments simply expanded into a day or a week.

"Mailon," he said into one blind room or another. In the last hour or day (or week, perhaps) a physical infirmity had overruled his need for drink, and he had drifted during some span of time from drink to *delirium tremens* without moving from his plank. "Mailon," he said.

"Daddy," came the child's voice as from across an immense space.

"Mailon."

"Daddy," came the faraway voice that was yet at his elbow.

He sensed the child beside him. "Mailon."

"I'm not Mailon, Daddy."

"Where's Mailon?"

"I'm here, but I'm not Mailon, Daddy."

"Where's my boy?"

"I'm here, Daddy, but I'm not a boy."

A cool breath found its way among the pilings of Sturdivant's Wharf to stir the air of the coal room, and Burne was shivering. It must have been day, for something like light sent gray feelers into the room so that he could almost see his child's face when it hovered above him.

"Daddy."

"Mailon."

"No, Daddy. I'm Melanie."

Burne fought with this notion. "How could you be?" he said. "I told you no. I told you, you're Mailon. Boys aren't so hard put as girls. I told you that. What if something happened to me?"

There was a silence.

"Mailon," Burne breathed out. He shivered. "Melanie," he breathed in. He hardly knew he had said it.

"Something did happen to you, Daddy."

Burne could not be sure in which dark room this was said. "Who told you?" he demanded as he struggled up on one elbow. It was indeed his little daughter beside him. It was his daughter standing yards away. Her hand was on his arm, but she was small and distant. He did not know how the sun had reached the blindness of the coal room. Her face was illumined in an orange light, and then the light shifted and he could see his son standing beside him. It was a boy—in boy's clothes.

"Daddy?"

"Who told you?" he said, and he struggled up on one elbow. He thought he had already done this and gaped down at the planks beneath him.

"You fell asleep, Daddy."

"It's cold," he said, but it was not the cold that made him shiver. He had had a terrible vision, just days, or perhaps only hours ago, of having killed his only child, and it occurred to him that this was but a ghost come to take him away. And then he was sure of it, as he was aware of other phantoms.

"Mr. Ring," said one of these specters—a dark, bearded creature, like something out of old-country ground in his grandmother's tales. "Mr. Ring," said this vision quietly, "you had better come with us."

"I wish there were more light," said a second, taller ghost.

Burne's daughter stood beside him. Her expression was so precise that he could suddenly accept that she was in the room (though *which* room, he still wasn't sure). She turned to the shorter, bearded phantom and said, "Daddy says not to strike a light in here."

"Hmmm," came the voice of the bearded face. That face turned away and disappeared into the shadows. In the light of a lantern, raised up by an invisible arm, a tendril of coal dust explored the room and, lifted by the incoming breeze, reached for the illumining flame.

There was another grunt.

"It's an old coal room," said the taller vision.

"It's too damp," said the bearded one. He was not worried about fire, but he caught sight of the searching spiral of coal dust and pulled the lantern away, as he might back off from the raised paw of a cat. Some current of air, drawn by the retreating lamp, tugged at the groping cloud, but it appeared to Burne (and perhaps even to the phantoms) as if the dust sought the light and flame of the lantern. "You had better come with us, Mr. Ring," said the bearded figure again, but with the smallest sense of hurry.

"Yes," said Burne. His reward was calling. He understood that now, though these attendants were a good deal less frightening than he had expected. He wondered that they would be worried about a little fire.

Burne struggled up on one elbow. He was used to thinking that he had done this already. "Melanie," he said.

"We'll have to carry him up," said the bearded phantom. "I hope the stairs will take it." He craned his neck and raised the lantern for a look at the ceiling.

Someone said, "Let's go," and the taller ghost simply lifted Burne's emaciated form from the hard, damp planks.

"I don't think you want to take me *up*," said Burne Ring. He didn't want to cause anyone embarrassment. He didn't want to chance his wife's waiting at the gate and seeing him.

"Come on, Daddy."

"Melanie, you can't come."

"Yes, I'm coming, too."

"Not where I'm going, child."

"Oh, yes."

"Hush," came a soft voice, and Burne couldn't say to whom it was speaking.

BOOK ONE
WEDDING AND DEPARTURE
June 4–5, 1897

I. The Members Were Early
(June 4, 1897)

Who knew whence Spruce Street had sprung? Several lanes up from the waterfront, it must once have commanded a view of Portland Harbor. Perhaps in the days of King Philip's War a cow path ran there, or even the rutted trail to a tiny cabin, from which a settler's family would have fled the Abenaki raids that razed the seaside village with fire and ax. Almost a hundred years later, when the colonies had raised the cry of rebellion (and the vicinity was still known as Falmouth), half a dozen homes along that former cow path might have watched the approach of the British fleet that would shell the town and the landing of the troops that would burn it once again.

And in 1866, on the very day set aside to celebrate the old rebellion, fire would once more blight the eastern view of what was then named Spruce Street, populated with handsome brick and clapboard houses. The Great Portland Blaze, purportedly the result of fireworks, would destroy half the town, but Spruce Street would be spared.

Who knew whence Spruce Street had sprung? Three times fire had visited the peninsula, and much of the perceived history had been swept away by war and the want of memory between generations, so that on the fourth of June, 1897, when the sun rose among a scatter of ambivalent clouds, when squirrels ventured the lawns and birdsong and sea breeze filled the oaks and maples and chestnuts along the old way, it might have seemed to the first solitary walker that it had always been thus, or even that this avenue had risen, persevered, and lingered solely for the purpose of hosting the day's significant event.

That first pedestrian on the heel of dawn was of less than average height for a grown man (which he was) and if he was more than average breadth (and again, yes), he was yet not fat but stout as a yeoman (which he was not). Consummately dressed in black, complete with gloves and top hat, he wore a brown beard that had twice been termed magnificent and that covered most of his face and a good deal of his upper torso. He held one arm against his side as if he were carrying something under it; the hour was too early for the newspaper that would normally occupy that position, but well-worn custom is hard to conquer.

Of three distinct and related figures expected on Spruce Street that day, he had the furthest to come, and it was not expected that he would walk the distance across town, or so in advance; but excitement had stirred him, and a powerful breakfast had fortified him beyond even his usual energies. He marched up to the gate of a Federal-style brick house and for all those energies, he looked uncertain when he stood there. With the phantom newspaper held in the crook of one arm and his free hand beneath his voluminous beard tapping arrhythmically against his chest, he considered the quiet home and the well-tended lawn.

"Hmmm," he said.

He wasn't very sure what he had intended, coming here at such a small hour. He had been roused by anticipation and drawn to this street by the coming event, but he hadn't the slightest notion of what do with himself, now that he was here. He was not even sure about the hour and was pondering this question when the answer began to toll from a nearby steeple.

The bearded man turned to face St. Dominic and the sound of the bell, whereupon he caught sight of a second pedestrian, likewise turned in that direction, who was consulting first one watch and then another and even two more that he pulled in sequence from various pockets about his person.

"Hmmm," said the bearded man again, and if the sound could not have actually reached the second man, something of its sentiment appeared to touch the back of his ear, for he turned and gasped with pleasure and amazement to see the yeomanlike figure upon the sidewalk.

"Thump!" came the second man's voice with more emphasis than volume. (It was, after all, still very early in the morning.) "How very remarkable!" added this fellow, who was of medium height, with black hair and mustaches, who was as well attired as the first man (though in brown), and who appeared also to be carrying something under one arm.

"Ephram!" came the low-registered voice of the first man. They met and shook hands with such enthusiasm that a spectator would hardly have guessed they had parted company not seven hours before.

"What an absolute delight!" continued Matthew Ephram.

"It is good to see you, my friend," said Joseph Thump. "High tide at 1:48."

"It's one minute past five," declared the mustached fellow. "I woke an hour ago and couldn't bear to lie in bed."

"I was the same."

"There seemed nothing for it but breakfast and a walk."

"A jaunt!" agreed Thump. They were still shaking hands.

"Even so!"

"And yet," said Ephram, "despite the excitement of the day, I have walked with a small degree of melancholy that puzzles me."

"I was the same," said Thump.

"Were you, really? I myself was loath to admit."

Thump raised his hands, taking care not dislodge the newspaper that was not under his arm, and gave the slightest sort of shrug.

"It is amazing how often we are got up with the same notions," said Ephram.

"I have often been amazed," Thump harmonized.

Their melancholy had all but vanished, though their uncertainty was redoubled as they approached the gate to the Federal-style brick house and wondered in unison (and aloud) what they might do to occupy themselves. It was not necessary for them to wonder long, for coming from the same direction as had Thump was a third figure, tall and blond and clean-shaven, his tan suit and top hat of recent vintage and his arm cocked in a now-familiar position.

"Eagleton!" said Ephram, and "Eagleton!" agreed Thump.

"Goodness' sakes!" declared the newcomer. "Ephram! Thump!"

The three men strode forth and met with a great deal of handshaking (some between Ephram and Thump again).

"It is extraordinary!" said Matthew Ephram.

"How very like you to anticipate me!" averred Christopher Eagleton.

"Ever in the fore!" declared Joseph Thump.

"Clouds scattering before a southwest wind," said Eagleton, "expected sunny afternoon, though more overcast by evening and possible thundershowers, clearing once again by tomorrow morning."

"High tide at 1:48," announced Thump. "That is, P.M."

"It's twelve minutes past the hour of five," said Ephram.

Now the full charter membership of the Moosepath League found itself before the gates of the Federal-style brick house with no better idea as to its purpose. Truth to tell, they were not, by habit, early risers and the hour was mysterious to them. Was it, perhaps, a little untoward to be up and about while so many people were yet abed? They might have gone back to their respective homes (and back to bed) themselves if they had not had one another's company to bolster their self-possession. But move-ment seemed necessary, and they began to amble, almost without con-scious thought, eastward on Spruce Street.

It was not long before they met with the first businessman of the day, trundling his milk wagon from the direction of Clark Street. They hailed the fellow cautiously, still not sure about the appropriate early-morning greeting, and they watched with fascination as he stopped before one of the handsome houses along Spruce Street to deliver his wares "round the back."

Further along the way they saw a fishmonger's cart rounding the cor-ner. In the distance they caught sight of other pedestrians or wagons trundling the streets. It was interesting to them how many people were out, and they felt less awkward about showing themselves.

"It is really a fine sort of hour," observed Ephram.

"It really is," agreed Eagleton. "Don't you think, Thump?"

Thump had paused when they reached the corner. From this vantage they could look down Clark Street and see the sunlit harbor over the buildings on Commercial Street. "It is quite handsome," said Thump.

"It really is," said Eagleton.

Thump's stomach growled. He was surprised how little his breakfast had done against the novelty of rising so early and the anticipation of the day ahead of them. Perhaps more breakfast was in order and he said so. It was a capital thought, and his friends' admiration was only improved be-cause of it.

And, now that a second breakfast had been decided upon, they had but to find it.

"Expected sunny this afternoon, overcast by evening and possible thundershowers," said Eagleton.

"High tide at 1:48," said Thump.

"It's early, really," said Ephram.

"It really is," said Eagleton.

Thump pointed them down the hill, and trusting his instincts, Ephram and Eagleton followed him.

"Eighteen minutes past the hour of five," said Ephram.

from the *Eastern Argus*
June 5, 1897

MAN ABOUT TOWN

Last night the Shipswood Restaurant on Commercial Street was host to a memorable dinner, celebrating today's wedding of Mister Tobias Walton of Spruce Street and Miss Phileda McCannon of Hallowell. Mister Walton is well known among the restaurant's patrons and, indeed, among the Portland citizenry as the chairman of the Moosepath League, which society has garnered a good deal of ink in the past months for several unusual exploits. The restaurant itself, in the person of Carlton Pliny, the proprietor, sustained the dinner with the help of the club's charter members, Mr. Joseph Thump of India Street, Mr. Christopher Eagleton of Chestnut Street, and Mr. Matthew Ephram of Danforth Street.

The event went off without a hitch, and the fêted couple showed, in their graciousness and jollity, why they are favorites among the Shipswood's employees as well as clientele. Once the largely invited crowd had expended a grand ovation, the happy pair visited briefly with each table before joining their fellows at the place of honor and commencing their meal. The evening was then much like any other night at the restaurant until after dessert was served, whereupon more socializing among the tables was evidenced. . . .

2. Bride and Groom

Phileda McCannon gently rapped at the door to the Nowells' hotel room. "Meer?" she whispered. "Meer? Are you there?" The upper hall of the City Hotel was empty and silent, the light of a promising day brightening the single window. Phileda was dressed a little haphazardly, and her hair was still mostly done up in the paper curls that Miriam had put in the night before. It was the short side of the morning, and the Nowells were not early risers. Nonetheless, when the door opened and Miriam peered into the hall, she wore an indulgent smile.

Parents look like that, thought Phileda, *when they are roused from bed on Christmas morning.* She smiled, too, if ruefully.

"Am I here?" said Miriam. "Did you think I had slipped off in the night?"

"Did you sleep?" asked Phileda as she was let in.

"I'm sorry, but I did."

"I think it very contrary of you, sleeping the night before my wedding."

"I slept the night before my own wedding."

"I know, you've told me, and I think that rests my case."

"Did you sleep?" asked Miriam.

"About that much," said Phileda, expressing the amount between a thumb and forefinger.

Miriam dropped onto the settee with a very unladylike yawn. Her husband, Stuart, came out in his pajamas and smoking jacket, squinting like a mole as he searched for his pipe. They had been more than handsome in their youth and had, by good humor and good fortune, retained the better part of their appearance. He was blond, gracefully turning to gray; she was as dark as ever, her own journey from wasp-waisted youth to a middle age with more figure unhindered by any terrible distress. Until Phileda met Tobias Walton, they were the easiest people had ever known.

Phileda herself was almost forty-two, but many a woman twenty years her junior would do well to stand at a distance from her today. She had lived out her own plain youth with humor and generosity, which attributes had repaid her middle age with slender grace. Brisk activity had retained in her a youthful vigor; a fierce sort of intelligence had only brightened her clear blue eyes. In the sunlight her chestnut hair showed a few strands of gray, but whatever lines the years had drawn upon her face were *lightly* drawn and generally served to point up that humor and generosity. Whenever she smiled, as she would many times that day, anything like age seemed to melt away.

"Do you suppose Toby is up?" she wondered aloud.

"Do you want to go visit him?" asked Miriam. Her husband let out a grunt of discovery and stuck his pipe in his mouth.

"Good morning, Stuart," said Phileda.

"Good morning, my dear," he said. "How splendid to see you." His eyes were closed.

"If I thought that getting married would make *me* look eighteen again, I might try it," said Miriam.

"You *are* married," said her husband when he had thought about this.

"Oh, that," she replied, and with a negligible wave of her hand. "What makes you think *that* would stop me?"

"I'm not sure," said Stuart. "Lost my head." He sat down beside his wife, and they looked very cozy together.

Miriam was still marveling at Phileda. "Should we wire ahead and warn the groom?" she asked Stuart.

He narrowed one eye toward Phileda, who managed to sit herself down in the chair opposite for a moment or two. "She *is* glowing," he said. "I thought it was the light from the window."

In seeming contradiction to her elated state, Phileda had to blink away the tears in her eyes, which predicament would be as common to her to-day as her smiles. "Do you like him?" she asked her friends. It was a question she had asked of no one, and it startled them.

"Like him?" said Miriam.

"Toby?" said Stuart.

"I think he is scandalously good," said the wife.

"He knows how to bid at whist," said the husband. Without any great ceremony, he took a handkerchief from the pocket of his smoking jacket and passed it to Phileda.

She thanked him and dabbed at her eyes without embarrassment. "Do you know what the odd thing is?"

Miriam sat up and leaned forward. "No," she said, taking Phileda's free hand. "What is the odd thing?"

Phileda was usually a person of such even moods, but on this day, after little or no sleep, she felt that she was careering over hill and dale on a fast horse. "Last summer—oh, a week or so before I went to Boothbay, where I first met Toby—it was the end of June and I was walking above my house, thinking I might visit you. But I kept walking along the ridge, and the day was just glorious. I could see the capitol and the ponds off to the west, and the river was beautiful and blue. Everything seemed very simple, and I thought to myself that I was just fine—that *I* was just fine. And not only did I understand that I wouldn't get married, I *decided* that I wouldn't get married." She dabbed at her eyes again and looked down at her shoes.

"That was some decision," said Miriam, not letting go of Phileda's hand.

"It was, wasn't it," said Phileda. She took a large breath and smiled. "He is scandalously good, isn't he."

"He knocked *that* thought out," said Stuart.

Miriam swatted at him, but she was laughing, and Phileda, too.

Phileda stood again. "It's terrible, waking you up at this hour."

"I wouldn't miss it for the world," said Miriam.

"The extra hour—" began Stuart. He looked about the room, as if for the exact time. "Well, the extra four or five hours will do us good."

Miriam swatted him again.

Phileda did not attempt to thank them for being here this morning, or for having been her friends for so many years (and, in Miriam's case, since early childhood), or for easing the loneliness since her parents and sister had died. All her words were in her eyes, but there were too many to get out in any order. She went to the window and looked out over Commercial Street. There was traffic, despite the hour. In the distance she thought she could see a flag run up on the observatory. Phileda leaned close to the glass and turned her head to one side, as if she might see Spruce Street and the Walton homestead and Toby Walton's very window. She took another large breath and said, "I wonder if he's awake."

Sundry Moss opened the door at the bottom of the back stairs and poked his head into the kitchen of the old Walton homestead. It was not a surprise to discover the male principal of the approaching nuptials up and boiling coffee. The portly frame of his friend and employer stood quietly by the stove, his bespectacled gaze abstracted by cogitation. "Good morning, Mister," said Sundry, his deep voice resonant with missing *r*s.

Mister Walton chuckled. It was a greeting with some history between them—in fact, the first Sundry had offered almost a year before. "Good morning," said the grand fellow, his hands folded over his rounded middle, almost in an attitude of prayer. Sundry had the vague sense that he had interrupted the man in more than just the aimless gathering of wool. "It should be a nice day," said Mister Walton.

Sundry stepped into the kitchen. "I don't see how it can miss, though the weather will have to work a little harder." He had glanced out his bedroom window and thought the sky was not as clear as had been predicted by Mr. Eagleton the night before. The pot on the stove was burbling, and the smell of coffee was almost enough to wake a body. Sundry got cups and saucers down from the cupboard.

"I may have made this strong," cautioned Mister Walton as he poured, and "My word!" he added at the first sip. "You could stand your spoon in it!"

"It's not indecisive," agreed Sundry.

The older man considered the dark brew in his cup. "Perhaps it will do me some good," he said. Then, looking up, he wondered aloud, "Who do you think will arrive first?"

"The milkman," said Sundry, and he opened the back door to reveal the very fellow perusing the note that had been left on the stoop the night before.

"Congratulations," said the milkman when the reason for such a large order of butter and cream was revealed.

Mister Walton bowed his head with comic formality.

"I have a cousin who was married on April Fools' Day," said the milkman, who did not often have the opportunity to chat during the appointment of his early-morning rounds.

"Do you?" said the groom-to-be.

"We still don't know who the joke was on."

"Many a serious word is *said* in jest," pronounced Sundry, which made Mister Walton laugh.

"It *was* serious, I want to tell you," said the milkman, but the statement was cryptic without further elucidation. Not offering further news about his family, he went straight off to fetch the required provisions.

The fishmonger, who was used to more discussion (and even debate) with his customers, arrived next, and earlier than usual. The milkman, on his return, transmitted news of the impending nuptials, and the fishmonger explained how he and his wife had been married on the stagecoach somewhere between Newfield and Wells. "We were hightailing it before the matter came to issue with our people and we happened to be riding with a preacher who believed in multiplication under *any* circumstance."

"And did you?" wondered a wry Mister Walton.

"Multiply? Well, we had the ten kids, so you could safely say we did."

"I think so."

"Which town got the marriage certificate?" wondered Sundry.

"We split the difference and called it Shapleigh," said the man. He was not a young fellow—a retired fisherman, perhaps—and the effluvia of his trade hung about him like a fog.

"I've never been there," said Sundry.

"We drove through it once," said the fellow before he left without selling any of the day's catch. Sundry asked him to leave the door open.

The iceman, who next arrived, had an uncle who claimed to have been lured, while sleepwalking, into a proposal of marriage.

"What did he do when he woke up?" asked Sundry.

"It's what he didn't do, I guess, that got him over a barrel."

"Dear me," said Mister Walton. "A breach of promise suit."

"That was the upshot." According to the iceman, his uncle had tried to wangle out of his purportedly somnambulistic proposal. "The judge had met my uncle over the bench and notioned that the old dodger had been drunk."

"Not dissimilar states in some people," said Mister Walton mildly.

"He fined Uncle Luke for disturbing the sanctity of his office and told the woman in question to find a man who knew what he was about when he proposed marriage. My father quite liked it, really."

"Your *mother's* brother," said Sundry.

"You guessed."

3. A Kitchen Full and a Chorus of Two

Something of a procession arrived before the iceman was gone. Sundry caught a glimpse of a head bobbing past the kitchen window, and a moment later Annabelle Spark entered, carrying a linen-covered basket and looking round for a place to put it. Mrs. Spark and Minerva were close behind. The iceman helped Sundry and Mister Walton clear the counters and lift the baskets and hampers of soups and meat pies and pastries from the ladies' collective arms.

The young women went out again, and Mrs. Spark directed the advent of *the cake*, which was yet in a state separate from itself and which she would construct to its ultimate glory on Mister Walton's kitchen table.

"How is Mr. Ring?" inquired Sundry when Mrs. Spark's attention could be caught between commands.

"It's why Thaddeus didn't come," she replied, and her daughters paused in their work as if they didn't know it already. "Get to it," she said, and when they had recommenced their preparations, she turned back to Sundry. "We had to truss the man in bed, he was that bad with the shakes, dreaming with his eyes open and shouting something about hurting his son—meaning, I guess, his daughter. We were afraid he'd hurt himself." Mrs. Spark shivered.

"Melanie, the poor thing, wouldn't leave him. We sent Timothy for the doctor." Mrs. Spark reached out and took Sundry's hand. "Thank you again for going with Thaddeus yesterday and for helping him and Davey bring the man back, though I can't guess what we'll do with him. 'Save a man's life,' Thaddeus says, 'and you're responsible for it.'"

Sundry thought he understood this.

"I don't know what we'll do with him," said the mother. "The poor soul may take the problem out of our hands by dying sooner than later."

"I never saw anyone look more dead already," said Minerva.

"Hush," said the mother, then: "God bless you, you must be Mister Walton." Mister Walton bowed, which pleased her. "Is your Mrs. Baffin here yet?" she asked. "I need to make amends for crossing her kitchen, you know."

"I don't think it's a problem," ventured Mister Walton. He considered Mrs. Baffin relatively peaceful for a mild and sweet and elderly woman.

"No, no," said Mrs. Spark with a shake of her finger. "It's bad business otherwise. Oh," she said to Annabelle. "Go pay Mr. McQuinn." She fished a coin or two from her apron pocket.

"Mr. McQuinn?" said Mister Walton, and "Not Horace McQuinn?" said Sundry.

"Yes, he brought us all over in his wagon. Do you know him?" Mrs. Spark seemed surprised.

Sundry raised a hand. "Please. I have it," he told her, and "I insist," when she objected.

"Bring him in, Sundry, please," said Mister Walton. "And Mr. Flyce, if he's with him."

"Oh, he is!" declared Minerva.

"You mean Cowlick?" said Annabelle, and her mother swatted her arm.

Sundry walked through the house to the front hall and went out to the gate, beside which lingered a gray mare (in fact, an *old* gray mare) and a couple of familiar figures seated on a crude sort of wagon. There was an ocean breeze that morning, and Sundry thought the clouds were tattering against the rising sun. Robins hopped the lawn, and a squirrel chattered down at him from the safety of the lofty chestnut.

"Well, Mr. McQuinn," said Sundry with about equal parts pleasure and skepticism as he approached the wagon.

"Gory, Hod!" said the fellow on the other side of the bench, his extraordinary cowlick like an exclamation point above his head. Maven

Flyce had been born with the heart and expression of perpetual astonishment. "It's Mr. Moss!" he declared, leaning forward to gaze past Horace McQuinn as if he'd never seen anything like Sundry in his life.

"Well, it is," drawled the lean and weathered old fellow at the reins. Horace did not tip his hat but only nodded, his steel gray eyes flashing with humor and observation.

"I am amazed!" said Maven.

"How did *you* come to bring the Sparks over this morning?" asked Sundry. "Did you volunteer, or was it strictly by chance?"

"Oh, I read the papers," said Horace McQuinn, looking shrewd. "A lot of news comes by post," he said with something near a laugh.

Sundry nodded. Horace's standard post was an actual one, and he leaned on it down at the Custom House Wharf on good days (and sometimes in rain, in the summer). Little got by him. "What do we owe you?" asked Sundry.

"I couldn't take your money today," said Horace gravely. Horace McQuinn was of a type who gets up early so as to have plenty of time to do as little as possible, but this fashion of living often brings with it a shrugging philosophy when it comes to the accumulation of wealth.

Sundry Moss hadn't seen Horace McQuinn since the previous October, but the old fellow had made his mark in the history of the Moosepath League and would have laughed to be so enumerated. His age was indeterminate; his health might have been better if he'd at all taken care of himself, but was perhaps a good *deal* better than appearance would indicate. Sundry knew him for Mother's own rascal and liked him.

"If you've nothing better to do," said Sundry, hooking a thumb in the direction of the house, "Mister Walton would be sorry to miss you."

"I can't imagine it," said Horace with another chortle. "What do you say, Maven? Shall we see if Mabel craves help with that cake of hers?"

"Goodness' sakes, Hod! You don't think?" said Maven.

"Not too much," said Horace. He nudged the wagon a few yards farther along the street till he came to a hitching post, then hopped down to the sidewalk with surprising agility. Maven scrambled down the other side and appeared from behind the wagon, looking concerned that he might be called on to work on Mrs. Spark's cake. "It is a day for it," said Horace.

"It is bound to be, I guess," said Sundry as he considered the sky. He thought the clouds were taking their time.

Horace slowly followed the young man's gaze and said, "It's just a patch. Mister Walton will have plenty of sun to see what he's doing." This made the rascal laugh till he broke into a fit of coughing, and they paused at the steps till he recovered. The delight never left his eyes, however, and when he was done, Horace said to Sundry, "She must be *some* female."

Now Sundry laughed to hear Miss McCannon referred to in this manner. "You'd think highly of her," he replied.

"Well"—Horace shrugged—"she'll keep him in line, no doubt."

Sundry did not blink. "We're hoping," he said.

"Well, *there* he is!" announced Horace when he saw Mister Walton waiting for them at the door.

"Mr. McQuinn!" The grand fellow shook Horace's hand, beaming all the while.

"Good heavens, Hod!" said Maven. "It's Mister Walton!"

"Odd to find him at his own house," said Horace evenly.

"A pleasure to see you again, Mr. Flyce," said Mister Walton.

Maven hardly knew his hand had been shaken; he gaped at the front hall as if he'd never seen anything like it—and perhaps he hadn't. The Walton home was plain enough for the older, well-to-do side of Portland, but Maven's entire existence had been something less than plain. Truth to tell, he would have gaped at a hovel or anything in between. "I'm so astounded!" he said.

"Come in, come in!" insisted Mister Walton. "There's coffee on." He led them toward the kitchen. "You know the Sparks."

"Mabel and I go way back," drawled Horace. He had a fierce way of grinning that looked like a leer to anyone who didn't know him.

Mabel Spark heard this, and she called out from the kitchen, "I've put up with him since we took up the tavern," but the amusement in her voice indicated that this hadn't really been a source of much perturbation.

Stationed by the corner cupboards, Horace McQuinn and Maven Flyce accomplished the role of chorus to ensuing events—Horace with his occasional dry commentary and Maven with his perpetual astonishment. Horace thought it proper to laud Mister Walton's courage in light of the approaching ceremony, and Maven gasped with each bit of praise. Mister Walton chuckled and even blushed, but with pleasure.

Sundry himself took pleasure in watching his friend amid these people. Mister Walton had been born and raised in prosperity, and Sundry himself had seen him move comfortably on the upper rungs of manufactured society; but here the portly fellow sat among the unassuming Spark family, a farm boy (Sundry himself), and the roguish figures of Maven Flyce and Horace McQuinn without the least sense of contradiction. Years later

Sundry would be heard to say that Mister Walton simply had "a knack for people."

Mister Walton was not the only target of Horace's drawly wit. Horace occasionally leveled his observations in Mrs. Spark's direction, as she was the sole married female in the room. She was up to this and took little in the way of wisdom from the old fellow, which made him snicker happily. She returned his best and never lost track of what she was doing, which was several things all at once. The Spark children, who knew Horace from his occasional trade at the Faithful Mermaid, were more easily distracted.

"I never had a woman to keep me in line," said Horace, while the younger Sparks produced fresh baked delicacies from sacks and boxes.

"There wasn't one born who could, is my guess," said Mabel without looking round.

"There wasn't one who'd want to, is mine," ventured Horace as he filled his pipe without lifting bowl or pouch from his coat pocket. He struck a wooden lucifer against the stove top. Maven watched, his jaw slack and his eyes wide, as if he'd never seen Horace smoke before. Horace took a satisfied puff, then gestured with the stem of his pipe and said, "I'll wager Mr. Moss, here, will be next in line."

Mister Walton had been pondering a pie that had been set before him, but he looked up now, to see how Sundry reacted to this prediction. Minerva, Annabelle, and Betty—aged seventeen to fourteen—also betrayed interest in the subject. Even the mother looked up to consider the young man; she was herself a large, handsome woman and understood that her daughters favored her in several characteristics that might be deemed pleasant in the eyes of a potential suitor.

"My sister might be married before the summer is done," said Sundry, expertly turning the conversation away from himself. "It'll be the first wedding in the family since my cousin was married—oh, seven or eight years ago."

"How'd he make out?" inquired Horace.

"I think he'll live," said Sundry.

Mrs. Spark let out a snort, and Minerva laughed aloud.

"It was the courtship that nearly did him in," explained Sundry. He was pouring coffee for Horace and Maven. "She was a widow—a little older than he was, and a decent arm with a shotgun, as it happened."

Mister Walton laughed ruefully, and Mrs. Spark, who had been considering the sections of her cake, turned now to wait for the balance of the tale.

"He was delivering a May basket," said Sundry.

"And she shot him?" said Betty.

"I am amazed!" said Maven.

"He was sneaking through the garden," explained Sundry, "past the kitchen window, and she thought he was a woodchuck. You can't get caught giving a May basket." They all understood the magical properties of the May basket and how easily its purpose might be frustrated by improper delivery.

"And she shot him?" said Betty again.

Horace let out a wheezing laugh.

"It's not a common form of courtship," said Mister Walton.

"She was sort of sorry, afterward," admitted Sundry.

"And then she married him?" said Minerva.

"He was crawling on his hands and knees when she looked out and saw the irises swaying. So she more or less caught him in the end that was, just then, uppermost."

"Who would have thought?" said Maven.

"I always thought the way to a man's heart was his *stomach*," said Mrs. Spark, which caused Horace to laugh himself into a coughing fit again.

"But they went and married each other?" said Betty, who was almost as astonished as Maven.

"She was startled, I think, when he came bolting out of the flowers," said Sundry. "They caught him down the road half a mile or so, she and her brother, and brought him back to the house and got the buckshot out of him. Considering the exact target of her aim, she thought she knew him pretty intimately, so marriage wasn't such a rash thing."

The Spark daughters looked both scandalized and amused. Mrs. Spark shook her head.

"*That* May basket did its work," said a pleased Mister Walton.

"My cousin always says it did, but he thinks the means were a little fierce. But here are the Baffins."

"Toby, Toby!" declared Lucinda Baffin when Sundry had let her and her husband Cedric in. Her sweet old face lit up at the sight of Mister Walton in the midst of the crowded kitchen. "Good heavens! What a day to sleep in!" It was now all of a few minutes before seven, and the elderly Baffins had probably been up for an hour or more. Mrs. Baffin squeezed Sundry's hand when he took her coat. "The two of us slept as if there weren't a thing to do. Good morning, good morning," she said to everyone, the burr of her Nova Scotian childhood evident in her voice. "We haven't had a crowd in the kitchen for years."

Mrs. Spark heard this distinct note, announced that her own mother's people were from Beaver Bank, and they greeted each other like long lost kin.

"Oh, my!" said Maven. He was looking into his mug of coffee and seemed astounded that it was empty. There was a rap at the front door, and he looked up as if this were too much to believe. "I am amazed!" he said, and there did seem to be a lot of traffic that morning.

4. Varied Species of Chickens Came Home to Roost

The man at the front door held a round brown hat to the breast of his checked jacket and with his other hand gripped the handle of a carpet sweeper. He was clean-shaven, and the smell of a fruity pomade in his coal black hair wafted in with the ocean breeze. "Good day to you, sir!" he declared, revealing with his smile a wide part between his upper front teeth. "I trust I haven't shifted you from your breakfast this fine morning!"

"Not yet," said Sundry.

"Is the missus in?" wondered the man.

"Not yet," said Sundry.

A frown barely flickered across the drummer's face. "I rarely pay a call so early, but I saw some traffic on its way through your yard—"

"It's really not a good day—" began Sundry.

"I won't take but a minute of your time," said the man. He perched his hat on his head and offered his hand. "My name is Felton P. Deltwire, sir, and here I have the ultimate expression of housecleaning ingenuity—the Artemis and Atlanta Company's *Queen of the Carpet Sweepers!*"

Sundry was not very fond of dealing with traveling salesmen on a typical day, but he allowed his hand to be shaken and waited for a moment to put in a word.

That moment did not immediately avail itself. "More than likely, sir," continued the drummer, "the lady of the house has some such device *right now!* occupying a pantry closet, but I guarantee that if it isn't a *genuine! Queen of the Carpet Sweepers!* it hasn't the double-patented contracirculatory bristle action or the unique compartmental reservoir—patent pending— designed to separate mistakenly swept valuables from the collected dirt."

The single minute that Mr. Deltwire had promised to expend was more figurative than actual; very quickly it was gone, but even as another was ventured, Sundry's rescue unexpectedly revealed itself upon the sidewalk.

"Now you may look at this mechanism, sir, and wonder—and *rightly* wonder—how the lady of the house is to get it under the dining room sideboard, the escritoire, or the upright piano—"

Three well-turned-out gentlemen stood by the gate and peered down the walk with amiable curiosity. Sundry exchanged a wave of the hand with them.

"The primary mechanism is, of course, too large to find its way beneath such furnishings—"

It was the Moosepath League, and as was so often the case, it had arrived in the veritable *nick of time*. Sundry again waved a hand over the drummer's head.

"And that is why we have contrived for the *Queen of the Carpet Sweepers* what is called, in carpet-sweeping parlance, *an attachment!* and which I hold before you—"

"Gentlemen," pronounced Sundry with more ceremony than was his habit, including the approaching members of the club in a formal and declarative introduction. "Mr. Deltwire," he said. "Allow me to present Mr. Ephram, Mr. Eagleton, and Mr. Thump. Sirs, this is Felton P. Deltwire and his *Queen of the Carpet Sweepers.*"

The tall, blond Christopher Eagleton hurried up the walk to shake Felton Deltwire's hand, saying, "Very pleased! Clouds scattering before a southwest wind, expected sunny this afternoon."

"Yes, it is a nice day," said Felton P. Deltwire.

"Hmmm!" said the broad-bearded Joseph Thump, who quickly mounted the steps. "High tide at 1:48." He took a turn at agitating the drummer's hand. "P.M.," he added.

"I'm glad to be informed," said Felton P. Deltwire.

"It's five minutes past the hour of seven," pronounced the darkly mustached Matthew Ephram, close upon the heels of his fellows and consulting one of his three or four watches even as he took Felton P. Deltwire's hand.

"The sun and Saturn will find themselves in opposition by tomorrow morning," replied Felton P. Deltwire. "The moon reaches apogee by Saturday, setting in conjunction with Mars on Wednesday next."

"I never knew!" said Eagleton.

"How marvelous!" said Ephram.

"Hmmm?" said Thump.

"Felton P. Deltwire," said the drummer. He raised his hat, returned it to his head, and offered his hand again.

"Matthew Ephram," said that worthy as he reapplied his hand to Felton P. Deltwire's. "Apogee, you say."

"Christopher Eagleton," said the next in line, and he likewise greeted the man a second time. "And the sun in opposition. I hadn't realized."

"Joseph Thump," said the third Moosepathian, who likewise agitated the salesman's hand once more. "Of the Exeter Thumps."

"Pleased," said Felton P. Deltwire. "Very pleased. You gentlemen look ready for anything this morning."

This observation surprised the members of the club, and they looked at themselves and one another with abrupt concern.

"As I have been trying to tell you, Mr. Deltwire," said Sundry, "there's to be a wedding here today, and we will not be able to consider your fine carpet sweeper."

"Is this the very item?" wondered Eagleton, appraising the long-handled instrument in Felton P. Deltwire's grip.

"By opposition," Ephram said, "do you mean that Saturn will be on the other side of the earth from the sun?"

"Mister Walton is in the kitchen," announced Sundry.

"Hmmm?" said Thump.

"My word, how very nice!" said Eagleton. "You must meet our chairman," he announced to the drummer, which was not exactly what Sundry had in mind.

"And how is Mister Walton this morning?" said Ephram to Sundry.

"Holding steady," said Sundry.

One could not fault Mister Walton's confusion (or anyone else's) when the gentlemen of the club arrived at the same moment as Mr. Felton P. Deltwire. These four men entered the kitchen in concert (with Sundry bringing up the rear), and between the drummer's practiced art of familiarity and the Moosepath League's inherent warmth they appeared like old comrades. "A man for our membership," Eagleton was saying to Ephram, and this, too, might have signified to those in the kitchen that the Moosepathians had known Felton P. Deltwire for more than the time it took to travel the front hall.

The gentlemen of the club were gratified to see Mrs. Spark and her pretty daughters, and they appeared almost Maven Flyce-like in their de-gree of astonishment when they discovered that cowlicked individual and Horace McQuinn in Mister Walton's kitchen. It was a crowd, to be sure, and that is no doubt why Ephram, Eagleton, and Thump knocked one an-other's hats from their respective hands as they synchronistically bowed to the women, and after they had begged one another's pardon, it was per-haps why there was a loud *thock* when, as with one thought, they bent to retrieve their brand-new toppers.

No one said, "Ouch!" (the members of the club suspected this inter-jection to be a small bit unrefined), but Thump in particular seemed startled by the chance impact, and Mister Walton insisted on giving the stricken man his seat.

"Well, I never, Hod!" Maven was saying.

"Not here, you haven't," agreed Horace.

There was some avid handshaking as the members of the club, emo-tional with the day's significance, introduced Mr. Deltwire to the assem-blage like a long-lost cousin. The chairman beamed with pleasure.

"You dear men," Mrs. Baffin was saying to Eagleton, who blushed, then almost gasped as she reached up to pat his cheek.

The drummer closed in on Mrs. Spark, saying, "The lady of the house?"

Mabel Spark was no more susceptible to a salesman's flattery than to Horace McQuinn's wisdom. "You get away from my cake with that thing!" she demanded, shaking a spatula at the *Queen of the Carpet Sweepers*. Fel-ton P. Deltwire displayed excellent discretion by making a short retreat. The kitchen had grown as loud as it was crowded, so that it was difficult, at first, to hear yet another knock at the front door, but Mister Walton let out a short laugh when he did hear it. Sundry raised an eyebrow.

"My word! Who could that be now?" said Mrs. Baffin.

"I'll get it," said Mr. Baffin.

But Sundry was up and accustomed to it by now; he gave a nod and made the trip back through pantry and hall. There was another knock be-fore he opened the front door to reveal a policeman on the step.

"Calvin Drum," said the constable, his hat in hand.

"Officer," said Sundry.

"That rig," said the policeman. He pointed down the street. "That wagon. Does it belong here?"

"For the moment it does," said Sundry.

"Oh," said the officer. "You see, I saw it once, last year."

"You say you saw it?" said Sundry.

"I say I saw it, you see."

"So you said," said Sundry. "I see."

The officer looked the slightest bit curt. "Well, I did," he said. "The horse is darker than I remembered, but I couldn't mistake her. Last year— oh, closer to July, I think it was—I spotted a wagon just like it with a suspicious load of kegs—"

"Didn't you speak to the driver?" wondered Sundry. The scenario painted by the policeman had an oddly familiar ring to him.

"Well, I did," said the man again. "And he just whipped up the horse and bolted. I never did catch him, being on foot, but he went like Absalom's mule down through town without a thought for cross traffic. Had his hat pulled down so I couldn't see him proper." Clearly the memory galled him.

It was a coincidence that three principals of that remembered event were that morning within hailing distance of one another. The man with the runaway wagon (the horse had actually taken off of its own resolve) was in fact ambling up the hall even as Sundry and the policeman were speaking.

"Good morning, Officer," said Mister Walton, and as he recognized the policeman, his expression altered just a whit. "Is there a problem?"

"Well, I don't know," said the man.

"Constable Drum is concerned about the wagon," said Sundry.

"The wagon?" Mister Walton leaned from the doorway. "Horace's wagon?" His memory of his unintentional involvement with Horace Mc-Quinn's rum-running continued to set in his mind, and his voice trailed off to a whisper.

"What's that?" snapped Officer Drum. "Horace? Just as I surmised."

"He brought the Sparks over this morning," said Mister Walton.

"Sparks? Which Sparks? Horace who? The Thaddeus Sparks?" He may have realized that this sounded more demanding than courteous, and he altered his bearing before saying, more slowly, "Horace, you say?"

"How's business, Calvin?" came an amused chortle from the hall.

"McQuinn!" said the policeman. He narrowed his gaze past Mister Walton as he attempted to reconcile the presence of Horace McQuinn at this respectable home. Then he said, "Thaddeus?" and finally, "Mr. Thump!", for the Moosepathians had left the kitchen to see what was about, and by further coincidence Mr. Thump (who looked so much like Thaddeus Spark) had rescued Officer Drum from certain injury and possible death less than a week before.

"Is that Calvin Drum?" Mrs. Spark called from the kitchen, but this was not enough of a crowd, it seemed, for the day provided a second wagon, which was just then pulling up behind Horace's.

"Is this the Walton residence?" called the driver.

"Walton?" said the policeman.

"Mister Walton is our chairman, Officer Drum," informed Thump.

"Ah, the Moosepath League! It's good to see you again, Mr. Thump."

"I'll need some help lugging this contraption," shouted the driver.

"It's Phileda's organ," said Mister Walton.

"Organ?" said the policeman.

"For the wedding," said Sundry. It seemed a good moment to add something to the expanding glomeration of words.

"Horace?" said Officer Drum again. The notion of a wedding made the rascal's presence only the more peculiar.

"I stopped by in case the preacher doesn't show up," offered Horace. Mister Walton chuckled.

From behind Horace, a voice said, "I am amazed!"

"Feeling your oats?" wondered Sundry of Officer Drum. He hooked a thumb in the direction of the newly arrived wagon.

The policeman returned his hat to its perch. "An organ, you say."

"Don't be hurting yourself, now," drawled Horace solicitously.

Sundry and Officer Drum climbed into the back of the wagon to unlash the organ, and with the assistance of the Moosepath League, they lifted it down to the sidewalk. Standing nearby and looking as if he might help if Sundry would let him, Mister Walton said, "It's going in the parlor. It's very good of you." Several neighbors were watching from their lawns, and he waved to them.

Sundry was securing his grip on the organ when he caught sight of still another member of society making his way up the street and necessitating a chapter all his own.

5. The Unpredicted Storm

Sundry sensed trouble immediately. No one who has anything happy to convey stalks the sidewalk with such solitary confidence coupled with a hard-eyed (even grim) focus upon his goal. The man was tall and broad-shouldered and with a great mane of gray hair. He strode toward Mister Walton's gate with the appearance of someone who is unaware of the people he passes, or at least that he believes himself above any interest in them. One of Mister Walton's neighbors wished him good day, but the gray-maned man did not reply.

"There'll be dancing this afternoon," Horace McQuinn announced with a lingering look of wisdom toward the members of the club.

"Oh, my!" said Eagleton. He and his fellows exchanged looks of alarm just as the voice of Mister Walton was lifted in recitation.

Of wedding bells and organ's note,
Great potency is spoken;
Upon true love the bells will dote,
And vows expressed betoken.

And maids the nuptial music calls,
To bach'lors, dance propose;
More love is born in wedding halls,
Than you or I suppose.

Everyone paused while this bit of lyric was recited. Mister Walton smiled, the smallest bit of wry warning to his friends. "I heard it from an uncle years ago," he explained.

"That's a good one," said Horace McQuinn, who was known for his own abilities in the way of verse.

Sundry glanced back at the approaching figure. The tall man had halted some yards away and looked as if he were growing angry simply watching the gathering ahead of him. "Muckle on," said Sundry, hoping to get them all out of the path of this discordant note before it arrived. Ephram, Eagleton, and Thump were not very familiar with *muckling on*, and they had been startled by Mister Walton's poem, so they did not immediately fall to.

"That's right," Officer Drum was saying to Mister Walton. "You're getting married!" He seemed to have forgotten Horace's wagon. "I met *my* wife at a wedding," he admitted. "Danced all night with her."

"Oh, my!" said Eagleton again.

"I suppose we should have invited some extra ladies," said Mister Walton without a smile, but with mischief in his eye.

"I hear Mrs. Roberto's in town," said Horace quietly.

For some reason Thump went into a fit of coughing.

"Are you all right?" asked Officer Drum.

Thump nodded vehemently, dragged in a ragged breath, and coughed again. Ephram and Eagleton leaned forward, as if their collective proximity might alleviate his sudden affliction.

"Oh, dear," said Mister Walton.

Officer Drum noticed a cloud cross Sundry's expression and followed the young man's gaze to the lionesque man approaching Mister Walton.

Ephram gave Thump's back some experimental taps.

"They say it alleviates a cough to raise your arms above your head," Mister Walton suggested.

"Are you Tobias Walton?" came a voice that managed something curiously unpleasant with those words.

The portly fellow was at a disadvantage; the stranger stood more closely than social protocol might dictate, and Mister Walton had to adjust his spectacles and lean his head back to see who was addressing him. "I am," he said.

The newcomer towered over Mister Walton, and his great bearded visage looked like that of an angry prophet. "I am Harold Trowbridge," thundered this awful vision, and through the commotion of Thump's renewed fit of coughing, there could be heard the words *underminer* and *daughter* and *philosophy*.

"Mister Walton suggests that you put your arms over your head," Eagleton said between Thump's booming *expellations*.

"I beg your pardon?" said Mister Walton, even as he cast sympathetic glances back at his afflicted friend.

"Something went down the wrong pipe," said Horace McQuinn.

Trowbridge shot his frown at Thump before saying to Mister Walton (more exactly than before but still in that dark, low tone of his), "I am Harold Trowbridge, and *you* are an underminer, your notorious doctrine a blot upon society! I have read extensively about your sort. My daughter may be taken in by your repellent philosophy, but you will not entangle her."

Sundry Moss could not hear everything the man was saying, but somewhere about the word *blot* he left the organ and stepped up to Mister Walton's side.

"Arms up. Arms up," Eagleton was saying to Thump.

"I am amazed!" declared Maven Flyce.

"Your daughter?" Mister Walton was saying. "I beg your pardon, but your daughter, you say?"

Notwithstanding Thump's coughs, which were impressive, everyone else was now fixed upon Harold Trowbridge. "Mister Walton—" said Sundry.

If Mister Walton was nonplussed, he was not to be daunted, and he said to the man in the mildest tone and with his mildest expression, "I am sorry, sir, but I don't believe that I *know* your daughter."

"*Of course you don't know her!*" roared the fellow.

"Here, now," said Calvin Drum under his breath.

"You are a pawn of women's suffrage and anarchy!" growled the lionesque man. "A busybody and an agitator!"

"Good heavens!" said Mister Walton. He had never been the subject of such a litany. "An agitator?" he said with some humor.

"Must be Moses, come down from the mountain," suggested Horace.

"He'll be someone come down from his *high seat* in a moment," said Sundry.

Harold Trowbridge straightened to his full height, which was impressive, and said, as if to everyone within hearing, "You had better stay clear of decent folk or someone is liable to clean house with you!"

"Clean house?" said Mister Walton. Contrary to Trowbridge's purpose, the phrase almost made him laugh.

"Perhaps," said Sundry, "you'd like to step back onto the sidewalk where you and I can clean up the street somewhat first."

"Now, let's not get all haired up," said Officer Drum.

Thump had both hands in the air now and was finding this helpful.

"It's all right, Sundry," said Mister Walton. "There has been a misunderstanding, is all."

"Yes, this fellow misunderstands who he's speaking to."

Ephram and Eagleton were incredulous. Thump was making deep harrumphing noises (which might have been indignation or might have been the remnants of his cough) as he held his arms above his head.

"Now, someone explain the problem to me," said Calvin Drum.

"I am sure there isn't one, Officer," said Mister Walton.

"And what can I do for *you?*" said the policeman to Trowbridge.

"I require nothing from anyone but that this *Walton*, here, *and* his cronies watch their step around decent people."

"That's *Mister* Walton," said Sundry.

"Do you know what day this is?" said Officer Drum. "Do you realize that this gentleman is to be married today?"

"Cronies?" Eagleton was saying. He'd never heard of such a thing.

"Good gracious!" said Ephram.

"You're a troop of *freethinkers*, aren't you," said Trowbridge. "Taking a *woman* under your order," and his means of expressing *woman* came as close to making Mister Walton bristle as anything the man had uttered. "I know your tactics," said Trowbridge. "A young, addle-headed girl might fall right into your schemes, and who can say how many haven't already—" Trowbridge paused to glare at Thump, whose cough had subsided, but who had forgotten to lower his arms. Standing there with his hands above his head, the bearded Moosepathian looked like a Scottish dancer or perhaps a man who is being robbed.

"Sir," said Mister Walton, and quickly (for it was plain that Trowbridge had little patience to listen), "I *must* apologize."

"Apologize?" For the first time, Trowbridge's threatening glare broke, ever so slightly, to let in a *mote* of doubt.

"Mister Walton," said Calvin Drum, "I've half a mind to run him in for breach of peace—and I don't care *who* he is."

"No, no," answered Mister Walton. "Yes, apologize, sir. For reasons, unknown to me, you imagine that I have strange designs upon your daughter, and I must believe that some error on my part is the cause of your confusion. I am very sorry that you have been led to this mistaken belief, and I assure you that previous to this moment, I have known no one by your family name, though I believe I can safely speak for all of us in saying that if your daughter *is* in any danger, we should be pleased to offer whatever help is in our strength. My best advice, of course, would be that you speak to this fine policeman here."

Miraculously Mister Walton managed this speech without the slightest hint of condescension, though he might reasonably have employed the tone that a person would use to placate an unruly child or even a madman; the embers of graciousness were so well banked within him that he was able to sympathize with this man's distress no matter the circumstance or how unpleasant the man.

"My card," said Mister Walton, who produced the item from his coat pocket. "Please call on me when we won't intrude upon everyone's happy day."

"I know where you live!" growled Trowbridge as he backed away. "You have not seen the last of me. I shall be watching, and the *devil* to the police!"

It occurred to Thump at this juncture to let his hands down.

"Good heavens!" said Eagleton. "He was very angry about something."

Mister Walton appeared shaken, now that the scene was finished. "Thank you, Sundry, for being so obviously at my side. And you, Officer," he said to Calvin Drum, "I was very glad to have you here."

"Don't mind him," said the policeman as he looked after the disappearing figure of Harold Trowbridge. "He's a loose cannon."

"Do you know him?" asked Mister Walton.

"I know who he is. He has a firm down by the Portland and Ogdensburg."

"I thought the name sounded familiar," said Mister Walton.

"Or you've *read* it in the court news. He's been brought up twice on charges of assault and has leveled half a dozen lawsuits himself. There are stores in town that won't accept his trade, or let him pass their threshold. His firm can't keep a captain more than a year, they say."

"He sounds like an unhappy man," said Mister Walton quietly.

"He's an idiot," said the officer.

"At least I'm not unique in securing his anger," said the portly fellow, "however mysteriously I may have done so."

"Not at all," assured the policeman. "He's very sure that everyone is out to fleece him. There are those who say his poor wife died as a last resort."

"How melancholy."

"And I am not sure his way with her was confined to shouts and accusations," continued the man.

Mister Walton blinked at this and nodded his understanding; but he was disinclined to pursue the subject, and Officer Drum judiciously turned to praising the weather, which theme Eagleton was quick to join.

"I was so amazed!" said Maven Flyce.

"What could he have wanted?" asked Ephram in honest wonder.

"I couldn't say," replied Mister Walton. "I think that no amount of discussion was going to reveal what perturbed him. But we shall not allow a single case of bad humor to dispel the good that fills the day."

"Begging your pardon, Mister Walton," said Sundry as they returned to the organ, "but I was a little perturbed with your apology—at first."

"An apology is easy, isn't it. I *am* sorry for anyone so distressed, and he seemed singularly unhealthy in his anger. But if I was able to wax sincere, despite his uncivil manner, it is because I was thinking about his daughter."

"Now, where did that drummer go?" wondered Sundry. "You don't suppose he's demonstrating his carpet sweeper on the parlor rug?"

6. Time and Tide

"Well!" said Miriam when she returned to Phileda's chamber from the little parlor fronting the bride's rooms at the City Hotel. "Your brother and Stuart are putting breakfast into them, and the management has sent flowers." She held a large bouquet of roses and white sprays of elderberry.

"How beautiful!" exclaimed Phileda. She was almost ready for the day, having been waited upon by her friend in the most ancient and gracious fashion. She took a breath of the flowers and directed their presentation on the low bureau by the window. Miriam stood back and admired her work before returning to Phileda's hair, which was dark and long with only a stray gray strand here or there. "Don't pluck it!" said Phileda when this possibility was offered the first one. "Two more will take its place."

"My mother used to pluck hers and give them to one of us children," said Miriam. "'Here,' she would say, 'you gave me this.'"

"Probably you had."

"I *was* a terrible child," admitted Miriam happily. "My own children have been benign in comparison."

"That was the *other* business I gave up," said Phileda.

"Children?"

Phileda nodded. She had not taken her eyes from the bouquet. "It was more difficult, in its way, than deciding not to have a husband."

"And as premature."

"One must be as careful of what one gives up as prays for."

"Perhaps they are the same thing."

"That sounds like philosophy, Mrs. Nowell."

Miriam smiled. "You don't know a thing about Toby's nephew, do you."

"He's the reason I'm getting married today, I suppose, though he couldn't suspect it. He couldn't suspect *me* at all."

"My children were almost what they were going to be when they were seven," said Miriam.

"I've done it very backwards, you know. Having a child by people I never met—years, in fact, before I ever so much as heard of them. It's not the usual way to begin a marriage, or the ideal one, I daresay." She looked at herself in the mirror and picked at the papers in her hair.

"Ideal is what ends well, I suspect," said Miriam. "Among my own people there have been family divided by tragedy, people raising their children's children, widows raising children alone, adoption . . . and desertion, I fear. Why, *you're* like a sister to me."

Phileda smiled. She had known, heard, and felt this sentiment before.

"Family is where you find it, my father used to say." Miriam began to help Phileda with her curled papers. "Of course, that was when he tried to trade me to your parents for you. Family is where you find it."

"It's not the usual way to begin a marriage," said Phileda again.

"Yes, well, marriage *is* unusual, no matter *how* usual it is."

"Oh, I do hope."

Miriam regarded Phileda in the mirror. "You didn't feel—?" she began, then foundered with the unspoken thought, shook her head, and left off entirely to return to her duties.

"No, I didn't," said Phileda, rather mysteriously and without the slightest hint of offense. "It was very mutual. And if it was quickly thought out, it was very *well* thought out, if you can believe me."

Miriam nodded. "I like him very much," she said.

Phileda only continued to smile. "It will be a great thing for him to be with someone from his own family again."

Mister Walton almost put Mr. Trowbridge from his mind when he returned to the prerituals of the day. He shaved while Sundry laid out his things, and he detained his friend from further chores by chatting with him from the washstand. "You'll know more about children than I," he admitted when the conversation chanced upon his nephew.

"We were all kids once, I suppose," said Sundry. " 'We raise as we have been raised,' my father said to Martha Stivvard, who was dressing him down for some sin she saw in us kids one Sunday at church."

"I met her when we visited your family last September."

"You did cross swords." The memory seemed to please Sundry.

"She was concerned for the state of my soul," said Mister Walton.

"You might as well be a full-bloomed heathen, I guess, as be a Methodist."

"Our fellowship cherishes certain wild creeds." Mister Walton dabbed at his face with a towel. "If your father is correct, however, then I may perform my duties pretty well. The older I grow, the more I admire my own parents. Perhaps I shall have learned something from them without knowing it. I am in need of some nice cuff links."

"You have a box of them on your bureau."

"I was thinking of a pair my father used to wear on special occasions. No, no, I'll go look for them, thank you, Sundry." Mister Walton paused in the middle of the room, the towel still in his hand and a dab or two of shaving soap dotting his cheek. "Do you know, my friend, it may sound odd, but I don't know that I would have half the courage to venture forth upon this new path without your steady presence."

Sundry simply shook his head and chuckled softly. "Miss McCannon is steady enough, I think."

"Yes, she is, to be sure. But 'duty shored by many things, and friendship lights the path it can not take itself.'" Mister Walton briefly gripped Sundry's shoulder but did not look at him as he stepped into the hall.

Mister Walton had visited the master bedroom several times since coming home last July, poking about his parents' things for whatever tidings and memory. He was surprised this morning when he opened the door to discover that the room had been transformed. The bed, dressed in new clothes, was facing the windows, instead of between them. Fresh curtains hung in the room, and a new carpet covered the floor. "Good heavens!" he said as it occurred to him for the first time that he and Phileda would be spending the first night of their married life here. Obviously someone else, probably several people, had reached this conclusion before him. Sundry and the Baffins had been hard at work while he was out making arrangements and getting a marriage license.

It was strange to find his parents' room rearranged, and he paused to take stock of his emotions. He looked out the window and over the front lawn, the gate, and Spruce Street. The past two days had been so hectic that he had not thought very much about his family; now a pang of regret visited him, and he went to the chair by the writing desk to sit down.

What a terrible thing that they could not know Phileda and that she could not know them. How very final that was. Only in God's heaven would they ever meet. But here they would not know the solace of one another's wisdom and kindness. How his mother would have doted on Phileda and with what pride his father would have claimed his new daughter-in-law as his own family! How Phileda would have loved them! And Aunt August. And his brother, lost at sea, years ago. How terrible, and terribly final, to think that they would not know one another on these shores.

Mister Walton forced himself to rise and walk to his father's old bureau, which itself had been moved to another corner of the room. In the top drawer, in a small compartment, he found several sets of cuff links and also the pair he had been looking for. He shot his cuffs, held his left arm before him, and fingered the cuff link hole with the first post. Slowly, but with a kind of deliberateness, something substantial and unexpected in this simple task seemed to revive him, and as he secured his shirt sleeves, he had the odd sensation of putting on more than just his father's cuff links.

Like all children, Mister Walton was a peculiar compound of hereditary gifts and conscious and unconscious upbringing; like most children, in his middle age he had begun to mimic the appearance and manners of his parents and even ancestors unknown to him with uncanny, if unintentional, accuracy. In certain facial characteristics Mister Walton took after his mother and by extension her father, but in his portly carriage and balding, bespectacled countenance he otherwise favored his father and his father's family as recorded in portraits along the front hall stairs. How much more deeply and truly did he favor one or take after the other inside himself, in his manners, his speech, and further into his faith and dreams than he could ever understand. What a lot of people it takes to make one person—parents and grandparents and ancestors termed great and great-great—all descending and joining, sometimes colliding, to strike a specific and previously unseen spark. Was it really doing justice to their labor, their laughter, and their love to think that they were gone, or that labor and laughter and love were able to quit the world at all?

Standing in his parents' bedroom, looking into the mirror above his father's bureau, he could see bits of those people in his own face and in the frame of his shoulders and even in the way he looked over his spectacles at his own reflection. Truth be told, Phileda had already met these people; she had laughed at an old joke that his father used to tell, smiled at a bit of homely wisdom from his mother, but more important, she had heard such small prizes couched in a voice and a heart specifically crafted by God and handed down by his dear mother and father. And what had he encountered of Phileda's family? He knew that something worthy had preceded her and that he was the blessed recipient of all that she represented of her people and also of every atom of her that was *only* Phileda McCannon, that could never have existed before and would never be reproduced.

There was a knock on the door. Sundry had heard enough silence to grow concerned, and he listened for Mister Walton's soft "Come in."

"Just wanted to be sure that you hadn't fallen asleep," said Sundry.

"What *is* she committing?" said Mister Walton.

"Phileda?" said Sundry. "She seems pretty rash to me," he said.

Mister Walton chuckled. "Let us hope she doesn't come to her senses in the next few hours."

"We'll see if we can't distract her," suggested Sundry.

7. A Rum Business

A riddle arrived just before noon. The back door was thrown open, and two men rolled the impending quandary across the floor, then propped it up in the corner without a word. Horace McQuinn, who (along with Maven Flyce) seemed content to linger in the kitchen, recognized these fellows but asked no questions. One of them did nod to Horace, and then they were gone. Mrs. Spark had returned to the Faithful Mermaid, but the daughters had stayed behind to serve the reception, and they were amazed to see this intemperate object in such a *respectable* kitchen.

For the moment the rest of the house remained ignorant of the matter and solely concerned with the coming ceremony. Not long after this arrival, Sundry came down the front hall stairs and found the members of the club in the parlor. They had the appearance of men who await profound tidings, hands behind their backs or folded before them, faces solemn. Ephram compared the clock on the mantel with his own three or four watches. He was troubled to find Mister Walton's timepiece a minute or two fast; it seemed ungracious to contradict the chairman's chronometer, so Ephram busied himself with setting his own watches forward to correspond with the mantel clock.

Eagleton, meanwhile, discussed with Felton P. Deltwire the portrait of a Waltonian ancestor that hung upon the wall. "They only had brooms in those days," said Felton P. Deltwire. His and Eagleton's conversation had run from apogees and conjunctions to carpet sweeping to sextiles and quartiles and lunar contradictions and back to carpet sweeping. (Eagleton was not very familiar with sextiles and quartiles and several other words and phrases, so he was not always sure what they were talking about.)

Thump simply stood with his hands folded before him, and when Sundry entered, the bearded Moosepathian looked up and nodded.

"Sundry?" came the sweet voice of Lucinda Baffin. She peered into the parlor from the dining room, where she had been arranging the crystal upon the sideboard. "There seems to be something unusual in the kitchen," she said. Sundry could see Minerva Spark standing behind the elderly woman.

Puzzled by their mysterious demeanor, Sundry stepped into the kitchen, where his gaze fell upon Horace McQuinn standing by the corner cupboard, arms folded, pipe in hand, barely smoking. Horace shrugged when he met Sundry's inquiring gaze, and when Sundry looked at Annabelle and Minerva Spark, they looked away. He did not immediately see anything unusual, Horace and Maven notwithstanding. Then he caught sight of Maven Flyce's perpetual expression of surprise and followed the path described by those wide eyes to the current object of their astonishment.

Something protruded from the other side of the baker's cabinet and Sundry crossed the room to consider the low barrel—and not just a barrel but a keg which had, stenciled across the top, the single surprising word: RUM.

"That wasn't there before," said Sundry.

"It walked in about half an hour ago," explained Horace.

"I was so amazed!" said Maven.

"Half an hour ago?" Sundry looked to the Spark girls for corroboration. The Faithful Mermaid served beer and small beer, stout and ale (and *that* against the exact laws of the state), but their mother would never allow anything stronger in the house, and consequently rum carried with the Spark children a wild reputation. Annabelle nodded. Minerva shrugged. Whatever arrived in Mister Walton's kitchen was hardly *their* business to discuss.

"Half an hour ago?" said Sundry again to Horace McQuinn.

"I don't know whose it is, but I was startled to see it."

Sundry frowned at the keg. "Rum?" he said. He couldn't imagine that Mister Walton knew about this—no, he *knew* that Mister Walton didn't know about it. "Someone's having fun with us," he said quietly.

"Someone *expects* some fun, is *my* guess," said Horace.

Minerva Spark laughed nervously.

Cedric Baffin poked his head into the kitchen and announced that Mr. Seacost and his wife had arrived.

"Am I straightened out?" Sundry asked Mrs. Baffin. She walked across the kitchen to study his appearance more closely, but Annabelle Spark was quicker (not to say bold), and she reached out and adjusted his tie. "Thank you," he said, only briefly glancing at her before heading for the front door. A moment later he stuck his face back into the kitchen and pointed a forefinger at the keg. "I'll take care of *that* in a moment."

The Reverend Seacost and his wife had arrived, and the members of the club were solicitous, informing the elderly folk what might be expected of the climate and the tide and also what time it was. "Mister Walton's clock," said Ephram. Without further explanation, this statement was mysterious to the minister and his wife, but they smiled and nodded.

"Indeed?" said Mrs. Seacost. She thought that they were supposed to admire the clock on the mantel (perhaps it was a wedding gift), and she studied the instrument with a degree of seriousness that Ephram admired.

"Is someone here?" came Mister Walton's voice from above.

"Mr. and Mrs. Seacost," replied Sundry.

"Please inform the reverend that I am in need of spiritual counsel and an opinion regarding which tie I should wear." So, leaving Mrs. Seacost to the kind attentions of the Moosepath League, Sundry and the minister went upstairs to offer their assistance in these two fields of discipline.

"I suppose," Mr. Seacost said, "you will not require the standard lecture concerning the *properties of marriage* and the *business of life*."

"Am I to miss the standard lecture?" said Mister Walton, giving his best *worst* appearance of solemn regret. He held out two ties before Mr. Seacost.

"I don't know that anyone has ever benefited by it," returned Mr. Seacost, who pointed to the tie on the left.

Sundry heard this happy repartee indistinctly. Another carriage had just pulled up to the gate, and he had a distinct feeling about it.

"What are you seeing?" asked Mister Walton, like a child at Christmas.

"Nothing for your eyes," said Sundry. "Yet."

"Oh," said Mister Walton, suddenly earnest.

"I'll go down and let them know the coast is clear," said Sundry.

"Sundry," said Mister Walton, still with that abrupt seriousness in his face and his bearing. Sundry turned, his brow raised in question. Mister Walton opened his mouth, looking ready to ask some profound question or favor or perhaps to forward some significant message to the new arrivals. In the next moment, however, he closed his mouth and laughed quietly. "Thank you," he said, for (perhaps) nothing at all or for everything.

Sundry was still smiling when he opened the door for the bridal party—Miss McCannon: her tall brother, Jared; her maid of honor, Miriam Nowell; and Mrs. Nowell's husband, Stuart, who carried the wedding dress in a long box.

"Is this the right house?" asked Miss McCannon puckishly.

There was something so very definite about her, so very *of itself*, as if she furnished her own source of light, that Sundry was startled. He simply bowed and extended a hand toward the back of the house, where they would find the birthing room just off the pantry. Mrs. Nowell took the dress box, and the women hurried off, leaving Sundry and Mr. Nowell in the hall and a stunned silence in the parlor. The Moosepath League had seen the bride pass.

"Hmmm," said Mr. Thump.

Sundry was going to see Stuart Nowell and Jared McCannon to the parlor, when Mrs. Baffin tremulously spoke his name again. She stood at the other end of the hall, looking anxious. "There's a policeman in the backyard."

"Is there?" said Sundry.

"I think he's going to come in," she said.

"Oh, he's a curious one," said Horace when they reached the kitchen.

Bravely, if uncertainly, the Spark girls stood their ground. Sundry suggested that Mrs. Baffin escort them to the parlor, there to await the guests and avoid any association with rising matters. "Who marks a keg *rum*, when rum is illegal?" he said when they were gone. He saw a flash of the policeman's hat pass the kitchen window and wondered which was more incriminating—the presence of the keg or that of Horace McQuinn and Maven Flyce. He considered rolling the offending object into the pantry and down the cellar steps, but then there was a knock at the kitchen door.

The officer was tall and broad-shouldered. He held his hat at his breast, and he ran a speculative hand through his reddish blond hair. "Good afternoon to you, sir," he said, looking Sundry's best man's outfit up and down. "Are you the master of the house, then?"

"I'm not," said Sundry.

"I'm Officer Rye. Would you mind if I took a look about?"

"I thought you had been," said Sundry easily.

The officer was pleasant enough, if a little stiff. He had a stiff pair of reddish mustaches, in fact, that bristled over his cheeks. "*Inside*, if you take my meaning, sir," he said.

"We're having a wedding in about half an hour," informed Sundry. The appearance of this police officer after the keg's mysterious arrival touched him with vague misgiving.

The officer looked surprised. "I regret the intrusion, but I have been sent by Sergeant Frith to investigate." His search past Sundry's shoulder was snagged by the sight of Horace McQuinn. "Well!" he said. "Well!"

"Cuthbert, how are you?" drawled Horace.

"McQuinn," said the officer tersely.

"What are you looking for?" asked Sundry.

"I'm not at liberty to divulge that at this hour," explained the policeman, sounding like a quote in the court news.

"You're not?" replied Sundry. "I might be able to help you if I knew what this was about."

The policeman shifted his feet, took a breath, and said, "Actually, the sergeant was small on detail."

"I think," said Sundry with a nod toward the baker's cabinet, "that what you're looking for is in the corner over there."

"What?"

"You're looking for a keg, I guess."

Officer Cuthbert Rye didn't ask for further authorization but pressed past Sundry and into the kitchen. He let out one or two low gasps as the keg hove into view, and he stood a few feet away from it, peering at it as if it were a bomb about to explode.

"Who marks a keg 'rum' when rum is illegal?" asked Sundry again.

"What's that you say?" said the gaping officer. "You stay right there, and don't you move."

Sundry simply folded his arms.

The officer let out a derisive snort. "You get the owner of this house, and be quick," he added, countermanding his previous order, though perhaps he didn't realize it.

"He's to be married in half an hour," said Sundry, more seriously.

The officer was large with suspicion, but it occurred to him that he had put his hat back on. Looking rueful, he took it off again and stuck it under one arm. "Yes, well—you had better go find the owner."

The last thing Sundry wanted to do was to put any sort of cloud over Mister Walton's day, and *almost* the last thing he wanted to do was put himself in trouble with the law by claiming (for Mister Walton's sake) any culpability regarding the object in question. "You mean the owner of the house or the owner of that barrel?" he said, and when the officer gave him a glare, he added, "I'd really like to keep Mister Walton out of this."

"Walton, eh?" Officer Rye found a notebook and a pencil in his jacket.

"*Mister* Walton, and he doesn't know anything about this. *We* don't have any notion where it came from, and *he* doesn't even know it's here."

"I guess *I* know where it came from," said the officer. He gave Horace McQuinn the hard stare.

"Who'd have thought!" said Maven Flyce.

"I'm as much in the dark as anyone," professed Horace.

"You spend enough *time* skulking around in it," replied Officer Rye.

Horace returned the officer's stare with an expression of profound bemusement. He hardly blinked.

"If he didn't bring it with him, who did?" the policeman asked Sundry.

"Horace said two men came in with it about half an hour ago."

"What did they look like?" asked the policeman, plainly dubious.

"One had hair," said Horace slowly, "and one had a hat."

Cuthbert Rye ceased scribbling in his notebook and considered what he was going to say. "I'm sorry to interrupt a man's wedding, but I was sent down here to see what was up, and I must speak to the head of the house."

"Now why would anyone mark a keg 'rum' when rum is illegal?" said Sundry for a third time.

"I guess you'd know something about it."

"I guess I wouldn't have to know much to understand that contraband would generally be delivered unmarked. How about you, Horace? Have you ever seen a barrel marked 'rum' before? Here in Portland?"

"I've never heard *tell* of it," avowed Horace.

"What are you trying to convince me of?" said the officer, looking almost ready to be convinced.

"Wouldn't it be a shame to spoil a man's wedding," offered Sundry, "simply on account of someone's bad judgment by way of a joke?"

"A joke? I don't know that illegal liquor is a joke, there, fellow."

"Mister Walton would consider it serious indeed," said Sundry.

"He knocked down old Adam Tweed with a single shot last fall," said Horace out of the blue.

"Adam Tweed?" said the policeman. "Is it *that* Mister Walton?"

"It is," said Sundry simply. Sundry wasn't the sort of man to curry favor for himself and he was sorry he hadn't thought to do so for Mister Walton.

"Hmmm," said the policeman. "We're not to show favoritism, you know. We were taken to task for that business with the mayor's brother-in-law."

"Once the wedding is over," said Sundry, adding fuel to the fire of the policeman's nascent decision, "and after I stand up with Mister Walton, I'll come back and we'll deal with this."

"Knocked down Adam Tweed, eh?" said Officer Rye. "*That* was a good piece of work. We'd been wanting that one for some time."

"Oh, he was poison, was Adam Tweed," asserted Horace.

"A joke, eh?" said the officer. Clearly he was a fair-minded man. "All right then. I'm waiting here with the keg, and Mr. McQuinn will wait with me, notwithstanding his declaration of innocence." Cuthbert Rye was fair-minded, but he wasn't above irony. "You go ahead and stand up with your friend now." He nodded curtly and with a frown.

"I'm much obliged," said Sundry. He turned back toward the front of the house and was startled to see that Mr. and Mrs. Baffin had come into the kitchen during the preceding dialogue. Their own expressions of elderly concern and shock had perhaps aided him in his campaign. "Let's not speak to Mister Walton about this if we can help it," he said as he passed them.

"But what are we to do?" she wondered aloud.

Sundry tapped the side of his head and said, "I have a thought."

"Gory, Hod!" pronounced Maven, when Sundry had left the room. "Isn't it something!"

"I guess probably it is," agreed Horace.

8. Gathered on That Day

Truthfully, Sundry did *not* have a thought, but it seemed too bad to worry the Baffins. For the span of a breath or two, he paused before the door to the birthing room or sickroom; near the pantry, and with its own fireplace, this smallest room in the house had been used to both purposes. Several people (Mister Walton included) had been born in that room, and some (such as Mister Walton's Aunt August) had died there; but Sundry did not consider the significance of a bride's donning her wedding dress there.

With no more than a general idea of what was being accomplished behind that door, he was abashed to hear, indistinctly, Mrs. Nowell express Miss McCannon's Christian name with the sort of pleasure and wonder that could only mean the bride was dressed and ready. Feeling that he had heard something, however unremarkable or oft repeated, that had not been meant for his ears, he strode into the hall and mounted the stairs at a clip.

"Ten minutes before the hour of two," came the voice of Mr. Ephram.

Mister Walton waited nervously in the master bedroom. "There you are," he said when Sundry came in. Mr. Seacost stood to one side, looking amused and meditative.

"Sorry," said Sundry, giving his own tie an extra pull.

"No, no," insisted the grand fellow. "I don't think you could call it a wedding if the groom wasn't ready to faint dead away."

"You might not call it a wedding if he does," suggested Sundry.

"Never fear," said Mister Walton. "You'll get me to the altar. I have every faith." He patted his brow with a handkerchief while Sundry led the way downstairs.

"Is it two yet?" asked the groom.

"I don't think so," said Sundry. He expected news of the hour to rise from the parlor at any moment.

"I think a breath of air is in order," said Mister Walton. Sundry opened the front door, and he and Mr. Seacost stepped out with the groom.

The day had become everything they could have wanted and an Edenic instance of summer on the coast of Maine. The sun was high and warm, the ocean breeze soft and restorative. The greens of the oaks and maples and chestnuts along Spruce Street could almost hurt the eye, and past roofs and the crowns of other trees on streets below them there was a glint of separate green from the harbor itself. Mister Walton appeared incapable of moving till he had taken it in.

But Sundry had a strange and fleeting consciousness of the dark interior of Pearce Eddy's waterfront flophouse, a vision that welled up from the center of his bright view, carrying with it equal degrees of gratitude and regret. He was at a loss to describe even to himself how that recent experience warred with the present moment, but Mister Walton expressed it for him and also spelled the darker haunt away by saying simply, "We are blessed."

Sundry would think about it later. "On to the next thing," he said.

"Gentlemen," said Mister Walton when he entered the parlor. He who had always carried his portly frame with unconscious savoir-faire appeared to the members of the club as dapper as they had ever seen him, and they were moved to spontaneous applause. Mister Walton blushed and bowed, and Sundry heard his bespectacled friend say, in a quiet, if delighted, voice, "I see Mr. Deltwire received his invitation."

Sundry had forgotten the drummer, or perhaps had merely accepted the stranger's presence in the house. It was a tradition in the Moss family that an uninvited guest brings good fortune, so it is not strange that Sundry was disposed to let the man in the checkered suit stay, even if Felton P. Deltwire looked a bit like the palace guard, standing to attention by the door with the *Queen of the Carpet Sweepers* gripped in one hand.

"So glad you could come," said the groom, the statement sincere and punctuated with a hearty handshake.

"It's very nice of you," said Felton P. Deltwire, as if he had received a formal letter of invitation.

Mister Walton met Mrs. Seacost with an embrace. "Mr. Ephram," he then said, and shook hands with that worthy fellow. Speaking the names of Mr. Eagleton and Mr. Thump, he did the same. The gentlemen of the club were visibly moved, and they hemmed and blinked as their chairman went on to speak to Stuart Nowell and Jared McCannon. The room was filled with greeting, and charter members joined in as if they themselves had only just arrived.

"Expected sunny afternoon," said Eagleton to Mr. Nowell, "though more clouds by evening and possible rain, clearing once again by morning."

"High tide at 1:48," Thump informed Jared McCannon.

"It's four minutes before two o'clock," said Ephram.

"Well," said Thump, "that was eight minutes ago then, wasn't it. Good heavens! The next high tide at 1:16," he corrected. "A.M."

Jared McCannon looked interested, though surprised. He had met the Moosepath League in the summer of the previous year but had perhaps wondered, in the meantime, if he had imagined it.

The Baffins came into the parlor; she stationed herself at the organ, and he stood beside her. Mister Walton insisted that the pretty Spark girls join them, and they demurely sat by the front windows and gathered appreciative (and all very proper) glances from the men in the room. Sundry feared that Mister Walton would insist on going into the kitchen in search of Horace McQuinn and Maven Flyce, whereby the groom would be apprised of the keg and the cop therein; but the groom was yet dizzy with the moment, and his memory was not so complete.

Ephram was consulting one of the three or four watches that he carried about his person, and Eagleton looked as if he'd been pinched. Thump offered to pump the organ's foot treadles, and the instrument wheezed into life under the exquisite notes of "If My Songs Had Wings."

Reverend Seacost, who had been talking quietly with Mr. Nowell, took his place beside Mister Walton and said in a low tone, "The moment of truth is at hand." Mischievously he said to Sundry, "Prop him up."

They stood by the hearth and awaited the coming revelation. Sundry thought he might *have* to "prop him up" as Mister Walton faltered a little. The groom was shaking slightly, and Sundry had a flash of that terrible moment, not a week ago, when his friend had fallen headfirst in a sudden faint.

"Are you all right?" asked Sundry under his breath.

Mister Walton took a breath, then appeared calm again. Fingering one of his cuff links, he said, "I have hardly been better."

"Watch closely everything that happens next, young man," said Mr. Seacost with continued good humor. "Our friend may ask you what occurred when all is done."

"I promise," said Sundry.

And anyone with a low degree of tolerance for what the skeptical world might consider "immoderate sentiment" herewith has permission to forgo the ensuing chapter. The Moosepath League offers no apologies.

9. The Wedding

"My word!" said Mister Walton. "Which way are they coming in?" There were two doors to the parlor—one from the dining room and the other from the hall—and he did not know by which door his bride would enter. "We never spoke about it," he said.

Sundry saw a flash of white in the hall and made a gesture in that direction. Mr. Thump tromped the organ treadle with admirable energy, and the instrument sounded like church itself. When the song was done,

Mrs. Baffin startled the bearded Moosepathian by touching his hand af-
fectionately. Then she nodded to him, Thump recommenced his labors,
and she began to play Mendelssohn's "Wedding March."

Miriam Nowell entered the parlor, wearing a beautiful sky blue dress
and a spray of white flowers in her dark hair. One eyebrow lifted when she
saw Mister Walton—a shot across the bow, so to speak, and a friendly
warning of what was to come. The portly fellow gave a small chuckle, and
Miriam, pleased with herself, took her place opposite Sundry.

The bride's brother then came into view; Jared McCannon was tall and
good-looking and appropriately serious. There was a white sleeve on his
arm, and then Mister Walton saw the white dress attached to the sleeve
and the very vision within the dress that he had so anticipated yet could
hardly have imagined. Phileda McCannon had tears in her eyes and a
smile on her lips that looked as if it might at any moment turn into happy
laughter. There was something wry in the way her glasses were perched
upon her nose. Then a visible pleasure touched her as she saw her beau
and, perhaps as important, what effect seeing her had upon him.

Nearly of a height with Mister Walton, but slender, she had designed
her white dress with as little bustle and furbelow as she could reasonably
do without. The lines of her shoulders were strong and elegant, and her
high collar accented a graceful neck. In the pattern of her dress there was
almost the hint of an Empire waist, which had been in vogue a hundred
years before and to which her slim carriage was very much suited.

On her breast shone a brooch of silver and pearl, and Mister Walton
recognized this piece of jewelry as one that his father had given to his
mother on the occasion of their marriage. Again, he fingered one of his father's cuff links and felt that sense of extended grace as delivered to him by
people gone before. The dress, the bride, his mother's brooch, and the
moment all seemed timeless, and Mister Walton felt the hair at the back
of his neck lifting with glad anticipation.

There would be no formal *giving away*. Phileda, with some humor, had
declared the phrase "scandalous" (but "many a serious word," as someone
had already said that day). Jared was content to kiss his sister's cheek when
he had escorted her to Mister Walton's side, then find a place to stand beside the other guests.

Mister Walton was as still as if he were observing some natural phenomenon (an *exquisite* natural phenomenon) that might evaporate were he
to take a single breath. The music had stopped, but he did not know when.

Their eyes met—his in wonder and hers with that same mixture of tears and mischief—and she took his hand suddenly in a fierce grip.

Sundry watched life pour into his bespectacled friend. The groom's expression of wonder slowly melted into a soft smile, and his eyes filled with their own kind of gentle disposition. Mister Walton took a long-delayed and much-needed breath. Mr. Seacost gave them this moment—there in the parlor, with the sunlight coming through the open windows, and also the sea breeze and the song of birds from among the trees. The old minister even bowed his head. Sundry looked away.

"We gather together to unite in the holy estate of matrimony these two people," said Mr. Seacost, "in the name of God the Father, and the Son, and the Holy Spirit. Amen." Then he prayed, asking for God's love to move among them and to bless them all with peace and harmony.

"Amen," said bride and groom with the minister. Sundry's lips moved in accordance, and the gathering joined in with a collective and whispered "Amen."

"Dearly beloved," continued the minister, "forasmuch as marriage is a holy estate, ordained of God, and to be held in honor by all, it becometh those who enter therein to weigh, with reverent minds, what the Word of God teacheth concerning it. And our Lord Jesus Christ said: 'Have you not read that He who made them from the beginning made them male and female,' and said, 'For this reason a man shall leave his father and mother and be joined to his wife, and the two shall become one flesh? So they are no longer two but one flesh. What therefore God has joined together, let no man put asunder.'"

Mister Walton's eyes were closed; Miss McCannon watched him, and he raised his head and looked up when Mr. Seacost next spoke.

"Tobias Elisha Walton, wilt thou have this woman to thy wedded wife, to live together after God's ordinance in the holy estate of matrimony? Wilt thou love her, comfort her, honor and keep her in sickness and in health, and, forsaking all others, keep only unto her, so long as you both shall live?"

Over a sudden frog in his throat, Mister Walton said, "I will."

"Phileda Katherine McCannon, wilt thou have this man to thy wedded husband, to live together after God's ordinance in the holy estate of matrimony? Wilt thou love him, comfort him, honor and keep him in sickness and in health, and, forsaking all others, keep only unto him, so long as you both shall live?"

Miss McCannon's blue eyes grew wide, almost as if she hadn't expected such a question. Then she said, "Oh, I will." Her eyes were brimming.

Mr. Thump stood and read in his deep tones the pertinent verses from Colossians 3:12–15, calling for kindness, forbearance, charity, and peace.

Mr. Seacost then spoke in meditation, calling upon the images of time and tide and climate to exemplify nature as experienced in the course of a life and the conduct of a marriage. Certain members of the gathering were moved by these metaphors, and Mister Walton and Miss McCannon smiled through them. Another prayer was offered, another "Amen" chorused through the room, and Mr. Seacost said, "I would enjoin you to take each other's hands—if you had ever let go of them," and there was a murmur of laughter. "Toby, if you would repeat after me: I, Tobias Elisha Walton . . ."

Vows very much like those they had already voiced were repeated, but to each other. Mister Walton very seriously captured his bride's eyes and spoke the solemn promise without hesitation.

"I, Phileda Katherine McCannon . . ." Mr. Seacost continued.

Miss McCannon, for all her aplomb, found herself tongue-tied, and she tripped on a word or two and had particular trouble when asked to say, "and thereto I plight thee my troth." The breeze from the windows tugged at a stray lock of hair, which tress was then the very center of Mister Walton's world and attention.

Sundry was asked to produce the ring for the bride, and Mister Walton slipped the simple gold band on Miss McCannon's slender finger, saying, "Receive this ring as a token of wedded love and troth."

Then Miriam Nowell offered the groom's ring, and Phileda worked this with a little more trouble over Mister Walton's ring finger, saying in turn, "Receive this ring as a token of wedded love and troth."

Said Mr. Seacost, "O God, who art our dwelling place in all generations: Look with favor upon the homes of our land; enfold husband and wife, parent and child in the bonds of thy pure love; and so bless our homes, that they may be a shelter for the defenseless, a bulwark for the tempted, a resting place for the weary, and a foretaste of our eternal home in thee; through Jesus Christ our Lord. Amen.

"Forasmuch as Tobias Elisha Walton and Phileda Katherine McCannon have consented together in holy wedlock, and have declared the same before God and man, I pronounce them husband and wife: in the name of the Father, and of the Son, and of the Holy Spirit. Amen."

"What God hath joined together, let no man put asunder."

Mr. Seacost said very softly, "Toby," and to Mrs. Walton, "My dear," then more loudly to Mister Walton, "You may kiss the bride."

Again Mister Walton's eyes were closed, and the new Mrs. Walton's spilled with tears, and when they had kissed, simply and gently, he opened his eyes and she reached up and very slightly adjusted his tie.

10. The First Shot of a Distant Conflict

"My goodness' sakes!" said Eagleton. "Wouldn't you say, Ephram?"

"I was indeed going to," said Ephram with no hint of vexation that his words had been presupposed. He was, in fact, delighted to be of such close mind with his friend and rather thought it a compliment to himself that they were.

"Wouldn't you say, Thump?" said Eagleton.

"Hmmm?" said Thump.

Hearty congratulations to the newly married couple had been offered all the way around, and the gathering soon wandered into the dining room for a modest reception served up by the Spark girls. The wedding cake, Mrs. Spark's grand creation, presided over the table, and Annabelle and Minerva were laden with many compliments to carry to their mother, along with a few to keep themselves, for they were really very handsome young women.

Though occupying the center of everyone's interest, the bride and groom were blissfully unaware of even their own side of various conversations, and sometimes their answers were at odds with whatever subject was at hand. Mister Walton said, and very happily, "Do you think so?" when Thump spoke of the hour in which to expect the coming high tide, and the chairman would never have willingly caused his bearded friend such resultant confusion.

"Mr. Moss!" came a portentous *Hsst!* of a whisper in Sundry's ear. Annabelle Spark stood just behind him and looked ready to pluck his sleeve when he turned about. "The policeman is getting anxious."

"Is he?" said Sundry, with very little thought in the words. He exchanged a look with Mrs. Baffin but managed a small smile. She appeared to accept that he had a plan and turned back to the bride and groom. But the day had not been conducive to *scheming* against the unforeseen. Sundry had been bent on enjoying himself despite the situation at the back of the house. Annabelle waited in the pantry, looking anxious, her wide eyes questioning Sundry as he strode past.

"Ah! There you are," said Officer Rye. He looked as if he'd been pacing all the while. Horace still leaned with his elbow on the cupboard. Maven Flyce's astonished expression had hardly shifted. "I told you he'd be on his way," said Horace.

Sundry was startled. A second policeman was in the kitchen now.

"Mr. Moss," said Calvin Drum sharply.

"Officer Drum."

"This *is* awkward," said Officer Drum. "I don't like to trouble a man at his wedding, but Sergeant Frith sent me back to see what was keeping Cuthbert."

"I am amazed!" said Maven.

Annabelle and Minerva had pressed their faces past the kitchen door, and in a moment they stepped in to make way for the Baffins.

"We'll need to see the owner of the house," said Officer Rye.

"I'm afraid you're going to have get Mister Walton," said Officer Drum.

"Mister Walton doesn't know a thing about it, I promise you," said Sundry, "and as I took care of the preparations, this must be my doing, however accidental."

The Spark girls gasped, and the voices of Lucinda and Cedric Baffin were heard to take the blame upon themselves. "I'm sure Mr. Moss didn't know a thing about it!" said Annabelle, looking sweet in her distress.

"I still should speak to your employer," said Officer Rye, looking unconvinced by Sundry's short speech.

"I wish you wouldn't." Sundry stepped toward the door, as if to block the policeman's way. The door then bumped him in the back of the head.

Excusing himself, Mister Walton came into the kitchen. "What's happening?" he asked. "Sundry? What's the trouble?"

"Nothing at all," said Sundry, though the presence of the policemen and the expression on everyone's face certainly put the lie to his words.

"No?" said Mister Walton, with perhaps the tone of a parent who is one statement away from demanding the truth. "Officer Drum," he said, "and Officer—"

"Mister Walton," said Officer Drum.

"Congratulations to you, sir," said Officer Rye. "I am sorry to interrupt your wedding day with police business, but I was sent by Sergeant Frith on the strength of an informant."

"Police business? Informant?"

"Toby?" The door opened again, and the recently installed woman of the house stood at the threshold, surveying the puzzled and anxious faces. "Toby? What's the matter?"

"I'm not sure, my dear. Sundry?"

"It's the keg, here in your kitchen," answered the policeman as he backed away from the object.

The short barrel did look guilty, and Mister Walton let out a small gasp as he approached it. "Now, what do you suppose—" He looked across the kitchen at Horace McQuinn, with whom he had some history regarding the conveyance of illegal spirits.

"I don't *suppose* at all, sir," the policeman was saying. He had perhaps reached the end of his patience. "Now, *some*one is going down to the station with me, or *every*one is."

The situation grew only more awkward, and in more ways than one, when Ephram, Eagleton, and Thump came into the kitchen. "What is it? What is it?" said one of them. "Good heavens!" said another when they saw the policemen. "Hmmm!" said a third. *Room* began to sound like a mistaken nomenclature for the space they subsequently occupied. In addition, the person of Mr. Thump, who had rescued Officer Drum's well-being only a week or so ago, only made that policeman's duty the more unpleasant.

"The devil of it is—I beg your pardon, ma'am," said Calvin Drum, "the worst of it is that if I didn't know a one of you from Adam, I might hoist that keg and dump it down the sink without another word."

"*I* don't know them, and *I'm* taking someone with me to explain things to the sergeant," asserted Cuthbert Rye.

Calvin Drum looked as if he didn't know what to be embarrassed about. He shifted his feet, shrugged his shoulders, and let out a low growl. "Ever since that business with the mayor's brother-in-law," he said.

"I wouldn't allow you to make such an exception," said Mister Walton.

"It is odd circumstance," drawled Horace.

"It's *very* odd to have the word *rum* painted across the head," observed Mister Walton. "I do apologize, Officers. And the fact that you hesitate at all is appreciated. Officer Rye, I must thank you for allowing our recent ceremony to carry on uninterrupted. I shall, of course, go with you to talk about this with your sergeant."

"*We* shall go," corrected Phileda.

"I have arranged to take care of the whole business," said Sundry.

"No, no, Sundry, I can't allow it," said Mister Walton.

Mister Walton looked around, as if for his coat, and Phileda took hold of his arm, and Sundry began to ask the policemen if *he* couldn't represent the household when still another voice made itself heard and the general babble died away so that its sentiments could be repeated.

"I'd taste what's in that barrel before I marched a man away from his wedding reception," said Felton P. Deltwire, who held the *Queen of the Carpet Sweepers* in one hand and half a pie in the other.

"Here, now!" said Officer Rye. "Let's not be making light of it, and perhaps you'd like to come down and talk a bit with the sergeant yourself."

"I sold a *Queen of the Carpet Sweepers* to an *army* sergeant's wife once," said the drummer offhandedly. He took another bite of his pastry and said, "I only meant that regret might fit the other foot if you took this gentleman to the police station without first determining the contents of that keg."

"I guess it's pretty plain," said Officer Rye.

"That's just my point," said Felton P. Deltwire.

"Never judge a book by its cover," said Thump suddenly.

"Oh, my!" said Maven Flyce.

Officer Rye considered the keg with a frown, then exchanged looks with Horace McQuinn, who looked amused.

"Latch on to that, will you, Mr. Flyce?" said Calvin Drum.

"Who'd have thought?" said Maven.

"Calvin?" said Cuthbert Rye.

"I'll take the heat for this one," said Officer Drum.

In a moment they had the keg in the dry sink, and Sundry had gone to the cellarway for a hatchet, which Officer Drum took, saying, "I'm an old hand at this. Stand aside." He went to the sink and broached the barrel-head with a crack of the hatchet and a splash. The room held its collective breath, but it was evident, almost immediately, that Officer Drum sensed something he hadn't expected. He dipped a forefinger into the barrel and brought it out dripping with a rummy-looking substance. He did not put his finger to his mouth but held it under his nose and declared, "Turpentine!"

"I'm glad you didn't pour *me* a portion," said Felton P. Deltwire, who appeared to have found another pastry in one of his pockets.

"Well, this *is* mysterious!" said Mister Walton.

"But, Toby, what does it mean?" wondered Phileda.

"It's a *rum* trick, if you don't mind the phraseology," said Officer Drum. He gave Horace McQuinn a sharp look.

"I'll be!" said Officer Rye. He went to the sink and dipped a finger. They all gathered around the dry sink to see and smell for themselves.

"I never thought!" said Maven.

"It is a peculiarity," admitted Horace. "And a pretty hard business to visit a fellow on his wedding day."

I I. Indications

"Well, God bless the both of them," said Mrs. Spark. "It must have been a lovely wedding. Minerva said she cried." Mabel Spark was pounding out bread dough and fanning flour over half the kitchen. She paused in her labor to look through the cloud she had made. "But what was this about a keg of turpentine and the police?"

Sundry guessed that she knew the story top to bottom from her daughters, but some tales ask to be repeated and from every point of reference; he did not mind explaining his while he ate dinner. He might have eaten in the tavern, but he liked the family bustling around him. The growing noise from the tavern room briefly shouted whenever anyone opened the swinging door. Thaddeus Spark, looking as Mr. Thump–like as ever, came into the kitchen during Sundry's recitation.

Thaddeus leaned an elbow on the counter and paused to listen to the tale. Three of the Spark children, Minerva and Annabelle and Bobby, came in and out, pausing as long as they dared to hear Sundry's version of things, and though the young women had been there, they seemed the most interested.

"I can't understand the turpentine," said Thaddeus.

"It was Felton P. Deltwire's idea to broach the keg," admitted Sundry. He was speaking to Mrs. Spark, who might appreciate this, having met the man.

"He came in useful after all," she said.

"I wish I had thought of it," said Sundry.

"It was someone's idea of a joke," said Annabelle.

"Do you think?" Sundry wasn't so sure. "It reminds me of the sick pig that Mister Walton and I met just last week. When we found the cure for him, it was still another day or so before we discovered what had made him sick in the first place."

"Did you get Mr. Moss's room ready?" asked Mrs. Spark when Betty came down the back stairs. The girl had, and she was hurried off to other duties.

"I'm glad you had a room," said Sundry.

"Give the dear folk some peace and quiet," said Mrs. Spark. "When Thaddeus and I were married, they kept us up all night banging pots and singing." She rolled her eyes at the memory. "We'll put you on the third floor, if you don't mind," she said to Sundry. "With the family. Your Mr. Deltwire took the last room on the second, I'm afraid."

"I can climb another flight of stairs," said Sundry.

"I wasn't going to put *that* drummer on the same floor as the girls, I can tell you!" said the mother. "I think he followed them back here after the wedding, though he made out as if it were pure chance."

"That wasn't what kept *me* up," said Thaddeus proudly. He had a talent for hanging on to subjects. It took his wife a moment to realize that he was still talking about their wedding night, and she flung a potato at him. He deftly caught the spud, laughing happily at his own joke.

Sundry did not immediately look up from his meal, but he heard Annabelle whisper, "Daddy!" as she hurried out to the tavern room.

Thaddeus was still chuckling, but he grew serious when Davey appeared at the back stairs. "Mr. Ring's awake," said Davey. "I think he's in his right mind, too."

"Where's Melanie?" asked Mrs. Spark, wiping her hands on her apron and making for the stairs.

"She fell asleep in the chair."

"We shouldn't leave her alone in there."

Thaddeus was vacillating between his duties in the tavern room and those upstairs. "I'll go with you," said Sundry to Mabel, rising from his chair.

Mrs. Spark waited at the first landing, then led the way up the next flight of steps, which were narrow and contained; she opened the door at the top and led the way down the hall. Sundry stopped at the threshold to the sick-room, where the heat radiated as from a fevered breath. In the grate burned a low fire, which Sundry hardly believed was necessary. The curtains were drawn, and the glowing hearth doubled as light in the dim room.

The man whom Sundry had helped carry the day before lay in a small bed by the window. His breathing was quick. His eyes were deep and fiery, his lips drawn back as if in pain. Burne Ring stared at the small form curled up in the chair beside the bed, and someone might have thought, by his wild expression, that he intended some harm upon the sleeping child.

"The doctor said small beer," said Mrs. Spark. Davey stood behind her and he hesitated a moment before hurrying off. "Mr. Ring," she said, as if greeting a familiar guest at the door.

Burne Ring rolled onto his back, his breathing hard and shallow, and Sundry had the stabbing thought that the man was going to expire. Calm and businesslike, Mrs. Spark stirred the fire and threw in a few pieces of coal. She dusted her hands and advanced to the bed. But Burne Ring's eyes were closed now, his mouth open, his breathing fast.

"He's asleep again," said Mrs. Spark. She turned to the little girl in boys' clothes who was curled in the chair. "Let's take her to Tim's room."

Sundry slipped his arms beneath the sleeping child, surprised that she hardly stirred when he lifted her.

"He's asleep again," Mrs. Spark said to Davey at the door. He stepped aside with his cup of small beer. Sundry followed the woman down the hall. The family rooms at the Faithful Mermaid were plain and comfortable. The rugs were braided by hand, the pictures on the walls were from old calendars, and the sturdy furniture was from estate sales at older, declining homes. Timothy's room, which he shared with Bobby, had a single window overlooking the tavern sign and they could hear the creak of this wooden emblem when the wind shook it. While they stood between the two small beds there was a tap at the window, then another. Mr. Eagleton's predicted rain had commenced.

Tim was asleep, his hair standing in cowlicks over his pillow, his arms and legs thrown in all directions. Mrs. Spark pulled the covers back on Bobby's bed, and Sundry laid the sleeping girl down. Melanie stayed as she had been situated, and there was in her openmouthed breathing and her thin limbs something of her father that touched them.

"You don't want a kid, do you?" said Mrs. Spark. Her voice was quiet, and there was something in her tone that indicated she had no intention of letting Melanie Ring go.

"Someday," said Sundry.

"Sometimes they come before someday," she whispered. "I'd send her father to the hospital; but she insists on staying with him, and that's no place for a child."

"You may not have him very much longer," said Sundry, turning away from the little girl and saying this more to his feet than the woman beside him.

"I don't suppose we will." She brushed the hair from Melanie's forehead. Having seen her pound dough a few minutes before, Sundry was taken by how gentle she could be. She was not unhandsome, Mrs. Spark, but she looked like some years of hard work and child rearing. A few of those years fell off in that moment, and she might have been a young mother stroking the sleeping head of her first child.

Timothy let out a groan and turned over. Mrs. Spark and Sundry left on tiptoes. They paused again at the door to the sickroom. Davey Spark had recommenced his watch over the man. He yawned in his chair. "It's long, sitting here," he said.

"You should take up knitting," said his mother, not pausing to find out whether her oldest born thought this funny. "I'll show you your room," she said to Sundry. "And then you'd better go down and have some pie."

"I can do that," he said.

12. Departure
(June 5, 1897)

"I wouldn't want to say anything in front of Phileda," Mister Walton began to say when the steam whistle of the *Manitoba* let out a blast. He waited, one finger raised and his posture eloquent of his unfinished statement. On their way down the pier, Phileda had stopped to peruse the wares of one of the wharfside vendors and they were a little ahead of her. When the last of the whistle shriek died and his ears had ceased to ring, Mister Walton said, "I am concerned to be leaving without first having solved the business of that keg."

Sundry wondered if Miss McCannon (*Mrs. Walton*, he reminded himself) would express something similar before the ship cast off and when Mister Walton was out of earshot. "I thought that business was done with," he said.

Mister Walton smiled. "I seem to remember that when our good friend Hercules appeared to have been cured, it was you who wondered what had made him sick in the first place."

"I was just concerned that any talk of *curing* might make a pig anxious."

Mister Walton laughed. "I am going to miss you, my friend."

"I can't believe that."

"Well—" The portly fellow took off his spectacles and rubbed them with a handkerchief. He stopped and looked back for Phileda. "It would be embarrassing to lose my wife at this point in our marriage."

Phileda caught sight of them, smiled, and waved, a newly purchased scarf fluttering with her gesture. This morning she was dressed a little more ornately than was her habit; this was the first evidence of her trousseau, after all, and she and her new husband were boarding ship this morning, no matter the serious nature of their mission.

While she paid the vendor, Mister Walton considered Sundry with an odd expression. "You're not thinking of leaving my employ?" he asked.

"Leaving?" Sundry pulled a frown. "No, I hadn't thought of it."

Mister Walton nodded to himself.

"I needed something bright to wave when we cast off," said Phileda as she caught up with them, and she had certainly picked the brightest scarf for the purpose. Taking Mister Walton's arm, she leaned close to him as they continued up the wharf. The porter with their bags was long out of sight.

In the shadows of buildings along the wharf there were patches of dampness from last night's rain; but the clouds had graciously disappeared, and the crowds had come out in force on this Saturday morning— the ladies with their bright dresses and parasols, the men striding about *looking business* whether they had any or not. Arriving passengers and the friends and relatives here to see them off milled at the foot of the gangplank and lined the upper deck of the steamship. There were ship spotters and children and vendors and even the occasional dog and the smell of peanuts roasting and the colorful flags of the steamship flapping in the harbor breeze above it all.

"Look who has anticipated us," said Mister Walton, and as if by fiat the crowd parted and three sprucely dressed gentlemen in top hats were revealed.

The charter members were looking up at the steamship's stack and were leaning so far back to do so that they had to hold their hats onto their heads to keep them from falling off. Contrary to appearances, Mr. Thump was informing his friends of the salutary qualities of the American walnut. "There are black ones and white ones, I was informed, and the one on High Street is nearly as tall." He directed their gazes with the day's edition of the *Portland Courier.* "The nut is said to enrich the blood," he added.

"Very good, Thump," said Ephram, shading his eyes with the *Eastern Argus.*

"It's a very nice tree," agreed Eagleton, who might have been looking at it instead of the stack of a steamship. This morning he was not without his *Portland Daily Advertiser.*

"The hull is very hard," said Ephram, speaking of the walnut.

"Steel this thick," said a man who was standing nearby. He held his thumb and forefingers apart.

Ephram, Eagleton, and Thump were not quite ready for this semantic leap; but Mister Walton greeted them in the next instant, and walnuts and ships' hulls were quickly forgotten. Ephram shook hands with Mister Walton, and Eagleton exchanged similar greetings with Sundry while Thump hesitated, then gently agitated Phileda's offered hand. Thump looked uncertain, and perhaps he wondered if she was going to buss him on the cheek—a thing she had done recently when she and Mister Walton first announced their engagement. She let him off with a warm smile, and he blushed anyway. Eagleton then pumped Mister Walton's hand with great vigor and Thump shook Sundry's hand and Ephram took his turn wishing his best to the new bride. Then the greetings and good thoughts continued round and finished with Ephram, Eagleton, and Thump's shaking one another's hands and seeming a little surprised about it.

"Who could have known," said Mister Walton, his hands behind his back in the attitude of unrehearsed oration, "and certainly I didn't, that when I returned to Portland last July, I would, in less than a year, gain such friendship? I have always thought myself blessed beyond my worth and yet now every former blessing, and even every trouble and dismay, seem ten times as fortunate, since they have added up in experience to this moment when I can call such men friends and such a woman friend and wife."

There was much blinking of eyes among the membership. Perhaps the sun was too bright. There was another shout from the steam whistle, and they had the impression that the ship was growing impatient.

"All ashore that's going ashore!" shouted the first mate from the head of the plank.

"They're very punctual," said Mister Walton. "And I fear we did not rise with the sun this morning."

To the members of the club, this last statement was suggestive in a manner that was wholly unintentional on the part of their chairman. It was perhaps the plural pronoun linked with the verb *to rise*, not to mention the state, that is the place, well, at any rate, perhaps it were best—!

Thump shook himself from a brief reverie, and Eagleton looked as if he had discovered a pebble in his shoe. Ephram meanwhile did not even think to consult one of the three or four watches that he carried about his person. Mrs. Walton did not help their state of confusion by invoking Mrs. Morrell's upcoming June Ball, which they had pledged to attend.

"Yes, well," said Ephram.

"Exactly," said Eagleton.

"Hmmm," said Thump.

"I shall expect descriptive summaries all the way around," Phileda insisted, "and an account of the lovely ladies with whom you exercise your dancing skills. And Mr. Moss?"

"I have my ticket," said Sundry, his arms folded before him and his expression a perfect composite of the amused and the doubtful.

She reached out and squeezed his hand, which was meant as a tacit expression of "Good luck."

Late arrivals hurried by, crossing paths with those who had said their farewells and were now returning to the wharf. There was often a festive atmosphere about the docks when a steamship arrived or departed, particularly on such a handsome summer day, when the sea breeze perfectly complemented the strength of the sun and the gulls and terns wheeled noisily overhead. The salt air itself invigorated a body, and the general bustle of the wharves lent constant interest to the eye.

But the attention of the Moosepath League, and of Sundry Moss, was wholly upon the Waltons as they mounted the gangplank, and Mister and Mrs. Walton's attention was almost wholly, and quite pardonably, upon each other. Happy as he was for them both, Sundry felt very mixed emotions to see them go; he thought himself a little adrift when he considered the weeks and maybe months ahead without the steady presence of his friend and employer and the happy wryness and wisdom of Phileda McCannon. And the June Ball, so quickly approaching, was of more consequence to him, and therefore answerable for more anxiety, than he would have admitted to anyone.

"I do believe they are the picture of a *handsome couple*," said Ephram when the newlyweds reached the top of the plank and waved again. It was a phrase he had read in a book not long ago.

Sundry and the members of the club returned the wave.

"You are very right, my friend," said Eagleton. "Don't you think, Thump?"

"Hmmm," said Thump. He lowered his bearded visage, as if in thought, then raised his head again and said, " *'They would benefit each acquaintance (and even the brief passerby) with their gracious mien and warm their surroundings by the kindness and happiness of their coupled tendencies.'"* Thump let this quote hang in the air before citing its source. "*The Rose Beneath the Street,* by Mrs. Rudolpha Limington Harold."

"Ah, yes!" said Ephram. "That was a fine story. And how very right." He could believe that these words were crafted to describe their departing friends.

Sundry took a moment to regard these men with whom his lot had been so unpredictably cast. They, too, had about them the wisdom of kindness and would never have guessed that the quote from Mrs. Harold might well describe themselves. They were, in fact (in their own way), as steady company as a person could want. Sundry felt a sudden confidence regarding Ephram, Eagleton, and Thump. It was as if the couple on the deck above them had indeed left behind a sense of warmth and grace, and that those left upon the wharf would know what to do simply by imagining what Tobias and Phileda Walton would have done in their place.

The steamship let out another whistle, and the final call was shouted from the deck. A bell rang. The air grew cacophonous with good-byes and last-minute instructions between those leaving and those staying behind. The Waltons did not attempt any communications beyond the occasional wave. A new and unexpected source of noise had risen from the other side of the wharf, and their attention was increasingly taken by something beyond the crowd.

Sundry was aware of a cheer and a chorus of laughter. A voice carried over the general din. He could not at first make out the words, but he was surprised, as he peered past and above the heads in the crowd, to see the paddle end of a great long oar rise like a sprout in the air. Beside him, Eagleton was getting a little better look, and Ephram almost as good a view, but Thump was standing on his tiptoes and seeing little or nothing past the swarm of people. There was more laughter as the oar was lowered and several people were obliged to move aside. Sundry glimpsed a vast bear of a man, unshaven, with ruddy cheeks, blond hair cast behind his ears, and a cap tilted precariously at the back of his head. The big fellow was carrying a haversack in one hand and that great sweep of an oar over his shoulder.

The fellow stalked through the crowd, and folks leaped aside till there was only the Moosepath League standing in the way and Thump at their center, leaning forward and looking amazed.

"I don't expect anything *this* close," growled the sailor, but he looked like a man not ready to take anything by chance.

"I beg your pardon?" said Thump. Ephram and Eagleton stepped closer to their friend. Sundry watched from a pace or two away, a little less daunted than the members of the club, but not entirely at his ease. "Can I be of assistance, sir?" said Thump.

"He's looking for Fiddler's Green, man!" shouted someone.

The wharf grew almost quiet, while Thump pondered this news. "I've never been," he admitted.

There was a roar of laughter from several sailors in the crowd, but the immense fellow before Thump seemed to consider it a serious business. "Fiddler's Green," he declared, as if reading from a stone, "is a form of Paradise; that is, Heaven; that is, anyplace that won't starve you, burn your hide, or freeze parts that you might be needing in port. Fiddler's Green takes some wandering to find, and there's only one way of knowing it. Throw an oar over your shoulder—"

"I do beg your pardon," said Thump again for no obvious reason.

"Take that oar with you wherever you go," continued the sailor, "and wherever you go, you go as far from the sea as the sea will allow (when you leave the sea, you'll *find* the sea if you go far enough, if you take my meaning), and you roam with that oar till you come to a place where they ask to look at it, and they peer at it, and they consider it, and they ask you what it is."

"Do they really?" said Thump. He was astonished.

"And then you've found it," said the fellow. "Fiddler's Green!" He patted Thump's back as if they had been friends all their lives. Thump looked as stiff as if he were expecting snow down his neck. Once again hefting his haversack and swinging his oar back over his shoulder (expertly missing several onlookers' heads by mere inches), the big man strode toward the street without further word or even a good-bye to his newfound confidant.

"Be sure to write, Robin!" shouted one wag, and the sailor simply raised a hand and waved.

The sound of the gangplank being lifted drew everyone's attention back to the *Manitoba* and a new volley of sentiments flew between the deck and the wharf. Sundry spotted the Waltons a little further up the rail, and he waved. Mrs. Walton looked elegant, waving her newly purchased scarf. It was the brightest scarf or kerchief on display, and there were many. Mister Walton took off his glasses and rubbed them with his handkerchief. Sundry knew that his friend was feeling a potent mix of emotions. Mister Walton had beside him his new and beloved wife, he was steaming to Hal-

ifax to meet his nephew, he was by nature a forward-thinking and opti-
mistic fellow; but he was waving good-bye to his friends. Life is unpre-
dictable.

Sundry sighed—a strange thing to hear from him if anyone had been
able to hear it among the noise of the crowd and the rumble of the *Manitoba*. He saw that Mrs. Walton was gesturing at her side, patting her waist,
and without thinking Sundry touched his own waist and then put his hand
in his coat pocket and felt a folded piece of paper there.

He nodded to her. She seemed satisfied and turned away. When the
tugs were escorting the steamship into the harbor channel, Sundry took
the piece of paper from his pocket and read it.

> *I did not want to say anything in front of Toby*, it read, *but I am
> concerned that the business regarding that mysterious keg is not fin-
> ished and that you have been left to deal with its sequel by yourself.
> Please take care and do not put yourself in the way of any trouble.
> Thank you for your friendship and particularly for your companion-
> ship with Toby. We will be anxious for our return to Portland and to
> our friends. Affectionately, Phileda.*

from the *Eastern Argus*
June 7, 1897

SEA AND SHORE

Various Happenings of Interest
Along the Wharves

A smokey souwester was holding forth on the waterfront yesterday afternoon and it blew so hard that many of the people who were
enjoying their usual Sunday stroll along the wharves had considerable difficulty in keeping their headgear in place. The surface of
the harbor was dotted with whitecaps and very few of the numerous
crafts that were flitting about carried full sail. The Thomson liner
Iona was expected to arrive but she had not been sighted at dark.

There was not much in the way of business, it being Sunday. The
only English steamer in port was the *Vancouver*, so a good deal of

talk along the wharves ran in the direction of that vessel, the officers and crew of which were kept busy during the afternoon receiving visitors. Others spoke of the *Manitoba*, which left port on Saturday, and some speculated where she might be, a day out.

Talk of another kind centered on a peculiar apparition of the day before, which ascended the Atlantic and St. Lawrence Wharf at about the same moment the *Manitoba* was steaming from the harbor. A large fellow—something of a giant, claimed observers—appeared in the crowd and was pretty hard to miss as he added to the height of his general person by his possession of an oar, the size of which itself would have done justice to Cleopatra's barge. He carried the sweep like a baseball bat over his shoulder and was last seen, by the wharfside walkers, peering one way, then the other, along Commercial Street, before striding away in a westerly direction.

The large four master *Wm. B. Palmer* arrived from Philadelphia yesterday with a cargo of coal for the Maine Central Railroad. . . .

BOOK TWO
MRS. MORRELL'S
ANNUAL JUNE BALL
June 8, 1897

13. Picking the Principals

Every spring, Philbrook Newcomb Morrell returned to Portland long enough to see his family properly situated in their mansion on Vaughan Street and to attend his wife's annual charitable ball, held on the second Tuesday in June. Only a few servants kept house during the off-season, but all year long the mansion that Philbrook's father had built captured the passing eye with its Italianate architecture and façade of unusual red-brown stone. The return of the Morrell clan was always duly noted in the papers, and at the first rumor of the approaching festivities, Portland matrons began to nose about the shops (or even foray to Boston) for the latest fashions in which to deck their marriageable daughters.

The Morrells had been away since fall, and letters from Portland may have neglected salient details of local gossip, such as the engagement of Cordelia Elizabeth, the daughter of James and Mercia Underwood, to one Dresden Ebuelon Scott of Millinocket. The Underwoods were respectable, if quiet, people in local society, their daughter thought to be unfortunately red of hair by the mothers of other daughters and a beautiful redhead by the sons of those mothers. The mothers clucked their tongues and said, "Wasn't it nice that the Underwood girl found someone?" and the sons shook their heads and wondered how the fellow could be so lucky. The daughters, on the whole, liked Cordelia, for she was a bright creature with a contagious sense of fun and a ready gift of laughter; but they were not sorry to see the field of competition narrowed.

It was not only Cordelia's beauty but also the romantic origins of her fiancé (and the tale of their *affair*) that made them the center of curiosity. Mr. Scott was a woodsman and a guide who called the trackless forests his home. The previous summer he had rescued Cordelia from abduction (with some help from the young woman herself, who knocked one of her kidnappers senseless with an iron ladle). There had been vague statements in the papers and much talk, but all that most people knew (or thought they knew) was that buried treasure had been involved and that the scheme of modern-day pirates foiled.

Now word was about town that those attending the Morrell Charitable Ball would have their first and perhaps only look at the mysterious groom before the wedding day. Adding to the anticipation of this year's ball was another rumor that the recently formed gentlemen's club known as the Moosepath League would be in attendance. The brief history of this club involved several extraordinary adventures, which were said to encompass (among other things) an escaped circus bear, the rescue of a police officer from a falling piano, and even the affair of Cordelia Underwood herself.

The weather had been cooperative during the first week of June, but clouds gathered on the morning of the eighth; the harbor became *squally*, and the streets of the city wet with rain. Those gathering at the Morrells' were undaunted; umbrellas were furled, wet wraps and coats and men's hats doffed to servants in the hall, and the bright chandeliers and music in the ornate ballroom warmed away all thoughts of inclement weather. The musicians were already playing when the first guests arrived.

While greeting their guests at the front door, Philbrook and Tabitha Morrell were conscious of an unspecified excitement this evening, and naturally curious about it—never more so then when a young lady waiting at the door hurried to the ballroom to announce that the Underwoods had arrived. "This is the beau, behind them, with their daughter, I suppose," said Philbrook. Mr. Morrell was an affable man, with large handlebar mustaches and a graying head of hair. "Who's that behind them?"

"It's Mrs. Underwood's sister, Grace Morningside. Her husband, Henry, captained the *Sea Beard*, you remember. They're from Ellsworth."

"Ah, yes. He died a few years ago, I think."

"That's their daughter, Priscilla, with Grace."

Six people were mounting the steps during this quiet dialogue, and Philbrook put a hand out to James Underwood. "Philbrook," said James, "you know my wife, Mercia, and my daughter, Cordelia. This is my daughter's fiancé, Dresden Scott."

The host greeted Mrs. Underwood, who was elegant and charming, and he mentally marked his dance card as he took her hand. Then he turned to the daughter. "Miss Underwood."

"Mr. Morrell." Cordelia looked like the very emblem of summer in her green gown and with her beautiful red hair piled up in the latest fashion. She fairly glowed, and Mr. Morrell was much affected.

He was a man of commerce, however, and used to playing with a poker face; he turned to the prospective groom without revealing his reluctance to leave off the hand of this beauty. "Mr. Scott," he said, "I have been hearing great tales about you all week."

Dresden Scott, a tall blond fellow with a beard and the look of little experience in a formal suit, shook the hand of Philbrook Morrell and said dryly, "I *try* to stay out of the court news, sir."

Philbrook liked this and was about to say something when his wife introduced herself to the much-talked-about Dresden Scott. The host, in turn, greeted Grace and Priscilla Morningside.

Grace was a wispy woman who would have been handsome if she had smiled more easily. Her daughter (who did smile softly) was mild and diffident; Priscilla was neither as effervescent nor as obviously beautiful as her cousin Cordelia, but she had lovely raven black hair and intelligent dark eyes behind her round spectacles. Her features were a shade too long, perhaps, but there was something pleasant and even sweet about her, and beneath this sweetness, Philbrook (who was a sympathetic old Yankee) sensed a hint of melancholy.

What she did possess was a *brimful* of figure, for if Cordelia was a willow, Miss Morningside had the requisite portions to do justice to the fashions of the day, and she was wearing (with visible uncertainty) a dress that made this fact obvious. Mr. Morrell guessed, however, that many a swain would rush past this young woman for the chance to waltz with other, more confident flowers, but he thought they would miss something for not cluttering Miss Morningside's dance card with their names.

Philbrook had a diversion he practiced wherever he went; he called it Picking the Principals, and it had come from a lesson he had been given as a schoolboy by an exacting professor of literature. The schoolboy had made a game of it, and since that lesson, whenever he was among a crowd of people, he tried to imagine the story that was taking place around him—though he himself might command only a bit part—and for this story he *picked the principals*. The object of the game was to eschew the obvious and find the players who would sneak up on the reader of a novel or the audience at a play.

It is the prerogative of a woman to shake hands or demur. Grace Morningside, who was herself dressed in a dark gown that did no injury to a determined widowhood, only inclined her head and, with a look toward her daughter, gave Philbrook the impression that she expected Priscilla to do likewise. The daughter hesitated but offered her hand while Mr. Morrell welcomed her to his home. "Thank you," she said, and made something very pretty and graceful with a slight curtsy. She had become his first principal of the evening. Several more were in the offing.

Four gentlemen stepped from a carriage at the gate, and among them was a short, stocky fellow with an extraordinary profusion of beard who prompted an elusive recognition in Philbrook's mind. The host moved out onto the bricks above the front steps, protected from the rain by the portico roof, and he watched as this quartet quickly traveled the front walk. Philbrook was searching his tongue for the bearded fellow's name when a new announcement ran from the front hall of the Morrell mansion to the ballroom; the news was relayed in stage whispers: "The Moosepath League is here!" The four men had reached the steps by this time, and the waiting host, with sudden recollection, called out, "Joseph Thump!"

The bearded guest halted and peered up the steps. "Mr. Morrell!"

"Philbrook, please. Good heavens, it's been years!" The host braved the rain to meet Mr. Thump halfway down the steps and accompany him and his fellows to the door. "And what is this I hear about you and your club jaunting about the state, rescuing people and fighting fires? Philbrook Morrell," he said, when they were out of the rain, and he offered his hand to a tall, blond fellow, who pumped Philbrook's hand with great enthusiasm.

"Mr. Moss!" came a delighted cry, and Cordelia Underwood ran onto the porch, saying, "Oh, Mr. Moss!" and pressing one of the other men's hands in hers. "You must tell me all about the wedding! Was Miss McCannon *very* beautiful?"

"I will," said this young man with a smile, and "Yes, certainly."

"Cordelia!" hissed Grace Morningside from the door, but the young woman's parents greeted the Moosepath League with almost as much warmth.

Mr. Thump introduced Philbrook to Christopher Eagleton (the tall blond fellow), who continued to shake hands, assuring their host that the rain would end by midnight and that clearing skies would herald a fine summer day.

"Joseph and I were friends at school," said Philbrook. To be truthful, they had not had much to do with each other, but he had always liked the quiet and courteous Joseph Thump. It was a wonder that he had recognized the man behind that extraordinary beard.

Matthew Ephram, whose fine dark mustaches rivaled Philbrook's own, was introduced next, whereupon this gentleman (with his free hand) produced a watch from his vest pocket and announced the time, which was seven minutes past eight. Philbrook was amused and a little confounded as

Mr. Ephram, still shaking his hand, consulted a second and then a third watch before nodding his assurance that this information was accurate. "Mister Walton's clock," Philbrook thought the man said.

Without further prompting, Joseph Thump said, "High tide at 3:14 A.M." as if everyone present were planning a cruise. The fourth member of this quartet was then presented as Sundry Moss, and the host was sure he had misheard till the young man smiled and indicated by a short nod that his name often required repetition.

Chatter and laughter filled the porch, and standing in the hall, Mrs. Morrell peered over several heads with exasperated curiosity. From one side of this flurry the impressive Dresden Scott watched with amused affection as his fiancée beamed at the Moosepath League and engaged Mr. Moss with a dozen questions about a recent wedding.

Grace and Priscilla Morningside stood back (and from different motives, it was plain). Philbrook caught an expression of specific interest, mixed with apprehension, on the younger woman's face, and following the flash of her glance, he caught its reflection, very nearly as reserved, from Mr. Moss, who was long and wiry and not quite handsome beneath his brown hair and the unaccustomed black silk hat. The young man remembered himself and pulled the hat from his head; it might have been a greeting to Miss Morningside on the other side of the crowd. When Philbrook shot a look back, Priscilla was turned away, head down, and talking to her mother.

But other people were arriving, and Philbrook must fulfill his duties, though he did not forget the Moosepath League and the Underwoods when they left his porch for the ballroom. A society known as the Moosepath League belonged in *any* story according to his lights; the members themselves must be included simply because they seemed so strangely at odds with what he had heard about them, but the young man—this Sundry Moss—interested Philbrook very much, the more so since he could imagine Mr. Moss imagining the initials S. M. on Miss Morningside's dance card. Philbrook had picked his second principal and the Moosepath League besides.

14. Partners Bow

Sundry Moss was aware of a genteel melody that carried the air from inside the Morrell mansion. Stepping into the front hall, he thought it looked large enough to hold a town meeting, and some people did linger there, watching as the Moosepath and Underwood parties entered. Miss Underwood chatted beside Sundry, all the while holding Dresden Scott's arm with both hands and peering ahead of them for signs of her cousin Priscilla. "I don't know where she and Aunt Grace could have gotten to so quickly," she was saying. A servant by the stairs passed them each a dance card and steered them to their right, and they stepped into the opulent ballroom.

Sundry took in the ornate columns along the immediate wall, the vaulted, two-storied ceiling decorated with articulate constellations, the parqueted floor, the elaborate furnishings, and the elaborately dressed crowd. He had never been to such a place, or to such an event, and he wished that the Waltons were with him. There were two elements in his favor: The first was that he did not mind being impressed, or even appearing impressed; the second was that the young woman with the dark hair and round spectacles, who stood with her mother some yards off, accounted for about all the apprehension and nerves that he could ponder at one time.

Sundry had met Priscilla Morningside only twice before that night. It had been enough. The first time he saw her he had been struck by a quiet beauty, which was increased (he had been convinced) by the sweetness of the person beneath. A little more than a week ago they had met a second time, and something lingering and unstated from their first meeting had risen within him at the sight of her and the sound of her voice. He had met Priscilla Morningside only twice before that night, and it had not been anything *like* enough. He realized that he was shaking.

It had been Priscilla's custom (or, rather, her mother's resolution) that she dress in a fashion less than her age, which was almost twenty-two. A small bout of rebellion on the part of the daughter (instigated by her mother's unkind remark regarding a certain young man) and Cordelia's exuberant insistence had put Priscilla in her present and intriguing dress. The result was more than Sundry could have anticipated. Miss Morningside's hair was coiffed in a manner that suited her longish features; the glasses on her nose had the effect of making her look thoughtful and mild.

Priscilla wondered if she was up to this sort of luster and feared that she looked like a child playing in her mother's gown. Standing beside Grace, fingering the ivory cameo that was fastened about her graceful neck with a velvet ribbon of dark blue, Priscilla must have looked, to the veterans of former balls, uncertain and a little lost. To Sundry she seemed so completely *of a piece* and so obviously the center of anyone's attention who had the opportunity to look at her that he felt himself diminished by his own blockheaded daydreams and a fool for ever imagining that she had ever imagined him as anything more than a chance acquaintance.

Sundry himself was tall and broad-shouldered. If he was on the narrow side, it was the narrowness of youthful vigor. He moved with ease and (as a rule) without self-consciousness. Tonight his natural *élan* was sharpened by the *high élan* of his clothes. When Priscilla Morningside turned at the sound of Cordelia's voice, she saw the *braw* Mr. Moss cut out in the finest togs that Mister Walton's purse and the former Phileda McCannon's impeccable taste could afford; the fact that he had not the slightest idea of the effect of his ensemble simply made it the more emphatic. His hair was perhaps a shade too long, his features a little less than handsome, but he looked gallant and the very image of the well-to-do hero in a dozen stories Priscilla had read in the *Century*.

Cordelia caught the look that passed between these two and was startled by their mutual and barely concealed panic. "Quick, Dresden!" said Cordelia in a near whisper. "Do something!"

"Do something?" said Dresden Scott with more volume. When enjoined to "Do something!" in such dire tones, he was usually required to deal with an emergency that could arise only in the depths of the northern forests. Ballrooms were not his forte, not to mention that he had never been in one before. He was more amused than piqued by the mandate, however, and proved a quick thinker, even in this thicket. "Mrs. Morningside," he said, his voice cracking only slightly with the unaccustomed effort. Cordelia's aunt Grace looked dismayed to see her niece's tall fiancé approaching her with such strange familiarity. "Mrs. Morningside," he said, "have you met the members of the Moosepath League?"

She hadn't.

"Christopher Eagleton, madam," said that worthy. She did not offer her hand, so he bowed, looking very courtly and proper—and properly so, as he was both these things.

"Matthew Ephram," said the second in line. "We have heard such fervent praise of yourself and your children from our chairman!" He bowed also, and certainly as well as Eagleton.

"I am sure I am quite gratified," said Grace nervously.

"Joseph Thump," rumbled the third Moosepathian. He did not bow as much as he simply leaned forward.

"Rain falling off, late this evening," said Eagleton. "Wednesday expected to emerge in a seasonable manner. Winds south by southwest."

If anything, she looked more startled than before.

"High tide at 3:14," said Thump.

"It's twenty-two minutes past the hour of eight," informed Ephram.

People across the room might have thought that the charter members were vying for Grace Morningside's attentions, and she inadvertently encouraged such rumor with the appearance of tender indecision. With a hand at her breast to still her own rapid heartbeat, Grace looked from one member of the Grand Society to the other as if unable to judge among them.

"Priscilla," Cordelia was meanwhile saying. She gave Sundry a slight tug as she walked around the knot of introductions that surrounded her aunt.

Sundry did his best to appear as if his entire reason for being there were *not* embodied in the dark-haired young woman, who turned toward him without speaking to Cordelia, gave a small smile, and said, "Good evening, Mr. Moss."

"Miss Morningside," said Sundry, without the slightest notion of what to say next.

Cordelia was at no such loss. "Mr. Moss has all the news about Mister Walton's wedding!" she announced.

Sincere interest and an element of inherent kindness lifted Priscilla Morningside above her reticence; her smile broadened, her eyes widened, and she said, "Was Miss McCannon *very* beautiful?"

"She was," said Sundry, who seemed restricted to sentences of two words.

"I don't suppose," said Cordelia, "you're equipped to describe her dress."

"Oh, Cord!" said Priscilla, almost with a laugh. "Leave him alone." She waved a hand at her cousin, as if she would swat her.

"It was white," said Sundry with such a comic look of competence in this field of inquiry that Priscilla did laugh and put her hand to her mouth.

Cordelia laughed as well. She was aware that other groups in the great hall were wandering toward their united parties, perhaps in hopes of overhearing something interesting about the mysterious Moosepath League. Cordelia cast a glance at her fiancé, who gallantly held the fort between Aunt Grace and the gentlemen of the club. *Well,* she thought, *I will be spending the most of my life in his forests, so it serves him well!*

Dresden Scott (all six feet four inches of him) looked so completely out of place in this highly decorated and decorous setting that she fell in love with him all over again. He met her eyes and she gave him her "best shot" (as she was wont to call a particular expression that managed something coy and something *come hither* in the same instant). It was a peculiarity of this look that it must be cut off a little peremptorily, and she turned her attention back to Mr. Moss, who was telling Priscilla about the wedding.

However, Grace had heard Priscilla's delighted laugh, and a quick glance informed her that the young man she had once characterized as "a servant" was talking with her daughter. The mother's stricken countenance grew so much more stricken that Ephram, Eagleton, and Thump were straightaway concerned for her and offered, in concert, to see her to a chair.

"What?" she said. "Oh, dear me, no!"

"Please, Mrs. Morningside," said Eagleton. "Allow us to find you a seat. You look quite pale." Eagleton himself paled to realize that he had suggested anything of such a personal nature to someone (and most especially to a woman!) whom he had just met. "Of course, it is very becoming," he said without further study, and he paled some more. "Wouldn't you say, Ephram?"

"Oh, yes, certainly!" said Ephram before he had thought very much on what he was agreeing with. He thought that perhaps they would do well to look for *several* seats.

"Thump?" said Eagleton when Grace Morningside appeared startled and perhaps just a small bit flattered by this attention.

"Hmmm!" said Thump with more volume than that vowelless syllable might readily suggest.

"The Moosepath is on the pursuit," said one mordant wag who stood beside the punch table.

"What's that?" said another man nearby. He scanned the ballroom. "The Moosepath League, do you mean? Where are they?"

"Those three fellows, just this side of the redheaded beauty."

"Oh?" said the second man—a tall, elegant sort, who carried himself with terrific confidence. "How do you know them?"

"I don't. I heard several people talking about them when they came in."

"The Moosepath League," said the second man.

"I believe," said the first man, "they must have decided upon a contest for that woman's attention—the one they are speaking with now. There's not very much of her, but she has a decent face."

"You have an *in*decent mouth," said the second man.

The first fellow was unfazed. "Do you know her?"

"No."

"Do you know them? The *Moose*path League?" He pronounced the name of the club as if in mild disbelief.

"I have met one of them," said the second man. "I wouldn't have asked you to point them out if I had known the others, would I? I think I will go rescue that woman."

"Now, now," said the wag. "No need of a fourth dog on that fox. There's hardly enough of her to go around."

"I believe, Mr. Pleasance," said the second man, "that you are a villain. And I believe that if I were willing to dirty my hands, I might use them to strike you." And with that less than implied threat, he wheeled about, his coattails flying, and marched across the room.

"And I believe, Mr. Thistlecoat," said Mr. Pleasance, "that you are a windbag."

15. Cutting In

Charleston Thistlecoat *had* met one of the Moosepath League and had crossed swords of disposition with Mister Walton in an unspoken rivalry over the attentions of Phileda McCannon. Charleston had proposed marriage to the woman, the offer having been made in a friendly, if rather businesslike, letter. He had been puzzled, and a little put out, by her declining him. In the past he had had much to say about the Moosepath League without having seen their membership, and now that he saw the Moosepath League, he thought he had quite a lot to say *to* them.

Charleston was a lofty man, or at least tall. Slender, with large features and dark, ironic eyebrows, he had a fine head of silver hair and a way of looking down his prominent nose that was not meant to put the subject of his study at ease. He was something of a self-made man (or thought of himself in this manner), and one wry observer had ventured that this relieved the Almighty of a great deal of responsibility.

The dancing portion of the evening had yet to begin, and the musicians at the far end of the ballroom were rendering a classic march to rouse everyone's blood. Charleston strode across the floor in time with the music and felt the eyes of the room upon him (whether real or imagined) without qualm.

"Well," he said when he arrived at his intended destination, "it is the Moosepath League." He stood next to a short, bearded man, the better to loom majestically, and he pronounced the name of the society as if he were amused with, and also highly indulgent, of other people's folly.

The members of the club turned as one, and the short, bearded man craned his neck so that he might look up at the newcomer. "Joseph Thump," said this fellow, and he offered his hand.

"Yes," drawled Thistlecoat. He accepted Thump's hand, but indolently.

Christopher Eagleton and Matthew Ephram introduced themselves as well, but the newcomer did not pronounce his own name till he turned to the small, pale woman standing nearby. "Charleston Thistlecoat," he said, as if this name should mean something to her, and passing an eye over the members of the club, he said, "It is cordial of the Morrells to provide entertainment," which may have referenced the ball itself or might have been meant to suggest that these men had been hired for the amusement of everyone else. There was a fourth man in the immediate vicinity who had not included himself in these preambles. "Are you a member of the Moosepath League?" asked Thistlecoat, who had to look up to this rugged, blond-bearded individual.

The man frowned in a suspicious way and folded his arms before him. "I'm not," he said, "but only because I haven't been asked."

"How extraordinary!" said Thump.

"Mr. Scott!" said Eagleton. "We would be honored!"

"I think you must excuse these gentlemen if they weary you," said Thistlecoat to the woman. "There is perhaps not much room for amenities on the Moosepath." And again he pronounced this last word with a sort of wry forbearance even as he insinuated himself beside her.

"I am a little worn out," said the woman, amid the astonished sounds that emerged from Ephram, Eagleton, and Thump. "I mean, I'm somewhat overwhelmed, if you understand."

"Of course," purred Thistlecoat.

"We were just suggesting that Mrs. Morningside take a seat," Ephram was saying, which statement was meant more as a general agreement with the newcomer than any defense of themselves.

Not far away three young people were talking, and the single beau among these broke away to approach Thistlecoat and the others. "Mr. Thistlecoat, did I hear you say?"

"Yes," said the man. He was prepared to be generous to youth.

"I have heard Mister Walton speak of you."

"Oh?" Thistlecoat's tone altered perceptibly.

"I'm sure that he would want me to forward his best," said Sundry Moss, who had marked the tenor, if not the details, of what had passed between the members of the club and Thistlecoat. He had not been present at the meetings between Mister Walton and this man, but he had inferred from Mister Walton's sedate descriptions that the fellow was trouble and that Thistlecoat had done his best to make Mister Walton appear small before Phileda McCannon. "And his wife," said Sundry pleasantly. "I know she would forward her best as well."

"His wife?"

Cordelia took her fiancé's arm, and Priscilla was drawn, by dint of having been left alone, back into her mother's orbit. Grace latched on to her daughter as if she would not let go of her the rest of the evening. "Miss McCannon and Mister Walton were married on Saturday," said Cordelia, who had added up the elements of this meeting very quickly, not the least portion having been Dresden's obvious suspicion of the silver-haired man.

"I'm Sundry Moss," said the younger man. He reached out his hand.

Thistlecoat was not in a position to refuse a handshake, but he hid his shock at the young woman's news and took Sundry's hand with a striking display of condescension and said, "Aren't you Walton's *driver* or something?"

The orchestra had picked up the first waltz of the evening and the ballroom hummed with conversation from a dozen circles, but in the immediate vicinity a hard silence faced Thistlecoat in the wake of his words. Cordelia took a breath, and Dresden pressed her arm to warn her from jumping in before Mr. Moss had the opportunity to respond. The members of the club continued to look perplexed, and Priscilla Morningside looked horrified, but her mother had the appearance of someone who had found an ally.

Sundry did not flinch. "My duties have often fallen under that title," he said, sounding and looking positively Waltonesque, his expression so mild and unoffended that clearly it was an honor for him to admit to such service.

At this point Grace had profited by two things, the first being the re-possession of her daughter. To the other constituent of her sudden fortune she said, "I *am* a little weary. Would you mind terribly finding me a seat?"

Thistlecoat gave a bow, took Grace's unoccupied arm, and escorted her and, by association (and her mother's firm grip), Priscilla to the chairs at the perimeter of the ballroom. Priscilla hardly dared look back at her cousin for fear of precipitating a scene. In a moment the three were en-sconced in the relative shadow between two pillars.

"How extraordinary!" said Ephram. He and his fellow members were perplexed by these swift events and conversation. "What do you think, Eagleton?"

"I do, yes!" said that worthy.

"Thump?"

"Hmmm?" said the bearded fellow.

Where are Mom and Daddy? wondered Cordelia. She was certain that her mother could have prevented this. "Mr. Moss," said Cordelia, and an entire train of heartfelt verbiage was ready to spill from her when Dresden renewed his grip upon her arm.

"You must allow me to attempt one of these dances you've made me practice," Dresden said to her. She looked up at him, but her fiancé shook his head and knitted his brow as if he knew something she didn't. What he *guessed* about Sundry Moss he might not have realized about himself.

While Priscilla walked away, Sundry experienced a lapsed sense of time; weighing upon him was an entire evening of lonely possibility, the prominent detail of which was that he might not talk with the dark haired young woman again, or stand beside her, or even watch her from anything but a distance—not just tonight but forever. He had been tested and he had returned his best (and perhaps the best he *could* have returned), yet she was walking away.

In for a penny, he thought. He clasped his hands behind him in the most casual fashion, lifted his chin just a bit, and said to the small gathering,

"Excuse me." Then he strode in time with the "Emperor's Waltz" toward Thistlecoat and the seated women.

"Oh, my," said Cordelia. She put a hand to her breast and resembled her aunt Grace just a little bit.

"Give him a chance," said Dresden, now that Sundry was out of hearing.

"What makes *you* so smart?" she asked him with a smile.

"I don't know that I was till I met you."

"Good heavens!" said Eagleton. He was not very sure what Mr. Moss was doing, and he was vaguely aware that Miss Underwood and Mr. Scott were making love in a subtle way.

"Yes, indeed!" said Ephram.

"Hmmm!" said Thump. He had been watching the engaged couple with a sentimental affection, but now his ears were red.

"Punch, perhaps!" said Ephram.

"Bravo, Ephram!"

"Thank you, Eagleton. Thump?"

"Very good."

The room was filled with people. The music had altered in tone. A *schottische* had begun.

The ballroom floor seemed to stretch out before Sundry, and that lapsed sense of time he had experienced compressed into a hard lump that lodged in his chest. His heart was pounding. Priscilla saw him first; she sat up straight and looked at her mother and Mr. Thistlecoat, then looked down at her feet, and finally looked back at Sundry. Thistlecoat was describing his business ventures to Mrs. Morningside and also tendering advice about investments when Sundry drew close enough to speak. "Miss Morningside," he said brightly, "you were asking about the wedding."

"Yes!" said Priscilla emphatically—somewhere between hope and fear. "I was."

To lay credit where it was due, Charleston Thistlecoat took in this situation and responded with perfect ease—all in a heartbeat. If he had missed Sundry's interest in Miss Morningside before, he realized it now in the instant, and also *Mrs.* Morningside's opinion of it. He said, "Mr. Moss, be so good as to get a cup of punch for Mrs. Morningside and one for myself."

Priscilla let out a small, hurt sound. Even Grace was startled, but she cleared all evidence of this from her face and gave a single nod. She understood how poorly she was acting yet seemed to have no power to stop herself. There was something very unhappy lying beneath her calm façade, and her cheeks grew red.

Sundry did not suffer a cloud to pass over his face. He had learned well from Mister Walton the power of a direct and magnanimous reply, and Thistlecoat, he was sure, had overplayed his hand. "I'd be very glad to," said Sundry, and as soon as his gray-haired opponent expressed mute surprise and then patronizing approval, Sundry said, "Miss Morningside, would *you* care for some punch?"

There was a moment of electric stillness among this quartet as something like confidence claimed the expression on Priscilla's face. "Yes, I would, thank you," she said, then added, "But you will be thirsty, too. Let me go with you, and I can help you carry my mother's drink." She turned to the elegant man seated beside Grace. "And Mr. Thistlecoat's."

Grace's mouth hung open. Thistlecoat looked stunned.

Priscilla stood and gathered her dress. Sundry thought there had been tears in her eyes, but now she smiled, her head tilted just a bit to one side. He offered his arm and she took it. Nearby clusters of people watched them as they moved across the floor. The floor had filled with dancers, and Sundry and Priscilla wove their way past several couples, almost dancing themselves. Sundry said something that made Priscilla smile again. They disappeared beyond the dancers and groups of conversation on the other side of the room.

"I'm terribly sorry about that," said Priscilla, walking with her head down to hide her emotions.

"You needn't be," said Sundry. He was interested that, having employed a Waltonian strategy against Mr. Thistlecoat, he couldn't be angry with the fellow. It helped, of course, to have Miss Morningside on his arm.

"Oh, but I must," she replied. "My father would have said that Mr. Thistlecoat is all manners and no courtesy."

"That's very good," said Sundry. They stopped as a knot of dancers passed by or perhaps so that they might have this exchange behind them before they went further. She had let go of his arm. "Mr. Thistlecoat had shown some interest in Miss McCannon," he said, "and I am guessing that he holds Mister Walton's success with her against me."

Priscilla smiled at this convoluted logic. "Then he has only proven, after the fact, that she chose the best man," she said.

Sundry almost said, "That's very good," again, but instead said, "I'm glad you came with me. I might get lost in this crowd."

Priscilla took his arm again and said, "I might not be of any help in that case. I'm not used to so many people."

"I'm used to more *cows* than people," said Sundry as they recommenced their progress across the ballroom. He wondered, for a moment, if he had gone too far with his self-deprecation, but when he turned to Miss Morningside, she was smiling. Though he hardly knew it, his self-image as a farm boy was at odds with his debonair appearance tonight. "At any rate," he added, "if we *do* get lost, I'll be in good company."

Miss Morningside bent her head, still smiling, so that there was a secretive look to her, though whatever secret she did have just then was kept only from him.

It would have been simple enough to keep anything from Sundry that evening, his well-documented powers of observation having been overwhelmed by the young woman on his arm. It was true, too, that he was not accustomed to such a press of people, and though he had spent time on the streets of Portland and wandered the crowded docks, there was something altogether focused about the *mob* at Mrs. Morrell's Annual Charitable Ball that demanded a level of attention he could not quite muster.

"I don't think he really did want punch," Miss Morningside was saying with more irony than was probably common to her.

"I beg your pardon?" said Sundry.

"I don't think that Mr. Thistlecoat really did want punch."

"But we should be sure to bring your mother some," he said.

Miss Morningside saw something past Sundry. "There's Cord and Dresden," she said. "I'm going to ask her to bring it to them."

Sundry was on the verge of objecting. He could hear Mister Walton's voice saying, "Not at all. I'd be very glad to get it." But a moment ago Miss Morningside had appeared almost as out of her element as Sundry felt. She had seemed bewildered and uncertain, as if she did not belong among these people or in that magnificent dress. She seemed like a girl in women's clothes, and looking at her, Sundry had felt a pang of sympathy that was not entirely comfortable.

Now, crossing toward her cousin with renewed self-possession, she seemed born to that dress and whatever circle she chose to occupy. Decision had lifted her sweet, bespectacled face, and a sense of right had given her otherwise careful step a level of confidence. Yet she demurely held one hand in the other, like a student preparing a speech, and tilted her head a little as she considered what she was going to say to her cousin, and these visible chinks in her poise made that poise the more admirable. Sundry was startled into following her by the sudden conviction that another fellow was bound to intercept her before he had the chance to occupy her dance card.

Grace waited with growing anxiety, only half hearing Thistlecoat's running commentary about those members of Portland's elite who passed before them. He attempted a witticism or two and eventually scrambled from his confusion and retrieved his usual self.

In a few minutes Cordelia appeared with two cups of punch in her hands. She presented these to her aunt and Charleston Thistlecoat without a smile. "Your punch, Auntie," she said. "Mr. Thistlecoat."

"Thank you," said Charleston stiffly.

Cordelia gave her aunt a stern look, but she reached down and squeezed Grace's hand and said, "Come join us when you are rested up."

16. A First Time for Everything

"Hasn't our chairman made mention of a Mr. Thistlecoat?" said Eagleton as he and his fellow members of the club voyaged the perimeter of the ballroom, their progress slowed by the numbers of gentlemen to whom they must nod and ladies who must receive a full stop and a bow.

"I believe he has," said Ephram.

"I was a little unsure what Mr. Thistlecoat meant about the Moosepath and amenities," said Eagleton, "but I am sorry if he thought we were wearying Mrs. Morningside."

"Yes," said Ephram. A sloe-eyed beauty holding court by the door had just touched him with her gaze, and she made some sport of watching him and his two friends pass rather than pay attention to the man who was talking to her. "That is troubling," said Ephram, perhaps as addendum to his previous agreement.

"She did appear weary," voiced Thump. He looked up to find that his friends had got some paces ahead of him and hurried after. "Though I do not mean to imply that she wasn't entirely presentable," he finished.

The music had shifted from waltz to schottische, and some people had the impression that these three were bustling to secure themselves dance partners. One man stepped from the milling crowd alongside the dance floor and looked after Eagleton and Ephram. "Whom are they in pursuit of?" he wondered aloud. Thump nearly ran down this curious onlooker, excused himself, and hurried on.

"She is a lovely woman," Ephram was saying over his shoulder, though the last of this sentence was actually delivered to the fore as he looked ahead to be sure of where he was going. The words *lovely woman*, amplified by the breath required to produce his present stride, carried over a nearby clutch of social aristocrats beside the punch table, and several members of the gentler sex who thought these syllables best described themselves turned to see who had been blessed with such profound discernment.

"What a nice thing to say," said one lady to Ephram with more humor than conviction. Of possibly advanced middle age, she made up for any physical loss, consequent to her years, with a sure knowledge of what might capture a gentleman's regard and a cultivated manner that was expert at putting that knowledge into action. She did seem to fit the phrase *lovely woman* rather well, and she raised a careless hand toward Ephram, who was himself broad-shouldered, square-jawed, and a good deal more handsome than he ever suspected. "And, yes," she said, "I will be pleased to put your name on my dance card."

Something of Ephram's recent training at Mrs. De Riche's Academy of Ballroom Sciences (and his deeply ingrained sense of chivalry) took charge of his subsequent behavior; he straightened his posture, took the offered hand, and bent over it as if he might place his lips upon it.

"Oh, my!" said Eagleton. Past his friend was a pair of gray-blue eyes attached to a soft smile, which was attached to a *grande dame* who stood beside Ephram's lovely lady. He said, "Oh, my!" again.

"Hmmm?" came a voice from behind Eagleton.

The lovely lady gave Ephram the benefit of an artfully arched eyebrow.

"Matthew Ephram," he said in a range slightly higher than was normal for him. "And this is my friend and fellow club member Christopher Eagleton. And here is also my friend and fellow club member Joseph Thump."

"Charmed," said the woman, without releasing Ephram's hand but turning that languorous gaze upon him.

"Are you?" said Ephram. In his confusion, he thought perhaps that this was her name. "Twenty minutes before the hour of nine," he informed her.

"You're members of the Moosepath League," said one of the other ladies.

The woman in charge of Ephram produced a dance card from a nook in her garments that he did not see fit to contemplate. She considered this document and, as it was almost filled up, put it back and retrieved a second card that was as yet unsullied by any man's signature. "My goodness!" she said. "You seem to be first on the list."

"Am I?" said Ephram, whose vocal range had risen an octave or two. Eagleton was forecasting the weather to one of the other ladies, and from outside Ephram's immediate view, Thump's voice rumbled to someone the hour of the coming high tide.

"Now you must wait with me for the next dance," said the woman.

"Must I?" said Ephram. "I mean, certainly . . . Miss—?"

"*Mrs.*," she informed him.

"Charmed," he said by way of address, and bowed again.

That exquisite eyebrow lifted once again, and when the schottische came to an end and the applause died, Ephram had hardly moved.

A waltz commenced, and Ephram found himself walking with the lovely lady onto the dance floor. Since graduating from Mrs. De Riche's institution, he had attended more than two dozen dance functions with Eagleton and Thump, but not till this moment had he ever actually exercised what he had practiced. Stiffly, and with no small sense of horror, he placed one hand in the general vicinity of *Mrs. Charmed*'s waist, though about six or seven inches away from actual contact. He allowed her to take hold of his other hand and looked, for a bit, like a music box figure whose function is to twirl in place slowly. He was perplexed by the swirl of dancers about him. He even had the odd perception that Eagleton and Thump had pivoted past him, each in the close company of one of the ladies from the punch table.

After a bit he did shift his posture, though it might be considered an exaggeration to say that he relaxed. *Mrs. Charmed* had a way of moving— her hip in particular—that caused herself to come into contact with Ephram's hand. "I beg your pardon," he said when this occurred.

"Please don't," she said lightly. She smiled.

Ephram swallowed. He was attempting to reconcile the name she had given him. "Mrs. Charmed?" he said, testing out the appellation.

She widened her eyes to indicate that she hadn't heard him.

"Mrs.—" he began.

She turned her ear close to his mouth.

"Charmed!" he said, more loudly than he had intended.

"You dear man," she said, "I will have to believe you if you are going to keep repeating it."

17. Principals in Play

Apart from her duties as hostess, the course of the evening for Tabitha Morrell was largely dictated by her desire to see her daughter, Fredrica, shown off in the best possible illumination, real and figurative. She had instructed her daughter on the most complimentary distance to stand from the nearest source of light and also how to stand so that the shadows (however vague) did no injustice to her pretty features.

Tabitha herself was more handsome than beautiful and had secured her own position in Philbrook Morrell's heart and home by way of disposition as much as appearance. There were women of much greater beauty who wore the trappings of wealth with a good deal less poise than Tabitha Brownlow Morrell. Contrarily, Fredrica was born with more beauty and less poise, though Tabitha was of the opinion that the young beaux today were less sophisticated than her husband's generation and consequently more readily prevailed upon by a pretty face. Several prospective suitors hovered about Fredrica, and the daughter was indeed looking pretty, if pretty well aware of it.

Philbrook dearly loved his daughter, but he was content to let his wife conduct Fretty's education in matters of courtship. He hardly understood the dynamics by which his own wooing had come to fruition and had only a vague memory of his and Tabitha's engagement and marriage. He hadn't a notion of what Tabitha was talking about when she instructed their daughter. "Can't she just wear a pretty dress and smile at people?" he had asked when, passing through the parlor one day, he overheard some of these strategies. Fretty had said, "Daddy!" Tabitha had simply enunciated her husband's name with an indulgent laugh. Philbrook had rolled his eyes, retrieved his newspaper, and gone back to the more rudimentary matters of politics and high finance.

The host of the June Ball was content to let matters run their course as regarded his daughter. He trusted that he would in time be provided with a fairly presentable son-in-law from well-to-do stock. It was all too predictable to interest him very much, and he had distracted himself already by *picking the principals* for the night.

Philbrook had that lucky knack for carrying on a conversation about one or another of the standard topics—the aforesaid politics and high finance—while occupying the bulk of his mind with the immediate and physical world around him. He fulfilled his duties, greeting the patriarchs and providers of other clans, trading observations about the ball and its participants, commenting about the weather, forecasting the fate of the local ball team and politicians. The mayor himself was there with his wife and daughter, "mending gossip," as Philbrook's mother used to say. The mayor's brother-in-law had recently run afoul of the state's laws against the sale and consumption of liquorous spirits, and the mayor had come under hot criticism for using his position to rescue his fallen in-law, but a certain amount of palm pressing and a hearty laugh or two did much to cloud people's memories.

Philbrook was amenable to having his ear bent, and he chuckled with the mayor and bowed over the hand of the mayor's wife. The mayor was not particularly corrupt, beyond the generally accepted bounds of nepotism, but politics are by nature like the iceberg that reveals only the smallest portion of itself above the surface of the water. There was a good deal of the mayor below the surface, and the present crisis would prove a small storm in his career, once the initial gusts had blown themselves out.

It was while laughing at one of the mayor's jokes (one that he would not recall at evening's end) that Philbrook saw one of the Moosepath League dance past with Mrs. Allglow—a three-time widow and notorious flirt, who was no doubt casting the roiling waters of the ball for a fourth husband.

Philbrook was fascinated by this Moosepath society (it wasn't a brotherhood inasmuch as a woman purportedly was part of its cadre). And this Ephram fellow had the appearance of an inexperienced juggler—his limbs stiff with effort, his mouth slack with concentration. Mr. Ephram's hand occasionally touched his partner's waist, and each time he might have received a static shock for the sudden jump of his eyebrows. Soon

Mr. Ephram and Mrs. Allglow swirled into the eddy of dancers and disappeared.

"So Francis said to me," the mayor was saying, "he said, 'I can't ask Mr. Williamson *that!* He's a deacon at church!'" and the mayor lifted his ruddy face and let out a great roar. "A deacon at church!" he said again, and several people who had not heard the anecdote were encouraged to laugh simply by his conspicuous jollity. Philbrook laughed also, and not insincerely. He knew enough of the actors in the story to appreciate the punchline without having taken in the entire tale that led to it.

Then Mr. Eagleton, the blond Moosepathian, whirled into view with Mrs. Nostrum in his tentative clutch. Mrs. Nostrum was another woman bereft of husband and only a little less obviously looking for the next than was Mrs. Allglow. Mr. Eagleton looked like a man who has had snow fall under his collar and doesn't dare move for fear of sending the chilly melt down his back, but Mrs. Nostrum was unconcerned for her frightened partner and animated enough for the both of them. They, too, moved out of Philbrook's view as other dancers made the rounds of the ballroom floor.

Philbrook was fascinated! Everyone in town was talking about the Moosepath League and marveling how, only last week, the members of the club had appeared at the terrible fire in Iceboro with a small army of hobos in tow to help save the town. Apparently Messrs. Ephram, Eagleton, and Thump had proved men of quick thought and action and no little pluck, though they had appeared so uncertain of themselves to Philbrook out on the portico and a deal more uncertain in the arms of these wealthy widows.

"So Williamson said to me," the mayor was saying, "he said, 'One should never be businesslike about one's religion or religious about one's business.'"

"Ah, yes," said Philbrook, smiling and nodding.

"Businesslike about religion and religious about business," said a newcomer to the conversation. "I like that."

Philbrook continued to nod, but here came Mr. Thump! and what a remarkable catch the bearded fellow had made! or rather, what a remarkable catch he had been made of! Mrs. Pleasance was not a widow at all, though she was perhaps as much on the lookout for something like a husband as the first two ladies. Once considered one of the beauties and fine wits of the city, she had been married off (it was commonly agreed) to a lout in order to save her own family from bankruptcy (a famous scandal!).

What had once been lovely about her had turned a tad bit hard; what once had been wry and admirable in her humor had fluctuated to the calculating and predatory.

With his extraordinary brush of beard, Mr. Thump looked like some mammalian prey in the clutches of Mrs. Pleasance. He, too, was swept into the general stream and disappeared. Mrs. Pleasance was still a fairly stunning woman, but Philbrook did not envy Mr. Thump—much.

Then his eyes were snagged by the two young principals of his imaginary tale. *How did* that *happen?* he wondered. Had he misread all these people? This young man and woman had seemed to him mutually enamored, completely unaware of each other's admiration, and about equally petrified. Now they came out of the crowd, she on his arm, he looking affable as he pulled a face and said something that made her smile. They looked like old companions, blessed with the sort of friendship that the happiest couples comprehend.

But he soon realized that they had not been dancing, and their being together at this moment was a surprise, perhaps a shock, to them both. They were putting a brave face on the situation, the young man staring off, hoping to formulate another complete sentence, the young woman looking down at her feet, still smiling, but not as easily as Philbrook had first thought. They were walking more stiffly than was initially apparent, too, and after some awkward decision-making, they approached one of the punch tables.

"So Williamson got up at the next board meeting," the mayor was saying, "and he took a collection plate from behind his seat and gave a little speech about tithing. They said Francis looked as if he'd been kicked by a horse!"

The mayor was laughing again, along with his wife and several other listeners, but Philbrook had lost track of the tale, which seemed convoluted. He nodded again, indicating just how much he liked this part of the recitation by way of old-fashioned Yankee underreaction. "I hope you folks enjoy the evening," said the host. "I must go perform my duties."

"Yes, Philbrook, of course," said the mayor, who may have suspected he was losing the man's attention.

Mr. Morrell shook hands with everyone in the immediate vicinity again and made his way toward the punch table in hopes of having a better vantage from which to view his chosen principals.

18. Charmed

"Mr. Ephram," declared Mrs. Allglow when Ephram had announced the hour for perhaps the fifth time, "I believe you are endeavoring to make me laugh."

"Good heavens!" said Ephram. "I wouldn't presume, ma'am."

Then she did laugh, and so close to his ear that the hair at the nape of his neck rose up. She had a deep and mellifluous voice, and when she was amused, those robust notes contrasted pleasingly with her delicate, if not youthful, features. There was something equally robust in her eye when she considered Ephram, and this did nothing to calm his nerves.

It did occur to Ephram that his duty was done and that a swift and honorable retreat was called for, but Mrs. Allglow (or Mrs. Charmed, as he continued to think of her) had a seemingly casual grip upon his arm, and they were standing by themselves in a relatively shadowed corner of the ballroom. The orchestra had commenced the beautiful waltz from Gounod's *Faust*, and he watched for his fellow Moosepathians among the elegant couples dancing by, but as it fell out, Eagleton and Thump had finished the previous dance in other corners of the room and were struggling with similar issues.

"Have I understood the rumors about you correctly?" asked the lady.

"Rumors?" said Ephram.

"That you are a member of this club everyone is talking about?"

"Really?" said Ephram. "I mean, I beg your pardon?"

"The Moosepath League, isn't it?"

"Yes, certainly."

"Oh, you dear fellows! How gallant you are!"

"Oh, my, that's very—" He was searching for words.

"Modern," she said with a sly smile.

"I beg your pardon?"

"I say, you're very modern."

"Are we?"

"With a woman in your lists?"

"Miss McCannon, yes. I mean, Mrs. Walton." Ephram had never thought of himself or the club as *modern;* it seemed so indefinite.

"The men view you with some misgiving, certainly, but we women are sure you're wonderful." Ephram caught that robust glint in *Mrs. Charmed*'s eye again and let out a sound that was very like one of Thump's *Hmmms*.

"Mr. Ephram?" came a new and (to the Moosepathian) welcome voice. A young woman, dressed a bit less lavishly than some of the other guests and holding a pencil and notebook, approached Ephram and Mrs. Allglow from out of the nearest group of talkers at the perimeter of the dance floor. "Mr. Ephram?" she said again.

Ephram bowed deeply.

"I'm Jenny Darwin. *Eastern Argus*. The social column."

"Oh?" Something about this information surprised Ephram.

"Mrs. Ephram?" the young woman asked with a smile.

"No, no!" said Ephram, who then realized that he was perhaps too zealous in the correction. He looked from Mrs. Allglow to Miss Darwin and back again with such an expression of astonishment that the young woman could be forgiven for thinking that she had interrupted an *intrigue*. "This is Mrs. Charmed," said Ephram.

Mrs. Allglow looked surprised to hear it.

"Charmed," said Miss Darwin, not sure that she had heard correctly.

"Thank you," said Ephram, who was not sure what he had done to be so addressed. "The pleasure is mine."

Now Miss Darwin looked surprised. In fact, all three of them looked so surprised that several people in other circles began to watch the ensuing conversation with immense curiosity.

"I believe that Mr. Ephram is having some fun with you," said the older woman, who did not mind suggesting that the younger woman was beneath his serious attention.

"Oh?" said Miss Darwin, looking vaguely offended.

"I am?" said Ephram, looking more than vaguely at sea.

"The name is Allglow," said the older woman.

"No, no," said the Moosepathian. "It's Ephram!"

"My dear *Mr.* Ephram," said Mrs. Allglow with an indulgent smile. She almost laughed at his antics and may have looked and sounded to Miss Darwin like a wife gently chastising her husband for too much levity.

Clearly, Miss Darwin was to receive very little in the way of information from this fellow. She turned to Mrs. Allglow, pencil poised over notebook, and said, "Mrs. Ephram."

"Charmed!" shouted Ephram, so that even people dancing could hear him over the music. A rumor began to circulate that the young woman to whom he was communicating was slightly deaf, and another story gaining momentum was that a romantic triangle had come to a sudden point, as it were, though experts on the subject disagreed which of the women in the affair was the injured party. "No, no," some said about Mrs. Allglow, "she's much older than he," and "No, no," said others about Miss Darwin, "she's much too young." Still others who could name one or more of the parties involved suspected even deeper waters.

Eagleton was shocked when the story traveled to his corner, where he was nervously keeping company with Mrs. Nostrum. (He would have been more shocked if the names of the participants had made the journey.) "Good heavens!" he said when an otherwise idle fellow informed him and Mrs. Nostrum of the scene that was *playing out* at the other end of the ballroom.

"Gussie Davis," said the man to Eagleton, offering his hand.

"Christopher Eagleton," said the blond Moosepathian.

Mr. Davis inclined his head toward Mrs. Nostrum. "Your charming wife?" he asked.

"No, no," said Eagleton. "Mrs. Delighted."

19. Priscilla

"Punch has been served," announced Cordelia when she returned from her errand.

"Thank you," Priscilla mouthed to her cousin, but when Cordelia was close enough, she said quietly, "Was my mother white as a ghost?"

"Pale enough, I should say, and rather startled to see me."

"Oh, dear," said Priscilla, looking crestfallen. "Perhaps I should go to her."

Sundry stood a small distance away and politely appeared unaware or uninterested in their *tête-a-tête*. Dresden stood closer, with his arms folded, and if he looked every bit the fish out of water, he was (in Sundry's later characterization) "a pretty big trout." The ball could last only so long, and it was not going to daunt Dresden Scott.

Cordelia took her fiancé's arm without looking at him and said with definite emphasis to her cousin, "Priscilla, I dearly love your mother, but you can't live in a shadow all your life."

"*She* is," said Priscilla sadly.

"God bless her," said Cordelia. "She thinks she's doing right by you, I know."

"No, I don't think she does," said Priscilla. It was a terrible admission, and she couldn't say why she let it out just then and in such a public place; perhaps that is exactly why she had let it out, for she could say it yet be obliged by her surroundings not to think about it or cry or look bitter. Cordelia studied her beloved cousin's face and wondered what exactly Priscilla had meant. "She doesn't," said Priscilla. "She doesn't think she's doing right at all, and that's what makes her miserable. She's just afraid to lose Ethan and me. Ever since Daddy died, she's clutched at us like a drowning person."

"She wouldn't lose you, would she," said Cordelia softly.

"She might, on her present course."

Cordelia shook her head. She leaned closer, looking less somber, and said, "And think what a nice son-in-law she'd get."

"Cord! Please!"

"He can't hear us."

"It doesn't matter. It's foolish—"

"Why?"

"I've met him twice before tonight, Cord."

"Mr. Scott believes that he fell in love with me when he saw me in my bare feet, and that *was* the second time we met."

"I always said you had pretty feet," said Priscilla with a short laugh.

"And I have never disagreed with you. But notice that he didn't fall in love with me when he saw my face."

"A lot of people here," Dresden was saying to Sundry. He did his best not to hear the women's conversation, his arms still folded and Cordelia upon one elbow; this dialogue could last only so long, and it was not going to daunt Dresden Scott.

"I wonder if there is any one person who knows everybody," said Sundry.

Dresden considered this with a frown. Priscilla almost laughed to see him looking as solemn as a cigar store Indian. Under her breath, she said to Cordelia, "Bare feet! Don't tell my mother!"

Sundry glanced at Priscilla just as she was saying this. She was smiling conspiratorially, looking particularly winsome, and this vision, added to the unfamiliar milieu of the ball and the accurate perception that there were those close to her who would think little of his wooing, suddenly felt too large and daunting. Sundry's chest was weighted, and his breath came hard. There was a moment when he thought everything would be a good deal less complicated if he simply excused himself, went outside, and hailed a cab; he was considering several possible reasons why he might have to leave when he was aware that the ballroom was growing quiet.

In fact, the musicians had been silent for a minute or so before the guests thought to turn and see what was going to happen next. Three or four hundred people were in attendance, and it was a great, grand assembly that waited upon the orchestra leader as he mounted the dais to announce his hope that an ovation from everyone might encourage Mr. Sampson Wyngarde, a celebrated tenor among them, to step forward and join the orchestra in a song. There was no doubt about the general consensus, and after a roar of applause a pleasant-appearing gentleman separated himself from the crowd and mounted the dais to shake hands with the orchestra leader.

Sundry was almost relieved. An artificial break in the evening's mood had been provided for him, and he had a moment of comparative quiet in which to explain that he must leave.

The orchestra leader and the singer conferred briefly. Then the leader returned to the floor and faced both singer and musicians.

Priscilla left her cousin's side to stand next to Sundry. He was conscious of her as he might a source of light or warmth and debated whether he should acknowledge her presence with a glance or affect a cooler attitude. He took a breath, turned his head, and smiled. Priscilla looked up at him and smiled in return. Sundry turned back to the orchestra and tried to swallow the sudden lump in his throat.

The room became quite silent, for a room with so many people in it, and in a moment there was the sound of the baton tapping on a music stand, till the orchestra began the first moving notes of "Where Is My Wandering Boy Tonight?" The voice of Mr. Wyngarde was like aural gold, gliding to the ceiling of the ballroom and piercing the hearts of his listeners.

> *Where is my wandering boy tonight,*
> *The boy of my tenderest care,*
> *The boy that was once my joy and light,*
> *The child of my love and prayer?*

Portland is a city by the sea, and few people living there toward the end of the nineteenth century were without some *wandering boy* in their family history. Many of those present at the ball had sons or grandsons who were somewhere on the high sea or seeking their fortune out west. The ball was a venue for intrigue and love affairs, for dancing with old flames and kindling new ones, but for this moment the mood of the evening was changed. Parents held each other's hands, and grandmothers and grandfathers lowered their heads.

Once he was pure as morning dew,
As he knelt at his mother's knee;
No face was so sweet, no heart so true,
And none so sweet as he.

Some in attendance were wandering boys themselves, and the words and notes filled their hearts and minds with intimations of a mother's soft kiss or a father's proud grip upon their shoulder.

O could I see you now my boy
As fair as the olden time,
When prattle and smile made home a joy,
And life was a merry chime!

The song was not yet done, but several handkerchiefs were visible among the crowd, some in the hands of the most stalwart-looking men. In their separate corners, the Moosepathians were greatly affected and momentarily forgot the perilous proximity of their recent dance partners.

Sundry was not unmoved; the voice was so fair and clear, like a fond sound carrying over a meadow. He felt a grip upon his arm and glanced carefully at Miss Morningside, whose eyes were wet with tears. Sundry thought she hardly knew she had taken his arm, and he had a sharp intuition that contrary to the subject of the song, she was thinking of her father. He lowered his head.

Go for my wandering boy tonight,
Go search for him where you will;
But bring him to me with all his blight,
And tell him I love him still.

When the song finished, soaring at the top of the tenor's splendid voice, there was a moment of silence in the ballroom and then a great round of applause. Priscilla did not let go of Sundry's arm to join in this, and Sundry chanced another look in her direction. Priscilla blinked, and Sundry produced a handkerchief for her.

"I'm sorry," she said, laughing ruefully. "It's such a sad song."

"Would you like to sit down?" he asked.

She shook her head.

Mr. Wyngarde stepped down from the dais and shook hands with the orchestra leader. He gave the nod to the musicians and disappeared into the crowd. The leader turned back to his crew, raised his baton, and the opening strains of *La Belle Hélène* incited the dancers once again. There was a languorous, wistful quality to the music, and everyone sweeping by appeared more serious and perhaps more appreciative of the person in his or her arms.

"Oh, my," said Priscilla, with another laugh. She gave Sundry his handkerchief and thanked him, tapping at her heart as if she felt herself recovering.

Sundry had fallen from one quandary to another. He thought perhaps here was an opportunity to ask Miss Morningside to dance, yet he feared intruding upon the previous moment or in any way taking advantage of the young woman while she was made vulnerable by memory. Mr. Scott and Miss Underwood glided by, and Sundry marked how sure the guide seemed. Presumably they waltzed in Millinocket, too.

"They do look marvelous," said Priscilla. She had let go of his arm now, and she stood with her hands clasped before her.

"They are handsome," said Sundry.

"You don't know the half," she said. "Cordelia is like a sister to me, *and* a best friend, *and* sometimes just a touch of a mother. Everything is a little better when she is around."

It seemed that the beauty of Offenbach's music had affected everyone, for the dance floor teemed with increasing participation. Sundry and Priscilla, concentrating very hard upon each other (while trying not to appear so), found themselves surrounded by waltzing couples till they had to shift to avoid one and then another brace of dancers that twirled in their direction. Sundry turned, unconsciously stepping in time to the music, and Priscilla pivoted so as to remain in the same position relative to him. Their coordinated movements were themselves so much like a dance that when they performed this tandem maneuver a second time, they laughed. Sundry put an arm out, meaning only to imitate a dancing posture as a small joke, but then Priscilla curtsied with a soft smile and took his hand.

Then they were dancing, waltzing at half an arm's length so that they could see each other and speak to each other as they coursed the ballroom floor. Just to rest his hand lightly upon her waist sent such powerful waves of longing through him that it took several bars of music before he could regain his breath and consider the necessity of saying something.

"I don't want to cause you any trouble with your mother," he said, certain that he had chosen the one statement that would doom any sense of romance between them.

A raft of complex emotions passed over her face and sparked, then troubled, then again sparked her bespectacled eyes. She smiled, a little sadly at first and then with a hint of impish humor. "Thank you," she said demurely. "But we just passed her."

20. Principally Speaking

There is always a point during such a function as the Morrells' Annual Charitable Ball when the hosts cease to have very much to do with anyone's pleasure or boredom. The guests have taken over, as it were, and they will eat and drink as long as eat and drink hold out, and dance as long as the musicians' fingers last; many a tryst in a lonely alcove or business deal in the front hall will be under way, and people will have gotten used to seeing one another in their finest trappings—gowns of every color swirling upon the dance floor and jewelry winking in the light of the chandeliers.

Each year Philbrook Morrell looked forward to the moment when his duties became moot and he imagined consequently that he could relax. He was just beginning to feel it that night when he caught sight of Mrs. Morningside and Charleston Thistlecoat. They were seated somewhat apart from their nearest neighbors, and by the look on Mrs. Morningside's face, Thistlecoat was holding forth on some dull subject. Mrs. Morningside stared into the crowd, the dance card in her hands looking the worse for having been worried. Philbrook had greeted Thistlecoat in the hall earlier that evening, the guest filled with pomp and flourish. The host might have forgone any further contact with the fellow if he hadn't thought it his obligation to offer Mrs. Morningside some respite. "Charleston," he said with guarded familiarity as he approached them.

"Philbrook, how are you," said the man, standing to shake hands with his host again. "Another successful event to add to your wife's laurels. Have you met Mrs. Morningside?"

"I have had that pleasure, yes." Philbrook gave Mrs. Morningside a formal bow. "I hope you're enjoying yourself this evening."

"Very much," said Mrs. Morningside, looking like anything but her words. She continued to exhibit an interest in the crowd upon the dance floor, and Philbrook guessed that she was watching for her daughter.

"How's business, Charleston?" asked Philbrook. This was the most bland question that came to mind at quick notice and he realized, regretfully, the one most likely to prompt a lengthy reply.

"Splendid, splendid," said Thistlecoat. "We had a strong first quarter on the P. and R. and I am looking to vary my profits into shipping."

"The railroad is doing very well for you, it seems."

"Yes, but it seems a stodgy business, on the whole, don't you think?"

"I don't know," said Philbrook. His own fortune had been greatly augmented by railroad stock, but he did not remind his guest of this.

"It's just trains," said Thistlecoat, putting on his best appearance of philosophy. "They're mundane, I think. The grand steamers have a sublimity about them that the railroads cannot hope to imitate."

"They both get you from one place to another," suggested Philbrook.

"There's a good deal more *mixing* on trains," said Thistlecoat, marking by his expression some distaste for this feature of railroad travel.

"Ah," said Philbrook without the least agreeing with the man.

"And speaking of which," said Thistlecoat, "I must say, your open door policy here at the ball is all very good, but it does invite some odd customers."

"Guests, not customers," said Philbrook, whose hospitable nature jumped with small offense at this last statement.

"This *Moose*path Club is laughable enough, to be sure, but to pay host to one of their servants must gall you."

"There are several people who give tickets to their employees," said Philbrook, not looking in the least galled.

"This *Moss* fellow, however, has been making an annoyance of himself regarding Mrs. Morningside's daughter."

"Oh? I did see this *Moss* fellow and Miss Morningside talking together, but she didn't appear very annoyed."

"That is precisely what concerns her mother."

Philbrook stole another glimpse of Mrs. Morningside. "Come, Charleston. A little flirtation? I daresay you or I won't travel too many generations back to find some humble origins."

Thistlecoat straightened his already impeccable posture and looked across his nose at Philbrook. "I have decided to speak to the boy," he intoned. "You say that you saw him?"

"I believe he was in the foyer," Philbrook lied.

Thistlecoat bowed slightly, said, "Excuse me," and returned to Mrs. Morningside. "If I may be so bold," he said, and with (Philbrook had to admit) a look of great elán and gallantry, he bowed, took the dance card from her hand and affixed his name upon it. "I will return," he said, and without informing her of his errand, he marched off to the cadence of *La Belle Hélène* in the direction of the foyer.

Philbrook did not feel the least bit guilty for misdirecting the man. "May I get you a drink, Mrs. Morningside?" he asked.

"No, thank you, Mr. Morrell," she said. "I am quite all right." Again her expression and manner belied her words. She was disturbed by the dance card in her hands. Until the moment before, it had simply been something to grip and fuss with, but now, with Mr. Thistlecoat's name registered upon it, she held it as if it had just come out of a bed of glowing coals.

"Charleston is a man of large opinions," said Philbrook to the woman in a kindly, almost fatherly tone. "I think they may get in the way of his seeing when someone is content to sit and watch." He could see Mercia and James Underwood making their way along the perimeter of the dance floor. "Here come your sister and her husband," said Philbrook quietly. "Would you like me to take that for you?"

Mrs. Morningside looked up, not sure what he meant. Then she considered the dance card in her hand, appeared to notice it for the first time (and unhappily), and held it out to him. It was an old custom that a woman without a dance card did not want to dance, and one that even Charleston Thistlecoat would silently honor when he returned. "Thank you, Mr. Morrell," she said.

He bowed again, waved to the approaching Underwoods, and hurried off. At first he slipped the dance card into a pocket, but then he halted in his step, pulled the card out again, and considered it with a frown. He scanned the crowd. As host, he thought, he had certain privileges *and* (when he came to think of it) responsibilities.

"You look pale," said Mercia to her sister, and she went so far as to touch Grace's forehead before she sat down in the chair previously occupied by Mr. Thistlecoat. Mercia and James, who stood nearby looking handsome and droll, had been closely watching Grace and Charleston and they approached after the man had made his bow and left. "I thought that man was going to ask you for a dance," said Mercia offhandedly.

Grace grew paler.

"I wager he's a good dancer," said James without turning about.

"I do hold you partly to blame for this," Grace said to her sister.

"For Mr. Thistlecoat?" said Mercia with wide eyes.

"You know what I mean."

"Yes, I'm afraid that I do."

"If you hadn't let Cordelia go wandering off with this Mr. Scott—"

Mercia gave out a short laugh. "She didn't go *wandering off* with Mr. Scott; she was *kidnapped*, if you remember—something that her father and I did not arrange. It was Mr. Scott—Dresden—who rescued her, and it occurs to me that they fell in love with one another without any assistance."

"You set a tone, and Priscilla has been touched by it through her cousin."

"If I did, or *we* did, I am not sorry for it," said Mercia. "Dresden is a grand fellow and everything a parent could want in a son-in-law."

"He's seems very nice, I'm sure," Grace conceded stiffly.

"Henry would have liked him very much," said Mercia.

Grace looked down at her knees at the mention of her husband's name.

Mercia was sorry, but not exactly regretful, for offering this salvo. She looked up and aimlessly watched the dancers reel by. Suddenly Priscilla and Mr. Moss came out of the crowd, waltzed past, looking more awestruck (the both of them) than happy, and disappeared once again in the massive entity that was the ball's ostensible purpose. Mercia almost said, "There's Priscilla now," simply out of surprise, but she stifled that comment and said, softly, "I do hope she is having a good time."

2I. Principals in Action

Whether dancing with him or simply standing beside him, watching the dancers, Mrs. Pleasance had not let go of Joseph Thump's arm since she first caught hold of it. Thump's expression was difficult to gauge, peering as it did from behind such a forest of beard, but his eyes hardly blinked, and his brow was perpetually furrowed *up* in an expression of unyielding surprise.

Mrs. Pleasance possessed certain material attributes that did not belie her (married) name, but she was otherwise something of a trial for a man of Thump's reticent nature; she had interesting, if not always flattering, things to say about the people who passed them, and she cooed in Thump's ear, which rather paralyzed him.

Thump said, "Hmmm," several more times than we are absolutely able to verify and was even heard to utter the occasional "Hmmm!" Once or twice he disclosed the hours of the week's remaining high tides; he generally didn't think this far ahead, so these announcements have been interpreted as a signal of a distracted mind. To be truthful, and to refer to his journal entry of the next day, he was *"much in mind of Mrs. Roberto,"* with whom he had danced almost a year ago at the Freeport Fourth of July Celebratory Ball and who had cooed in his ear (if it can be so called respectfully) to a much more salutary, if similarly paralyzing, effect. For all her self-assurance, Mrs. Pleasance did not coo as well or as nicely as the beautiful and noble ascensionist.

Occasionally Mrs. Pleasance did say something that required a specific answer from Thump—for instance, when she said, "Don't you think Miss Carruther's bustle is a bit lavish?" and he said, "I wonder where Ephram and Eagleton got to."

He continued to wonder this and continued to hope that they might emerge from the dance floor and assist him in bearing the weight of Mrs. Pleasance's generous regard. They continued not to show up, though help was in the offing from another, unforeseen source.

Philbrook Morrell was looking for someone else when he came through the crowd along the edges of the dance floor. He had decided to place himself within striking distance of Miss Morningside and Mr. Moss for the purpose of heading off Thistlecoat if that man should come *meddling* around. He thought he might enjoy telling the overstuffed fellow what station he could get off on his railroad. Mr. Thistlecoat would do well to leave Philbrook's *principals* to their own devices.

As he wandered the periphery of dancers, it was not with the purpose of rescuing his old school chum, but when he did spot Mr. Thump with Mrs. Pleasance stuck to his side like a barnacle, Philbrook was moved by a sudden concern for the bewildered fellow.

"Mr. Thump," Mrs. Pleasance was saying, "I think it quite wayward of you to ask for the one dance of a lady and then to let her simply pine upon your arm the rest of the evening." It was very prettily (and pretty fervently) said, and the suggestive intensity of Mrs. Pleasance's gaze upon Mr. Thump seemed to have a direct correlation to the accumulated heat beneath his collar. Mr. Thump couldn't remember having asked Mrs. Pleasance to dance, but he didn't like to contradict her.

"Joseph," said Philbrook when he reached them, "I hope you're enjoying yourself." Mrs. Pleasance had to let go of Thump's right arm so that the two men could shake hands.

"Hmmm," said Thump. "Yes, yes. A felicitous gathering." It was a phrase he had read in the *Portland Courier* recently.

"*Mr.* Morrell," said Mrs. Pleasance, "I believe you have just interrupted an invitation to the next waltz."

"Mrs. Pleasance," admonished Philbrook pleasantly, "you're not monopolizing the Moosepath League, are you? There are only the four of them, you know, and not really enough to go around."

Thump looked startled to be described somewhat along the lines of a scarce comestible.

"We ladies must watch out for ourselves," sang Mrs. Pleasance.

"Oh, Mr. Thump," said Philbrook suddenly, as if he had just remembered something of importance, "Mr. Ephram was looking for you, I think." He had seen Mr. Ephram in the clutches of Mrs. Allglow and could well believe that the fellow *might* be looking for help.

"Hmmm?" said Thump.

"Something about club business, if I'm not mistaken."

"Hmmm."

"I'm sure Mrs. Pleasance will excuse you," said Philbrook, proving none too subtle for the woman in question and probably just subtle enough for Mr. Thump. "I will do my best to entertain her in your absence."

"Yes, well," said Thump. He shook Philbrook's hand, offered to shake Mrs. Pleasance's hand as well, then realized his *faux pas*, withdrew his hand, and bowed. Reflexively, Mrs. Pleasance put out her own hand, and when Thump bowed instead, she pulled it back again. Thump, who saw the offered hand, lifted from his bow and reached for her hand, which had so far retreated that it looked as if he were reaching for her instead. Embarrassed, Thump pulled his own hand back again and bowed. Mrs. Pleasance almost extended her own hand a second time but corrected herself and said something, possibly indelicate, under her breath.

Thump, who was sure he had heard wrong (though perhaps not quite sure enough), walked away. Not being very particular about the direction of his escape, he was nearly run down by several polka dancers.

"Mr. Morrell," said Mrs. Pleasance, turning her smoky gaze upon Philbrook, "I'm not sure whether you are bad for depriving me of Mr. Thump's company or worse for wanting to dominate *my* company yourself."

Philbrook had not intended anything like this and, truthfully, was constructing his plans purely out of the moment. But circumstance did not leave him in the lurch. He was exchanging practiced badinage with the provocative woman when he saw a tall head of silver hair overtopping the nearby crowd. The man caught sight of Philbrook, gave his host a frown, and approached. "It was not for my company that I was attempting to secure you," Philbrook said to Mrs. Pleasance pleasantly. He passed her Mrs. Morningside's dance card and said with a sort of humorous gravity, "I acquired this by means that I am not at liberty to divulge."

It did not harm his sudden plan that *Mr.* Pleasance was not very fond of Charleston Thistlecoat. Nor did it harm his design of the moment that Mr. Thistlecoat was really a striking individual with his shock of silver hair, neatly coiffed, his patrician features and long nose, and his self-assured manner. Thistlecoat was dapper to the very laces of his shoes, and he carried about him an aura of wealth.

"I looked all over the foyer," said Thistlecoat, upon his approach, and these odd words, spoken so stuffily, almost made Philbrook laugh.

"Did you?" said Philbrook. "Perhaps what you're looking for is closer to hand."

"Oh?" Thistlecoat unknowingly made the mistake of looking a degree more satisfied even as he turned to Mrs. Pleasance.

"Mr. Thistlecoat," she said musically, "I believe I have something of yours."

"Oh?"

"You didn't have to be so . . . indirect." She waved the dance card before him, and Thistlecoat tried to peer at it as it fluctuated past her pretty nose.

"That looks like my signature," he said.

Mrs. Pleasance laughed slyly.

Philbrook made a simple bow and said, "I leave you to it, Charleston."

"Philbrook?" said Thistlecoat uncertainly.

"Mrs. Pleasance," said the host, including her in his bow. Then he hurried off in search of his former concern.

"Mr. Thistlecoat," said Mrs. Pleasance, "I believe you must make good on this promise."

Thistlecoat, still at sea as to how this promise had come to be in her hands, allowed himself to be escorted to the dance floor while the orchestra picked up the quiet flow of the *Danube*, and being nothing if not gallant in his conduct toward people "of his own station," he exhibited all his outward charm and elegantly fell in.

Philbrook Morrell stumbled across *Mr.* Pleasance not half a minute after he'd left *Mrs.* Pleasance's side. Philbrook thought Thistlecoat was a stuffed shirt, but he considered Sterling Pleasance a thoroughly bad sort. Pleasance was obsequious when he was in need of something and derisive when he thought he had the upper hand. There were those who thought that he had ruined a decent woman, in the person of his wife, Sybilla, as if she had been a horse run badly, but Philbrook was of the opinion that Sybilla Pleasance had probably always been something of a schemer. "The best tricks are learned in the cradle," his father used to say.

But there was no doubt in Philbrook's mind—Mr. Pleasance was the worst of the match. "To put it delicately," Philbrook had once said to his own wife, "Sterling Pleasance is a lout." Not duplicitous by nature, Philbrook approached people like Sterling Pleasance with something like apprehension, and having perpetrated something *like* duplicity on Mrs. Pleasance and Mr. Thistlecoat, he was doubly startled when Sterling's smirk loomed out of the crowd.

"Well, Philbrook," said Pleasance, "it's all very grand, isn't it."

"Thank you, Sterling."

"The ladies are looking fetching, don't you think?" The man cast his gaze about like a vaguely irritated snake.

"I have noticed a high degree of admirability," said Philbrook dryly.

"Take that one," said Pleasance, "no, take *that* one," and astonishingly, he indicated the young bespectacled woman who stood only ten or twelve feet away from them. "She hasn't left that fellow's side all evening."

Philbrook tried to view Miss Morningside and Mr. Moss as if he had never seen them or (at least) considered them before. "She's very pretty."

"Do you think? I don't know. She looks uncertain about it all to me. But there is no doubt she is otherwise presentable. 'Put together,' I believe is the phrase."

"She's very young," said Philbrook.

"I thought I might ask her to dance," said Pleasance unpleasantly. The Morrells were a highly respected and respectable family, and Sterling Pleasance, who had capped a wayward youth with a wayward adulthood, had never tried to hide his disdain for Philbrook. "You should have seen Thistlecoat, a while back," said Pleasance. "All straight and narrow, striding off like the proverbial knight to rescue that girl's mother from the *Moose*path League."

"I believe he's dancing with your wife at the moment," said Philbrook without warning and in that same dry tone.

Pleasance looked puzzled. Philbrook's flat statement sounded more like one of his own, and Sterling was not used to having his general scorn being reflected from this source. "Really?" he said.

"Yes," said Philbrook as if this were neither surprising nor cause for distress. It occurred to Philbrook that his unrehearsed machinations might be found out if the three people upon whom he had exercised them actually spoke to one another, but he really wasn't very concerned about it.

"Thistlecoat," said Pleasance. The news of his wife's dancing (or even *carrying on*) with *any*one was not very shocking to him, but the source of the news, as well as its offhand delivery, had given him pause.

"Have a nice evening, Sterling," said Philbrook.

"All very grand," said Pleasance as the host stepped past him. There was a long moment (or at least long to Pleasance) while he sorted through what had just occurred. "The Blue Danube" seemed to him trite and annoying, and he watched as placid dancers drifted over the pretty notes, swirling past him like so many leaves on a steady breeze.

He cast his eyes over the dancers, once or twice thought he saw a silver-topped head, and, when the waltz was finally over, prompted himself to movement and began to weave through the crowd.

22. Much Might Occur

By the time he finished his second dance with Miss Morningside, Sundry had ceased trying to say anything clever. By the time he finished his third dance with her, he ceased trying to say anything at all. He had used up all speech, or all the speech he dared employ; his emotions were that close to the surface and only waiting for the smallest excuse to boil over.

They hardly looked at one another directly. Sundry found himself gazing at the side of her head or past her shoulder, though she otherwise filled the memory of his vision that night. Occasionally he did address her with a plain look, and inevitably she would be turning her own gaze to steal a glance at him. Once their eyes met, he found it difficult to pull his gaze away so that when he finally did, he was red to the ears.

When they waited out a dance or two, Miss Underwood came wandering by with her fiancé and applied her happy wit toward conversation. Sundry was grateful, as his own well-documented social abilities seemed profoundly truncated. He did reveal further details concerning the marriage of Mister Walton and Miss McCannon, and Miss Underwood was prevailed upon to divulge some of her own plans under this theme. "Of course, Dresden just wants to get it over with and go home," she said breezily.

"I do want to go home," agreed Mr. Scott without a smile, which made his fiancée laugh.

"Dresden!" said Priscilla, who would have sounded like her mother if she hadn't laughed as well; then she wore that sweet, secret smile as she looked down at the floor before her feet.

Sundry took the opportunity to look at her again. He did like these people, and Mr. Scott was a man to admire, not the least for his dry humor, but he wondered: Could he even *joke* about such a thing if, by any stretch of fate and the imagination, it involved the young woman standing beside him? Miss Morningside's beautiful dark hair was gathered behind her head and fell thickly past her shoulders, the combs holding it back gleaming and the glass of her spectacles winking when she moved. The natural abundance of her, all in marvelous relationship with itself, called to the depths of his young man's heart; her hands when she moved them seemed not entirely delicate like Cordelia's, but altogether feminine.

She looked up, unexpectedly, caught Sundry looking at her, and said with an endearing smile, "It's such a nice evening."

Sundry looked to one side, which was timid of him, and said, "*I* can't remember one better spent," which was not.

"There you are," came a voice from the nearby crowd, and Miss Underwood's father ambled up to the small group.

"Daddy, why aren't you dancing?" asked Cordelia.

The older man regarded the present *quadrille*. "I don't like any sort of dance where I have to share your mother. I'll stick to waltzes. I don't see *you* out there."

"We're resting, thank you."

"Your aunt isn't feeling well."

"Oh?" said Cordelia. Priscilla said something that couldn't be heard over the music, though her shrinking posture spoke well enough.

"She's having one of her headaches," said Mr. Underwood without the use of an ironic tone. "Your mother and I are taking her home," he added, still addressing his daughter.

"Oh, no, that's not fair," said Priscilla.

"We've been to many dances—" he began with an affectionate hand on Priscilla's shoulder.

"But it's the biggest event all summer!"

"And we'll be to many more, God willing."

"*We'll* take her home, Daddy," said Cordelia cheerfully. "Won't we, Dresden?"

"Very glad to," said Mr. Scott, who was perhaps telling the truth.

"No, no," James was saying.

"Uncle James, *I* will go home with Mother," said Priscilla in a tone that rang of finality.

"Now *that's* not fair," he replied. Grace was known for her headaches and fainting spells, a large proportion of which, it was suspected, were more *motive* than *ailment* in their origin.

"If anyone should go home with her, it's me," insisted Priscilla.

"Your aunt and I are leaving, at any rate," said her Uncle James.

"I'll go," said Priscilla, after only the smallest hesitation.

"Priscilla," said Cordelia.

"I'll go," repeated Priscilla. She turned to Sundry and with clear eyes, but with an obviously heavy heart, said, "Thank you for the dances." She even reached out and touched his arm.

Sundry had been listening to the preceding conversation with something like horror and an increasing inability to breathe. He shook his head and tried to express to Miss Morningside how very much his pleasure it was. "Thank you," he finished, and (he thought) lamely.

"Good-bye," she said, almost below hearing.

Miss Underwood looked as if she might cry. Mr. Scott looked grim.

Mr. Underwood put on his most placid expression and nodded to Sundry. "Mr. Moss," he said almost with a note of query.

This address was meant as a nudge, and Sundry appeared to wake with a start. "I'll see you out," he said, surprising even himself. He couldn't think what had been the matter with him; certainly he didn't want to hang back, like some small conniver hiding from sight. He hurried up alongside Miss Morningside, and she smiled as she took his arm.

"Thank you," she said again.

Somehow the air and circumstances had cleared. Sundry could breathe, and he wondered, did she perhaps grip his arm a little tighter than need be? Was she walking a little closer to him?

Mercia Underwood looked vaguely amused when Priscilla and Sundry emerged from the crowd. "How good to see you again, Mr. Moss," she said pointedly. He exchanged genteel pleasantries with her and included Mrs. Morningside in these, expressing his hope for her speedy recovery.

Grace Morningside looked as grim as had Mr. Scott. She held her forehead between a thumb and forefinger and thanked him. "Are you coming, Priscilla?" she asked with more graciousness than directive in her tone.

"Yes, Mom," said the young woman. They went out to the wide, high-ceilinged foyer, and James retrieved their coats.

"This must be quite an event for you, Mr. Moss," said Mrs. Morningside.

Priscilla flashed a look of anger at her mother, and both of the Underwoods seemed dismayed by the statement.

But in his sudden decision to accompany Miss Morningside to the Underwoods' carriage, Sundry had regained a measure of his usual equanimity, and he was not to be shaken from it. "It certainly is, Mrs. Morningside," he said with all honesty and an honestly warm smile.

Even Priscilla's anger was somewhat mollified by this reply, and the mother herself looked every bit the party in arrears. "I'm glad if you're enjoying it," said Grace quietly, and with enough sincerity that she almost exonerated herself. She even took Sundry's arm when he offered it and allowed him to escort her to the street.

The rain had fallen off, though the walk was still wet. A dim light from the sky strained through several layers of ragged cloud. The moon was up but invisible.

"Pay us a visit," said Mrs. Underwood to Sundry while her husband was calling up their driver.

Mr. Underwood, when he had handed his wife into the carriage, gave Sundry's shoulder a warm grip. "Good night, Mr. Moss." James offered assistance to his sister-in-law, and after only a brief hesitation, Grace entered the carriage on his hand.

"Good night, Mr. Moss," said Priscilla. "And thank you." She let him hand her in after her uncle stepped aside.

"I hope to see you again," said Sundry, but Miss Morningside only smiled softly and looked down where she was stepping.

"Pay us a visit, Mr. Moss," said Mrs. Underwood again, a little more loudly this time and none too subtly.

Sundry chuckled. "I will," he promised. Then Mr. Underwood was ensconced beside his wife. Sundry had a glimpse of Mrs. Morningside leaning her head back against the seat with her eyes closed, and the driver whipped the horse up and took the carriage away. After a few minutes in the cool of the evening air, Sundry went back inside to make his excuses to the Moosepath League and to say good-bye to Miss Underwood and Mr. Scott.

The affianced couple were in the foyer. A grand schottische was under way in the ballroom, and even out here they had to speak louder than usual. "Mr. Moss," Miss Underwood said, almost as soon as she saw him, "you must come by and visit us."

"I've already promised your mother that I would," he said.

"Very good." She seemed satisfied, but then she wanted to be sure of him. "Mom will be very put out if you don't, you know."

"I will do my best not to disappoint."

"And of course, the rest of us will be looking for you, too."

"I think Mr. Moss will probably come by when he has the opportunity," said Mr. Scott with the sort of expression that indicated his beloved may have stretched the subject far enough.

Miss Underwood very nearly made a face.

"Mr. Moss!" came a familiar voice, and Mr. Ephram strode into the foyer. He looked rather out of sorts, and he sported a bewildered cowlick that would have done Maven Flyce proud. Mr. Eagleton and Mr. Thump were in close order behind him, and if they did not wear the bewildered cowlicks, they did wear the expressions. Mr. Thump was very wide-eyed, and Mr. Eagleton walked as if he expected to be prodded from behind at any moment.

"High tide at 3:14 A.M.," said Thump.

"Rain expected to clear, sunny and seasonable tomorrow," said Eagleton.

"It's five minutes before the hour of ten," said Ephram. Eagleton and Thump were considering his cowlick with polite interest, and Ephram reached up and touched the wayward plumage. "Oh," he said, as he brushed the hair back in place, "Mrs. Allglow thought I had something in my hair . . . I think."

He *hoped* she thought this, but in truth, she thought he had said something amusing, and when he professed that he had not, she only laughed more and impishly ruffled his hair, which she thought handsome. Thump had appeared soon after with the news that there was business concerning the club, and Ephram had hastily excused himself from Mrs. Allglow's company. Eagleton was quickly discovered, and though none of them had actually called a meeting, they were each quite sure that one was in order.

"Business to attend," said Ephram.

"Glad to have you with us," said Eagleton to Sundry, though the young man would have to be quick to catch up with them as they hurried for the door.

"Thank you," said Sundry. "I think I'm in need of a walk."

"Mr. Thump?" came a feminine voice from the ballroom.

"Hmmm?" said Thump as he followed his friends into the night.

"Mr. Thump?" Mrs. Pleasance was standing in the entry to the ballroom, calling after the bearded Moosepathian as her husband whisked past her to retrieve their coats. A few feet behind her stood Charleston Thistlecoat, who looked nearly as provoked as her husband.

"A great deal can occur at one of these functions," said Miss Underwood with dissembled innocence. "Why is everyone leaving so early?"

Several other people were lingering, for whatever intrigues, in the foyer, and a buzz went up on the heels of the Pleasances' departure. Mr. Morrell sauntered into the hall and spoke to the three young people there. When Thistlecoat traipsed past him, Philbrook inquired of the man why he was leaving so soon. Thistlecoat stopped in his tracks, rose to his full height, and regarded the host very seriously before turning on his heels. He snatched his coat from the servant holding it out for him and made his swift leave.

Philbrook said good night to Mr. Moss, who was also leaving, and thanked him for coming.

"It's been my pleasure," said Sundry. "Thank you."

Miss Underwood and her fiancé said good-bye and watched him go; then Philbrook stayed in the foyer and watched *them* return to the dance. Another waltz was slowly revolving the many stories upon the ballroom floor, and the handsome young couple considered the transient display of bright gowns and black tails before facing one another, clasping hands and waists, and disappearing among them.

"That was quite an exodus a moment ago," said an old acquaintance of Philbrook's. The man approached, his hands clasped behind him.

"Yes," agreed the host.

"They weren't all going to another party, were they?"

"I don't believe they were all going to the *same* party," said Philbrook. The old acquaintance chuckled. "Another successful evening," he said.

"Yes." Philbrook had rather lost interest in it now. He suspected that the ball had lost some of the best and worst in about five minutes' time. "Ah, well," he said, as if the man standing beside him could understand his thoughts. "I had better find my wife and dance with her, I think."

"I think you would be wise to do so."

Philbrook smiled and nodded, then wandered back to the ballroom. He was humming the tune to the waltz, trying to remember the name of it. The old acquaintance walked back to his previous station, hands clasped behind his back, and looked as if he were waiting for someone.

It was a few minutes after that a late arrival appeared at the doorway to the ballroom and the name of Mrs. Roberto filtered through the glittering crowd.

23. Chasing Solace

Sundry Moss had found it increasingly difficult (or at least increasingly oppressive) to wander the rooms and halls of the Walton home on Spruce Street now that Mister Walton was out of residence. He had grown up in a large family and was used to noise and bustle; living on Spruce Street with Mister Walton had taken adjustment, as his employer was a quiet man and the house was often loud with the voiceless shadows of past inhabitants, its unused rooms affecting Sundry as a little sad. Now Mister Walton was gone to Halifax, and the house was truly empty when Sundry arrived that night to turn up the lights in the hall and sit in the near dark in the parlor by the unlit hearth. He missed the presence of his friend, and without the distraction of another person, his romantic melancholy was harder to bear.

Contemplating the short arc of the evening, Sundry wondered what sort of fool he might have made of himself and what Miss Morningside might have meant with a smile or a kind word (beyond a smile or a kind word) and thought that he was about as despondent as he'd ever felt. It did seem a terrible contradiction that he had actually danced with her only an hour ago, that she had taken his arm, and that they had talked quietly, if cautiously, together; but now his heart was in his boots because he was no longer dancing with her, and she was no longer holding his arm, and they were no longer talking quietly together.

How soon could he reasonably visit the Underwoods, where Miss Morningside, her mother, and her younger brother, Ethan, were staying until Cordelia's wedding later that month? He didn't think he could really visit them tomorrow, but even then, sitting in the Waltons' parlor and the hall clock striking the eleventh hour, he was pretty sure that he would. For now he was sure he couldn't abide the silent house and he went upstairs to change his clothes and pack a bag before heading back into the night.

The clouds must have been listening to Mr. Eagleton, for they had run off from the local atmosphere and left a bit of moon hanging in the east. As he reached the nearest corner and descended Clark Street, Sundry caught glimpses of the dark bulk of Peak's Island in the dim sheen of Casco Bay. A breeze came off the water, and he lingered at the foot of the hill to feel it in his face. A policeman ambled by, slowing his stride long enough to consider Sundry and his bag. They exchanged tentative *good evenings*, the policeman not sure about Sundry and Sundry not sure that he wanted company. The officer continued on his beat.

There was more waking life on view as Sundry neared the waterfront: A carriage trundled by, and a group of men further down the hill seemed to be arguing about something. Sundry worked his way east, carefully skirting the potential melee, then south until he strode the sidewalk of Brackett Street and found himself beneath the sign of the Faithful Mermaid. He had not known the Spark family very long, but he enjoyed their company and thought the tavern's business would prove diverting. Thaddeus Spark hailed Sundry the moment he stepped inside the front door, and the regulars greeted him with friendly nods or a wave of a tankard. The smell of ale and beer was strong and the air was blue with smoke.

"Davey," Thaddeus called when he took note of the bag in Sundry's hand. Then, with a wink, he said, "The air get a little thick over on Spruce Street? I can't stand a quiet house myself. Davey!" The oldest Spark boy hurried in from the kitchen and Thaddeus told him to open the west room on the third floor. "Sit down, and we'll feed you, boy," said Thaddeus.

Sundry nodded to several people he had seen the time or two he'd been in the tavern room before. He was surprised that the thought of food appealed to him. He thought he could do justice to a pretty big meal and wondered why. It was while looking for a place to test his appetite that he caught sight of Horace McQuinn's half grin and sharp steel blue eyes and the exclamation point of Maven Flyce's hair rising from the dimness and smoke of the nearest corner.

"Well, old boy," drawled Horace, "sit down and tell us all about it."

"Gory, Hod," said Maven. "It's Mr. Moss!"

"I thought it might be," said Horace.

Sundry struggled between the need for solitude—contrary to the impulse that had brought him to the Faithful Mermaid—and society, which was his natural inclination. It was a desire not to offend that tipped the scales; he pulled a chair up and sat with the two professional idlers. "What do you want to know?" he asked.

"What do you have?" replied Horace after a profound shrug.

"About a day more than I had yesterday," said Sundry, which nonsensical remark could be taken for what it was or for profound philosophy. Horace gave a wheezing laugh, but Maven said, "I can't imagine it," and looked astonished. Horace could, however, and he put a ditty into the air:

> *Will the next day be mirth?*
> *Will the next day be sorrow?*
> *Looks like we'll wait,*
> *And find out tomorrow.*

Upon which assertion he raised the mug of ale in his hand and toasted all. There were those who heard him and raised their glasses in salute to the fellow's wisdom, and those who hadn't heard and raised their glasses anyway.

"Honestly, Hod, where do you get it!" said Maven.

"The well isn't very deep, Maven," informed Horace McQuinn, tapping his head, "but it's close to hand."

"Are you gentlemen frequent callers here?" wondered Sundry.

"We like to spread it around a bit," said Horace. "Don't we, Maven?" Maven looked as if it were news to him.

"We've been over the Weary Sailor lately and the Crooked Cat a time or two," said Horace. "But seeing Mrs. Spark the other day reminded me where I might get a decent meal." Horace nodded slowly, pulling a long face to indicate how serious he was.

"Mr. Moss," said Mabel Spark, who might have heard her name spoken as she came through the swinging doors from the kitchen. "I thought you were going to the ball tonight." Betty Spark poked her comely head through the doorway, then followed her mother to the table.

"Well, I did," said Sundry.

"You're out early," said the mother.

"Was it very grand?" asked Betty. She raised her shoulders like a child who expects sweets, her hands at her sides and her eyes wide and pretty with the sight of grand things beyond the tavern room. Put *her* in a fancy gown, thought Sundry, and she would have given the celebrated belles of Portland a potent challenge. It was a pleasure just to watch her think about it.

"It was very crowded," said Sundry, wavering between an urge to fulfill her wistful imagination and the concern that he might sadden her with grand descriptions of something she had missed.

"It must have been wonderful," she said, lost in her thoughts.

"I think it's who you're with, not where you are," he said, sounding like an old man reminiscing on younger days.

Betty thought about this, but not very much.

"Have you ever been to a ball, Horace?" asked Maven Flyce.

"I was at the *Governor's* Ball, once," admitted Horace.

"Good heavens!" said Maven.

"Horace McQuinn!" declared Mabel Spark as if it hurt to hear something so preposterous. Thaddeus had circled back, and Davey, too, stopped on his way to serving another table, so a small crowd managed to assemble in that corner to marvel or scoff at the thought of Horace attending a Governor's Ball.

The old man's blue-gray eyes sparkled happily, and he raised his mug again. "Horace has been a place or two, I can promise," he said.

Sundry believed him and felt better just imagining the old rascal at such a function. He was going to inquire after further details when Mabel spoke up on a subject more current and less amusing.

"Mr. Ring is a little recovered," she said.

"Is he?" said Sundry.

"He hasn't told Melanie, but he has some idea about taking her up-country to live with cousins of his."

Thaddeus had yet to change subjects. "Whoever *you* were with must have left early, too," he said to Sundry.

Sundry was noncommittal.

"Did you dance?" asked Betty.

Sundry nodded, and there was a brief and telltale expression upon his face before he turned to Mrs. Spark again and said, "Where are his cousins?"

"Up Brownville, I guess."

"We dance, sometimes, here in the tavern room," said Thaddeus, who wasn't to be shaken from his theme.

"Oh, Daddy, it's not the same thing!" insisted Betty.

"I don't know. We have a good time."

"Tell him it's not the same thing, Mr. Moss," said Betty.

"I wouldn't presume," said Sundry. He was thinking that if Miss Morningside were on his arm, almost any time or place would suffice.

"Go get Mr. Moss a plate of stew," Mabel said to her daughter, and Betty reluctantly hurried into the kitchen. "And a loaf of bread," the mother called after. Then she returned to her previous concern and said to Sundry, "I don't like the idea of Burne Ring traipsing off with a six-year-old girl. He's not in enough shape to cross the street."

"Why are you telling Mr. Moss?" asked Thaddeus.

"He's not planning to leave tonight, is he?" asked Sundry.

"I was just telling him," said Mabel to her husband, and to Sundry she said, "He says he's leaving tomorrow."

"Oh."

"He thinks his cousins will take the girl in, though he hasn't seen them for years."

"Wouldn't a telegram or a letter work?" wondered Sundry.

"I guess he doesn't know exactly where they are—just up Brownville way, and he figures he's going to look for them." Betty almost stumbled, hurrying back into the tavern room with a steaming plate and a loaf of bread on a tray. Mabel took the serving from her daughter and set it down before Sundry, saying with half a smile, "It's a bit of a climb down the ladder, coming from the Morrells' ballroom to the Faithful Mermaid."

"Not at all," said Sundry. "You notice I didn't waste any time coming back for something good to eat."

She smiled at the flattery but was flattered nonetheless.

"And the company is not to be faulted," said Sundry, taking in Horace and Maven and the several Sparks by way of a gesture with his spoon.

"We're not too bad," agreed Thaddeus.

"Better than my mother expected for me," said Horace sagely.

"My goodness!" said Maven.

Betty took after her father in her allegiance to a favored topic. "It must have been lovely," she said.

Mabel put a sympathetic arm around her daughter. Thaddeus stood and nodded. Horace produced a pipe from a pocket and considered it like a previously unknown specimen. Maven gaped.

"On to the next thing," said Sundry.

24. Tending Teacup

Priscilla lay in the dark, listening to the occasional traffic on the street and the steady snores of Teacup, her family's fox terrier, who slept at the foot of the bed. She never heard the carriage pull up to the gate, or did not separate it from the other night sounds, but she sensed (as much as heard) movement in the house below. After a while there came the rustle of skirts on the stairs. A quiet voice called from down the hall, and Cordelia must have stood for a while at her parents' door, talking to them.

Priscilla closed her eyes, then realized that her cousin was in the room, quietly readying herself for bed. "I'm awake," said Priscilla.

"I'm sorry."

"No, I was awake."

Teacup made a drowsy sound.

"I thought you were asleep."

"I might have dosed after you came in. But I was waiting for you."

Cordelia sat on the bed, half dressed, her hair still up. She reached out and found Priscilla's hand. Teacup made another, more articulate noise and raised his small head from his paws.

"I hope you had a good time after we left," said Priscilla.

"I'm sorry to say, just a little." Cordelia looked regretful. She stroked the dog's head, and Teacup clambered into her lap.

"Don't be. I was sure Mom's headache would ruin everyone's evening."

"I daresay it ruined Mr. Moss's," said Cordelia blithely.

The veneer of Priscilla's response was matter-of-fact. "I daresay he found other girls to dance with."

"I don't think so. He left as soon as you were gone."

Priscilla sat up in bed and considered what this meant. Cordelia was smiling softly. A chip of moon afforded a dim light through the window to the east, and by this Priscilla could see her cousin's pretty face. "I shouldn't be glad of that, should I," said Priscilla.

"I would be," said Cordelia without hesitation.

"I'll probably never see him again."

"That's what you said the last time." Cordelia set Teacup aside and rose from the bed so that she could change into her nightclothes. "I wouldn't have been surprised if Mother asked him to come and visit."

"She did. Twice."

"Count on him knocking at the door tomorrow then."

"But we're leaving first thing in the morning," said Priscilla.

This news occasioned a brief silence. "Leaving?" said Cordelia. "You can't be leaving. What about my wedding?"

"Oh, we'll be back for that, of course. But Mom says we've been gone too long and should be home for a while."

"Do my parents know this?"

"I thought your mother would turn ten shades of red, but she didn't say very much. Your father, bless his heart, tried to talk Mom out of it, but she was set."

"Then let her go," said Cordelia, her pique barely *sounding through.* "Ethan can go with her. There's not much for him here, following Papa around."

"No, I can't," said Priscilla softly, almost as if she were speaking to herself. She scooped the little dog into her arms and snuggled him like a babe. "I can't stay behind yet, Cord. Mother is still so angry about Daddy and still so lonely, and to be truthful . . . I understand her all too well." She took another breath before speaking again. "I know she seems stiff and prudish, Cord, and I know how tiresome you must think her—"

"I love your mother! You know I do!"

The night's mix of emotions seemed too much for Priscilla. It surfaced in her voice and weighed her head toward the dog in her lap. "There are days when she's in the parlor playing the piano, or when she is up in her room sewing, and Ethan and I are both in the house, and I can almost feel that she's content, that she's *not* so lonely, if only for an instant." Priscilla was weeping, now, but softly, and Cordelia sat on the edge of the bed again and hugged her. Teacup let out a little noise, as if he were afraid of being smothered between them. "Do I seem an awful martyr?" asked Priscilla.

"I've *never* thought that."

"Did I seem one tonight when I left with her?"

"To Mr. Moss? I don't think it would have occurred to him." Cordelia held Priscilla at arm's length and tried to read her cousin's sweet features in the half-light. "You just seemed every bit as kind as you always do." Cordelia reached for her dress on the chair by the bed and pulled a lace handkerchief from the sleeve. "He's quite smitten, you know."

Priscilla dabbed at her eyes, shrugged, and shook her head.

"Dresden thinks so, too."

"I bet you told Dresden that he didn't know a thing about it," said Priscilla with just the hint of admonishment.

"I didn't, this time." Cordelia made a face that would have been hard to read, even in the daylight. Priscilla, without her glasses, squinted at her cousin. "I do love to tease him," said Cordelia.

"He does love to be teased by you," said Priscilla.

"He's good for it," said Cordelia. She always acted so *nonchalant* about her fiancé, but Priscilla understood what depths of feeling lurked beneath the surface of her cousin's playful humor. Cordelia was in her nightgown now, and she stretched out on the bed, propped herself up on her elbows, and said, "I do like him very much, Priscilla."

"I should hope so!"

"No! Not Dresden. Mr. Moss."

"Oh."

"Oh?"

"He's a very nice man," admitted Priscilla.

"He's quite smitten."

"So you say."

"So I saw! And if you could have seen yourself tonight, you'd understand why."

"Perhaps Mrs. Walton will want a maid," said Priscilla, taking a page from her cousin's book and plying some wry humor upon the subject.

"Do you think that's what Mr. Moss is? A butler or valet or something?"

Priscilla was startled by this for reasons Cordelia couldn't know. "I don't think of him that way at all," she said. "What do *you* think he is?"

Cordelia shifted her posture, turning over on her back, to encourage clear consideration. "I think he's Mister Walton's best friend," she said. "Well, aside from *Mrs.* Walton, perhaps."

Teacup let out a terrific yawn, and both the young women followed close upon this display with yawns of their own. Cordelia climbed onto her side of the bed, and they lay quietly with their own thoughts for some minutes. Teacup trudged a portion of the bed in circles, then dropped down between them with a low, troubled growl that made them laugh. There was more quiet in the room. A soft breeze came through the open window. The hour tolled from some steeple on a street below.

"He'll be at the wedding," said Cordelia when the bells were done.

"Do you think he will?" asked Priscilla hopefully.

"I can't imagine anything keeping him away."

25. The Indian Bridge

The little room at the top of the tavern stairs was close, and Sundry opened the window to let in the breeze from the harbor. Lying on his back in the narrow bed, his arms behind his head, he conjured the excuses he might offer to the Underwoods for intruding upon them so soon as tomorrow. On a street somewhere above, the hour tolled a single bell. The ball would still be carrying on. Other romances would germinate or bud or come to fruition. (There would be two engagements announced in the social columns later that week.) Some affair might come to loggerheads and be finished. Somehow he felt both apart from and a part of it all.

Sundry thought Priscilla Morningside would be sleeping now, and he imagined her curled in a large bed with her glorious dark hair spilling about her head, and he did so without shame.

Some natural constructs exist so long that they become part of the spiritual landscape of being human, yet they stand out against the rest of the world when we are part of them, so that we wonder if we haven't invented them or inherited them directly from some clever ancestor. Some constructs seem too straight and regular for the hand of chance. Truthfully, they are.

To Sundry, a single, specific smile was the width of the world, and a particular voice all that he could hear. He would have been surprised how quickly and easily he fell asleep if he had been awake. Ardent love in an honest heart is like a lullaby.

BOOK THREE
THE SINGULAR ADVENTURE
OF SUNDRY MOSS

June 9–10, 1897

from the *Portland Daily Advertiser*
June 9, 1897

CITY INCIDENTALS

A car-load of Bangor extension ladders went through Portland yesterday for the Lindgren-Mahan Fire Engine Co. of Chicago.

Ivanhoe Lodge, Knights of Pythias, will confer the rank of knight in the long form tomorrow evening.

A brawny fellow, bearing the mark and accoutrements of a sailor and carrying over his shoulder an outsized oar, attempted to make ingress at a Commercial Street establishment on Saturday evening without first leaving that tool of his trade at the door. When the tavern keeper requested that he "put his oar in" somewhere else, the sailor informed the proprietor that he was loath to part with it, even for the fleeting length of time it would take to refresh himself.

The oar was estimated by several onlookers to be at least ten feet in length and carved from some hardy tree not indigenous to these shores, but size and strangeness aside (not to mention the possibility of exaggeration), it is difficult to understand why he held it in such esteem. The tavern keeper was adamant that the instrument stay out-of-doors, or at least out of his door, and the sailor was equally convinced that it should go in with him. The upshot of this contest of wills was that the police were called for, and after a slight altercation, the sailor received the wisdom-inducing end of a stick at the top of his tall skull and was then carried by cart and four strong officers to the nearby precinct.

A man who works for Stanwood, the blacksmith, was seriously injured Saturday afternoon. While a helper was swinging . . .

26. Leaving Without Knowing
(June 9, 1897)

Sometimes she heard a voice from the other room (or from outside or from within her own head) that called that other name. She had already grown accustomed to looking up when she heard her *real* name (the old name that was new again), but she had not left off saying, "Huh?" or "What?" or "Who's that?" when she heard the name she had previously lived under for as long as she could remember. At first she thought that some of the children from the neighborhood were teasing her, particularly when she and Tim were sprinting the sidewalks or climbing roofs along the waterfront. Once she turned to Tim and said, "What?" and then, when he replied by saying, "What?" she said, "Did you hear that?" but he hadn't.

Sometimes she thought her father was calling her. She would pause to assess the voice that spoke the discarded name, and once she hurried back to the Faithful Mermaid, fearing the worst—that her father had died and had communicated the name he had given her across some ghostly expanse. But he was sleeping when she came to him and never knew she had been there to look in on him as a mother might look in on her child in the middle of the night.

Once, since the discovery of her real name and her real person, Tim called her Mailon out of habit, though he was embarrassed afterward and apologized shamefacedly. Melanie was only surprised and then bemused. She could not be mad at Timothy Spark. He had not abandoned her, though she had not been what he thought all those long summer days hunting with the Abenaki along the forested trails of the city streets or fleeing enemy tribes with Daniel Boone on homemade sleds down the snowy slopes of the Western Promenade. It seemed a hard thing to be a girl after all those adventures, to ask a friend to carry on as if nothing had happened or changed, but Tim (according to his father) had proven a philosopher. Melanie didn't know what a philosopher was, but she suspected it meant that he was forgiving.

On the morning of her and her father's departure for Brownville,

Melanie woke up with the name Mailon in her head or spoken in the next room or from outside on the street. She thought it was a woman's voice this time, and she wondered if it was her mother calling, though she couldn't say why her mother would have employed a name she had never known.

"I'm here," she said under her breath. The bedchamber under the eaves felt close and warm after nights spent in the ancient coal room. She sat up in the trundle bed, the covers cast off since the middle of the night, and paid heed to the sound of the early-morning traffic below her window and the sense as much as the sound of movement in the house around her. "I'm here," she whispered again, hoping for a response. She wondered if she would hear that name the rest of her life or if someday the voice, be it man or woman, adult or child, would speak "Melanie" to her, which prospect loomed in her fancy like Tim's forgiving philosophy.

A steam whistle blew from the southeast, and it was a moment (during the echoes rather than the original sound) before she realized that it was a train and not a ship. Another, deeper sound boomed from the harbor—the oceangoing speaking to the railbound. Shod hooves, clopping the cobblestones of Brackett Street, masked an intermittent rap upon her door till the horse and wagon had passed out of hearing. "Melanie?" came a voice. "Melanie?"

"Tim?"

"Your dad is up. He's gone down to the kitchen."

"Wait for me!" she said, and scrambled into her boy's clothes. She hadn't thought what this news boded when she opened the door with her socks and shoes (Tim's socks and his old shoes) in her hands and her light brown hair, only now beginning to grow out in search of an acceptable female length and sticking out at startled angles. Tim's own blond head looked far from a recent combing, but this disarray seemed to indicate more concern than wonder. Tim was a year or so older than Melanie, rangy and rawboned. He had freckles across his nose, and his eyes were the blue one could trust against clouds. "He's says you're leaving," said Tim solemnly.

Melanie's mouth hung open. She couldn't guess what he meant.

"He says you're leaving," said Tim again. Melanie stood before him, dressed in boy's clothes (not her old ragged things, but mended pants and a shirt that Tim had outgrown), but Tim could not see the boy anymore. He didn't wonder, as his parents and everyone else did, how he had ever seen anything other than a girl in those delicate features. He didn't entirely understand the difference between a scrawny, possibly stunted boy of six and a small-boned, even dainty girl of the same age, but he could see it. The change had not slowed her down, however, dodging pedestrians and wagons along the sidewalks and streets, or made her less fearless as they scurried the rooftops of the waterfront. He didn't know if he admired her any more than before, but he admired her differently.

"I'm leaving?" said Melanie. How could that be, now that the Sparks were taking her in and she would be one of them? There was a time when Mrs. Spark had refused to let the dirty waif into her kitchen and *Mailon* had only hovered outside the door, taking a plate of breakfast or a bit of supper in the alley; but after the adventure with the Moosepath League and Mr. Thump's gratitude in the form of a substantial sum of money, Mabel Spark would not allow the gift into the hands of a father who would drink it up, and the child was taken into the warmth and bustle of the tavern. "If Mailon has a bath, we will take him in," said Mabel Spark, and even the discovery that *Mailon* was *Melanie* had not altered the promise, though the woman of the house insisted that the newly discovered girl must soon adopt proper attire.

But Melanie was to be one of them now, and she couldn't be leaving if she was going to be one of them. She thought that she and her father must be going back to the coal room below Pearce Eddy's flophouse, but she couldn't understand why.

"No," said Tim. "It's someplace else. He said you're going to Brownville." Tim searched Melanie's face when he said this, looking for some sign of knowledge.

She had none. "Where's that?" she asked. It sounded like a place far away, if for no other reason than that she had never heard of it.

"Daddy says up north somewhere," he said. "Is your family there?"

She shook her head. The children had not moved from their positions on opposite sides of the threshold, and Melanie suddenly wished that Tim would step aside so that she could hurry down to the kitchen and look at her father.

"Are you going to leave?" he asked. Whether Mailon or Melanie, whether greeting him from the stoop outside the kitchen door or rising from her own bed down the hall, he had got quite used to her and wasn't very sure what he would do without her. Life had taken some unexpected turns as of late, and he had not begun to catch up with them.

"There's just Daddy and I," she said. Timothy shifted his posture, and she intuitively used the moment to step past him, her shoulders hunched and her gait stiff as she walked the hall to the back stairs.

"Do you want me to hide you?" asked Timothy. He had not moved from the doorway. "There's a hundred places you could go, if you want." It was true; they knew every niche and cubby along the wharf district.

She stopped to look over her shoulder. "Maybe later," she said, but she couldn't really imagine it. She had not the understanding or the words to say what she felt, but she had been hiding all her six years, and it would have seemed like going backward simply to find a hole to crawl in. She picked up the pace as she neared the stairs, and soon Timothy could hear her small feet clattering down, socks and shoes still in her hands.

Timothy shook himself into movement and hurried to the stairwell. "Maybe I can come, too," he said softly behind her, but she was gone.

27. Quick at Figures

"God bless you," said Mabel Spark when Melanie sneezed. She almost said, "Start a journey with a sneeze, and you'll never get where you mean to," but she wasn't as sure of this tenet as she was of certain other laws of nature. You could cause trouble if you put a hat on a bed, that was certain, and setting an extra place at the table almost always drew an unexpected guest (purposely setting an extra place didn't work, of course, or every taverner in the world would have business); but Mabel wasn't so sure about sneezing before travel, and she didn't want to worry the child. Mabel shot a troubled look at Burne Ring, who sat at the kitchen trencher looking lost and out of breath. The taverness gave the little girl the handkerchief in her apron pocket and told her to keep it. Burne looked at his daughter as if he couldn't quite remember who she was.

"It's the sun," said Melanie.

"The sun?" said Mabel. She fretted for this broken-down man and his boy-clad daughter, but the Faithful Mermaid must continue business, and there were hungry breakfasters in the tavern room. She busied Minerva and Annabelle with a look and a wave of the hand.

"The sun makes her sneeze," said Tim. He stood in the doorway to the back stairs, looking uncertain. He pointed to the window, where the rising sun, reflected from another window up the hill and across the way, lit the table before the little girl.

"Nonsense," said Mabel Spark, but she glanced from the little spot of brilliance on the table to the window and back again. "Close the door," she said, which was more a precaution for winter than June, but habit with her.

Tim closed the door to the back stairs and came further into the kitchen. "She can sneeze just coming out of the shade," he said. "Mr. Ealing gave her a nickel once, just to see her do it." He was proud of Melanie's unusual talent, and just looking at him, Mabel wanted to go over and hug him but forbore for the sake of his seven-year-old dignity. Instead she made a noise of disbelief, though she didn't actually suspect her youngest child of lying.

"Horace and Maven's breakfast," said Thaddeus as he entered the kitchen.

"Yes, yes," said Mabel.

The bearded taverner stood by the door and considered Burne Ring, who stared down at the plate of sausage and egg and biscuits that Mabel had provided for him. Thaddeus had applied a razor to the man's face the night before and even trimmed his sparse gray-blond hair, which had been hanging like old straw over his ears, but Burne still had the look of a man who had not been recently groomed. His cheeks seemed in shadow, and his eyes were shot with red and sunk beneath what once had been a handsome brow.

Thaddeus and Mabel were troubled. They had explained to Burne about the money Mr. Thump had given Melanie, or at least about part of it; they had given the stricken man a portion of the generous sum—what Mabel considered enough to get them to Brownville and put them up for a week or so while Burne searched for his relatives. She would send the rest when she'd heard they were safely settled or that Melanie was safely settled, which was more to the point, since Mabel couldn't imagine the father would ever be safe *or* settled between here and the grave.

The requested breakfasts were assembled, and Minerva took them out to the tavern room. "No need to hurry off," Thaddeus said to Burne. He took a biscuit out of the warming oven as he passed it and approached the table. "Might be a good idea to stay a little longer and get your strength back." Thaddeus, like Mabel, thought it more likely that Burne would "up and die" than "get his strength back," but he might as well do it here where friends (or at least people willing to watch after him and his daughter) could tend him.

"We'd better be going," said Burne quietly, though he seemed to have wakened to this notion only when he stated it. He looked up at his daughter, who looked doubtful. "I'm grateful for all your help," he said, but with more peevishness than gratitude in his voice. "I'll give you something out of what this Mr. Thump gave us."

Thaddeus shook his head. Mr. Thump had given the money to Melanie, not her father, and the father hadn't even thought "Why?" though they had explained to him how his daughter had helped do Mr. Thump and his friends a service. Burne asked for no other explanation and truthfully might not have understood it if it had been offered.

About the time Minerva returned with an armful of dirty plates, the door to the back stairs opened again, and Sundry Moss came into the kitchen with a good morning meant for everyone present. Annabelle tugged at the back of her blouse and straightened her apron. Once she had rid herself of the plates, Minerva brushed at an imagined spot of flour on her cheek and left a spot of flour there. Sundry was surprised to see Burne at the kitchen table.

It occurred to Mabel Spark that Mr. Moss was a free man while the newlywed Waltons were off to Halifax, and he was, as it happened, just the sort of steady fellow who could escort two poor souls like Burne and his daughter to their cousins in Brownville. She wondered how to suggest such a thing without actually seeming to do so.

"Mr. Ring and Melanie are off to Brownville," said Thaddeus, who may have been on a similar tack.

"Not this morning!" said Sundry.

"It seems they are," said the taverner.

"Let me fix you some breakfast," said Mabel.

Sundry paused over one or the other of these statements. He had taken note of the little girl's expression. Tim, too, stood nearby, looking indefinite. "Yes," he said. "Thank you." He went to the table and sat opposite Melanie. "You have cousins in Brownville, Mr. Ring?" he said.

Burne looked as if he might say, "What if I do?" or, "There are a lot of people who know my business," but he vaguely recognized the tall young man. For almost a week, Burne had been drying out (and not entirely of his own will and choosing). He had seen visions and shaken his bed to pieces till he thought he was near death, nursed on small beer and barely aware of several people watching over him, including his tiny daughter. He could not say to whom he was indebted, and so he said nothing.

Sundry appeared not to notice the scarcity of reply, but he surveyed the faces of Melanie and Tim before going on to other things.

"Betty says you had a wonderful time last night," said Minerva.

It was perhaps more than Sundry had actually revealed, or actually meant to reveal. "It was very nice," he said, and they were not sure whether this was meant as wry understatement or a signal of indifference.

"The gowns must have been beautiful," said Minerva.

"They were," said Sundry, "and some of the people in them, too."

"Don't go pestering Mr. Moss about his night," said Mabel. She was frying up some eggs and sausage for Sundry.

Burne stared at his plate but didn't appear to see it. Thaddeus stood to one side of the table, and leaning against the baker's cabinet, he picked at the biscuit in his hand.

"That must have been some dance," said Melanie, who had heard Betty extolling the event (by way of her imagination and prematurely) the day before. Timothy made a face.

"I don't know that I was much use," said Sundry, who continued to represent himself as ill suited for a society ball. "But a waltz is a waltz, I guess, and I don't think I stepped on anyone's feet."

"It's a shame there isn't someone to go along and help Burne find his relatives," piped Thaddeus without preamble. He did not specifically regard Sundry when he said this, but Mabel otherwise gave the lie away by quickly turning her eyes from the young man.

Sundry did not appear resentful, though he may have sensed what was intended by this remark; he simply said, "Thank you," when Mabel laid his breakfast before him. Mabel felt shamed. He was a young man, after all, and not required to bear the burdens that others had taken to themselves. He had an air of competence about him, and they had come to respect the members of the Moosepath League, but it was not for the Sparks to weigh anyone else down with their concerns.

She would have sent Thaddeus with Burne and his daughter if they could have spared him from running the tavern. She had a raw feeling about Melanie going off with her father. Burne was not fit company, in her mind, and if she could have prevented him from taking his daughter with him, she would have. She and Thaddeus had tried to convince the man to wire the authorities nearest Brownville for information about his relatives or to go ahead himself and send for Melanie when he found them; but he would have none of it, and it was too far a leap of vision for them to consider telling him what he could or could not do with his own daughter.

Sundry Moss tended to breakfast with the concentration one exerts when one is trying not to concentrate on something. Mabel wished Thaddeus had not spoken, and Thaddeus himself perhaps wished the same, for he simply nodded at nothing when he had finished his biscuit, then returned to the tavern room. Melanie watched him leave, then regarded Mr. Moss as if something had been said and not answered, or as if something had been passed from one man to the other and she wondered what the second man would do with it.

Mabel was thinking, *Uncle Gillie has been putting the rum to him for twenty years or more, and here's Burne Ring but six years drunk and dying by feet rather than inches!* She was indignant with the man for not holding up better, though of course, when she thought about it, she remembered that Uncle Gillie was still in jail for almost flattening a police officer with a piano, so favorable comparisons against Burne's use to society were a little tenuous.

"My Uncle Elbridge went to Saco once," said Sundry without any discernible prompting. "He was looking for a man who owed him six dollars." No one said, "Oh?" or, "Do tell," but there was an atmosphere of inquiry in the kitchen. Even Burne frowned and turned to Sundry, but the young man went back to his breakfast.

Mabel smiled. The children looked more puzzled than ever.

Annabelle asked, "Did he find him?"

Sundry looked as if he had forgotten the topic of conversation. "Oh," he said. "No, he didn't. But he was down by one of the old tanneries and found a twenty-dollar gold piece in the street and came home."

Mabel liked the young man more for this bit of wise nonsense. Mr. Moss might have no intention of going with Burne and Melanie, but he would not hold it against the Sparks that they had almost asked him to. Mabel wished Thaddeus had stayed just a minute longer.

Burne was still watching Sundry with that puzzled frown.

"My uncle said he was ahead eleven dollars and thirty-five cents," Sundry informed them. "After he counted the train fare. He never did see the fellow again."

"Did he spend the money?" asked Burne, his voice shaking with weariness. They all were startled to see him come out of his lethargy.

"Well," drawled Sundry, "Uncle Elbridge was a saving sort of man, but I think he bought a hat for eighty cents."

This seemed to satisfy Burne, and he turned to his breakfast and nibbled on a bit of egg. The two younger children watched him eat, and Mabel tapped Tim on the back of the head to remind him of his manners.

"I think I'll be back tonight," said Sundry, which was as good as a promise. "I might go home to Edgecomb and visit my family tomorrow.

No, thank you," he said to the offer of more breakfast. At the door to the tavern room he stopped to consider Burne and the little girl, looking as if he might say something—perhaps good-bye or good luck. He nodded, raised a hand, and left. They could hear him speak to Thaddeus on the way out.

"I thought he might go with them," said Minerva in a low tone.

"Hush," said Mabel.

"Ten dollars and fifty-five cents and a new hat," said Annabelle. She was quick at figures and sometimes helped her parents with the ledgers. "Pretty good for a trip to Saco."

Thaddeus almost apologized to Mr. Moss as the young man came through the tavern room, but the young man was too brisk and the apology too uncertain. Sundry had his hat in his hand, and he waved it to Horace McQuinn and Maven Flyce, who looked as if they hadn't left the corner table since the night before. Thaddeus stood at the window and watched the young man go down the sidewalk.

"*He's* all business," said Horace.

Maven had a substantial portion of his breakfast in his mouth, and he ruminated largely as he stared about the room, his extraordinary cowlick like a signal flag of surprise above his wide-eyed expression.

"Something sweet in mind," agreed Thaddeus. "I had half hoped he might have the time to help Burne and his kid make it up to Brownville."

"They in need of escort, are they?" said Horace.

"I'm not sure about the little girl, but Burne is," said Thaddeus. "She might be better off going without him. Leastwise, people would know to look after her."

"Maven will take them," said Horace.

"What?" said Thaddeus.

Maven continued to chew and to look amazed.

"Oh, Maven's good at looking after things," said Horace, himself with wide eyes and a solemn nod. "Steady as an oak."

Thaddeus looked almost as puzzled as Maven. The cowlicked man's narrow form hardly conjured up such a vision, and he appeared, if anything, a little less steady while Horace volunteered his services. The astounded fellow gazed about the room as if he had missed something or as if there might be another Maven Flyce he hadn't heard about.

"Maven's helped me out many a time," said Horace proudly. Thaddeus guessed that Horace was referring to his occasional forays into the transportation of unauthorized spirits, and it did seem that if Maven Flyce could help to deliver a cartload of smuggled goods, he should be able to accompany a grown man and a little girl from one railway station to another. Looking at Maven Flyce, however, Thaddeus wasn't so sure.

Maven finally swallowed that substantial portion of breakfast, took a breath, and said, "I am so amazed!"

"Doesn't surprise me a bit, Maven," said Horace. He patted his companion's shoulder as if he were *that* honored to be his friend. "A regular member of the Moosepath League," pronounced Horace. "That's our Maven Flyce."

28. Sundry Puts in His Own Oar

No one back at the Faithful Mermaid could have guessed at the troublesome thoughts behind Sundry Moss's untroubled expression. Having gone to sleep the night before contemplating his mind's image of Miss Morningside, he had been wakened by a dream in which Burne Ring and his waiflike daughter had assayed leading roles. It seemed a little unfair, but on that day, almost a week ago, as he carried the stricken Mr. Ring from his filthy bed to the affable compass of the Faithful Mermaid, Sundry had been burdened by more than physical weight. The dark room and the man's dark-circled eyes and the innocent face of Melanie Ring hovered like insects at his shoulder, and he had been startled to find Burne sitting in the kitchen when he opened the door to the back stairs that morning.

Last night the Morrells' Annual Charitable Ball had seemed a world away from the earthy existence of the Faithful Mermaid; this morning the memory affected him as strange and off-putting and, as he sat across from the ill-starred remnants of the Ring family, almost beyond the range of suitable discussion. A practiced equanimity, rather than a real and present one, had seen him through his breakfast in the company of Melanie's wide eyes, but innocent as those eyes were of any conscious plea (and perhaps because they were so innocent), they followed him from the kitchen, through the tavern room, and out into the street. Only the perfection of the day could lift his spirits, and only his intended destination could distract him from that persistent sense of burden.

Sundry strode the sidewalk as if he were in a hurry, though the morning was much too young to be paying anyone a visit. He thought he might go down by the harbor and buy a sack of roasted peanuts from one of the vendors there, then find a lonely piling at one of the quieter wharves where he could lean and think. Brackett Street was dense with business—people walking and haggling at the corners and by the storefronts, and wagons and carriages trundling past. Peddlers and laborers rubbed shoulders with local shipping magnates and captains (and lesser officers) of industry and captains of ships and sailors. Toward Commercial Street and the water, gulls wheeled the sky and a steam whistle carried over the roofs between.

At the corner of York Street, Sundry spotted the business end of a large oar bobbing over the immediate throng and then intermittent glimpses of a blond head moving at a similar metronomic pace beneath this heroic implement. Sundry didn't imagine that the sailor would recognize him— there had been many people on the wharf the day of Mister and Mrs. Walton's departure, and the man in search of Fiddler's Green had spoken most specifically to Mr. Thump—but he searched the sailor's eye as the man came out of the crowd, and the two men paused on the sidewalk like acquaintances who chance to meet.

Sundry nodded, and the sailor nodded, too. "That shrunk some," said Sundry with little expression. Indeed, the great long sweep was not as long as when he last saw it and but a remnant of its former self.

"It broke," said the sailor.

Sundry considered the oar, which had been separated into two distinct, if not matching, pieces. The big fellow hefted them over his shoulder like a pair of rifles. "I hope no one's noggin counted for that," said Sundry.

The sailor shook his head. "I didn't ship oar before crossing the threshold."

Sundry nodded again, and the sailor nodded again, too.

"Do I know you?" asked the sailor.

"I saw you down at the wharf last Saturday."

The sailor nodded. "I need to get this put back together," he said.

"Do you?"

"I can't be looking for Fiddler's Green without it, and I don't mean to find Fiddler's Green in two pieces, so it must be put back together." The sailor raised his head and straightened his shoulders as if he were about to repeat his lecture concerning this paradise and how to find it. No one in the vicinity but Sundry was listening, however, and he only eyed a young woman who was walking by before he returned to the matter and the person at hand.

"You need a smithy," said Sundry.

"I need a smithy," said the sailor.

"I was about to say that," said Sundry.

The sailor blinked at him. He was wearing the canvas trousers, rough linen shirt, and dark pea-coat common to his kind. He had a knitted hat in a back pocket and a canvas bag on a stout rope. He was a powerful-looking fellow, and when he spoke, it was with an unexpected precision. When he didn't speak, he regarded the rest of the world as if he expected it to hold up its end of the conversation and was puzzled when it didn't.

As if on some secret signal, the two men ambled the sidewalk together, the sailor changing course without hesitation, craning his neck and gawking about as if he hadn't already seen the lower portion of Brackett Street moments before. Sundry knew of a blacksmith's down by the waterfront, and the sailor seemed to understand this, though no such words passed between them.

"Sundry Moss," said Sundry.

The sailor registered no surprise. "Robin Oig," he said.

When they reached Commercial Street, they paused for half a dozen wagons loaded with lumber that turned up the hill; then they crossed to the opposite corner and made their way past a gauntlet of street peddlers. When the noise of the horses and wagons had softened behind them, Sundry said, "You expect to find this place."

"What?" said Robin Oig. "Fiddler's Green? Why shouldn't I?"

"Exactly," said Sundry.

Several kids ganged by, skittering a leather ball before them and jostling their elders. Upon colliding with the sailor, one of these scamps looked up at the tall, bearded man and dodged off after his fellows, impishly unrepentant. A piebald dog came barking behind. Sundry pointed across the way at a low-roofed building in the shadow of the warehouses and shipping offices near Perley's Wharf. The ring of hammer and anvil chimed from the interior of the smithy, and diverse rough-looking fellows stood in the doorway, looking serious about watching someone else work.

Weaving through traffic, Sundry and Robin Oig found themselves at the blacksmith's door just as a short fellow with massive arms and permanently sooted cheeks came out of the comparative shadows. He had a pair of tongs in one hand and by these held up a smoking piece of iron that he plunged into the trough outside his door. There was a satisfying burble and hiss, and the smith pulled his work from the water for inspection.

"That's a piece of work you've got there," said the blacksmith without looking around. "What happened to it?"

"It broke," said Robin Oig when he realized he'd been spoken to.

The blacksmith looked up to consider the oar. The idlers who stood about formed a chorus behind him and also peered at the device.

"That's some oar," said one of them.

"Did you try to row the schooner all to yourself?" said another.

Robin Oig frowned at the man as if he had said something rude.

"He was cutting a wide path through a narrow door," said Sundry.

"I hope no one got in the way," said the first man.

"You're not the fellow the cops laid out?" said a third.

Sundry added his own inquiring look, but the sailor ignored the question. "What can you do?" he asked the blacksmith.

"I'll have to shorten it," said the man.

Robin Oig was sorry to hear this.

"What I *could* do," said the blacksmith, "is to mortise this one piece, tenon the other, then jacket and pin it all together."

"I need it put together," said the sailor by way of hiring the man.

The blacksmith nodded. He was interested in the job, and Robin Oig said to Sundry, under his breath, that this boded well for the efficacy of the oar in performing its duty. "I'd hate awfully for someone to work unwilling over it," he said. "I'd probably find Philadelphia as soon as Fiddler's Green."

"You can't be too careful," agreed Sundry.

Another whistle blew from the harbor, and there was talk about an English steamer expected in today. No one at the forge went to look, however, as everyone was concerned about Robin Oig and his oar. The sailor explained to the unwashed crowd how that oar was going to take him to Fiddler's Green, and no one appeared to doubt him, though whether these men simply thought him *touched* and in need of humoring or just too big to argue with, Sundry could only guess. The blacksmith seemed content to work.

Sundry himself was of farm stock and interested in the manufacture and repair of gear. The present company was not without its own rough charm, and he learned numerous things on topics the idlers clearly knew nothing about.

Robin Oig tugged at his beard, however, and looked as if he might try fishing for largemouth bass with a bare hook that had been kept in a drawer with an old shoe for three weeks or to avoid the deleterious effects of spirituous liquors by rubbing lard on the backs of his ears. One fellow, wise with pipe smoke, told of a friend who had heard of a farmer who'd taught a porcupine to sit up and beg and guard his house at night and shoot his quills with the skill of an archer at foxes and weasels that harassed his chickens (the farmer's chickens, specified the fellow, not the porcupine's).

Listening to this rare news, the sailor had the appearance of a man who wished he had pencil and paper to write down the regimen by which these wonders were obtained. Observing the idle fellows and gauging the level of sincerity in their discourse, Sundry began to doubt if *touched* or *too big* had ever entered their assessment of Robin Oig.

But Sundry's plan to visit the Underwoods' home wavered in his mind like a mote at the corner of his vision, and the wide and wondering eyes of Melanie Ring were not long in catching him up. He began to lose interest in Robin Oig and the oar and the group of idle men, and he wondered that they had held his attention at all. He stood back from the forge, considered the passing traffic—on foot and hoof and wheel—and then the sky and the gull-crowded roofs of the waterfront, and took a deep and uncharacteristic sigh.

"I think I'm off to other things," he said, perhaps addressing the group as a whole but catching the attention of Robin Oig.

"Where are you off to?" wondered the sailor.

"Before the day is out, I might be off to Edgecomb. Or maybe tomorrow."

"Edgecomb. Is that inland?"

"A little further than Portland."

"Oh."

"Good luck finding Fiddler's Green."

"Luck if I don't fall into a hole first, I guess," said Robin Oig. "I thought you might come with me."

Sundry almost laughed, but not unkindly. "I'm not fit for paradise yet," he said, and tipped his hat as he turned down the street without any clear notion of where he was going next. Somewhere a bell chimed the hour, and it was yet only eight o'clock. Sundry crossed the foot traffic between Perley's Wharf and Commercial Street and looked back only once. The sailor was craning his neck and standing on tiptoes to watch him disappear among the throngs.

29. Someone's Mr. Moss

"Here comes your Mr. Moss," said Dresden Scott. Cordelia Underwood's personal Maine Guide had been gazing out the parlor window as if hoping he might see more than a tree or two in one direction.

"Oh, dear!" said Cordelia. She leaped from the desk where she had been counting their answered invitations and went to her fiancé's side. "If only we could have delayed them awhile longer."

"I thought probably you had delayed them quite enough, letting the dog out the back door to chase after the neighbor's cat."

"Teacup needed exercise before a long trip."

"I thought Teacup was going to be eaten. It's a good thing the cat didn't turn around to see who was barking at her."

Cordelia hung on Dresden's arm with her cheek against his shoulder. "And he's not *my* Mr. Moss. He's Priscilla's."

"Is he?" Dresden looked both indulgent and wry. "Have you told Mr. Moss about these plans of yours?"

There came a rap at the front door. "I don't have to," she said, hurrying to the hall. "He has plans of his own, can't you see?"

Dresden followed her. "I thought I had plans once, too," he said without a change in expression, though he chuckled at her next sally.

Cordelia posed with her hand on the doorknob. "Before you met me? Nonsense. Mr. Moss!" she declared when she opened the door, looking delighted and surprised.

The young man stood at the top step with his hat in hand and looking spruce, though one collar of his jacket was turned up. He seemed to realize this deficiency at the last moment and laid the wayward corner down. "Miss Underwood," he said, "I beg your pardon for accepting your mother's invitation so soon, but I thought I would inquire after Mrs. Morningside this . . . morning."

It was a pretty piece of artifice, and Cordelia admired it. "Her headache was much better when she got up, thank you for asking. Come in, come in, please." She stepped aside and drew Mr. Moss into the front hall.

Cordelia's father was out on business, but her mother came down the stairs in a swish of skirts and petticoats. "How nice to see you so soon again, Mr. Moss," said Mercia, offering her hand.

Dresden, too, shook hands with the visitor, who looked grateful for the sight of another male creature.

Cordelia thought it best to get the bad news out as quickly as possible. "I'm afraid you won't be able to inquire of my Aunt Grace personally," she said. "Something unexpected came up, and they all had to take the train home to Ellsworth this morning." The fact that Mr. Moss was the *something unexpected* was left out of her statement, and she assured him, when he asked, that "It was nothing serious, really."

Mr. Moss considered one of the lower treads of the front hall stairs. Cordelia had been brokenhearted for Priscilla when her cousin left this morning, and now she felt more melancholy as this good man did his best to hide his disappointment. Would Priscilla be pleased to know that he had visited so soon or be doubly hurt to know that she had missed him? Cordelia almost reached out to grasp Mr. Moss's arm, she had such a rush of motherly affection for him.

He looked up, then, as if he had just now totaled a column of difficult figures. "I am sorry to miss them," he said, nodding again at some inner agreement. "Please forward my best wishes when you see or hear from them."

He was preparing to leave, which surprised Cordelia. Mercia was quicker to discern deeper motives in the young man's decision to withdraw, even if she had no specific knowledge but only a well-developed intuition. "Won't you come in and stay awhile, Mr. Moss?" she said with the sort of amiable manner that would not make him feel uncomfortable should he accept or decline. "It won't be long till lunch, and I am sure that Dresden craves talk of something besides wedding gowns and guest lists."

"Thank you, Mrs. Underwood," said Mr. Moss with evident regard. "But really, I should be going."

"Then you must come for lunch another time," she insisted.

"I would enjoy that very much." The young man shook hands with Dresden again and nodded to the ladies, raised his hat in salute, and went out.

Cordelia could not keep herself from following him onto the stoop. "We trust we'll see you at the wedding, if not before," she called after him.

"I hope so," he replied over his shoulder, but when he was at the bottom of the steps, he turned back and said, "Please tell your cousin that she was the most pleasant part of my evening last night."

"I will," said Cordelia. She was a little misty-eyed, remembering her own emotions when she had first been parted from Mr. Scott before she had the opportunity to speak or hear words of attachment. "I will certainly tell her you said so." She was about to say that Priscilla felt the same about him, but Dresden loomed beside her as tacit warning not to meddle. Good-byes were traded once again, and Dresden was escorting his bride-to-be back inside and Mr. Moss was traversing the front walk when Cordelia called out, "My parents thought you made quite a lovely couple!"

Now Mr. Moss turned again, looking vaguely surprised, and this time he bowed his head in a very Moosepathian fashion before finally taking his leave.

"Did we?" said Mercia when Cordelia came back inside. Dresden went into the parlor, apparently in search of something.

"Didn't you?" said Cordelia, undaunted.

"I like him very much," said her mother with careful diction. "But—" The word hung in the air.

"You think him a servant, crashing the royal door."

"I certainly do not, but the fact that your Aunt Grace *does* must count for something."

"An obstacle to leap over," said Cordelia.

"Then it is for Priscilla to leap," said Mercia. "A person needs to leap but once, God willing, and *you* have used your quota for the time being."

After a moment Cordelia said, "I hate to see anyone sad."

"I know it only too well," said Mercia.

Mercia was off to the kitchen to ask Mrs. Lerber to start lunch when Cordelia cleared her throat and said, loud enough to be heard in the parlor, "And just think how happy Mr. Scott would have been, back in Millinocket, if he had known my parents approved of him!"

Her mother did not stop, but she may have laughed.

Cordelia stepped back into the parlor, but secretively—peering round the jamb to locate her fiancé. *Mr. Scott* (as she liked to call him when she was feeling the most affectionate) was reclining in her father's favorite chair, his weight more or less on his collarbone, his feet on a hassock, and his neatly trimmed beard resting on his chest. He was tall and powerful-looking, even stretched out like a big cat, and his clear blue eyes did nothing to contradict her last statement as he assessed her standing in the doorway.

Cordelia took a long breath and said for his ears only, "And think how happy I would have been if I had known that Mr. Scott approved of me."

30. Sadness and Possibility

"They left ten minutes ago," said Mabel Spark when Sundry stepped into the kitchen of the Faithful Mermaid and inquired after the Rings. "Thaddeus tried to talk him out of it, but Mr. Flyce went with them."

"Mr. *who?*" said Sundry.

"Maven Flyce," said the woman, shaking her head as if she couldn't believe it herself. "Horace got him up to it, and I guess Thaddeus is right: Half a head is better than none at all." She thought about this for a moment, then added, "Or maybe it isn't."

"He can't have spent all that time in the company of Horace McQuinn without picking up a trick or two," said Sundry. "It's pretty light duty, after all." There was a moment when he felt the burden almost slip from his shoulders, but it wouldn't quite dislodge. He was recalling Maven's endearing slack-jawed expression and the cowlick crowning the man's perpetually astounded head. "I'll get my things," said Sundry, and he hurried upstairs.

"God bless you," Mabel called after him.

Timothy, who had been much shaken by Melanie's departure and who was being fed biscuits and jam for his sadness, asked if he could go, and his mother shushed him. When Sundry came back down, Mabel handed him a box packed with several sandwiches and told him that Thaddeus had hailed and paid for a cab. Timothy ran out after Mr. Moss and was snagged by his father before he could hop a ride on the back of the carriage.

Sundry felt partially absolved when he reached the station on time. He wished he hadn't had to leave the Underwoods in such a hurry, but upon hearing the news of the Morningsides' departure, he thought it no more than he deserved and only wanted to catch Burne and Melanie Ring.

For all his youth, Sundry knew that there are some burdens less heavy when they are borne than when they are left behind. He had never heard the word *karma* (though it had entered the language seventy years before), but he might have understood the philosophy. The Puritan concept of *retribution* may in theory have amounted to something like it, but in practice (or sermon) it weighed too heavily on stern punishment for Sundry's view of God and Grace, and so a certain faith was both answered and increased when he found that he had not missed the train and that he was partially absolved for having previously denied the innocent and unpleading eyes of Melanie Ring.

Sundry found the father and daughter and Maven Flyce's cowlick in the second passenger car and was struck by how small they looked at the other end of the aisle: the waif in Tim's old shirt and jacket, knickers, knee socks, and brogues, the father in whatever else the Sparks had been able to cobble together from their collective wardrobes, and Maven sitting with his back to Sundry but communicating a complete and continual wonder at his surroundings.

Sundry caught Burne Ring's eye as he approached them, and when he registered that man's vacant frown, he said, "I thought you might like some company." Maven stared, openmouthed, and Melanie only a little less so while Sundry arranged his clutch beneath his seat and leaned back, as if prepared for a restful journey.

"Good heavens, Mr. Moss," said Maven. "Where are you going?"

"Brownville, I guess," said Sundry, not understanding the depth of Maven's inquiry.

"Good heavens!" said Maven again. "That's where we're going!"

Sundry almost started to explain his presence to Maven but decided simply to nod and say, "That's what I understand." It occurred to him that he might send Maven home, but he could not, on short notice, think of a graceful way of doing so. Sundry could not think how to tell the man that his services were no longer needed without the risk of sounding (at least to his own ears) arrogant and pompous. Maven would probably have been amazed but unoffended.

There was a moment in which Maven's astonished look was the loudest expression among them. Then Burne said in a hoarse growl, "The Sparks sent you," his face more rueful than angry, and after he spoke, he let out two or three low grunts.

"They told me what train you were boarding," said Sundry.

Another grunt or two rose from the sick-looking man, and he said a little more fractiously, "I can't pay your fare."

"I've already bought it," said Sundry.

Burne Ring let out more of those short, low grunts, like some haggard animal that had been moving too fast. Melanie was looking from her father to Sundry. Maven gaped out the window. Sundry turned his attention to the passengers around them, hoping thereby to relieve the ailing man of the burden of conversation, but then Burne said, "Mailon—" and stopped himself. "Melanie says you were with Mr. Spark when he came and got me."

"Yes," said Sundry, "I was there," but in a voice he might have used if he had admitted to having been at the park.

Burne laid his head against the window glass. He said, "The Sparks are good people, I suppose," but with so little conviction that Sundry wondered if he could care about this man very much. "I've been ill," said Burne between more of those low sounds. "It'd be best if someone's around for the girl were I to take a spell. Pay me no mind if I speak strangely," he instructed Sundry. "Sometimes I see things other people don't," he added, as if this were a consequence not of drink but of perception.

Maven stared at Burne, then looked around for some of these visions, and Sundry was reminded of the previous fall when Horace McQuinn had conveyed similar watchful duties to Messrs. Ephram, Eagleton, and Thump.

The call to board the train was given from the platform; Sundry could almost feel the engine ahead of them straining, and just as a billow of steam rolled past the windows, he thought he caught a glimpse of a large, blond-bearded man standing on the platform with a great long oar over his shoulder.

Sundry leaned closer to the window, and when the steam no longer obscured his view, he could see that there was indeed a large, blond-bearded man standing on the platform with a great long oar over his shoulder, but also the conductor and another man in railroad livery talking with apparent heat on either side of the sailor. Robin Oig only frowned at one and then the other, and finally the conductor said something sharp to the other railroad man and then something to the man with the oar and jabbed the air with his forefinger in a direction, Sundry guessed, meant to indicate the figurative door. The conductor wandered off and shouted the final all aboard.

Clearly Robin Oig had wanted to board the passenger car with his oar and had been refused. The sailor only shrugged, nodded his head, and walked off in the direction pointed out to him.

Sundry sat back and considered little Melanie Ring, who, along with Maven Flyce, had viewed the scene on the platform. Any other day, or any other moment, Sundry might have gone out and seen what he could do to help the peculiar Robin Oig, but he was sure he had quite enough on his hands already.

"That was some oar!" said the little girl.

"I was so amazed," said Maven.

"He's off to Fiddler's Green," said Sundry without irony.

Maven and the child stared out the window, but the sailor was gone. The conductor had returned to his train, and the railroad man left standing there looked as if he smelled something unpleasant. Sundry was about to explain to them about Fiddler's Green but the car lurched forward, and the little girl, who had never been on a train before, seemed to have enough to interest her. Certainly Maven did. The sounds of the great engine ahead of them were dulled through the distance and body of a car and a half, but the strain and pressure of its work could be felt, thrumming the length of the creature to life.

Sundry himself had seldom traveled by locomotive before he met Mister Walton, but he had regard for the experience. It was true, there was nothing like having the flesh and sinew of a living creature beneath you or pulling the traces before, but he understood why the steam engine was once known as the iron horse and why railroad men loved a particular specimen like a pet.

The ever-shifting nature of a person's fellow travelers was of great interest: drummers and businessmen, visiting relatives and hopeful suitors, families moving out to the summer cottages and laboring people seeking employment in new surroundings. People getting off at the next stop were brisk and tentative; long-haul travelers indulged in whatever comforts they brought along, reading newspapers or fanning lunch out from a picnic hamper. Up the aisle, two children were asking their mother when they would "get there," and a young woman, who may have thought that Sundry was watching her, touched her "best hat" to be sure that it was becomingly tilted. The essence of a cigar rose from some seats beyond, where a man was slouched and presumably attempting to smoke himself to sleep. (He would, and a neighbor would rouse him to give warning of a smoldering vest front.)

The train passed below Portland's beloved observatory and the bowling lanes, and the engine whistle shrieked as it neared a bend in the tracks at the corner of the Eastern Promenade; a cow had gotten loose down on the tracks the other day, and presumably the engineer was leaning from his window and peering ahead for any sign of further bovine encroachment. They picked up speed when all was deemed clear, and the old almshouse whisked past them on the right. Then they were crossing the eastbound trestle that divided Casco Bay from Back Cove, bound for the first stop in Falmouth Foreside. Maven Flyce's nose hardly left the window.

Everyone seemed animated with the motion of the train and Sundry watched Burne Ring for some moments before he realized that the man was actually shaking, independent of the general tremor beneath them. The air was noisier, too, as they accelerated down the tracks, and it was difficult to hear those small grunting sounds that rose from deep in the stricken man's throat.

Melanie's mind was on several things, it seemed, for she looked at Sundry and said, "You're in the Moosepath League?"

Sundry Moss had never thought of himself as an actual member of the Grand Society, though the charter members always spoke of *six* Moosepathians in those days. Perhaps he did not trust that he loved good deeds more than adventure, or perhaps it was his unusual relationship with Mister Walton—part employee and all friend—but in his mind he had always kept himself a little aside from the rest of the club. For the purposes of the little girl before him, however, it seemed meet to avoid splitting hairs. He nodded and said, "Yes, I am a member."

"Oh, my," said Maven.

The little girl seemed satisfied, and she even smiled softly. She and Timothy equated the Moosepath League with adventure and grand exploit, and having one of their number with her and her father on this journey lifted it above sad farewell and propelled it into the realm of dangerous and desirable possibility. She could look ahead instead of back, though she did turn in her seat to peer past her father to see the only place she had ever known as it disappeared beyond the groves of the old Mariners' Hospital. Watching her, Sundry realized that she had a cap in her lap and that she had taken it off, like a polite young boy, when she came into the car.

31. Setting Course

Robin Oig stood outside the smithy and looked east, the direction in which Mr. Moss had disappeared. There had been something capable and right about that young man (Robin himself was bearing down on thirty and perhaps had weathered to the appearance of something a little further), and meeting Mr. Moss on the busy sidewalk was the sort of seemingly chance business to which the sailor believed a body should pay sharp attention.

One of the idlers outside the forge watched Robin gaze down the length of the wharf district and said, "I suppose you'll miss the salt air."

"Not a bit of it," said Robin.

"The feel of the deck rolling beneath you," chanted the idler as if he were reading a poem from a column of newspaper. (In those days there wasn't a journal that went to press without at least one stab at verse.)

"It doesn't make me sick, but it doesn't make me hanker for more."

"You don't say," said the idler, visibly disappointed of his romantic woolgathering. Two of his fellows came out of the smithy to consider the waterfront as if they had not seen it before.

"Where's Edgecomb?" asked Robin.

"That's near Portsmouth," said one fellow.

"Is it?" said another.

"New Hampshire or England?" said still another.

"I don't know which," said the informant. "Maybe both."

Another fellow joined them, and they looked around, shuffling their feet and craning their necks; it seemed that Edgecomb might be in sight if they looked hard enough. Robin saw that there wasn't a page of geography among them. "It can't be near New Hampshire," he said. "It's east of here."

"I guess I knew that," said one of the idlers, and his fellows watched him for further intelligence.

"It's across the river from Wiscasset," said the blacksmith.

"I know Wiscasset," said Robin.

"Why didn't you say so?" said one of the idlers, though it wasn't clear to whom he was speaking.

When the blacksmith had the oar restored, more or less, to its former glory, the sailor and the hangers-on stood around and appraised the art that had gone into mending it. There was a mortise and tenon a carpenter would have admired, and an iron sleeve with two pins.

The sailor tipped his beard back and looked over the work. He turned the device in his hands, nodding his approval. "That'll answer," he said, which was all the blacksmith wanted to hear. They settled up over money, and the sailor said, "Across from Wiscasset."

"There's a bridge, I think," said the blacksmith.

"Yes, I've seen it," said Robin, and without much more than a backward wave he shipped the oar over his shoulder and proceeded to march east.

It was pretty fine along the water and about all that June can offer. Gulls banked in an almost cloudless sky, and there was enough of a sea breeze to temper the heat of the sun. The wharves were crowded with business, and everything known to man seemed to exchange hands from ship to shore and back again, carted in wagons and drays up the cobble-stone avenue. Peddlers and vendors lined the street, and ladies in bright dresses and elaborate headgear strolled the sidewalk with men of important appearance and shadowed the sidewalks with their frilly parasols.

Robin counted a dozen dogs, eight parrots, and a monkey, and he stopped to look over a monstrous lobster occupying a tub before the fish market by Union Wharf. Slowly he read the sign above: 1 FOOT, 9 AND ONE QUATR. INCHES, AND A SMIDGEN. 31 POUNDS, 4 OUNCES. NAMED McKINLEY AFTER THE BIG MAN IN WASHINGTON. DON'T TOUCH. McKINLEY IS NOT PEGGED. WATER NOT FOR HORSES. Robin thought the lobster looked like a great peevish insect. He had eaten lobsters when he was young as they were considered poor man's food (and, before that, good for little more than fertilizing the fields), but he was more fond of a good chunk of salt pork or fried beefsteak.

With his oar shouldered like a battle standard, Robin garnered his own share of interested stares, and people only looked more inquisitive as he neared the Grand Trunk Railway Station. Mr. Moss had said that he was heading for Edgecomb, and the blacksmith had said that Edgecomb was due east, so Robin thought he might find Mr. Moss on an eastbound train. He was hardly surprised when, with a sailor's sharp sight for the proper landmark, he distinguished the very man stepping from a cab before the station fifty yards away. Robin didn't even shout but only followed Mr. Moss, he was that confident of affairs as they were playing out.

"I want a ticket for that train," said Robin to the ticket man inside the Grand Trunk Station.

"That's all well and good," said the fellow, "but where are you going?"

"Where does the train go?" asked Robin.

The ticket man considered the great long oar on the sailor's shoulder, then the large, blond-bearded face. He looked round to his schedules and said, after a moment, "It switches engines in Brunswick, then by way of the Springfield Terminal heads for Bangor and Mattawamkeag. You'll have to board the Eastern Maine if you want to go any further from there."

"I'll take it," said Robin.

The ticket man only shook his head. "You could have left *that* outside," he said, frowning at the enormous sweep.

"I wouldn't leave it outside," he said. "I just got it mended, and who's to say I won't cross paths with the person I'm looking for if I let it out of my hands for a minute?"

The ticket man didn't know what Robin was talking about and didn't ask. He had seen people attempt to board trains with all manner of objects; there had been the drummer with several boxes of rum bottled and disguised as *Auntie Tisrod's Dauntless Nerve Tonic* and a fellow from Prospect Harbor who had bought his ticket with his coat pockets fidgeting with a dozen high-strung rabbits. "You'll want a receipt," said the ticket seller as he prepared a baggage claim tag with a length of string.

Robin watched the man without any signal of understanding. Soon the sailor was sizing up the entrance to the first passenger car and holding the blade of the oar in front of him like the barrel of a rifle when a platform worker in railroad livery came up and asked him what he thought he was doing.

"I'm trying to see how to get this inside without clunking someone on the head," said Robin thoughtfully. He had backed away from the steps of the car several times to let others pass, and now he set the grip of the oar on the platform and held it like a flagpole. "Take one end of it, would you, and help me guide it in."

"I'll do nothing of the sort," said the platform man. "What made you think you could take that thing aboard?"

"What's this, Mr. Heath?" said the approaching conductor.

"He's trying to get aboard with this mile of lumber," came the reply.

"I don't know if the car is long enough," said the conductor with more humor than Mr. Heath had thus far displayed.

Robin looked more puzzled than daunted. "Where can I ride then?" he asked.

"You can ride where you want," said Mr. Heath, "but the oar goes in with the baggage."

"No, it doesn't," said the sailor. "I told the fellow inside I wouldn't part with it," and he proceeded to explain why.

The engine let out a gust of steam, and so did Mr. Heath; but the conductor liked the whole business. "I suppose you could dangle your legs off the back porch," he said offhandedly, meaning the landing at the end of the caboose. "Set that boom over your knee and snag the mail when we go by."

Mr. Heath was one of those people who often recognize dry wit half a beat after they have reacted to it. He had already snapped, "He can't ride there!" before wondering if the conductor had been serious when he offered the "back porch" to the sailor. Befuddled, he added, "It's not regulation."

"It's not your train," said the conductor mildly.

"It doesn't matter a lick," said Mr. Heath.

"I think it probably does," drawled the conductor.

"You're not letting him ride that back porch," said Mr. Heath, who was not above telling the conductor his business.

"Who's captain here?" said the conductor. Indeed, men of his profession were often called captains and enjoyed a similar omnipotence upon their craft. He was, aside from his present pique, a pleasant enough appearing fellow—short and gray-haired with thick muttonchops. This colloquium did much to attract the attention of boarding passengers and people who otherwise had business on the platform, but Robin paid little heed.

"You head right back to the end of the train if you want to carry that oar of yours," the conductor told the sailor with a defiant jab of a forefinger past Mr. Heath's nose.

"What?" said Mr. Heath. "It's not regulation!"

"Go frighten someone else," said the conductor.

Robin shrugged and nodded and walked off in the direction indicated.

It was a moment before the platform man understood that the conductor had exercised his dry wit once again, and then it was too late to respond. The captain called the all aboard as he walked the length of the train, his watch in hand. Mr. Heath did wish people would smile when they were joking. "Frighten someone!" he growled. A little boy was walking by, and Mr. Heath gave the kid a stare. The little boy was undaunted, however, hanging close to his mother's skirts, and he turned back to Mr. Heath as they walked to the nearest car and stuck his tongue out at the platform man.

32. Mr. Normell

It was at Brunswick, where the train changed engines before heading north, that the portly, bespectacled man with an amiable smile and thinning hair came aboard, catching Sundry's attention immediately. Having excused himself to each passenger as he went, the newcomer meekly inquired if the seat across the aisle was taken; then, with a nod, hat in hand, and a bow, he settled himself with a small sigh.

The conductor walked past Sundry's window, calling the all aboard. Several track switches, up ahead, would alter the train's course from its eastward bent and send them north through towns that Sundry had recently visited and past people whose tales he had briefly observed.

Sundry had been telling Melanie and Maven about some of these, specifically about Hercules, the heroic pig that lived at Fern Farm and had recently suffered a mysterious bout of melancholy. Mr. Ring said nothing during the story. His head lay against the window; his eyes were sometimes closed. Often he seemed to be shivering. Otherwise, Sundry's audience was quite taken with his portrait of the porcine Hercules, the pig's strange ailment affecting the little girl and the openmouthed Maven Flyce with all the potency and sentiment of a Greek tragedy.

Sundry's description of the eccentric farm and its denizens, once the shadow of trouble had been driven off, sounded to the little girl like paradise. "Is he still there?" she asked.

"Hercules?" said Sundry. "He was a week or so ago."

"My word!" said Maven. Melanie looked startled. The tale had contained all the elements of an historic event and Sundry had made no mention of himself, so that the little girl could be forgiven for imagining that it had taken place during some epic period and that George Washington or Daniel Boone might have ridden through at any moment.

"That was some business!" said the little girl. "I'd like to see that pig."

"You'd grow fond of him," promised Sundry. Melanie watched him watching her father. Burne let out a series of low grunts, and Sundry was put in mind of a dog chasing rabbits in its sleep. "You could climb his back and ride him like a horse," said Sundry.

"I'd like to see him. That must be some farm."

"It is. I grew up on a farm, so I can be trusted, I guess."

"Did you? Did you have pigs?"

Sundry nodded.

Maven shook his head in amazement.

Melanie seemed taken with the whole idea of a farm. "Did you have cows? Did you milk the cows?" she asked, so Sundry described Moss Farm in Edgecomb, and he perhaps did not spare any gold leaf on the oaks or sapphire in the brook that ran past the house. It all sparkled like a dream, and he talked about his mother's apple pie and his father's funny way of stating the obvious and his brothers and sisters (and his twin brother, Varius) and the dogs that slept in the barn.

It was in the midst of this description that the portly, bespectacled gentleman arrived, and when Sundry was finished with his encomium of home, the newcomer beamed with great happiness; he might have been sitting by old Crispin Moss's stone wall with his feet in the brook or on the rock ledge below the present Mr. Moss's woodlot, basking in the summer sun.

"It is an idyll, no doubt," said the newcomer, still smiling.

The young man felt awkward, now that he had gone on at such length and with such apparent feeling. "Home, you know," he said. "I suppose everyone thinks he comes from some wonderful place."

"On the contrary," said the man. "I have known those who are sure they have not. It is what drives so many beyond the horizon and across seas and over mountains. Forgive me, please, for eavesdropping."

"Not at all. That's not eavesdropping."

"You're very kind," said the man with frank admission, "but I was listening with complete intent and enjoying myself, too."

"You're right, though," said Sundry, turning the conversation away from the man's apology. "About what drives people to new places, I mean. I met a sailor the other day—and met him again this morning—who was quite seriously in search of Fiddler's Green."

"Ah!" said the portly man. "The sailor's bliss." Then he sang in a respectable baritone.

> *Where the weather is fair and there's never a gale,*
> *Where the fish jump on board with a swish of a tail.*
> *You lie at your leisure, there's no work to do,*
> *And the skipper's below making tea for the crew.*

"I think that is it exactly," said Sundry. Melanie was looking from one to the other of them with those wide eyes, and Sundry said to her, "You saw the fellow carrying a great long oar on his shoulder before we left Portland," and he explained to her about Robin Oig and how the man only needed to find someone who didn't know what the oar was and he would follow that person till they came to the sailors' paradise known as Fiddler's Green.

"Won't everyone know what an oar is?" she asked innocently.

"I do believe, my lad, that is why the task evades most applicants," said the stranger across the aisle.

"Oh," said Melanie, with almost as much understanding as syllables. The gentleman addressing her as "my lad" hardly seemed to register.

"I expect," said the portly fellow with a broad smile, "that he is wanting some young elf-child to come out of the woods and take his hand. I do beg your pardon again," he said suddenly. "I am Jeffrey Normell."

"Mr. Normell," said Sundry, trying the name out. "Sundry Moss."

"Really?" said the fellow as they shook hands. "That's quite likable."

"It's gotten me this far," said Sundry with a smile.

"*Normell* itself is something one must work to live up to."

"This is—" Sundry did not like speaking an untruth to a complete stranger, particularly to one who seemed so amiable and so very reminiscent of a good friend, but neither did he relish the thought of having to explain Melanie's situation in front of her, as if she were the attraction at a sideshow. All this was weighed in an instant, and he said, "Mailon Ring."

"Mailon," said Mr. Normell.

The little girl did not flinch, and she said, "Good morning."

Mr. Normell's smile broadened further.

"And Mailon's father," said Sundry, "Burne Ring, who has not been well."

"I am sorry."

Beneath the ailing man's pale lids there was an almost baleful glimmer reflecting the light from Mr. Normell's window. Sundry wondered if the man was awake or just dreaming with his eyes partly open and, if he was awake, whether there was any real emotion in that stare or the brilliance of day simply caught his dissipated features in a harsh and hateful light. It was a pity to dislike someone so ill. Sundry felt guilty for it. He turned back to Mr. Normell and was comforted to see a look of pity and understanding on the pleasant face. Mr. Normell met Sundry's eyes and nodded solemnly.

"And Maven Flyce," finished Sundry, who suddenly realized that he had not heard any astounded outbursts for the last few minutes.

Mr. Normell looked amused. Maven Flyce's superior cowlick was horizontal, his nose raised to the ceiling, and his mouth gaping open. Even as Sundry turned his attention to the man beside him, a *Herculean* sound rose from Maven's throat.

Sometimes astonishment simply wears a body out.

Sundry wished he could have gotten off at Bowdoinham Station just to stretch his legs and stop in at Jonas Fink's General Store and Post Office and discover how Hercules was doing or to look in at Johnny Poulter's smithy and hear how the young blacksmith fared in his wooing of the lovely Madeline Fern. These were tales he had brushed shoulders with a week or so ago, and he took in what he could from his window, only recognizing one of the loafers who held up a porch post at the corner of the store. Sundry was not one to leave a post himself, and he sat back and waited out the short stop without revealing his curiosity or impatience.

His curiosity was more easily satisfied from the train window when they came to Iceboro. With help from the surrounding towns, the community had done an extraordinary job of cleaning up after fire had destroyed one of the icehouses there; still, there was the great hole left in the midst of the houses and storefronts and churches. There was much talk about the fire on the train, and someone a few seats back seemed to have heard or read a good deal about it, and pretty accurately. Sundry said nothing about his involvement on that awful night, but he did have a piercing memory of Mister Walton's collapse on the street in the midst of the firefighting and was glad enough to quit this station and move on.

Maven slept, and Burne Ring lay with his head against the glass, the countryside and towns speeding by without his notice. As they approached Gardiner, Sundry could no longer see the man's eyes, peering from beneath heavy lids, and he began to have small hope that the man was actually on the mend; sleep seemed such a healthy thing for someone so sick and weary.

"I have been looking for a dowser," said Mr. Normell without preamble.

"Have you?" said Sundry. It might have been the most common sort of statement for the complete lack of wonder in his voice.

"I have," said the man. "Without success."

"I've dowsed before," said Sundry.

It was Mr. Normell's turn to conceal any apparent surprise. "Have you?"

"About that much," said Sundry, holding a thumb and forefinger an inch apart. Melanie was looking at him with the curiosity and wonder that he and Mr. Normell had not betrayed. "Dowsing is a way of finding water under the ground," Sundry told her.

"Do you dig?" she asked, which was a sensible question.

"You use the stick from an apple tree or a crab tree stick," he replied, which didn't sound sensible at all. "The stick has a fork in it, and you hold

it out, like this." He positioned his hands so that he looked like an awkwardly rendered cowboy in a dime novel, invisible six-guns drawn and
ready to fire. "Then you walk around till you feel a tug at the end of the
stick, and that, presumably, is where you'll find water."

"How does it happen?" asked the little girl. "What tugs on the stick?"

"I'm not sure anything does," said Sundry. Like many a veteran
dowser, which he certainly wasn't, he didn't know if he really believed in it
or not.

"Oh, *some*thing tugs!" said Mr. Normell with more excitement than he
had previously revealed. "Certainly, it does."

"To be honest," admitted Sundry, "I don't know very much about it."

"Oh, *some*thing tugs," said Mr. Normell again.

"I've tried it only a time or two."

"If you have the gift, that's all you need."

"My mother's Uncle Cedric has the gift, I guess," said Sundry.

"Oh? Where is he?"

"Norridgewock."

Mr. Normell turned his head forward and nodded slowly. "The gift
does seem to run in families."

"I learned it from Uncle Cedric years ago, when I spent summers up at
his farm. Two or three times when I was there he was asked to find water
for someone. He'd let me walk around with the crab tree stick after he had
already found something to see if I could feel the pull. Then, the last time,
I think, he let me go first."

"Did you find anything?"

"I did," said Sundry in a matter-of-fact way. "I think."

Mr. Normell took on an entirely separate appearance from his former
cheer and looked as serious as Sundry could have imagined him. "Would
you allow me to hire you?" he asked.

"To dowse?" Sundry laughed softly. "I don't think you'd get your
money's worth."

"I am quite sure that I would," said the portly fellow. "I am struck by
a sense of"—Mr. Normell searched for the words—"your abilities," he
finished.

"I'd be glad to take a stab at it, but unless you're going to Brownville,
I'm afraid it will have to wait."

"Brownville," said Mr. Normell. "No, no. Not Brownville."

"I'm sorry I can't help you," said Sundry. "I'm going to travel with

Mel—" Here he struck the first snag of his previous untruth. "Mailon and his father," he amended, "and help them find their relatives in Brownville."

"Not Brownville," said Mr. Normell again, and regretfully. "I'm going to China."

"Don't you need a ship for that?" asked Melanie.

"No, no, my dear boy." The man chuckled amiably and took off his spectacles to wipe them with his handkerchief. "I am going to China, *Maine*. It's a town, northeast of us at the present moment."

"Oh," said Melanie.

"China," said the man again. He replaced his spectacles on his nose, then nodded to Sundry and repeated, "I'm going to China," as if the young man might not have heard him.

"I see," said Sundry.

"Very near the border of Albion," said Mr. Normell.

"They are near one another?" said Sundry.

"Oh, yes," said the man. He held his hands together, as if in prayer. "Very near. Dutten Pond," he added. "China and Albion, right through the middle." He held his hands together again, then shot one hand through the imaginary border he had created.

"I'm surprised you couldn't find a dowser," said Sundry. "I thought every town had one or two."

Mr. Normell pursed his lips and nodded once again.

"Next stop, Farmingdale!" called the conductor as he came into the car and walked past them.

"China," said Mr. Normell again.

33. A Bad Juncture Between Stops

The car took on more passengers than it lost as they neared the capital. In Farmingdale, two women came down the aisle looking for a place to sit, and Mr. Normell, who had occupied a brace of seats by himself for some miles, quickly rose and offered the ladies the bench facing him. The portly man smiled and attempted to engage the women in conversation, but they proved reserved, or perhaps they were unhappy to find themselves across the aisle from someone as obviously ill as Burne Ring. Maven's snoring, too, sometimes rattled the window next to him.

At Augusta's South Station, west of the Kennebec, the car thinned out, and when they came to the second station across the river, it thinned out some more. Here the train took on water and coal, lingering longer than at some stops. The women across the aisle rose from their seats, chatting between themselves, though loud enough for their neighbors to hear that they were stepping out for some air. They did not come back, and Sundry suspected that they had changed cars.

He hardly blamed them. Burne Ring shivered in his sleep, and Mr. Normell asked an attendant to find a blanket for the man. While they waited, talk ran along several cheerful subjects, and Sundry thought the portly fellow did his best to engage the child, asking *him* what *he* thought of Portland's ball team and had *he* ever ridden a bicycle. Mr. Normell had attempted driving one some years back and had a story about the adventure that made Melanie smile.

"That must have been some mule," she said.

"His hind quarters were *some* powerful," said Mr. Normell with a hearty chuckle. "And I believe those were the very words of his owner."

"Were you hurt?" asked the little girl.

"Mostly my pride," admitted the man. "The bike was not to be recovered, however, and went back to the shop to provide some small parts for future generations of wheeled vehicles and more astute riders than myself." He grew quiet of a sudden, and a serious expression overtook him. The attendant returned, and Sundry leaned from his seat to tuck the blanket about Burne, but the man continued to shiver violently.

"I need something," said Burne.

Sundry was startled by the voice, which was shuddery and overloud. He knew the sort of *something* Burne needed—or wanted. The Sparks had been giving him small beer in small drafts—sips, really—by recommendation of a long-retired doctor who resided down the street from the tavern, but Sundry had no idea where to get the man a drink.

"I need some medicine," said Burne again.

"Does he have medicine?" asked Mr. Normell, then said, "Ah, yes," when Sundry gave him a significant glance. "I did wonder."

"There must be someone at the next stop," Burne hissed. "There'll be a tavern or someplace can help me. Just small beer or a drop of rum."

Sundry felt out of his depth. It seemed only merciful to find something that would chase away the man's demons. "I hate to drag him off the train," said Sundry, "and beat about some small town, looking for someone or someplace to serve him a drink." He spoke quietly, though he knew Melanie could hear him; he was thinking of her and how unseemly it would be to haul a six-year-old girl to an illegal saloon or a rumrunner's still.

"If I may venture a thought," said Mr. Normell. "It may be that a small supply of *medicine* is kept at hand by the conductor for the sake of emergency and that if our conductor understood that you are trying to deliver this man and his son to the bosom of his family, he might consider Mr. Ring's condition emergency enough."

Sundry was skeptical but decided he would attempt it. Standing, he swayed as the train negotiated a corner. Uncertainty touched his face as he realized that he was abandoning his post. He shook Maven's shoulder once, but Mr. Normell touched Sundry's shoulder and said, "I'll be here. Let him sleep." Sundry thanked the man and hurried down the aisle in the direction of the caboose, envying everyone else who seemed only to be traveling between two points and not in the act of delivering a drunkard and his daughter to a set of unknown relations. He realized, too, that he was hungry.

Sundry found the conductor in the last passenger car, talking with three men who were togged out in wilderness gear and obviously heading north for some hunting and fishing. Sundry stood by, choosing his words before he had to say them. The conductor took his time getting to him, though he caught sight of Sundry almost as soon as the young man pulled up an arm's length away. Sundry was the smallest bit annoyed by the time the man straightened his posture, gave him a one-eyed peer, and said, "Yes, young man?"

"I have a sick man on board," said Sundry, attempting a demeanor that would suggest a need for guarded conversation.

"Oh? Why didn't you say so? What's the matter?"

Sundry turned his shoulder to the three sportsmen. "Friends, down in Portland, have been drying him out—"

"I have the authority to toss drunks from the train—"

"He's not drunk, he's drying out—"

"He's having the rum horrors, is my guess, and you're looking for a place to wet him down."

"Not at all," said Sundry. He backtracked and said, "In a word, yes, but we're trying to get him and his daughter to relatives in Brownville."

"Brownville? You have a few miles to go, don't you?"

"He just needs the edge taken off." Sundry had never felt so ill at ease asking for anything in his life. He shifted his feet and came as near to hanging his head as he was capable. His former annoyance had not entirely left him, and he struggled to speak calmly. He thought he had probably come upon a temperance man; the conductor looked at him as if he had two heads.

"What is it you're looking for?" asked the captain.

"A gentleman riding with us suggested that something might be put by on a train for medicinal purposes."

"Did he?" The conductor was looking sterner by the minute. "And what sort of train has this gentleman been riding, do you suppose?"

Mr. Normell was not Mister Walton, but Sundry took umbrage as if the latter man's virtue had been questioned. "Quite the best, I'm guessing."

They considered each other for a moment, and Sundry decided if he wasn't to get satisfaction from the man, he wasn't going to give any. The conductor broke the stare first, nodding slightly. "Come on," he said. "We'll see what we've got back here and then go look at the fellow."

Sundry breathed a sigh, and all the annoyance and embarrassment flew out of him. "Thank you, sir," he said with gratitude.

"I haven't given him anything yet," said the conductor.

The room inside the caboose was neat and tidy. A stove stood against one wall and a table, bearing a newspaper and a deck of cards wrapped in an India rubber band, occupied the space beneath the single rear window. The conductor had made his decision, and he did not act coy about knowing what he was looking for or where it was. He went directly to a cupboard beneath one of the overhead berths and pulled from it a small brown bottle.

The engine whistle blew, and the conductor took a step or two before realizing that he had other duties to fulfill. He almost put the bottle in his coat pocket but seemed to think this was courting an embarrassing situation, so he went to the cupboard, put the bottle back, and said, "You sit down and stay put, and don't be touching that bottle. I'll get the stationman to call the all aboard and be right back."

Sundry looked uncertain, but the man repeated his order to stay and left the caboose. Sundry's stomach growled. He sat down at the table and read a line or two of an item in the newspaper without taking any of it in. He had finally decided to hurry back to Burne Ring and his daughter when the conductor came through the door, saying, "There. No one boarding." He returned to the cupboard and snatched the bottle from it. Sundry thought the man resisted looking to be sure nothing was gone from it, but barely. The conductor found a cup behind another door and led the way out.

Sundry breathed easier. If he had had time to think the business out, he would have realized that his troubles would not be solved by a shot of whiskey; but he had passed some of the burden on to this older man, and he was glad to be rid of it. They moved through one Pullman, then the other, and Sundry thought for a moment that he had miscounted cars, but there was Maven's telltale cowlick marking the spot. The other seats were empty, and he peered ahead, wondering if Maven's snores had finally driven them to other seats.

"All aboard!" came the call from without. Sundry caught a glimpse of the stationman walking the platform. "All aboard!" The train gave a lurch forward.

The conductor slowed his pace and turned. "What's the problem?" he asked. "Which is he?"

Sundry pushed ahead of the man and crossed into the next car, hoping to get a glimpse of the little girl sitting in her boy's coat and knickers, dangling her legs into the aisle. The train was chugging slowly forward, gaining speed.

"I thought you said the second car," said the conductor.

The engine let out a shriek, and steam fell past the windows. They were moving out of the station. Sundry reached the first passenger car and knew immediately that Burne Ring, Melanie, and *Mr. Normell* were not in it. "They're gone!" he said.

"What?" The conductor stood in the doorway, casting his eye over the puzzled passengers—ten or twelve people who had looked up from their newspapers or their conversations or a doze.

"They're gone!" said Sundry again. He hurried past the conductor once more and walked the aisle of the second car as if they had been hiding under the seats. "They must have gotten off at the last stop. But you said—" Sundry thought about this for a moment. "No, you said no one was getting on."

"Some people got off," said conductor, "and there was a fellow I thought might be yours, looking sort of ill, but you said he had a *daughter.*"

"Maven!" Sundry shook the sleeping man's shoulder, and Maven Flyce came to with a snort and a start.

"Oh, my!" said Maven. "Is it Brownville?"

"Maven," said Sundry. "Did they speak to you?"

"What? What? We're still moving."

"You did say a daughter?" said the conductor.

"Yes, I did," said Sundry.

"Where are the Rings?" asked Maven Flyce.

"Well, this was a boy," said the conductor. "Knickers and an old coat."

"Was there another man with them?"

"Yes. A plump, nice-looking fellow. They were carrying bags and marching into the station house liked they belonged there."

Sundry watched as Vassalboro rolled by.

"I thought the kid was kind of a brat," the conductor said, "pulling on his father like that when the old man didn't look so well. He was giving the both of them a fit."

"My bag," said Sundry, for he realized it was gone from under the seat.

"What's happened, son?" asked the conductor. He knew the look of a predicament when he saw one. Maven Flyce pressed his nose to the glass, as if he might see the missing people running alongside the train.

"I don't know," said Sundry, "but I'm going to have to change trains and do some backing up."

"Hayden Corner is the next stop. We don't always make it if there isn't a flag out indicating passengers to board; but I'll signal the engineer, and we'll let you off."

"Thank you."

"I thought you said a daughter," said the conductor.

Sundry nodded slowly and to himself. "Yes. I'm afraid I did."

"Don't feel you have to help me find the Rings, Mr. Moss," said Maven Flyce for perhaps the fifth time while they were standing on the platform at Hayden Corner. "It's a shame to miss your trip to Brownville."

"That's not a problem, Maven. And call me Sundry, please."

"I can't understand how they got off at the wrong station," said Maven. He shook his head solemnly, and it was clear that he felt bad about losing them. "I'd hate to tell the Sparks if they can't be found."

Sundry wondered whether they should wait for the next southbound train or if it would be quicker to hire a carriage and ride back to Vassalboro. He turned to look up the tracks, after the departing line of cars, and was startled to see Robin Oig standing at the very end of the caboose with his oversized oar stuck out from under the canopy.

Sundry raised a hand and waved to the sailor, who looked amazed to see the man he was following left behind. Robin Oig had been leaning against the back wall of the caboose, and he now stood and craned his neck to be sure of what he did see. Sundry watched as the man studied the tracks and the ground whizzing beneath and past the train; then the caboose disappeared around the next bend.

"Do you know people up to Brownville?" asked Maven.

34. Lillie in the Fields

They went straight through the station house when the next southbound train dropped them off at Vassalboro. Sundry stood on the wooden sidewalk, looking up and down the main street as if the Rings and Jeffrey Normell would be waiting for him.

"My goodness' sakes!" said Maven.

"What is it?" said Sundry.

"I don't see them."

It had taken Sundry and Maven a little more than an hour to return to this depot, getting off at Hayden Corner and waiting for the next southbound train. Sundry went back inside the station, and there the ticket man remembered the trio that had arrived earlier. "They might've hired a rig," he said when Sundry asked where they had gone.

The livery down the street seemed deserted. Sundry called two or three times at the barn before a head peeked in through a back door. The man had just returned from the *necessary*, and he looked in a contemplative mood while Sundry described the "two men and a kid."

"They took a rig," said the liveryman. "Heading for Winslow, they said. The big fellow did most of the talking. He said the other was ailing and they were heading for a doctor. I told them Doc Domus was just a nick up the road, and they allowed how they'd stop by and see what he could do. I think a stiff charge of rum was about all that fellow needed, if you ask me."

Sundry hadn't, but he resisted saying so. While Maven peered about at things, sneezing at the hay dust, Sundry explained to the liveryman that he was looking for a horse and saddle and wanted to buy them. The liveryman thought the two men had come in together, and he asked Sundry about his friend.

Sundry let out a sigh and stood with his hands on his hips. "Maven," he said, which startled the fellow. "It sounds as if the Rings went north from here. I'm going to buy a horse and saddle and try to catch them."

"You have to catch them first?" wondered Maven. It was a moment before Sundry realized that Maven thought he was speaking of the horse and saddle. "I am amazed!" said Maven when this misapprehension had been corrected.

"Yes, but are you ready to head back to Portland?"

"No, no. I'll go with you. I wouldn't like to go back till we find them. Horace was quite sure I could do it."

Sundry nodded, took another breath, and said, "Can you ride a horse?"

Maven thought about this and nodded, but not with great energy or conviction.

"Do you have any money?" asked Sundry.

As it happened, he did. The Sparks had taken up a collection for his trip from concerned patrons of the Faithful Mermaid. (Horace himself had ponied up two two-dollar bills.) Still, it was not quite enough to get Maven on a horse. Sundry made up the difference.

"I thought they had food on trains," said Maven.

"We got off the train, Maven."

"My, but you're right!" He thought that Mr. Moss's perceptiveness almost rivaled Horace McQuinn's.

The liveryman squinted at them. He led Sundry over to the stables and talked up one or two of the horses before Sundry made a quick decision on a dark mare. Maven got talking with a dappled gelding that appeared gentle.

"And a couple of saddles?" asked Sundry.

"I haven't much for sale," said the liveryman, but he dragged one old piece of gear out from a corner and a second saddle from an outbuilding behind the barn. Sundry harnessed the mare while the liveryman helped Maven with *Topper*.

"What do you call her?" asked Sundry about the mare.

"Name of Lillie."

Sundry stopped in the midst of tightening the cinch and looked over the horse's withers at the liveryman. "That'll be odd," he said.

"Is that your sweetheart's name?"

"No. My mother's."

"There's that bay we passed by," suggested the man.

"What's her name?"

"P they call her."

"Oh?"

"Stands for Priscilla."

Sundry threw his arms over the saddle and considered the liveryman as if he hadn't seen him before. "Do I know you?" he asked with an odd expression.

"I don't think so," said the liveryman.

Sundry led the dark mare out of the shadow of the barn. Topper was disobligingly walking in circles with Maven's foot in his stirrup, requiring the fellow to hop on his free foot to keep up. Once he had his fill of this, the liveryman caught the gelding's head, and Maven was able to make a pretty good show of mounting the animal.

Sundry climbed into the saddle and stroked the mare's neck. He didn't know which was the larger responsibility—finding the Rings or not losing Maven. The liveryman squinted some more. Sundry rode the mare around the yard a couple of times, then leaned down to pat her neck again.

"She handles pretty nicely," said the liveryman.

Sundry agreed. "How are you making out there, Maven?" Topper had taken to walking circles again.

"He'll follow her, I'm guessing," said the liveryman, pointing first to the gelding and then to the mare.

Sundry nodded.

"Were those people trouble?" asked the liveryman.

"No," said Sundry. "I owe them money." He counted out the required bills for the horses and gear, thanked the man, and spoke, not to Maven but to Topper. Then he rode out of the yard, and the gelding seemed willing to follow. On the road and heading north, he looked back to be sure that Maven was keeping up and saw the liveryman still standing outside the big barn doors of the livery. Maven's feet were out ahead of the saddle, his knees unbent, so that he looked like a man trying to brake himself down a steep hill.

It was not long before they reached the house described by the liveryman as belonging to Dr. Domus, but Mrs. Domus said her husband was out on a call and she hadn't seen anyone since early this morning when Clay Stale came by with a rip in his shoulder from tousling with a bull. Not half a mile on, they came to a part in the road, the inner angle of which cradled a small cape. An old woman sat in front, sewing in the afternoon sun. They took the better-worn road that pointed north, but just as the little house was about to disappear behind him, Sundry wheeled the mare around and led the way back.

"Nice afternoon," he said to the old woman.

"That's why I'm out in it," she said without looking up from her work.

"We were trying to catch some friends—" he began.

"Then you're going about it wrong," she said.

"Are we?"

"The only people you could be catching up with came through here— oh, an hour and a half, almost two hours ago, headed east there." She did not look up but gave a nod in that direction.

"East?"

"Well, near east. It'll take you more or less east. That's where they went. Kind of in a hurry, I thought. They raised a power of dust. I went back inside till it cleared."

Sundry tipped his hat and thanked the old woman. Maven didn't have a hat, but he made a stalwart salute, temporarily lost control of his mount, then trotted off with a joggly sounding "Thank you, ma'am."

The old woman looked up and called out, "Take care, young man."

The road dipped, and it rose again, heading northeast for half a mile and toward a tall hill that Sundry imagined commanded the sort of view he was in need of. He hoped that the road would take them there; the land hereabouts was without any great amount of forest, and he might be able to spot a carriage or its dust from some distance away. But the road veered almost directly east, and they followed their shadows past an ancient cellar hole, down into a wet hollow where a marsh was taking hold, a smooth shelf of rock glowed in the sunlight, and willows grew in a tangle over a small stream. The sight of running water made Sundry realize that he was thirsty, and this made him remember that he was hungry.

What am I doing? he wondered. He had ridden off without a thought to food, and here it was well past noon; the Rings and Mr. Normell had taken the box of sandwiches that Mrs. Spark had given Sundry, and neither Maven nor Sundry had eaten a bite since leaving the Faithful Mermaid that morning. Sundry stepped down from the saddle, eased the horse up to the stream, and stretched out by the water, upstream of the animal.

A moment later Topper came splashing into the stream, and Maven dithered back and forth on the saddle, trying to decide how to dismount and also how to dismount without getting wet. While the gelding's broad stomach was straddling the stream, this last problem was not to be solved, and Maven didn't. Sundry was a beat too late trying to catch the man as he pitched out of the saddle and into the water.

"I am amazed!" said Maven when he had righted himself. He was soaked to the skin, water spewed from his face when he spoke, and even his cowlick drooped. Topper jumped away from the floundering man, and Sundry only just caught hold of the animal's reins before the gelding had the chance to bolt. Sundry almost imagined he could hear laughter.

Maven made an effort to walk out of the stream but went upstream instead of to either side. Sundry caught hold of Maven's collar and somehow managed to get them all—mare, gelding, and Maven—onto dry turf.

"That was a near thing," said Sundry.

"I am dolorous," said Maven.

"Are you still thirsty?" asked Sundry.

"I think I've had enough, thank you," said Maven. He looked like a man who has lost his hat, then like a man who remembers that he doesn't wear one.

When Sundry had slaked his own thirst, and a little more conventionally, he stood and surveyed the road and the land thereabout. There was a farm house off to the south and stone walls and wooden fences enclosing a large acreage to the east. It was June, and the grasses hadn't yet reached a person's calves. The countryside was sparse of trees, and he could see past a crease in the land toward the east that he suspected banked more running water, to a hill beyond. There was a deeper shade of green to the south of the hill—a grove, perhaps—but he could see no movement or sign of life except a dark wedge of wings circling over that fold in the land.

Maven sat on the grass, holding Topper's reins, and the gelding almost knocked his rider over, nudging him. Sundry thought he heard a tickle of laughter behind him—a light, airy sound that carried on the breeze so that he could not be sure of it. He watched the slope to the west where dandelions and king devil bobbed untidily around the old cellar hole.

"Did you hear that?" he asked Maven.

"What was that?" asked Maven.

"Someone laughing."

Maven looked around.

"Who was it?"

Sundry shook his head. Then he heard it again and was sure a woman was laughing. He had the uneasy notion that someone was observing them from the little knoll beyond the ancient stonework. Another day, perhaps, he would have gone back and looked.

They returned to the road, Maven dripping, and Sundry tried to read the marks he found there. He was not a trained tracker and could only hope that the newest-looking ruts were made an hour or so ago by those he followed. *More like two hours, the old woman said, and they haven't been stopping to ask directions, presumably, but know where they're going. Or Mr. Normell does.*

Sundry had been subject to a hundred speculations. Who was Mr. Normell? And did he and Burne Ring have some history together? What were their motives for leaving the train without him? And were their motives alike? Burne was perhaps only wanting a drink, and Mr. Normell had taken advantage of that for his own purposes. Sundry wondered where the nearest law was, then wondered what the law could do about a man taking off with his own child. A small shudder ran through Sundry, and Lillie sensed this, for she shied away from him when he tried to mount her again.

"Come on, girl," he said, patting her side. "Good girl." He stroked her face and said, "Lillie." He didn't know if he could accustom himself to that name; but the mare's ears went up, and she seemed calmer. Sundry stepped into the saddle, and they trotted a few yards before he thought to pull up and inquire after Maven.

Maven Flyce was more or less in the saddle, and Topper was more or less progressing up the road. Sundry waited for Maven to catch up. Facing the hill that they had just left behind, he half expected to see someone step out from the old cellar hole—a bonneted head, a flash of brightly colored skirt. There was nothing, not even laughter, and they recommenced their progress north and east.

"I don't know how that happened," Maven was saying. He was still dripping. "I was so surprised."

35. Proof the Day Would End

The ramble-down shack at the side of the road looked to Melanie like an ancient man whose face had fallen into his jowls and his jowls into his neck. Two bleary windows reflected the shadows of the surrounding grove of hardwood, and weeds grew like stubble round the front stoop. There was even a gone-wild stand of bamboo (brought years ago by some sailor fresh from the Orient) lifting its leafy stalks from behind the hut like unkempt hair. That dark hollow through which an unseen stream rippled beneath the sound of birds was Melanie's first hint that the startling day would end. The sun had barely entered this place, and her eyes, dazzled by the brilliant fields and bright and cloudless skies, could not discern beyond the hut or between the trees on the other side of the road.

Her father had passed through a terrible fit of the shakes, and with the movement of the carriage she could not be sure if he was still breathing. Since she could remember, she had known a quiet fear of finding him lifeless in the shack by the railroad tracks below Munjoy Hill or, in more recent days, on his rough pallet in the old coal room beneath Pearce Eddy's flophouse. Many a time she had come back to one of these places and stood over his racked and intoxicated form to listen for the rale of his breathing or to peer after the shiver of a muscle.

To begin with, she had gone with her father and Mr. Normell without argument. Mr. Normell had leaned across the aisle to Burne Ring, who heard in the portly man's whisper something that roused him from his terrible withdrawal and onto his feet. "Come," her father had said, mumbling one name or another, and she had followed them quietly enough.

"Where's Mr. Moss?" was all she asked, and—almost musically—Mr. Normell replied, "Mr. Moss knows where he can find us. Come along." When she realized that Mr. Normell was hurrying them—that he was in a sudden and highly nervous state—she stopped on the platform at Vassalboro and said, "We should wait for Mr. Moss."

Burne Ring may have resented Mr. Moss and, in fact, he may have resented the Sparks and Dr. Hermann and everyone else who had offered help, for an unfamiliar anger lit his face, and he growled as he caught hold of her elbow and tugged her almost from her feet. She had let out a shout or two, hoping that Mr. Moss would hear her or that she could delay them long enough till he found them missing from their seats and came looking.

But Mr. Normell had said, "Nothing to be frightened of. Your father is very ill. Don't be pulling on him." Then he swept her up beneath a pudgy arm and marched with her through the station house and into the main street.

The conductor came down onto the platform and frowned at her.

The carriage Mr. Normell hired was an open chaise with two seats, and the horse a lean white mare with a frisk in her step. The day itself was the picture of driving weather, and the open fields, golden with dandelions and yellow hawkweed, might have elicited admiration even from a six-year-old under other circumstances. Once they were off the main road, Mr. Normell glanced back only a time or two.

"Is Mr. Moss coming?" she asked hopefully.

"Oh, yes," he said. "He knows where to find us."

"Will he come then?"

"Oh, yes. Certainly. I couldn't miss. Dowsing is not just for water, you know." He looked over his shoulder.

"Do you dowse?"

"Oh, yes, my boy. There isn't a member of my family who can pick up an apple stick near water without having it snap in his hands."

Melanie took this in, casting back through recent happenstance and conversation, but she could not make very much from this information. "Why did you want Mr. Moss?" she asked.

"Why, indeed!" he said, and what she could see of his face grew a little hard. "Why, indeed. You are a very astute young man." A sharp thought occurred to him, and he glanced back at her, then faced the road and shook his head.

Melanie pressed against her father's frail body, hoping to cushion him against the movement of the carriage. His head lolled back and forth when they came to a corner, and she cradled it in her small arm.

"Are you taking us to a doctor?" she had asked flatly. She was afraid her father would fall out.

"Oh, yes," said Mr. Normell. "We will find someone to take care of your dear father. Don't you worry."

"I think he's dying," she said, and she thought the portly man would stop the horse again.

Instead he sat motionless, except for the rocking of the carriage, and stared at her openmouthed. "Oh, no," said Mr. Normell. "Not at all. Don't you worry." It was an hour or so later that he took the carriage off the main road and brought them to the decrepit house at the edge of a dim copse.

Melanie Ring had seen a good deal that had gone to seed, and not a little that was absolutely corrupted. She had followed her father from low rung to a lower rung and slept and lain awake in places where the breathing of strange people could be heard in the darkness; but this shack and the enveloping trees, so still in the breezeless afternoon, the birds calling and the invisible water sounding as if the hut itself spoke in a clammy voice, were worrisome in the midst of luminous pastures and rolling farmland, almost as if a degenerate force had erupted from the granite bones among the feet of trees and beyond the hands of fern and bracken.

Having climbed down, Mr. Normell peered up at her, wondering (she thought) if she would run away. He went inside the hut and she heard low voices. Melanie half expected some wild creature to come out and peer at her father. She imagined that a bear lived in this hut, or a wolf perhaps.

Turning to look over her shoulder, she kicked the bag at her feet. It was filled with the girls' clothes that the Sparks had given her. She would have forgotten it when they left their seats on the train so abruptly, but Mr. Normell had snatched up the clutch and the boxes of sandwiches.

The sound of the stream seemed to fade. The shape of a face appeared at one of the dirty windows, and she was startled when the door opened. Mr. Normell looked at her again before climbing into the driver's seat. He considered Burne Ring for a full half minute—watching him shiver, listening to the sick man grunt whenever he drew breath. Mr. Normell took a moment to daub his own forehead with a handkerchief before he pulled a small bottle from his pocket, uncorked it with a deep-throated *dunk*, and reached the open end toward Burne's lips, hovering the bottle over the gray face.

Melanie almost reached out and pulled his hand away. "The doctor said small beer," she said just as Mr. Normell dipped the bottle onto her father's lips. The liquid ran out over the shivering man's mouth and down his chin. It was a moment before the taste or the sting of the liquor took hold and Burne opened his mouth wide and took a great breath.

Mr. Normell applied a little more of the rum and Burne lay with his eyes closed, but held his hands out like a blind man seeking alms. Mr. Normell helped him with the drink two or three more times before Burne took hold of the bottle, pushed himself up in the seat, and held it close to his chest as if it were a source of warmth. The grunting sound was coming out of him at a swifter rate, but not so loudly.

"The doctor said small beer," Melanie said again.

"Yes, yes," said Mr. Normell. "Yes. Small beer later. This will tide him over, but small beer later."

Soon they were breaking out into the sun as from the depths of the earth or from under a storm cloud. Melanie thought her father looked worse in the bright light, and she turned around to look ahead of them. "Where are we going?' she asked Mr. Normell.

"You'll see," he said.

"Mr. Moss should have come with us," she said.

"Don't you worry," he said. "He will."

When they reached the main road again and Mr. Normell turned the horse's head east, she looked behind them, hoping to see Mr. Moss striding over the nearest hill.

36. Odd Enough

Sundry and Maven crossed the China Lake outlet, stopping at the mill there to inquire about recent traffic. Curls of water from the wheel winked in the afternoon sun, fascinating Maven, who was beginning to dry out, and the lake itself shone several hundred yards and a smattering of over-watered maples in the distance. The lake was still high with recent rain, and the miller and his crew were making the most of the runoff, but heads went up when a carriage passed in those days, and they had taken note of the open chaise and the white mare. By their account, Sundry and Maven had not made much time against them, and the travelers did not linger.

Soon they had ridden through the hamlet of North Vassalboro and picked up further news of the passing rig ahead of them. After another twenty minutes or so they breasted the northern end of Priest Hill. To their right the road followed the ridge south; to their left it diverged again a quarter of a mile away. But there was life evident in the latter direction— two men working in a field with a horse and sledge, building a stone wall. Sundry led the way past evidence of recent labor to the place where these two men had paused to rest and to watch his and Maven's approach. It was a hot day for early June and the farmers squinted against the glare of the sky.

Sundry leaned over Lillie's head and stroked her neck. He was fond of wall-building himself and could admire the work before him. Halfway between the horse drawn sledge and the growing wall there were several large rocks and one object that might have come under the heading of "a pretty good-sized boulder." The massive brown horse looked content and lazy, standing in the sun and swishing flies with his tail, shifting his heavy feet with dull thumps. He looked over his shoulder at the mare, and they nickered at each other.

"A good day for it," said Sundry while Maven bumped up beside him.

"The breeze died about an hour ago," said the older man, "and we got blackflies instead, but otherwise it's not too bad." Both men were *horse people*, for they came round the end of their work and considered the dark mare and the dappled gelding almost with as much curiosity and regard as they did Sundry and Maven. The younger fellow, who was perhaps thirty—a broad-shouldered son of the earth with a sunburned face and a perpetual smile—reached up and patted Lillie's nose, and she blew out a polite greeting.

Sundry took a moment to glance up the length of wall; he did admire how such irregular objects could be formed into so handsome and regular a composition. "That's a pretty wall," he said.

The older man let out a guffaw. "They're just rocks. Hard and gray and lumpy. But . . . put in order, they do treat the eye. The Lord knows there's no scarcity of them."

"My father once met a geologist," said Sundry. "He told Dad a glacier dragged all those rocks into the state. Dad wondered when another one might come by and take them back again."

The farmer nodded. "There isn't one due, is there?" he asked dryly. "I would despise to go to all this work for nothing."

There were similar walls in every direction, only hidden at varying distances by the rolling hills they ranged. Maven seemed to think the two farmers were responsible for it all; he gazed about and whistled. "You sure have done a terrific lot of work!" he said admiringly. "Hod will hardly believe it." His cowlick had recovered from the dunking, and it afforded a focus of some interest for the farmers. Sensing that Maven had relinquished control of him, Topper walked some yards off to a clump of dandelion.

Sundry faltered between hurrying after the Rings and an innate sense that *taking your time will get you there faster*. "Could you use a hand with that piece over there?" he asked, indicating the boulder with a nod.

The older man looked at the rock. "Feeling your oats?"

Sundry didn't know that he was, although the first wave of hunger had passed him by. The day was warm for June, and if he was bearing down on his prime, he hadn't exactly put his shoulder to hard labor for more than a year now. Nonetheless, he wrapped Lillie's reins over a maple sapling and left her to pull grass while he went with the two men to confront the boulder.

"My goodness," Maven was saying. "That's a terrific lot of work!" Topper had wandered off for another grove of dandelion, and Maven with him.

The two farmers and Sundry each took up one of several stout poles lying by the sledge and in concert tottered and muscled the boulder toward its place. They were moving it slightly uphill, and they had to pivot it at the last minute; but one might have thought the huge stone had been cultivated for that spot alone, once it was couched and settled.

Sundry had put his back into the business and felt good about it. He hadn't realized how much he had missed such a straightforward problem as a big rock, a place to put it, and a means to put it there. There were several smaller stones—only a little bigger than his head—lying nearby, and he lifted one of these and laid it between the boulder and the existing wall where it set like the piece of a puzzle. With a nod, the farmer acknowledged Sundry's eye and asked him if he could stand a drink.

There was a covered bucket of water on the sledge, and Sundry took a long draft from it with a ladle. Smacking his lips, he said, "Sundry Moss. And this is Maven Flyce."

The older fellow shook Sundry's hand, saying, "Abner Cook and my boy, Abijah."

Abijah was less of a boy than Sundry, but he did not flinch at the description. He took his turn shaking hands with Sundry and gestured to Maven. The younger farmer was a big, bluff fellow—not made smaller by his labor—with a wide, open face and an unruly shock of blond hair.

"We've come up from Portland with some folks," said Sundry, "and lost track of them somewhere between here and Vassalboro."

"There hasn't been many pass by today," said Mr. Cook. "We did hear someone . . . oh, an hour or so ago, when we were down the meadow pulling up likely stones." He pointed a little east where the land dipped down. "Ab could only see the tops of them go by. Did you see anyone, Ab?"

"I just saw the fellow's hat, I guess," said the son.

"They're in an open carriage, I was told," said Sundry. "Do you know anyone by the name of Normell round here?"

For the first time since greeting Sundry, the older man appeared reserved, and the smile left Abijah's face. Abner Cook let in a bit of air and lifted his head in a reverse nod. "There are Normells in China," he said.

"Yes," said Sundry. "He did mention China."

"Up on Dutten Pond, just this side of the Albion line," said Abijah.

"You look surprised," said the older man. He had not turned unfriendly, but there was a sense of caution about him.

Sundry was, because it was just where Mr. Normell had said he would be.

"You following them or chasing them?" asked Abner Cook, after he explained to Sundry how to reach the Normell acres.

"I'm not sure anymore," said Sundry with a smile. "There are a couple of people with him, and I was supposed to be traveling with them."

Maven was doing his best to hear this conversation, leaning farther and farther from his saddle as Topper foraged farther and farther away till the man's cowlick was almost horizontal and a good bump would have unhorsed him. The farmers might have been more on their guard if not for the absolute innocence of Maven Flyce's demeanor, not to mention the easy manner and unhurried way in which Sundry had climbed down from his horse and helped with the big stone.

From the shadowy side of the wall, Ab took up a sack and fished in it till he found what he wanted and pulled out a hard-boiled egg. He was peeling this when he glanced back at Sundry and said, "Care for some?"

Maven's eyes were at least as good as his ears, and he began to cluck at the gelding and to wobble his knees against the animal's sides.

"I wouldn't want to take a man's dinner away from him."

"Just something to bide an afternoon's labor," said the father. "Help yourself."

Sundry reached in among most of a dozen eggs and took two. They insisted that he and Maven each take three or four and also gave them half a loaf of bread. Sundry was very much obliged, and he said so. Maven made gracious noises as he wolfed his portion down.

Abner Cook looked from Maven to Sundry with something on his mind. "Watch your step, over Dutten way," he said finally. "Those Normells are well named, in a contrary manner, if you understand me."

"How so?" asked Sundry.

Mr. Cook looked abashed. "Oh, I don't know. I shouldn't speak of people I haven't had truck with, but they're a clannish bunch. They stick to themselves mostly, and folk over that way aren't sorry for it, I guess. People seem to think there's reason enough to keep their distance."

Sundry gathered up Lillie's reins and swung up onto her. "Is that a warning?" he asked bluntly.

Mr. Cook looked up sharply, but his face softened when he saw Sundry's broad smile. "Not all of it, I guess. There's another family, the Droones, over the other side of the line, and they're about as normal as the Normells and just as tight. There's some sort of disputation between the two—people hardly know what about—but we catch the name Droone or Normell round here, and our ears perk up. Small-town affairs, you know."

Sundry nodded. "I come from a small town myself."

"Do you? I thought you said Portland."

"I've lived there the past year or so; but I hail from Edgecomb, and I sort of yearn for knowing what the neighbors are up to."

That made the farmer smile again. They thanked one another for help and food respectively, and Sundry herded Maven and Topper in before trotting Lillie off. "I wondered how those stones got there," said Maven. When Sundry looked over his shoulder, the farmers were still watching them go. Father and oversized son waved.

Sundry wasn't sure whether they needed to hurry or not if he really did know where Mr. Normell and the Rings were going. He had the oddest feeling about the events of the day, though, to be fair, they were odd enough. Riding beside him, Maven found too much out of his customary realm of experience to be astonished about anything in particular. He simply gaped in general and let out a gasp every eighth of a mile or so.

"It is a beautiful day," said Sundry.

"I am amazed!" said Maven.

What Sundry really would have liked to do was spend the rest of the afternoon with the Cooks and help them build that stone wall.

37. Laughing Water

Robin Oig was not accustomed to navigating on his legs. (Truth to tell, he was a simple sailor and not accustomed to navigating at all but only to following the commands of his superiors aboard ship and of no one onshore.) A sailor did some standing about, keeping watch and the like, but rarely exchanged feet as much as he had that day. A ship held its course as a general rule, too; he knew that at least. Set your course in fair enough weather, and there were minor adjustments now and then—a degree or two on the helm—but he had forgotten just how fickle landsmen's roads were in the way of direction. A vessel did its best to describe the shortest distance between two points, but land paths always seemed to be following the unmotivated wanderings of a dutiless cow—or an inebriated sailor.

Sometimes the road almost doubled back on itself, and he would stop and look behind him as if he might eyeball it into *straightening out.* The oar, too, was not unburdensome, and he might have shifted it from one side to the other if he had not got it into his head that it belonged on his right shoulder. He marched on, not reveling in but only marveling at the thousand shades of green and the hundred shades of yellow and gold and several of red and orange among the fields and rock walls. It was all a little *too* fecund somehow and, like mushrooms rising around the trunk of a great tree, looked ready to take hold of anything that paused long in its midst.

Robin thought he must be an hour or more behind Mr. Moss. It had taken him that long to get back to Vassalboro Station from Winslow and Hayden Corner, and it would have taken him a good deal longer if he hadn't been offered a ride from a young fellow with a battered buckboard who seemed to be training his horse for a race. The driver hadn't shown the least curiosity about Robin's oar, but the man at Vassalboro Station had frowned at the device and sent the sailor across to the livery, and the man at the livery had frowned at the device, scratched his head, and pointed the sailor up the road to Winslow.

"Winslow?" said Robin. That did seem circuitous. He'd just been there.

"The fellow with the sick man and the little boy said they were heading for Winslow," explained the liveryman. "And the next two fellows who came along went after them."

Robin didn't know about two fellows, but there had been someone standing with Mr. Moss when he saw him on the platform at Hayden Corner.

"Are there any more of you?" asked the liveryman. He looked past the sailor as if he expected a whole line of folk to be bringing up the rear.

Robin turned and looked himself. "Where?" he asked.

"What?" said the liveryman.

Robin thought the fellow was peculiar. "Winslow," he said. He might have saved himself some shoe leather, but then again, certain mysterious processes, such as finding Fiddler's Green, required roundabout methods. When he stopped to think about it, he was encouraged.

"That's some stick of wood," said the liveryman.

"Do you think so?" asked Robin, the light of suspicion brightening his eye.

"Never seen an oar like it."

"Oh."

Up the road, the doctor's wife seemed daunted by the man and his oar, but she reported a man of Mr. Moss's description who had inquired about some people in front of him and also a fellow with an exceptional cowlick.

The woman sewing in front of her house hardly looked up when he asked if anyone had come that way. "Goodness' sakes!" she said. "There must be some goings-on up the road!" She did point him east and looked up when he was a distance off. She took off her glasses and put them back on again several times, squinting after him to see what he was carrying over his shoulder.

It was while passing an ancient cellar that Robin first heard laughter from over the hill to the north. He stopped by one corner of the old structure. Trees as thick as his arm grew out of the hole and blooms waved in the crevices of rock. Robin watched the top of the hill and listened. A stream ran the length of the next crease in the land, wetting the road in its passage, *marshing* the field, and shading the immediate way with a nest of willows. Robin intended to have a drink.

He had recommenced his long stride when he heard laughter again, and curiosity took hold of him so strongly that he almost laid the oar down before climbing the short slope to his left. When he did make the top of the hill, he was greeted with simply more of the same: rolling fields of green, dotted with wildflowers and broken occasionally by a stand of birches or a single oak or maple or chestnut. Stone walls crisscrossed the land, and a small herd of cows grazed, a field or two beyond. A bird banked the sky.

From his perch atop the hill he looked down to the stream and was startled to see two women seated on a large gray rock by the water. They were dressed in near white, and their hair was long and loose past their shoulders. He had not seen them before, and though he had heard the laughter from over the hill, he was certain that it had been theirs. He could not place their ages as he drew near. Their graceful demeanor and knowing half smiles seemed to make them mature; their reckless locks and mischievous eyes marked them almost as children. Robin's heart raced on his approach; he thought a moment of dire import had arrived and didn't dare speak first.

He did not have to. "Where's the boat for *that* paddle," said the dark-haired woman, "and where's the water that will fit them both?"

Robin was crestfallen. "It's not a paddle, it's an oar," he said.

Both women laughed, a sound not very different from the water running at their slippered feet. "Are you lost?" asked the yellow-haired woman.

He set the boom end of the oar on the ground. "Don't you think it precarious to be laughing at strangers?"

This only made them laugh again.

"Is there more than one of you?" asked the one. She did not bother to look for those other souls implied by his use of the plural.

"I don't think there has to be," said the second woman. "There's enough of him for two or three of us and a little more to boot."

Robin Oig had suspicions about these two. Aside from the color of their hair, he had thought them very much alike, but now he saw that the one had a round face and the other a narrow one. He had thought them very striking, too, when he first laid eyes on them; they were basking in the sun by the stream, dressed in almost white with almost white slippers on their small feet and their long hair falling loose past their shoulders. Now he thought them very nearly plain, and they would have been altogether so, he was convinced, but for their smiles and the brightness of their eyes.

"I thought you were sisters," he said.

"We're friends," said the first.

"Where do you live?" he asked. It was not a meddlesome question (or not meant to be) but simply a declaration of natural curiosity. He looked around and saw no farm or house nearby.

"Nearby," said the first woman.

Robin felt his scalp prickle as he remembered the ancient cellar hole above them; it had been there that he had first heard their laughter. This was more mystery than he was inclined to pursue. "Well, you should be cautious about laughing at strange men," he said.

"*You're* not so strange," said the second woman.

He could make no sense of her inflection. He laid the oar on his shoulder again. He was disinclined to drink from this stream. These two women, if they weren't pixies, were pixilated, to be sure. (He could not have imagined that someone had recently suggested the same about him.)

"Hello!" came a voice, small with distance but round from between cupped hands.

A man stood atop the hill. The women waved and laughed, then, without a good-bye, leaped across the stream like does and ran up the small slope. They shouted to the man at the top of the hill, but Robin could not make out their words. The day seemed hot, though the sailor stood in the shade of the willows near the stream. The women and then the man waved to Robin when they gathered together on the hill. Robin waved back as they disappeared down the further slope. Strangely (or, at least, it seemed strange to him) he was sorry to see them go.

Robin drew the back of his hand across his forehead. He wondered if he might drink from the noisy water after all. He kicked at a stone and watched it *plip* into the current. A dark depression in the wet soil upon the bank drew his attention, and he leaned over to inspect the mark of a horse's hoof that had filled with water. Mr. Moss was on horseback, and here, he was sure, was a sign that the man had stopped at this very stream. He remembered his reason for being out in these fields and forgot the two women and the figure of the man at the top of the hill, and letting out something like an annoyed grunt, walked off without refreshing himself.

38. Tim's Burden

Timothy Spark was miserable and didn't quite know it. He understood that he had taken little Mailon Ring for granted when they scurried the waterfront in search of adventure or scaled the roofs of Brackett and Danforth Streets to view the incoming ships. He had been disconcerted to learn that Mailon was Melanie, that the boy was a girl, and that he had been sharing adventures with an Indian maiden and not a brave, but he had accommodated this sudden change with philosophy and moved forward.

Now both Mailon and Melanie were gone, and their combined absence did very little to solve the muddle between them in his mind. It rather made it seem a dream.

Earlier in the day he had hurried after Mr. Moss with grand designs to hitch a ride on the back of the departing carriage, but his father had caught him by the breeches, sent Timothy back to the kitchen, and enjoined him to "take some steam off."

Tim sat at the family trencher and hardly moved for half an hour. His mother thought he looked lost and friendless, sitting with his head half down and his face expressionless. "You miss your shadow," she said to him while sliding a piece of dried-apple pie and a chunk of rat cheese under his chin.

Tim did not respond, either to his mother's voice or to the pie, and when he did acknowledge the food before him by eating it, it was without any outward sign of relish.

"Where are your other friends?" asked Mabel in the midst of cutting potatoes into a stewpot.

Tim was not without further companionship, and he and Melanie (under the guise of Mailon) had joined the local kids, chasing many an imaginary enemy along the waterfront and many a real fly ball by the Western Promenade in the last year or so since the scrawny waif had first shown up at the kitchen door of the Faithful Mermaid. Tim had friends of longer standing than Melanie, just not better ones. It was not enough to characterize the little girl as his shadow or to imagine that Tim (as the older child) missed someone he could order about. Timothy was not a *boss* at heart; but he was a leader, and Melanie was a loyal and generous follower. She would do what he wanted most to do because that was what made him happy, and Timothy would often ponder on what she would most like to do before suggesting it.

Tim was not a big boy for his age, and he had developed a scrappy, if well-meaning and good-humored, manner that was not unlike that of his father. He was, besides, from sympathetic stock, and if he could not completely understand what it meant to Melanie Ring to walk in disguise for most of her young life, he could yet understand that she couldn't understand it herself. She was not much more than a minute (in the way of physical presence), and since the revelation of her identity, Tim had taken on the role of guardian when they were in the streets together. The black and purple bruise surrounding one of his eyes attested to his mixed success in this field, but also to his determination.

"Do you think Mr. Moss caught up with them?" he asked his mother some while after the pie was cleaned from his plate and he had been staring into the middle distances.

"I think he would have come back if he hadn't."

The next question was more difficult to ask, and for several reasons. "Do you think she'll ever come back?" he said, trying to look as if it didn't matter to him.

Mabel Spark had been clattering pans in the dry sink, and she stopped suddenly, not to hear what her son was saying but to realize what he had said. "I don't know, dear," she sighed. She had almost said, "I wished we'd never let them go." Even as Mailon, the dirty waif at the kitchen door, Melanie had become part of their family; now that Mabel had bathed and dressed the little girl and fed her at her own kitchen table, her heart was burdened by those wide, unpleading eyes. "There's no telling whether Burne will find their relatives in Brownville. He hadn't heard from them for years, and they might be anywhere." Then she almost said, "They might be back tomorrow," but didn't want to raise his hopes.

"Maybe they'll be back tomorrow," said Timothy.

She wouldn't have credited how keenly he had felt the little girl's leaving. Timothy had once announced to Melanie (back in the days when she was *Mailon*) and to the rest of the world that he didn't have much use for girls, and at seven years of age there was small reason to doubt him.

"Maybe," said Mabel. "But you have to remember who she is . . . and that she is, well . . . a *she* and that if she does come back, she will have to commence dressing and acting like a girl." Mabel expected some reaction—anger or even disgust—to register on Timothy's face, but he only frowned, as if he didn't really believe her.

"Simon Daily's little sister plays baseball with us sometimes when we need to even up the teams," he said.

"I wouldn't do everything the Dailys do," was her reply.

She went back to the pans in the sink and didn't see the slow process of change that speculation wrought upon his face. There is nothing like a plan for chasing sadness, and Timothy looked like someone who had found his breath. Mabel didn't hear him as he left the table, but she called after him when his footsteps clunked on the back steps. She went to the door and looked up the stairwell, but he had already flown from the top landing.

A few minutes later he came down the front way. The family had strict orders to use the back stairs, and Thaddeus would have spoken to him if Tim hadn't managed to sneak down to the tavern room and out into the street without his father's notice. Tim ran along the sidewalk with only one hand swinging, the other gripped close to his side. Anyone looking carefully at the towheaded seven-year-old might have noticed that he was carrying something under his shirt. He charged round pedestrians and took only the briefest looks for traffic before darting past alleyways.

With one hand he pulled himself onto the tar-papered roof of the shed behind the old molding mill, and still holding his secret prize close to his side, he scurried over roof and gable till he came to a place that perhaps only he and Melanie had ever visited since it was last shingled. There was a bell-like cupola above the soap factory, and nearing it, he could smell strange odors wafting from the vats below. Several slats on the back side of the cupola were loose, and he removed them before pulling his prize from beneath his shirt and stashing it inside.

He was pleased. Once he had replaced the slats, he moved along the rooftops more slowly, almost ambling as he climbed to the widow's walk above Mr. Ealing's Shipping Firm. From there he could see the harbor and the observatory on Munjoy Hill; more important, he could see the Grand Trunk Railway Station. Maybe Mr. Ealing would come up to view the signal flags on the observatory or to watch the ships come in with his spyglass. He might have a bag of peanuts. Timothy would tell the businessman about Melanie, and the old fellow would certainly be surprised. He was a kind man, Mr. Ealing, and Timothy actually looked forward to his reaction to such strange news.

Tim scrambled over the railing onto the widow's walk and sat in the afternoon sun beside the trapdoor, looking out over the water, watching for a plume of smoke, and listening for the shriek of a locomotive whistle from the north. They would not be back today, he knew, but he would wait. A fellow had responsibilities.

39. Among the Droone and Normell

Burne Ring did not wake up dead that afternoon, though he expected this to happen "sooner than later." But when he opened his eyes and realized that he wasn't rocking on the Bosom or rafting the Styx, he felt only the smallest comfort. Before him sat his only surviving child, slumped in sleep against the portly driver, representing life's tenuous hold and the single frail argument for living a little longer. There had been a time when he saw his lost wife in Melanie's face, but in the past week, gazing from his bed at the Faithful Mermaid, he had been sensible of her standing over him and also how much she resembled his own father's mother, who had raised him. Looking at Melanie, he sometimes wondered where Mailon was.

Burne had difficulty remembering things; this afternoon he couldn't remember the name of the young man who had been traveling with them on the train, but he did wonder where the fellow was. He vaguely recalled the man who was driving the carriage, but didn't know *why* he was driving it or why they were rattling through a small town beside a long expanse of lake. The bottle clutched to his chest afforded him queasy comfort; sometimes he lifted it to his mouth without knowing what he was doing till the harsh liquor touched his lips.

The carriage flickered beneath lengthening shadows, and the breeze near the lake was almost cool. They were not far past China Lake before the blue of another water gleamed past the intervening fields, and the scattered trees assembled into something like a wood at either side of the road. The driver hummed tunelessly as he looked around and caught Burne's gaze. Mr. Normell turned back to the horse and did not look back again till the carriage came to a halt before a wide gate in the shadow of a parklike wood.

Burne sat up, as awake and aware as he had been in days. A boy of about thirteen appeared from somewhere, looking alarmed. He watched them from the other side of the fence and asked, "Did you find someone?" in a small tone when the chaise pulled up before the gate.

"Don't quiz your elders," said the driver. "Open the gate." Jeffrey Normell shot a glance back at Burne Ring that was as startled as the boy's.

The boy obeyed, head down, shoulders up. Melanie roused as they ambled forward. She sat up quickly and leaned away from the portly man, her cheek red with the reflected heat from his side. She saw the boy by the open gate and turned her head to watch him as they passed. He looked as if he wished he could follow, and when they were almost out of sight, he raised one hand and waved uncertainly to her.

"Daddy," said Melanie when she realized that Burne was awake. "Daddy, Mr. Normell says there's someone down this way who can help you."

Burne pulled a frown and looked down at the bottle in his hands. "Are we in Brownville?" he said, his voice hoarse with disuse.

"No, no," said the driver hurriedly. "Not Brownville. China. We're in China. You were so sick."

I wasn't sick, I was dying, thought Burne. "What are we doing in China?" he asked.

"There'll be people down this way who can help you," said the man, but with less conviction and a good deal less bonhomie.

"Where's the young fellow who was with us on the train?" continued Burne with more energy than he would have credited. He gripped the bottle with both hands as they went over a series of ruts and bumps.

"He was very insistent that you go on to Brownville," said Mr. Normell, "but I thought you needed help sooner than that. We can get you another of those, if you like." He turned ever so slightly to indicate the bottle.

"Oh," said Burne, after a brief silence, and then added bitterly, "You *are* my friend." He wondered if he had strength enough to strangle the man, and some of this inclination may have carried with his voice, for Mr. Normell glanced back several times. Burne wondered where they were. It wasn't enough to say that they were in China. Where *were* they? And why had this man taken custody of them?

The mare clattered over a granitic hump, and the carriage bumped up and over the rock. The hooves quieted, and the rig dropped off the hard plate with a jolt and descended in more gentle degrees down a wooded slope. Stone walls lined the way, and irregular piles of rock and the occasional lone boulder stood among the gathering trees like figures poised to watch them pass. It seemed very quiet among these trees. Burne felt uneasy, though his daughter looked brave enough. She was in boys' clothes, and he wondered if the man in front knew her real identity.

They came to Dutten Pond, or within sight of it, for the blue water flashed between the trees and bushes along its eastern shore. The westering sun hurt Burne's eyes, and he shifted his gaze to the darker side of the wood, where patches of light touched the boles of trees, and clumps of bright leaf shone like faces peering from holes in the shadows. Burne thought he was having visions again—the leaf faces appeared so real—and then, with a start, he knew they were real and that people were coming down half a dozen paths toward the road the chaise traveled, wary creatures of the forest pausing at the sight of the newcomers.

And seeming to rise out of the very ground but only coming into view as the carriage topped the next little knoll was Mr. Normell's taller, wider self standing like one of those glacial castoffs, but in the midst of the road. The shell of his ruddy face appeared unmoved and imperturbable, but his eyes had the same frightened shine as the boy's at the gate.

As the chaise approached him, the large man held his hand out, palm up, till it stopped, whereupon he stepped up to the driver and said, "What is this, Jeffrey?" His voice as well as his face and figure marked him as close kin to Mr. Normell. "Who are these people?" He did not consider Melanie for very long but turned his gaze to Burne and, for a moment, the bottle in Burne's grip.

"I looked for three days and finally found someone," said Mr. Normell. "I looked for someone for three days and couldn't wait any longer. Suppose the Droones had found someone and *I* was away?"

"Is this him then?" Before the driver could answer, the larger man looked at Melanie and said, "And who is this?"

"He's coming," said Mr. Normell weakly.

"Who is coming?'

"The man I found. He's on his way."

"But who are these?" asked the larger man again.

Mr. Normell cleared his throat, considered his next statement, and, instead of talking, looped the reins on the carriage rail and clambered down. The two men walked off and conferred, Jeffrey Normell steeling himself with paper-thin courage and the larger, wider man once more taking on that rocklike aspect as he listened to Jeffrey's explanations. Twice the larger man looked back at the passengers in the chaise, and once, to Jeffrey Normell's obvious relief, he nodded.

Burne heard a series of broken phrases from the mouth of Mr. Normell—"his own free will" and "looking for them, I'm sure" among them—and the father pricked up his ears without otherwise shifting his slumped posture. Mr. Normell stopped to glance back at the carriage with a nervous sort of smile that set Burne's teeth on edge.

The larger man came back to the chaise and looked at the father and child. "Very well," he said with a wheezing sigh. "I'm Charles Normell," he said. "Welcome to Normell Acres. Get them down to the summerhouse, Jeffrey."

Jeffrey Normell scrambled his portly frame back into the driver's seat, and they recommenced their progress. Burne wavered between apathy for his own well-being and vague dread for that of his child. He leaned to one side, then the other with the rocking of the chaise, and with each tilt to his left he turned his head a little till he had Charles Normell in sight again. The man wore a strange expression—wild and perhaps hostile; then Charles caught Burne's gaze, and a startled smile wrapped around his broad face.

They met and passed several other people further down the road—large, round-faced folk with stolid faces and curious, anxious eyes—plainly dressed country men and women and their scrubbed-faced children.

Jeffrey Normell did not look at them, but he glanced back at the bottle in Burne's hand and asked, "Hide that, would you?"

One handsome, round-faced woman, with her hair in a bun and an apron tucked under one arm, reached for the two children before her and gathered them in as the carriage passed. Burne was not surprised to find the cork for his bottle in a pocket. Even in a stupor he knew enough to take care of comfort. He corked the bottle and slipped it into his coat. His small energy began to evanesce till breathing itself sapped his strength.

Further down the road the assembly took on the size of a small mob, the chaise drawing people in its wake as a troller hopes to draw fish. They walked alongside or fell in behind the rig, a ruddy, heavyset clan with the occasional trim figure standing out like a birch among rugged oaks. They had dark hair, as a rule, though Burne saw a red head or two through the haze of his renewed weakness; these people were so obviously of a single lineage that he had the dreamlike sensation of having crossed into another country or discovering the land of a separate and previously unknown race.

The carriage came within sight of several homes—neat little capes and a single larger edifice of colonial origin—then left these dwellings for a rougher lane that led to the pond, a small clapboarded house, and several outbuildings of stone and wood. The crowd followed. On the pond itself there were several boats, each manned by several people—some with nets—who took interest in the gathering at the shore. Beyond the outbuildings, as if waiting on the other side of an invisible line, stood a separate group of men and women, girls and boys, narrow as the Normells were broad—taller, paler, and blond. The two groups were like distinct hives, humming just below the level of dangerous agitation.

"Who are they?" asked Melanie.

"Droones," said Mr. Normell, and a very unjolly timbre took possession of his voice. "Beyond one or two of their elders, I can tell you no more. We know they are Droones because we do not recognize them or know their names."

One of these people, a tall, narrow woman of indeterminate years, came forward, past the unseen margin that fenced the others in, and approached the carriage. "What have you there, Mr. Normell?" she asked.

The portly driver blinked, surprised to see her or perhaps to see where she was standing. "Visitors, Mrs. Droone," he said with a nervous laugh.

"Have you found someone?" she asked, looking at Burne and then Melanie as if she thought this unlikely. "Our Bradford is not back yet."

"I did," said Jeffrey, but as if she had accused him of something and he were denying it. "And he will be along presently."

Her head came up like a watchful eagle's. Burne tried to muster the energy to meet her gaze but found himself considering a little girl in a white dress who stood some feet behind this tall woman. The girl carried a doll over her shoulder and added her own uncertainty to that of the elders around her. Further back, beyond the unseen demarcation, there were other children with narrow faces and similar expressions, but the adults in the two crowds had the look of fear and barely concealed desperation.

The tall woman's face was itself hardened with apprehension and doubt. Only Melanie appeared undaunted, exhibiting more self-possession than the whole lot of them. She was a six-year-old child having an adventure—and almost enjoying it. This poise did not come from her father—he knew that better than anyone—but was more of his grandmother, whose own self-possession had not been a dark thing but full of humor and wit and promise.

Charles Normell came puffing down the road and his presence among them appeared to balance that of the tall woman's. She did not retreat, but she drew herself up as if ready to squeeze herself through a narrow passage.

Burne felt himself fading. "Where are we?" he said. He was slumped in the back of the chaise, frail and ashen.

"You are in China, sir," said Mrs. Droone, but in a tone that suggested he could do better.

"He told me that," said Burne. "But *why* are we here?" After a breath or two, he said, "What's this mob all about?"

"It has nothing to do with you, Mr. Ring," said Charles Normell.

"Who are these two?" demanded Mrs. Droone.

"We're waiting for Mr. Moss," said Melanie.

"Moss?" said her father angrily. "Then *he* brought us here."

"No, Daddy," said Melanie. "*You* made us leave while he was gone." Burne remembered this, but not clearly.

"Mr. Moss is coming," said Melanie. "Didn't you say?"

"Yes, I did, lad," came the voice of Jeffrey Normell, almost sounding as he had on the train.

Burne understood nothing and had reached the end of his strength, barely propped up by the bottle in his coat pocket. He dwindled visibly, like a clouding patch of sunlight on a bedsheet.

"Daddy?" said Melanie.

A muddle of voices rose up, frightened and angry and petulant. "Take them into the summerhouse," said Charles.

"What are they here for?" said someone.

Burne perceived it all through the fog of his sudden relapse. Hands grasped him; an arm reached behind his back, lifting, then carrying him to the house and to a bed. He was looking up at his daughter's anxious face. Beyond her were tall screened windows and a maple branch swaying in the breeze and the leaves on the tree were alike yet each different (he knew) and he was wondering about them and the branch and the tree and how it looked if you stood outside the building and saw the tree beside it and how the tree gave shade and the sun lit the top of the tree and the water beyond and the breeze that moved the branches was why he noticed the tree in the first place and the air and a bird sang and there was shadow—shade and shadow and shadow.

"Daddy?" said Melanie. She stood by the bed and clutched at his arm. "Daddy?"

"Mailon," said Burne, which utterance he intended to be his last act of parental responsibility.

40. The Deafened Man Thought Whispers Were Silence

They came to a room where the sun picked its way past a toplofty maple to fall across a four-posted bed. Burne looked small and ineffectual on the brightly quilted counterpane, his graying hair damping the white pillow and his face as pale as the sheets.

"Daddy?" said Melanie, standing by the bed and gripping his arm. "Daddy?" In her other hand she still held the clutch, which she had thought, this time, to snatch hold of as they left the carriage.

"Mailon," said her father softly. She almost corrected him, but she remembered that Mr. Moss had introduced her to Mr. Normell as Mailon and that, dressed as she was, everyone here would think her a boy. "Boys aren't so hard pressed as girls," her father had said. Oddly, she had been feeling a little less like a boy in the past few days, but she would honor what she perceived as her father's intent in using the old name.

"Stand aside, stand aside," said a wide and elderly woman who was coming into the room. Jeffrey Normell and then Charles came after, echoing her "Stand aside." People shifted and moved but did not leave the room as she leaned over the stricken man, instructed that his coat and shirt be unbuttoned. She felt his face and wrists and finally his neck.

"What is that?" she said when his coat was turned back and she heard something hard in his pocket fall upon the bedcovers. Reaching into the pocket, she retrieved the bottle, saying testily, "What have you brought me?" She turned upon her heel, her round, rosy face twisted into an almost childish expression of pique. "What have you brought me?"

"That's Mr. Ring," said Jeffrey, as if this would explain everything.

"Not anymore, it isn't," said the old woman.

Melanie did not look at her or Jeffrey Normell or even her father but considered the faces of the men who had carried Burne to the bed. They were respectable-looking fellows, their shirts rolled up to the elbows and some with hats in their hands. Similarly, the little girl did not glean the import of the old woman's words from the words themselves, but from the faces of these men as *they* understood and cast sidelong glances at the child.

"He hasn't been very well," said Melanie, and for the look on her face, she might have been defending him against accusation.

Jeffrey looked past Charles's shoulder from the other side of the room. "What do you mean, not anymore?"

"Who are these people?" said the old woman.

"Now, now, Auntie," said Charles, stepping forward.

"Who was this man?" she amended.

"There is another man coming who will be able to help us," said Charles, not sounding very convinced himself.

"I should hope so!" said the woman.

"Aunt Gisselle!" said Charles with a little more severity than he had heretofore exhibited.

"How do you know he's coming?" she said. For all her pique, and despite the general noise of agreement from the others in the room, she appeared uncertain of her strength against Charles. She gained an inch or two of height, however, and considerable more assurance by turning back to Jeffrey and saying again, "How do you know he's coming?"

"He's following these folk," said Charles.

"Is he? And what is he going to say when he finds one of them dead?"

"He hasn't been well," explained Jeffrey.

"How much excuse do you think that people around here need to burn every one of us out of the county?" declared the woman.

"That was years ago," said one of the otherwise silent men, but without much conviction.

"Aunt Gisselle," said Charles.

"It's not like that anymore," said someone.

"It will be again, mark my word!"

"Auntie, you should go out," said Charles. "Now."

"Mr. Moss understood that this fellow was unwell," said Jeffrey.

"And you!" she said, pointing an accusatory finger. "All of us in more trouble than we know what to do with, and *you* bring a man to die here, and a boy to watch it! It's a good thing he *is* dead, I suppose, or what will the Droones think?"

"That's enough," barked Charles. One of the men who had carried Burne looked ready to speak, but then Charles said, "Out of the room, Auntie! Out of the house!" And when she did not move to obey, he laid hold of her arm, pulled her away from the bed, and shoved her none too gently toward the door.

There stood Mrs. Droone, almost at Jeffrey's shoulder, and none of them knew how long she had been listening and watching.

"The idea!" said Aunt Gisselle, slapping her nephew's hand till he let her go.

"In*deed*," said Mrs. Droone.

"Mrs. Droone," said Charles, "I do not remember inviting you into this house."

"*I* do not remember inviting *you* to keep secrets."

"This has nothing to do with the problem at hand," said Charles.

"Doesn't it?" Charles Normell might prod his own aunt toward the door, but he was not so sure about showing Mrs. Droone the same. "This is not a time to be crossing the Droones, Charles Normell," said the woman.

"This not a time to threaten the Normells, Bridey Droone."

"Do you see what you have got us into!" said Aunt Gisselle to Jeffrey. She had the look of near hysterics. "How can you be so stupid when there is so much at stake!"

"Take her out of here!" Charles shouted, and the other men looked glad to comply—and to follow her out. "And you, too, Mrs. Droone, if you please. Unless *you* would like to deal with this situation."

"I may need to, by the look of things," said the woman.

"I will call you if need arises," said Charles without revealing any irony.

The woman startled him by advancing into the room, and before anyone could stop her, she approached the bed and laid a hand against Burne
Ring's neck.

"Are you satisfied?" asked Charles.

"Perhaps," she said.

Melanie moved to step out of the woman's shadow. "That's my father,"
said the little girl with her own note of warning.

The woman regarded Melanie for the first time. "I am sorry, child,"
she said, not sounding *very* sorry. "But there is pressing business hereabouts that you could not be expected to understand."

"Are you satisfied?" asked Charles again.

"Not very," said the imposing woman. "The fact that he is dead may
only mean that he died sooner than you expected."

"We have not forgotten our agreement," said Charles.

"Nor what might occur if you do, I trust."

"Jeffrey could not find anyone willing to come with him," said Charles,
"but he did meet a man traveling with these two and is certain this fellow
will follow them. *This* man came willingly, and his son with him. Your
Bradford hasn't returned, has he?"

"Mr. Moss will be along presently," Jeffrey assured everyone. "I am
quite sure. Don't you think so, Mailon?"

Melanie thought before answering. "Yes," she said finally. She very
nearly added, "And you had better take care when he does, for he is a
member of the Moosepath League," but she had heard enough about
Daniel Boone's dealings with enemy tribes and the hairbreadth escapes of
Mountain Wilma to know that one did not reveal the strength of one's
forces. "He'll come," she said. She had complete faith in Mr. Moss.

Mrs. Droone scanned the room with her hawklike eye, then turned
about and quit the room. It was clear, from the sound, that a crowd had
gathered in the fore of the house.

Charles's round face was red with anger, his eyes protruding as he
stared after the woman and his relatives. He leveled this gaze on Jeffrey.
"This Mr. Moss of yours had better be prompt," he hissed.

"Oh, yes," said Jeffrey. "I'm sure he will be."

Charles cast a glance toward the outer room. "She's right, you know."

"What? Who?"

"Aunt Gisselle."

"But it won't matter once Mr. Moss sets things aright—"

"Won't it?"

"I looked and looked," said Jeffrey. "It's very enervating, and I thought I had done quite well. To find someone with the gift is complex, but to find someone with the gift who is willing to come here—" Jeffrey pointed at Charles and almost shouted, "You try that! I thought I was very clever."

"That remains to be seen," said Charles. He had calmed somewhat, and it must have occurred to him that they were speaking in front of the *boy*. "How do you know this Mr. Moss can help us?"

"He told me so," said Jeffrey, and when Charles did not respond, or not in so many words, he added, "I had a feeling—"

"How could you have a feeling?"

"I did. About him." There was a brief silence; then Jeffrey finished with, "He seemed trustworthy."

"Then I guess we shall see if *trustworthy* serves. If you think it has been difficult traveling about and looking for someone, you should have stayed and stared across the line at Droones. Or watched everyone else stand about and fret and brood. I'm not sure you didn't have the better portion."

They had reached an impasse or at least a lack of anything further to say. Charles walked past Jeffrey and went out of the room. Jeffrey began to follow him but stopped and turned to Melanie. "Come, lad," he said, uncertain and distracted. "We'll find something for you to eat."

"I should stay here, I think," she said.

"What?" he said. "Oh, yes." There was a dead man on the bed whose remains should be arranged in a dignified manner and also the child who must be dealt with. "There's a great deal happening," he told her, as if this would excuse everything. "It's very important that your Mr. Moss arrives," he said, looking at his own hands. "And soon, I think." He was talking to himself now, and nodding to himself.

"I should stay here," she said.

Jeffrey Normell seemed honestly troubled to leave the child in this room alone, but perhaps not honestly enough. "We'll find you something to eat," he said, and left.

Though hungry, Melanie did not want anything from these people. Letting her little clutch drop to the floor, she sat in the chair by the bed and watched her father as she had done countless times before. The sun had lowered, and the shadows of the maple tree had crept up the inner wall. The room was even nicer than her room at the Faithful Mermaid—or finer, at least. Tim had told her about Mr. Thump's apartments, which he had visited a week or so ago with his father, and she wondered if they were as well decked out as this: framed prints of cows and fields and flocked wall-paper, a beautiful bowl and pitcher on a highly wrought washstand, a dresser, and a pretty blue and green rug beneath the four-posted bed.

There were sounds coming from the next room and voices from outside.

She didn't think this very different from sitting up with her father when they were living below the Portland wharves, except that it was in choicer surroundings and there would be no answering rale from him when she keened her ear against the silence. She imagined what the Sparks would have done if her father had died in *their* bed and tried not to think how very much better off she would have been if he had. It puzzled her that he looked so much better; often when he was asleep, she feared he was dead, and now he looked as if he *were* sleeping, and peacefully.

She put her hand in her father's open palm, and the rough fingers gave two or three sudden jerks. For a moment the little girl held her breath, holding his hand in hers. "Daddy," she whispered.

Burne himself felt only surprise. "Well, not yet," he said loud enough for his daughter to hear.

"Daddy," said Melanie.

"Not yet," he said again.

"They said you were dead," she told him, so that the two statements seemed to have come out of order.

Burne lay quiet, trying to recall a dream about a crowd of people who all had been gifted with extraordinary hearing. Somehow they had been deafened to the level of common men, and they did not know when he told them, "Not yet." He could hear himself, and any other person might have heard him; but these people, who had known such unusual percep-tion, now mistook a whisper for silence.

"Mr. Moss will be coming," said Melanie. "Mr. Normell says he will."

"I'm awfully tired," he said.

"I won't tell them," said Melanie to her father. She had not let go of his hand. "They won't bother you if I don't tell them. And then Mr. Moss will come."

"I will wait for him," said Burne. He looked at her from the corner of his eye, scarcely having moved from his deathly stillness. He was shocked to see that his daughter was only six years old.

41. Meeting Horace

"They call *all of* it Dutten," said the boy whom Sundry and Maven caught up with about half a mile east of China Village. "They mean the pond *and* the woods, *and* the Normells and the Droones who live there. 'Over to Dutten,' they say."

It was the right time of day to view that pond and those woods from a knoll south of the road and about a quarter of a mile southwest from the pond's closest shore. A consummate June day was taking its long golden time to close shop, and the shadows of the people and horses atop the slope seemed fit to stretch forever across the yellowed fields. The faint hint of night sounds tested the air on the eastern slopes. A breeze from over by China Lake ruffled the grassy hilltop. Sundry took note of a carriage, though not the open chaise he was looking for, heading north and raising dust past the western perimeter of the pond.

"Mail stage," said Henry Schmidt. About ten or eleven, he was the picture of bucolic youth with brown boots and overalls and an old white shirt, a hat that had once belonged to his father, perhaps, and a stem of June grass in his mouth. Sundry thought he knew the fellow well. "What's your business over *there?*" asked the boy.

"I'm not entirely sure," admitted Sundry. "A friend of mine is there."

"With the Normells or the Droones?"

"Does it matter?"

Maven was gazing with such apparent awe at the pond that the boy reasonably thought the man must see something to warrant the expression. "I don't know if it does," said Henry, who stood beside Maven and squinted against the afternoon light.

"They have an odd character hereabouts, I'm told," said Sundry. He was rubbing Lillie down with handfuls of wadded grass.

"They're talked about, for sure." Henry couldn't see what Maven seemed to be looking at, so he pulled another stem of grass and fiddled with it. "People say they're witches."

"Oh, my!" said Maven.

Sundry did not evidence any skepticism or even any very strong opinion about this. To say that someone was a witch was not necessarily to say that they truly had any supernatural powers, though the implication was perhaps not far behind. Witch folk were not uncommon in the old hamlets, even in that recent generation, but they were often identified under other callings—herb doctors, people with second sight and evil eyes; even certain established churches had members with *gifts* that were not so far off from strange practices otherwise frowned upon. Earlier in the day, he had guessed at just such a reputation for the Droones and Normells while hearing about the two clans from the farmers at the stone wall.

"They call themselves dowsers," said Henry. "They do have a talent for finding water, I guess. And other things."

"Dowsers?" said Sundry. "Really?" Mr. Normell had said that *he* was looking for a dowser.

"Their old folks sleep all winter, like squirrels."

"That might be convenient."

"They call it *hand sleep*."

Sundry had heard similar tales of families in Edgecomb, but from years ago in his grandfather's day. The elderly members of a household were put into a state of *winter sleep* by a means some called 'the laying on of hands.' Then the old people were wrapped in quilts and put in the cellar like cord wood or a sack of potatoes. It meant fewer mouths to feed through the lean months and in the spring old Aunt Mabel or Granny Skyler would be revived and refreshed for having slept through the winter doldrums. Sundry had never put much stock in such stories, but that didn't mean he cherished walking among people they were told about.

"You don't seem too worried," said the boy with a grin.

"Is there anything else I should know?" asked Sundry.

The boy shook his head and Sundry liked him. There were some folk who would have made a hair-raising tale of it, but Henry Schmidt only chuckled. "Dad says it's just a pond and a wood and people living in it."

Sundry nodded. It was difficult to reconcile any sense of threat or danger with the scene before him. And yet, he wondered why Mr. Normell would take the trouble to run off with the Rings but first make certain that Sundry knew where they were going. And why had Mr. Normell asked after a dowser if his entire clan were famous for the gift?

"They've been *out* on the pond a lot the past few days," said the boy.

"Is that unusual?"

"People noticed it."

Sundry nodded. "Whoever owns this hill," he said, "I trust he won't mind if Maven and I sit down on it and take a meal."

"Old Wilbur Post," said the boy, "and he won't much care."

The travelers had stopped in China long enough for Sundry to pick up some sustenance at the local grocer's, and the sacks hanging from Lillie's saddle were proof enough of the dangers inherent in shopping on an empty stomach. "Crackers and canned herring?" he asked the boy.

Henry Schmidt laughed. "They'll be looking for me at the dinner table," he said, presumably, the intimation being, with something more to his taste.

"Pickles?" said Sundry. "Moxie? Canned biscuits and jam? I even thought to buy a can opener."

"*Did* you?" said Maven.

Henry Schmidt waved as he descended the low hill to the road, then said "Good luck finding your friend," and waved again as he crossed an angle of field and took the north road in the direction the mail stage had gone. While Lillie and Topper contentedly pulled grass, Sundry opened the sacks and picked through his purchases. He tossed Maven his can opener and a can of sardines.

The noisy confluence of afternoon and evening rose up around them—the birds and creatures of day saying good night and their nocturnal counterparts rousing themselves with the frog boom, the nighthawk's squeaky gate cry, and what Sundry thought was the bark of a fox. The blackflies had retired, and the breeze was enough to ward off mosquitoes, though a vigorous fly, buzzing in the lee of the horse's broad sides, did its best to annoy.

While he ate, Sundry wondered what lay beyond the pond and within the woods. Young Henry Schmidt said that *they* had been out on the pond lately, without being specific between Droones and Normells, and deemed this unusual enough to have noticed it. He imagined Jeffrey Normell driving Melanie and her father in among those woods to the shore of that pond, and a wave of uneasiness washed over him.

It was such an odd business, to roam off with an ailing drunk and his six-year-old kid, that he could hardly imagine a suitable motive for it. If there had been a single added degree of menace to the affair, he might have looked up the local authorities, but however badly the man was ailing, Burne Ring would be deemed sufficient to his own choices, and of course, Melanie would come under her father's heading.

But there *was* a degree of menace to it, if only the sort that is lured by negligence. If Burne Ring up and died, which seemed not unlikely, what would become of the little girl among strangers and under the aegis of a man who would steal her and her father away in the first place?

Sundry had decided to approach Dutten (as Henry deemed it) after sunset. He was unsure about steering through unfamiliar woods at night, but the moon's attenuated disk was already pale in the east and would not be setting till well after midnight. The sky was clear, and he expected he would have some light to go by. He was more uncertain still of bringing Maven Flyce with him.

"Do you think you should stay up here, Maven?" asked Sundry, "or back down in the village while I go looking for the Rings?"

"I'd better go with you," said Maven, looking wide-eyed and serious. "I promised the Sparks I'd look after them, and I'm awful sorry I fell asleep. Horace promised them I could do it, too."

Sundry nodded. "I guess if *Horace* promised," he said with some irony.

"Oh, yes," said Maven. "He did." Maven seemed to be gaping at a cloud that hung over the darkening east, but Sundry wondered if he was just thinking hard, or remembering, or wondering about something not plain before them.

It was too simple to say that Maven Flyce was simple, unless it was meant as praise. He was not complex by the common gauge of the world, but Sundry had watched him handle Topper with kindness and even deference, and the man with the remarkable cowlick was determined to fulfill his duty, though it was not self-imposed or even entirely comprehended.

"Have you known Horace a long time?" asked Sundry.

"My goodness!" said Maven. Sundry waited for more, but the fellow only continued to gape at the horizon and just when Sundry had grown accustomed to the lack of reply, Maven added, "I was having a terrible day. Poppa died, and they drove me out where we lived and never told me where they buried him. I slept some under a bridge and found a thing to eat here and there, till someone thought I might find something to do in Portland." Maven thought about this for a while, or perhaps he needed to recoup his thoughts and his breath. Sundry had never heard him say so much in one draw.

"I hadn't a notion those fellows were stealing chickens," said Maven apologetically. "Goodness' sakes!" He shook his head. "Goodness' sakes! And I would have returned that milk bucket, once I got my foot unstuck, and I would have helped put the fence back together, too! But that farmer was some angry! Goodness, didn't Horace laugh!"

"Horace was there?" said Sundry.

"'You just leave old bucket-foot be,' he said to the fellow. I was so astonished! He was talking about *me*," Maven helpfully explained. "Then he gave the farmer an extra jar of rum and told him to call it good if he ever wanted to see any more. 'Don't worry about that bucket,' he told me. 'I paid for that, too.' Then he told a poem about me and the bucket, but I can't remember it."

It was a picture. Sundry wondered how long ago this event had transpired. He guessed that Maven was thirty years old or more, but the incident with the chicken thieves and the milk bucket might have happened two decades or two years ago.

"And off we went," said Maven. "I couldn't have imagined!"

"I guess none of us could have imagined Horace McQuinn," said Sundry. Horace of course would have denied the whole tale with a dismissive wave of the hand and a rude face.

"*I* didn't!" said Maven. "I was so amazed!" He shook his head in awe.

He gaped at the horizon, and again Sundry wondered what the fellow might be thinking about.

"Look at that cloud!" said Maven.

42. Dutten Lane

Lillie had let out an unladylike snort, which may have wakened Sundry, or it may have been the mosquitoes that roused him. His back itched in several places that were complex to reach, and he stood up and rubbed his shoulder blades against Lillie's saddle till he felt a little relief. The air had cooled considerably, and by the light of the moon's portion he could see mist rise out of the hollows and skate the waters of Dutten Pond. Beyond Lillie, Topper stood at his tether, staring off in the direction of the pond, and further on lay Maven, huddled in sleep.

Shaking off an errant shiver, Sundry stroked the mare's neck, then gathered up their small bit of gear. Maven sat up and gaped about confusedly till he remembered where he was, and then he only looked a little startled.

Sundry was tying the remains of their provisions on Lillie's saddle, and looking at Maven over the mare's back, he said, "It might be best if one of us stays here while the other one goes down to find out what the story is with this Mr. Normell."

Maven's mouth hung open, and his eyebrows came together in a frown of concentration. "OK," he said. "I'll go down. Where did they go?"

This of course was not what Sundry had in mind. "On second thought," he said. He could hardly imagine leaving Maven here alone, so once he had finished packing, they led the horses down to the road. The animals had been standing in the cooling air while the men dozed, and Sundry thought they might be a little stiff; but they came willingly enough. He spoke quietly to Lillie when they reached the bottom of the hill, gently rubbing her shoulder. She nudged him, and he was glad to have her steady company.

Sundry Moss was no more than ordinarily superstitious, and by day he wasn't even *that*. He was as familiar with tales of herb folk and witches as any country fellow would be. There had been people up Mount Hunger way, in Edgecomb, in his grandfather's day (or so people said) who had practiced something like this laying on of hands that Henry Schmidt had talked about—putting the elder folk to sleep and rolling them in carpets on cellar shelves to wait out the winter. And there was also a stand of lilacs, up near Edgecomb Heights, that bloomed almost blood red every June, and the story was that a great herb man had been killed there by outlaws back in the days when old Parson Leach was still roaming the countryside.

Sundry was not unfamiliar with such tales, and if he took them "with a grain of salt," like any good Yankee, he still didn't discard them; it was hard to know when you might find use for the oddest item. Those stories lived inside him, dormant for the most part and on most days like something inherited rather than learned. A fascination, a predilection, and an apprehension of the mystic walk with the race of man, and our most practical associates can experience something dark and primitive when they are alone in the early mists of night, walking the vicinity of purported haunts and spellmakers.

Then again, Sundry had been known to say, "Just because you can swallow it, that doesn't mean it's good for you," and he reminded himself of this as he neared the edge of the meadow between the road and the pond.

Farther along his present track, there was a road entering Dutten Wood, but he wondered if they would be wise to split some of that distance and ride the diagonal through the meadows and past the water. He thought the horses would mind their feet getting damp a lot less than he and Maven would their boots, so he swung atop Lillie and waited for Maven to mount before taking them into the field.

Lillie was a surefooted creature and not without her own foresight, so Sundry gave the mare a general direction and allowed her the specifics. Her broad chest broke the rising mists, and he had the illusion of riding above a thin cloud. A loon laughed out on the pond and something moved past them, shushing the grasses beneath the fog. The pond gleamed dully in the moonlight, and the trees, as they approached, had the appearance of a solid battlement. He thought he had outsmarted himself when he came to a stone wall ranked with bushes on either side; but close to the pond, mounting over a stand of granite, he found a break among the rocks, and it was not long before they stepped onto the path that would take them into Normell territory.

Sundry peered up this lane and toward the main road. It was not thickly wooded here, and the moon leaked through a latticework of limbs and leaves to dapple the ground, and beyond the silhouettes of Maven and Topper, the end of the path glowed like a dimly lighted room. There was a gate by the main road that they had avoided, but he thought he caught the brief movement of a shadow there. In the other direction, further down the lane, which did in fact descend, the way appeared murky and dense.

Sundry wasn't very sure what he planned to accomplish; probably he would simply get a sense of who and what was down here before he finally did the only thing he could think of, and that was to knock on the first likely door. He encouraged Lillie into the greater darkness.

It was a beautiful night, cool after a warm day, the damp, mist-haunted air rich with smells from tree and pond. It was sound that warned him first, but with the clop of eight hooves to account for, he had to pull up and wait for Maven to do the same before he could be sure of several deep thumps separate from Topper's shuffling feet. A human cough from among the trees touched at the back of his neck like a cold hand.

Maven did not ask why they had stopped but leaned down as if he might hide behind his horse's head. Another mount was moving from the direction of the main road. Sundry resisted the urge to look over his shoulder and was estimating the distance between themselves and this other rider when another set of hoofbeats sounded hollowly ahead of them. He didn't notice that the immediate woods were quiet of any natural sounds till he heard, from a relative distance, the call of a whippoorwill.

The horse ahead of him let out a blustery snort, and Lillie jerked her head up. Sundry's heart raced, and he looked back the way they had come. A tall, amorphous figure occluded the pallid light from the far end of the lane, stopped after another step or two, and sat there, eerily silent. The horse before them stopped as well, and now there came the sound of someone, maybe two or three *someones*, walking.

"Hello?" he called into the dark of the lane.

"Hello," answered Maven. "I'm right here."

"We're not alone, Maven," said Sundry. "Hello?"

"Mr. Moss?" came the unexpected reply.

After a moment he said, "Yes, it is."

"It's good of you to come," came the reply from that nebulous shape, but there was an edge to the voice that belied the friendly welcome. The other rider moved his horse closer, and Sundry had the impression of a younger person, tall and thin; then the mental echo of that voice came back to him, and he realized that he was speaking to a woman.

"Mr. Moss?" came another voice, but from further down the path. Several people were walking toward him, flanking a third rider and making no pretense of silence. The strangeness of it all had gathered enough force inside Sundry so that he was on the edge of telling Maven to ride up the lane and get away as best he could. Then he turned to speak and saw the blue metal gleam of moonlight on a gun barrel wrapped in the shadow of the mounted figure behind.

"Mr. Moss?" came the voice again.

"Yes," said Sundry.

A broad shape flickered beneath the specks of moonlight, and Sundry had quick glimpses of a round, familiar sort of face. "You met my uncle Jeffrey earlier today," said this person—a man of about Sundry's years, and twice his thickness. There was a forced heartiness in the greeting that reminded Sundry of Jeffrey Normell and also gave him a sense of imminent hazard.

"I believe I did," said Sundry.

"We're glad you've come," said this fellow as he laid a hand on Lillie's bridle. "We've been expecting you."

43. What Abner Saw at the Fair

"And then you've found it," said the fellow. "Fiddler's Green!"

"Well, I never!" said Mrs. Cook. She served Robin Oig another help-ing of beef brisket and potatoes, then ladled out half a pint of her county fair–winning green beans, canned last summer and cooked up this evening in pork scraps. Robin Oig smacked his lips. He was powerfully famished and had said so several times, even after he had put away enough to feed two or three rugged men.

Mr. Cook leaned back from the table and folded his arms before him. What he needed now was his pipe. Beetle, their black and white dog of uncertain parentage, shifted at the farmer's feet. "Fiddler's Green," said Mr. Cook without much more than a little humor lighting his eyes. "I do believe that some farmers have reached the same spot from the other end."

"Oh?" said the sailor. He was surprised to hear it.

"You take up a hoe, you see, or a pitchfork—"

"Abner!" said his wife.

"It's true!"

"*I* never heard of it."

Their son, Abijah, chuckled.

"I promise you," said Abner, one hand up as a sign of his solemn honor. Robin Oig looked ready to be convinced.

"Abner!" said Mrs. Cook again.

Abner laughed. "You remember old Curtis Hanke, over at Palermo."

"No, I don't, particularly."

"He used to sing a song, you know. Let's see. How did it go?" After mum-bling to himself for a bit, he rendered the tune in a serviceable baritone.

> *Oh, I was off to Fiddler's Green,*
> *To Fiddler's Green I boldly stepped,*
> *And never veered from off that path,*
> *For any bother once except—*

There was the time I smelled a pie
A'cooling on a windowsill;
A pleasant widow baked it up,
And, so, I bode with her until—

"Abner!" said Helen, but her husband only laughed and sang some more.

I was off to Fiddler's Green,
To Fiddler's Green I set my prow,
And never steered but toward that end,
When one odd day, I don't know how—

A flash of ankle caught my eye,
A pretty maid stuck up a tree;
I helped her down and bode awhile,
Till one bright day she looked for me—

But I was off to Fiddler's Green,
To Fiddler's Green I took my way;
And kept my bearings straight and true,
And walked the course till came the day— ...

He stumbled on this last verse, which gave his wife a place to put her foot down and look unpersuaded by his melodic endeavors. "All right, all right!" she said, but she was laughing underneath the grim expression.

"You see, *I* don't have to look for Fiddler's Green," said the farmer. He was a little carried away with his own performance, and when he said, "I've got everything I need right here," he gave his wife an affectionate swat on the backside and received, for his troubles, a portentous rendition of his name as well as a grim expression that concealed very little laughter at all. "Guess it's my turn to milk the cow," said Abner suddenly, and he leaped from his seat and grabbed his hat on his way out the door. Beetle sprang up and clattered after him.

"I never!" said Helen Cook again, and without thinking she patted that portion of herself that her husband had assailed. "Pay him never mind, Mr. Oig," she told their guest, but the sailor was tucked back into his supper and caught little of what had just occurred.

It was Abijah who watched Robin Oig with the *loudest* appearance of doubt, although his interest in their guest was more amused than his sense of logic offended. The Cooks were straightforward people but could put up with a little nonsense if it was delivered with sincerity. They may have felt sorry for the man or perhaps had the capacity to admire windmill tilting. Ab had greeted Robin's travel plans with doubt and a guffaw or two. His father had prodded the guest into explaining the intricacies of discovering his intended destination. Mrs. Cook simply fed him. She may have been fueling his fire or attempting to quiet it by stuffing him, but in the end she was more concerned that he was set on following the mysterious Mr. Moss (as she thought of this man, since she hadn't met him) to Dutten and the Normells and Droones.

"I've had an *accountability* about that fellow since I first met him this morning," Robin Oig replied. It did seem like a lot of miles and steps since he left Portland, and the roundabout nature of his wanderings had only managed to convince him that following Mr. Moss was the wise thing to do.

"He knew how to build a stone wall," said Ab.

Robin Oig didn't. He had helped the Cooks move a large piece of rock, but the sailor did not have Mr. Moss's eye. Robin had lifted the boulder onto the stone wall and propped it up with some smaller rocks, then stepped back to survey his work. Even he saw that his contribution looked more like accident than art, and he had frowned and pouted till the Cook men muckled onto the boulder and set it right.

"You wouldn't know there was a right way to set one stone atop another," said the sailor at the dinner table.

"The right way, the wrong way, and *my* way," said Ab.

Robin understood this; it might explain what he was doing in Vassalboro that evening. Helen Cook herself rarely followed a recipe to the letter.

"In the morning I'll show you a shortcut for catching up with Mr. Moss," promised Ab, who had felt his own accountability about the two wanderers.

The meal accomplished one thing, and that was to exhaust their guest's remaining powers. He yawned at the table and never thought to excuse himself. "I'd better search out your hayloft," he said. "I can't tell you when I last ate like this," he added without specifying whether he was referring to the quantity or the quality of the meal. "I am obliged," he said as he rose from the table, and with a simple good night, retrieved his oar, which was laid out in the hall, and tromped outside.

Inside the barn, the smell of the cow, a calf, and Cram was a bit like too much spice in the air for Robin Oig, or at least like the sort of spice he was unaccustomed to. Salt and seaweed, fish and tar he wouldn't take note of, but a horse clopping past, even in the open air, smelled of earth and greenery and labor. He sneezed first thing, and Beetle, lying near by, let out a startled *woof.* Abner Cook said, "Bless you," and leaned down so that he could regard the man from under the cow while he milked her. "So, what's driven you to it, Mr. Oig?" he inquired.

Robin frowned, listening to the rhythmic squirt of milk in the bucket. He said, "There does seem to be a lot of fussing about."

"Oh?" The farmer didn't catch his meaning.

"You see, on board they're always fussing about with sheets and halyards and the like, and in port they're always fussing about with laws and regulation, and excuse me for saying so, but even out here there seems to be some fussing about with rocks and cows."

Abner straightened his back with a crackle or two and laid his cheek against the Jersey's side. "A man has to make his living," said the farmer without having taken any offense.

"I suppose that's generally the case," said Robin Oig, but he had not thought about it very much before agreeing.

"There was a fellow, come to the fair last August," said Abner, "had himself a *perpetual motion* machine. There was a wheel going round, and it pushed a gear here and a lever there that lifted a ball bearing a step at a time up a little ramp, and when that ball bearing reached the top of the ramp, it slipped onto a little dumbwaiter, you might call it, and turned the wheel, by pulley and lever, riding to the bottom of the ramp again, and the whole thing just kept up—wheel and ramp, wheel and ramp. Perpetual motion, he called it. I said I hoped it didn't get away from him somehow as it didn't appear to need him to start *or* stop."

"What did he say?" asked the sailor.

"Oh, I said it to myself, really. Or to Helen perhaps."

"Something had to keep it going." Robin pulled on his beard.

"Yes, *I* thought so."

"I'd like to see that."

"Maybe there'll be one where you're heading," said Abner without irony.

Robin only nodded and looked for the ladder that would reach him up to the hayloft. He sneezed again, and Beetle *woofed.*

"Beetle," said the farmer, and "Bless you," again to Robin Oig.

The sailor thanked him as he climbed. Settling himself in the hay above, he went into a fit of sneezing till the dust had settled. A whippoor-will called from the lilacs in front of the house. The rhythmic sound of milking altered subtly as the milk bucket filled.

A powerful snore rose up from the loft.

Abner Cook set the full bucket aside, then grained the animals and spent a few moments *making* of Cram in his stable. He listened to the res-onant snores from above and hummed to himself the tune he had sung in the kitchen. Then he took up his lantern and the milk bucket and, with Beetle close upon his heels, went across to the house.

44. On the Cusp of Knowing

"We're glad you've come," said Jeffrey Normell when Sundry Moss and Maven Flyce came riding, under escort, out of the darkness and onto the lawn before the summerhouse at Dutten Pond. The round-faced fellow and his round-faced relatives had not been expecting anyone beside Sundry, but Jeffrey hid it well. "We've been expecting you," he said.

"Yes, I know," said Sundry flatly. Whatever *he* had expected, it had not been this solemn crowd—man and woman and all ages down to the youngest child still in her mother's arms—standing about in their shirts and ties, their linen dresses and practical hats, as if they were Fourth of July picnickers at dark, waiting, though with apparent dread, for the fire-works display.

"Oh," said Mr. Normell, "very good," but was at a loss for further statement or deed. He appeared to infer something deeper from Sundry's reply.

"I'm so surprised!" said Maven, looking about at the staring crowd.

The moon was not high enough to send its unhindered glow beyond the trees, but lamplight filled the yard and dotted the way past the shore to a separate group of people some distance away. Boats, half beached, swayed with the vague movement of the pond or the wind. Sundry looked for the Rings, and particularly for Melanie, pausing once or twice upon the face of a similarly sized child. Jeffrey Normell followed his gaze, look-ing abashed, but another man—wider and more red-faced than Jeffrey—approached Sundry's horse and attempted a placid expression.

"Where are Mr. Ring and his child?" said Sundry, hoping to garner some advantage by the first demand. There was no guessing how much these people had learned about Melanie, but intuition favored keeping secrets.

"They are in—" began the larger Mr. Normell, "inside," he finished, but with little conviction. "I am Charles Normell, Mr. Moss," he said after gathering his thoughts with a nervous cough. He began to offer his hand, but hesitated, and Sundry did not encourage the familiarity by either gesture or expression. "There has been an unfortunate turn of affairs," said the man.

"That is what brought me here," said Sundry, making use of his height upon the horse to *look down* upon Charles Normell and the people behind him.

"The man is dead, Mr. Moss," said a tall woman of indeterminate years and polar appearance to Charles Normell.

"Oh, my!" came Maven's voice.

Expected news can yet startle a person, but Sundry's face betrayed more anger than surprise. He left a hard gaze on the woman to study the crowd but received only blank or, at best, uncertain stares. He wondered if such tidings might merely be a means of keeping the man in question out of his sight, and he said quietly, "Where's Mailon?"

"This is Mrs. Bridey Droone," said Charles Normell, as if he hadn't heard Sundry's query. It was odd how no one else stirred or shifted.

"Where's the boy?"

"He's with his father," said Jeffrey after a general look of inquiry proceeded from face to face.

"I am amazed!" said Maven.

"Mr. Moss," said Charles Normell, after a brief and puzzled look at the man with the cowlick.

"Where are they?" said Sundry.

"Yes, in due time," replied Charles, but several others glanced guiltily toward the house.

Sundry swung a leg up over Lillie's saddle and dropped to the ground in front of the man. He kept Charles's eyes locked in his own stare till he had passed the man. The crowd had been silent, but now a murmur followed him, as did several senior members of both the thin clan and the thick. Sundry walked to the house and mounted the front steps, but here he showed the first sign of hesitation; he couldn't say if he would be doing Maven a disservice by leading him in with him or leaving him outside and to his own devices. When Sundry glanced back at his traveling companion,

Maven was gaping with evident astonishment at the back of Topper's head.

The house was informally arranged with a kitchen at its front, an open stairway, and a pair of rooms at the back. The door to the left-hand room was open, and the space beyond unlit; a pale line of light shone beneath the right-hand door, and Sundry rapped twice at this entrance before he heard a small voice. Shaking with complex doubt and emotion, he steadied his hand on the knob before looking over his shoulder at the small crowd.

Charles Normell was attempting to form a cogent remark, but Mrs. Droone simply said, "We must speak with you, Mr. Moss."

"That much we do agree on," replied Sundry, and he went inside, closing the door on a sudden uproar behind him.

Of the two of them the little girl had the most reason to look surprised and appeared least so. As it happens, there is a difference between faith and expectation. "I am sorry," said Sundry, just loud enough to be heard above the ruckus on the other side of the door.

Melanie shook her head slowly, her eyes wide.

"I suppose that's small comfort," he admitted. "I shouldn't have let you out of my sight." Sundry stopped. He had the presentiment of seeing something beyond the realm of the natural and the canny. Stretched upon the bed was the form of Burne Ring. Melanie sat in a chair beside him, her shadow large against the wall. The little girl's hand was rested in her father's, and as Sundry watched, the larger fingers appeared to grip hers lightly.

The scene had been suggestive of every terror advertised by temperance preachers and every sharp pang of melancholy and suffering sought after by writers of cautionary tales. Now Sundry was not sure what he was seeing. Several thoughts went through him about the *clutch of death* and the *rigors* of the deceased. He heard that strange grunting noise—once, twice, three times—that Burne Ring sometimes accomplished when he took a breath, and he approached the bed to lean over the ashen face. "They said . . ." Sundry's voice trailed off. It seemed indelicate, somehow, to finish the sentence while he was standing next to the man.

"They think he's dead," whispered Melanie.

"Not yet," said Burne Ring quietly.

"Apparently not," said Sundry.

"They think he's dead," Melanie said again.

"Where did *you* get to?" rumbled Burne Ring without opening his eyes.

"They *said* you'd be coming," said Melanie. "Mr. Normell said so."

There was, in this statement, a hint of the little girl's odd faith in him, and Sundry was reinvested with the strangeness and possible danger of their circumstances. "Has anyone told you why Mr. Normell brought you here?"

"He just said you'd be coming."

Sundry couldn't imagine what he had stepped into. "What would they want with me?" he wondered. He looked back at the door and attempted to pry a single voice from the heated discussion beyond.

"There's a lot of people out there," she hushed. "They seem awfully worried about something."

Sundry thought they seemed more frightened than worried.

"Where's that bottle?" asked Burne. He was remembering that there had been a bottle in his coat pocket.

Sundry laid a finger aside of his nose and said quietly, "Let's not disabuse them of the notion that you've left us."

Burne Ring opened one eye and gave Sundry a doubtful glare.

Sundry leaned close to the man and said in a sharp whisper, "Do you know what we're doing here?"

The man on the bed said nothing.

"Then for the sake of your daughter, if not for yours or mine, you had better play along." Sundry looked at the wide-eyed, openmouthed face of Melanie Ring, and his heart went out of him. "What they don't know can't hurt us," he said with more confidence than he felt. "You will be Mailon for a little while longer."

"Is Mr. Flyce still on the train?" asked the little girl.

"He's just outside," said Sundry. He went to the door and tried to sense what was happening beyond it. The angry words had diminished, and Charles was saying something in a low voice that Sundry could not quite catch, even when he pressed his ear to the door. When he did return to the front room, Sundry shut the door behind him, as if in respect for the dead and the mourning. The crowd awaiting him looked alert and anxious. "If someone would get that chaise turned around," he said, "we will be leaving."

"Not yet, Mr. Moss," said Charles Normell. "We have an important task for you here, and you are not going anywhere till we have had use of you."

The faces before him were implacable—apprehensive yet unyielding. Sundry recalled what his father had often said: that there was no more dangerous dog than a frightened one. He was a little frightened himself. He was not getting past these people, and certainly not with a child in his keeping. It was time to discover what they wanted of him.

"What am I dowsing for?" he said.

Charles Normell's head rose a fraction of an inch. Others seemed surprised. Mrs. Droone stood by the front door, and she reached out to swing it open even as the crowd parted for Sundry and Charles.

"Come," said the big man, "and we will tell you."

45. One Why but Not Another

With the moon on the ascent and lanterns lining the walk from the summerhouse to the pond, Sundry thought the night well lit—and well populated with the distinctive face of the Normell on the one side, and that of the Droone on the other. There were a hundred people or more—middle-aged men and women standing in conference, parents with their children and young men with their hands in their pockets. Those near the end of the line leaned forward to peer up the human corridor.

Maven was still on Topper, looking more surprised than frightened, and Sundry gave him a significant look—one that Sundry hoped would indicate the need to beat feet and rouse the neighbors. Maven leaned forward to see Sundry's face more clearly and almost fell out of the saddle.

"Help the gentleman down," said Charles to the crowd in general. Someone took hold of Topper's halter, and two or three men pulled rather than helped Maven off the horse. Charles stepped up to Sundry's shoulder and surveyed the hushed crowd. "Our troubles began down by the pond, Mr. Moss. Your friend can stay here. Come with me."

Mrs. Droone walked behind them, and the crowd came next. Patches of moonlight grew broader as they approached the water; from across the pond, Sundry heard peepers and frogs, but the near shore was oddly silent. The boats had not been entirely abandoned, but their lanterns were extinguished, and the figures left along the gunnels were faceless in the relative dark.

Reaching the very edge of the water, not far from that imaginary line that must divide the Normell Acres from those of the Droone family, Charles took a lamp from someone and held it over the ground ahead of him. "It began here," he said. "Or at least what we know of it." Charles looked at Bridey Droone. "Or at least what *I* know of it."

"Keep something in reserve, Charles," said the tall woman.

The large man ignored this. "Four days ago," he continued, "a member of our family—a Normell—disappeared, and also a Droone. Two young women, Beatrice Normell and Adina Droone, disappeared that morning, and the last we know of them was here in the sand."

"Footprints," said Sundry, though he could not see any in particular that told the tale.

"Ending here at the edge of the water," said Charles.

"There has been foul play, Mr. Moss," said Mrs. Droone.

"Has there?" said Sundry.

"Their footprints ended here," said Charles again. "The boat that one of them escaped in was found on the opposite shore."

"And the footprints on the opposite shore?" inquired Sundry.

"It's a grassy bank on that side."

Sundry looked across the water and considered the places where the pond was dark with the shadow of the farther bank and the trees. The moon washed one tall elm in its cold glow, and the spectral image of this tree's crown made something like a face in the water. "But foul play?" said Sundry.

"It is our belief," said Mrs. Droone, "that my granddaughter was murdered by Beatrice Normell, that the murderess dumped the body overboard, weighted down with stones, and escaped across the pond in the boat."

"It is *our* contention," said Charles, "that my niece was murdered and similarly disposed of by Adina Droone."

"Did either of them have reason to be out slaying their neighbors?" asked Sundry, and when he received what amounted to puzzled looks, he added, "Aside from one being a Normell and the other a Droone."

"We older folk," said Charles, "practice what might be termed a guarded truce between us, but the younger people sometimes become hotheaded."

"Beatrice," said Bridey Droone, "and, to be truthful, Adina both were quick-tempered."

"They were zealous in their devotion to family," said Charles.

"They were reckless and wanton in their anger," corrected the woman. "I myself have told Adina to curb her tongue *and* her actions."

"I am thinking she didn't pay heed," said Charles.

"*I* am thinking that *you* should have so instructed your niece."

"It's a matter for the law," said Sundry.

"It is a matter between Normell and Droone," said Charles.

Sundry took in those faces lit by Charles's lantern. "It's a matter for the law," he said, "and that's the end of it."

"The law, Mr. Moss," said Mrs. Droone, "is not so fond of either of us."

"To tell you the truth, ma'am," said Sundry, "you haven't gone a long way toward winning *my* heart. If the law likes neither of you, then you can count on it being impartial. I can only guess what you want me for, but hiding a crime from the law is a crime itself."

"We have reasons for separating from the law, Mr. Moss," said Charles Normell, "*and* from society in general."

"Yes, well, divided you fall, you know."

"Mr. Moss!" spat Bridey Droone. "We are not amused by your attempts at levity."

"Mrs. Droone, I should think you'd be pleased if I found *anything* amusing at this point." Sundry leaned forward just a trace, leading with his left shoulder like a man who is ready to take a poke at someone. The image of a young woman's body tangled in the weeds and rot at the bottom of this pond had shaken him, but he was resolved to show nothing but anger and dissent. He leveled an eye on the tall woman, who didn't move but looked less indignant and more uncertain. "Perhaps," said Sundry, "it's time you tell me what you think I can do for you and *then* why you think I would be disposed to do it."

"You are a dowser, Mr. Moss," said Jeffrey Normell, who had fidgeted his way to the fore of the crowd.

"I told you I'd taken a lesson or two from my uncle," corrected Sundry.

"I sense that you are modest about your abilities, sir."

"I assure you, my abilities are at best modest."

"We wouldn't trust someone who came in here boasting of what he could do," said Mrs. Droone.

"Then I've taken the wrong tack, haven't I. I thought *you* folk were the potent dowsers."

"And so we are," said the woman, but quickly and almost as if Sundry might doubt it.

"But what would finding water have to do with your problem?" he asked.

"As you very well know," said Jeffrey, "dowsing is efficacious for more than discovering water."

"I've heard of the odd fellow searching for gold and silver with a dowsing rod, but I don't know that any of them is rich."

"It's searching for something *in* the water, as well as finding water itself, that is the dowser's strongest suit," said Charles.

"I was afraid you were going to say that," said Sundry, and he was, though he didn't look it.

"We need you to find the body," said Charles.

Sundry looked out over the dark surface of the pond, and a curious presentiment about what was out there, or perhaps *where*, touched him so that his heart flinched. "It does seem like shipping coals to Newcastle."

"*We* can't do it," said Mrs. Droone.

"And why is that?"

"That should be only too apparent."

"It's not that we *can't*," said Jeffrey, as if he were correcting a student, "but that neither can allow the *other* to attempt it."

"Because you don't trust one another?"

There was no immediate reply, but the Droones and the Normells did each regard their opposites with obvious *dis*trust.

"There seem to be so many ways out of this," said Sundry, "that there must be something more."

Charles Normell and then Mrs. Droone blinked at him. "Whoever found the body first could hide it from anyone else," said Charles, and Jeffrey added, "There are ways of preventing the next person from finding anything, Mr. Moss."

"A spell, you're saying," said Sundry, barely withholding a note of scorn. It was the first plain suggestion of anything like true witchcraft or magic, and several people in the lamplight started.

There were those, however, who did not flinch, and Jeffrey actually smiled, saying with a graceful indicative gesture, "It's like brushing footprints from the snow." Pleasure touched his round face, as if he were calling upon a cherished memory.

They're as odd as owls, thought Sundry. He hadn't realized how close the night had grown. Sweat stood out on his brow, and he chanced revealing his nerves by producing a handkerchief and brushing it over his forehead. "So you mean for me to go out in a boat and dowse the pond for a body?"

"There are springs and currents under there that might shift an object all around," said Jeffrey. Something about his statement disconcerted Charles, and he raised the back of his hand toward Jeffrey, who pulled his head back like a pigeon.

"We will send someone out with you to row," said Mrs. Droone.

"A Normell and a Droone," said Sundry.

"Several of us will be observing from other boats," said Charles, recovering himself. "It is that simple."

"Simple doesn't describe." With a raised eyebrow Sundry challenged Mrs. Droone to make something of his *levity*, however little of it he actually felt. They had explained the reason they needed his assistance, but still had not touched on why they thought he would offer it—or, in other words, *What would they do if he didn't?* Taking stock of the frightened faces in the crowd, he suspected that this came under the heading of *"questions you may not want answered."*

"Mr. Moss?" said Mrs. Droone.

Something else had just occured to Sundry. "If you don't trust one another," he said to the woman, "how is that you let a Normell go looking for someone and not a Droone."

"There *is* a Droone out looking now," she said.

"Someone you trust?" asked Sundry of Charles.

"My nephew, Burnham," said the woman sharply.

"And is he zealous in his devotion to family?" said Sundry. "Or maybe he's smart and won't come back."

"Your friend, Mr. Moss," said the woman with a nod up the shore toward Maven. "And the boy."

It was as blunt a threat as had been offered, and perhaps it was time for Sundry to tell them that several people knew where he and Maven were (three, at any rate). Caution suggested that he keep this to himself a little longer and, to be truthful, he may have sinned in his fear of appearing fearful. He was fearful, even if he did not show it—of the crowd, which was so strange and so intent, and of what lay at the bottom of the pond. "Let's have done with it," he said.

The crowd let out a collective breath, but Charles said, "Not yet," and Mrs. Droone pronounced, "You will be more assured of success in the hours immediately preceding and following sunrise."

Sundry doubted it. "You will be able to watch me more closely with daylight on the way," he corrected. He shrugged. "It's the best time to go fishing," he said with a grim expression.

"It's a very similar phenomenon," said Jeffrey.

Sundry let it go. "In the meantime, my friend can go for the proper authorities to deal with Mr. Burne's body."

"No," said Charles.

Mrs. Droone's face was set in hard lines. "We've gone this far, Mr. Moss," she said. "We would not care to have your search interrupted."

"We suggest you take the time to rest up from your day," said Charles.

"You're not separating us from the boy," said Sundry.

Charles Normell and Bridey Droone considered this and one another.

"Take their horses up to the old house," said Charles to one of the Normell men standing near.

"*We'll* take his horse," said Bridey Droone. "You are showing him hospitality enough," and when Charles only frowned in reply, she added, "It's the least we can do."

"You see?" said Sundry dryly, though suppressing a shiver. "A little levity is a wonderful thing."

46. Moths Through a Window

Melanie sat by the wall, her hand in her father's open palm, and wondered, as countless minds have, what drives a moth to the flame that will sear its wings. Shadows trembled on the ceiling as two insects battered the lantern glass across the room, and she felt a pity for them.

Sometimes her father's hand trembled against hers, and perhaps only she could have felt it. The skin about his fingers was loose, as if his bones had shrunk, but his palm had a pleasant roughness about it, a signal to his daughter of what had been his working life on the day that she was born and in the days before their family had been carried away by influenza.

It was another derelict soul who told her, months ago, that her father had been the assistant to a chief mason, on his way to becoming a master of his craft. A spark of grace had touched Burne Ring from a clear blue sky—or a clouded one. He had been a chief in the making and there were homes within sight of Philbrook Morrell's grand ballroom windows that

Burne Ring had helped build, though they were not visible from the black room—from either black room he had recently inhabited. His daughter had seen their lofty chimneys from the waterfront roofs.

Burne's hand trembled against hers, and she could sense movement outside the house that seemed part and parcel with the beat of moth wings on the glass of the lantern across the room. She had heard some of the conversation from the front of the house and was worried that the Normells and Droones wouldn't let them leave. She was hungry but nurtured something stubborn that was ready to refuse anything from these people.

They had lacked sympathy for her father's apparent death, and Mr. Normell provided the bright flame of rum when the doctor said small beer. Melanie had decided not to like them very much. She was glad that Mr. Moss was here and sorry that he had to be, but she understood the force that brought him to Dutten Pond. Hadn't it brought Daniel Boone to the Congo to rescue his children from pirates? And hadn't it brought Wilma of the Mountains to Lake Moosehead, where she warned the Micmacs of the Mohawk army on the warpath? Timothy had told her so.

She left the bedside to blow out the lantern, and enough of the waxy moon found its way upon the braided rug so that she could find the nearest window sash and raise it, shuddering in its frame, till it banged against the jamb. She had not known how to lift a window until she came to live at the Faithful Mermaid, so all things seemed to have their reason. The night air cooled her face, and after a short while she felt something patter, almost like gratitude, past her cheek. She leaned over the sill and wondered why no one had come to investigate. Peering into the night, she saw the glimmer of many lanterns paling the trees from around the front of the house.

As the moths beat into the night, she had a terrible thought. She went back to her father and leaned over him, listening for a breath or sensing for a heartbeat. She held her mouth open, her eyes wide, and in the same moment that she caught a whisper of movement in his chest, she understood what surprising opportunity had revealed itself.

It was night but moonlit, and she had piloted darker places. It was lonely, but not as lonely as her sojourn among the drunks and transients, the broken men and hungry looks in the darker corners of the Portland waterfront.

The little clutch was at the other side of the bed, and she pulled from it several strange garments, which she laid on the counterpane. Melanie had been feeling less like Mailon in the past week or so, but perhaps not *this* much less. Mrs. Spark had given her a complete lesson in female attire, and especially the underthings, but the little girl had been more puzzled than enlightened. She thought it odd that she could live among people, half of them women, and not understand more of what was expected of her. She dared not dawdle; she did not want to be caught in the middle of her transformation, even by Mr. Moss. The thought in fact horrified her, and she felt a profound and previously silent modesty. Almost in panic, she hurried.

The clothes seemed peculiar and vulnerable, and she felt peculiar and vulnerable in them. The slip and petticoat were like a breath of wind, and the dress hardly more. It was not a cold night, but she was glad that the clutch produced a light coat to cover it all. The shoes were troublesome, more like slippers than proper footwear. In the guise of a boy she had traveled many a city mile in bare feet or barely shod; but in recent days she had worn a pair of Tim's old brogues, and she decided that these were more appropriate to an adventure. Even had she been aware of the incongruity of boy's shoes beneath a girl's dress she would not have changed her mind.

She put Tim's cap back on but thought better of it. The cap and the boys' clothes went into the clutch, and the clutch went under the bed. She went to the mirror on the dresser, where a shadow looked out from the glass; she ruffled her hair and made faces, hoping to squeeze more sight out of the darkness. It was hard to reconcile herself with the silhouette in the mirror; it made her satisfied and perplexed and daunted all at once, and if she had been old enough to think very far upon the subject, she might have been thankful not to have had much time, just then, to think about it at all.

Her father's clothes smelled smoky when she leaned over him, and the aura of rum hung upon his faint breath. She kissed him on his damp temple, something she had never done before. If she ever had a son, she thought, she would do that while he slept.

In another moment she was outside, having pulled the sash down as she touched the earth. She hunkered in a crouch, though she knew she mustn't hide or appear uncertain; true concealment would rely on being seen without being noticed. Hawk of the Hurons had walked among the Iroquois in just that manner. That's what Tim had told her.

"What are you doing here, Droone?" said a plump red-faced boy to

Melanie when she appeared from around the side of the summerhouse. "You had better get back down with the rest of you," he added belligerently.

She was pretty sure she could handle him in a fair fight and was tempted to throw a fist at his broad nose. Instead she moved closer to the center of the crowd, where Droone and Normell alike either avoided her or dismissed her by taking no notice. She looked more Droone than Normell—small and narrow—but there were a few exceptions to the Normell girth, and her hair was neither dark nor light but a medium brown. People of both sides imagined that their lack of recognition was simply a sign of her belonging to the *other* clan. One or two noticed her boy's shoes and scoffed at their neighbors' inability to dress their children. They looked no further.

Mr. Flyce was standing in the midst of the crowd, and Mr. Moss was walking back up the path from the pond with the two Normell men, Jeffrey and Charles, and the tall Mrs. Droone. Everyone seemed anxious that some agreement had been realized. Melanie searched for a neutral place among them, but this portion shifted as Normell, then Droone gave her the look to indicate she was standing on the wrong side of things. Every glance was a danger to her scheme, but she knew she must be seen by Mr. Moss, so that he would know where she had gone and what she was doing, and so that he would not suspect anyone else of making off with her.

It suddenly struck the little girl that he might not know her any more and her heart plummeted into a moment of icy fear and loss, as if she had died in her father's place, and were but a ghost and invisible even to those who cared about her.

But that look of loss on Melanie's face was what drew Sundry Moss's attention, and it was her strange resemblance to someone he knew that kept it. He was coming up the path to the summerhouse when he saw her, and a natural sympathy caused him to wonder what so troubled the little girl. His second look must have hinted at more recognition than he experienced, for Melanie's face glowed with sudden relief.

Sundry's heart came into his throat, and it was only because he was so astonished that he didn't show how astonished he was. She was a pretty child in a plain pale blue dress, a yellow coat, and a crude pair of boys' brogues. If anyone between the Droones and Normells had been willing to claim her, they might have noticed that her dress was on backward. She was so happy to be comprehended by him that her smile might have given her away if Sundry had not distracted everyone else. He stopped to take off his boot and shake an invisible stone from it.

"What was that?" asked Charles Normell, who was on the alert for tricks.

"That rock has been digging my heel, I guess, since before I noticed it," said Sundry, which was just the sort of backward statement Charles would have to pause to consider. Mrs. Droone eyed the crowd like an alarmed bird. "I guess there isn't any trouble knowing which side anyone is on," said Sundry. He himself was tall and narrow like a Droone, but dark of hair and eye like a Normell.

"We are not very fluent in the details of one another's individual members," said Jeffrey, sounding almost cheerful. "So I recognize anyone I *don't* know as a Droone, and I guess you judge by the same coin, Mrs. Droone, if on the other side."

She turned that hawklike gaze upon Jeffrey, but he was undaunted.

"In your words, Mrs. Droone, that makes it simple," said Sundry.

"That makes it simple, yes," she said, looking suspicious.

"Just like brushing footprints from the snow," said Sundry. There was no reply, and Jeffrey, to whom he directed this statement, only blinked at him. Sundry cast an eye over the crowd for Melanie Ring, but she was gone. "If that's a bedroom," he said when they brought him and Maven into the summerhouse, "we'll leave Mr. Ring's unfortunate remains where they lie and sleep in there." He nodded to the left-hand door at the back of the house

"I'm sure that's fine. We can help you arrange the body."

"No. Thank you. You've done quite enough."

Jeffrey did not respond to Sundry's irony. Charles was bustling into the summerhouse kitchen with three members of the opposite clan. "You'll be wanting something to eat," said Jeffrey.

"We'll keep to our own provisions," said Sundry. Someone had brought his sack into the kitchen, and he lifted it from the table. Without asking for permission, he took up a lantern.

"It's all right," said Jeffrey to Charles. "I went through the sacks."

"You will be wanting your rest," said Charles. "Don't let anything disturb you. We will be watching the house carefully."

"We'll sleep like babes," said Sundry, who was not going to be outdone in wry delivery. He let Maven go before him into the room that housed Burne Ring, then stepped inside himself and closed the door behind.

Maven had said nothing, or very little, since they arrived at Dutten Pond, and even now he stood in the room and simply gaped at the two framed pictures on the other side of the bed. "Oh, my!" he said, finally, when his eyes shifted to the form on the bed.

Burne Ring was doing such a good job looking the part of the deceased that Sundry leaned over him to be sure he really wasn't. Sundry held his own breath in hopes of hearing Burne's, and for a moment he thought the man might have breathed his last after all.

"Not yet," said Burne Ring in a hoarse whisper.

"I am amazed!" said Maven Flyce, though perhaps no more so than he was at any given moment of the day.

"For some reason, they think he's dead," whispered Sundry. "But as Mr. Ring informs us, not yet."

"Who would have guessed!" Maven did not spend much time on this particular marvel but peered a little more closely at the bucolic pictures on the wall. "Isn't that something!" he said. "That looks just like a cow I saw today!" He took in the rest of the room and said, "Where's the little girl?"

"Where's my daughter?" echoed Burne.

"She's asleep," said Sundry.

Burne grunted three or four times, looked paler than he had a moment ago, and said, "I think I'm feeling better."

Sundry stretched out on the bed in the next room. Maven had settled himself in the chair by Burne and fallen into a snore-rattled sleep in a matter of moments. Sundry could hear him drag each breath like a stick along a picket fence and didn't think he could sleep with so much to think about and so much racket. In a moment he roused himself from a doze and sat up.

After dull reassessment, he fashioned the facsimile of a child beneath the covers. Then he lay down beside the lump of pillow and stared at the lantern-yellowed ceiling. He was tired. He had napped on the hill after eating, but the day had been trying and filled with unexpected miles. Could it have been only last night that he danced with Miss Morningside at the Morrells' ball? Could it have been only this morning that he went to the Underwood's, to find Miss Morningside had left?

A wave of sadness washed over his tired bones like a current strong enough to drag him out beyond his ability to swim. He lay there with his chest constricting till he might have drowned had he not reminded himself of the little girl who depended upon his being there if she was caught sneaking down Dutten Lane in search of help.

Looking up from the bed, Sundry considered the shadows cast by the lantern on the ceiling. His heart grew more regular in its labor. His breathing slowed. He had no intention of going to sleep, and when he woke, it was with the sensation of falling and he gripped the covers to steady himself through that instant of panic. He sat up and considered the still-burning lantern, the quality of light and sound from outside and from the front of the house. With the sort of presentiment that he did not usually believe in or trust, he was quite sure that someone stood on the other side of the door, waiting for another minute to pass to rap upon it and rouse him.

47. The Path of Best Intent Went Both Ways

She wondered where the moths had got to and half expected them to kiss her cheek with their wings again and guide her. As she walked, even skipped down the moonlit lane, her eyes were up to the task, but her heart and her lack of knowing and her expectation of the woods sometimes called out to startle her and stop her in her tracks, not unlike that unidentifiable voice she heard so often.

The breeze itself was like a voice, and the trees squeaked and groaned and rubbed one another's backs. It was not an old wood; but she was not an old person, and it seemed old to her. Neither were the trees tall (for trees); but she was not tall even for a six-year-old and she felt almost, but not quite, beneath their notice. Melanie Ring had usually been beneath notice, which circumstance had eased her disguise as a boy for the most of her life and also greased the skids of her recent escape. She hoped to remain invisible just a little longer.

Thaddeus Spark often read to Timothy from those grand adventures written by a Mr. Benjamin Granite Gunwight—books filled with the exploits of Boone and Hawk and Wilma. Tim would relay these exploits to Mailon Ring and, in recent days, to Melanie while they sat on the roofs overlooking Portland Harbor, or waited in ambush for a rival tribe in the oaks at Deering Park. These tales were not diminished for having been heard third or even fourth hand. (Who knew where Mr. Gunwight got them?) They were not diminished as she moved among the pools of moonlight. They were what gave her any understanding that she could have done what she had already done and any belief that she could finish doing what she intended. Before long she was not walking or skipping but running. She did not consider that the way might be guarded, that the boy might still be at the gate, or that others might be watching the path from Normell Acres to the common road.

She would have no memory of touching the fence as she vaulted over it and no recollection of her awkwardly shod feet pounding the rutted path to the road above Dutten Pond. She was out of breath, looking east, then west for a light or some other sign of habitation, but there was only the moon hanging over silver fields. A bat wobbled, mothlike, in the cobalt air. For no good reason that she could have explained, she began to walk, panting, toward the east, the night's pale light casting an outsized shadow before her.

It was a mile or so along an unpopulated stretch of road that she began to flag. Even the stories could only lead her so far or carry her so far. In a little grove of birch she lay down and fell asleep before she knew what she was doing, and when she woke, however many minutes or hours later, she had the rested sense that she had been going in the wrong direction.

48. Light and Dawn
(June 10, 1897)

Growing up on a farm in Edgecomb, Sundry had often risen when first light had yet to pink the east, more usually in winter months, when snowy fields embraced their own blue shimmer against the stars and the milk cow gave off welcome warmth in her corner of the barn. In summer months a person must rise early to beat the sun, but when Sundry did, as in this morning hour, he thought it quietest just before dawn, when the owl takes her ghostly flight home and the nighthawk hides his head beneath a wing, but the robin and the veery have yet to wash their faces and greet the day.

He came out of the bedroom before anyone could knock or enter. Charles was by the door, looking as if he had expected their guest to rouse himself at the proper hour. Both Normells and Droones sat at the kitchen table. Sundry asked them to let Mailon and Maven sleep. "It's been a rough night for the poor kid. He had a dream that his father was still alive, so every noise he hears he thinks is Mr. Burne in the next room. But he's asleep now."

"It's just as well if they do sleep," said Charles. "No one will bother them." Sundry might have warmed to the man if there had been more sympathy and less business in the response.

The frogs and peepers were still, and the wind made no ripple on Dutten Pond; even the people down by the shore, standing in pools of lantern light, seemed to have lost their voices. Charles and Jeffrey Normell led Sundry down to the boats without a word, and Bridey Droone greeted him with only an expectant look. The crowd had not thinned or its anxiety diminished. Their chiefs seemed to be on their nerves; even Jeffrey's normally light expression was pulled into a grim frown.

"You people should go to bed," said Sundry offhandedly. "I can take care of this." It was his backward humor employed in backward circumstance, and perhaps a shade or two of contempt, but he was sorry for it in the next moment.

Everyone was startled by his flippancy, and a low note of discomfort ran through the crowd till one man—a Normell—said to Charles, "You're not letting a stranger drag it up?"

"Be quiet!" said Charles.

Bridey Droone looked as if she might say something herself, but the man who had spoken, a large enough fellow moving gingerly, stepped forward. "But he's not to bring it up," he said. "Not a stranger—"

"Be quiet, you idiot!" said Jeffrey this time, but it was too late. Charles had already come around with the back of his hand and as much weight as he could put into it on short notice. He caught the man on the side of the head with a loud crack, then drew back and hit him again in the face. There were shouts from the others—more in fear than anger—and people on both sides leaped and fell back (sometimes over children) as Charles Normell waded into his kinsman, knocking him down and pummeling him with hands and feet.

The attack was silent, but for the sound of blows and the gusts of expended breath. Charles's face was purple with rage, and his eyes started from his head like a madman's. Sundry did not know when he had seen such awful fury, the more awful for manifesting itself in someone who might otherwise have looked the part of a jolly uncle.

Sundry snatched at Charles's collar and violently yanked him back. Charles rolled onto his feet and looked about for whoever had the temerity to step into his wrath and intent. Charles was large in every sense of the word, but Sundry knew better than to imagine that the size of the man's girth indicated he was either soft or weak.

Charles had not entirely lost his mind, however, and was perhaps the more dangerous for his ability to regain his head and alter his course. Sundry thought he had the look of a bully with the upper hand, almost smiling as he gasped. "The house is still guarded, Mr. Moss," he said between breaths. "And the boy is still in there. And your friend."

Sundry would have liked nothing more than to disabuse the man of some of this, but for all he knew, Melanie was still sneaking away or hidden someplace in the woods, and he did not want to chance a general search for her. With the level of suspicion between the two clans, he might easily set the Normells and the Droones at each other's throats, but he likewise feared endangering the children in the crowd. He must take his satisfaction from his own secrets and go forward. They expected him to perform as commanded on the strength of the *boy's* tacit imprisonment in the house, and he would play the part.

From someone in the agitated mob, Bridey retrieved the fork of an apple bough, which divided a foot or so from its base and was, in overall length, about three and a half feet long. "We have picked some others," she told Sundry as she passed this to him, "in case you find this one ineffectual. Take the bow, Mr. Moss." It was a moment before he realized she was indicating not the branch, which she had already handed to him, but the end of the boat that he was supposed to occupy.

"Be thorough," advised Jeffrey.

More astonishing to Sundry than Charles's sudden fit of violence was the relative calm with which everyone else—Droone and Normell included—accepted it and went on. He took the apple bough and weighed it in his hand.

The boat swayed as he stepped past the Normell steadying it. The Droone in the stern said nothing but lifted the lantern by his side as Sundry took the bow, and by this light Sundry saw ropes and weighted nets at his feet. The boat dipped and rocked as it was cast off and the Normell climbed in past Sundry to sit at the thwart. Drifting beyond the encompassing trees, turning slowly beneath the gap of bluing sky, Sundry was conscious that day birds chorused the more distant tracts of field and wood, but that the nearer groves remained quiet and hardly seemed to stir, even with the breeze that lightly roughed the pond and moved the trees on the opposite shore.

His companions were silent, and the people on shore watched without comment, waiting at the water's edge like unhappy ghosts staring after life. In happier gatherings, Sundry noted, it was usual to see children at the fore of a crowd, watching fireworks or a parade, but here the elder Normells and Droones lined the front ranks, their forms dim and amorphous in the near dark, their faces strangely lit by several lanterns.

"Where do we start?" asked Sundry. Experimentally he held the forked bough out over the water by its two *tines*.

"In the northeast corner where it becomes too deep to wade," said the man in the stern, whom Sundry was to refer to as *Mr. Droone; Mr. Normell* rowed them across the border into Albion and Droone territory.

Sundry had his own idea of where they might find something but said nothing. There was birdsong and a rising breeze in the wood on the other shore; water purled against the freeboard, and the oars rubbed in their locks; but otherwise silence had mastered the air, and Sundry had long moments to think as he hovered the bough above the water. He suspected that he had not been told the truth about this business, or at least not all of it. He could understand that both families would be apprehensive to know who had murdered whom, but their fear and their stagnant dread, rather than anger and action, indicated to Sundry that more than knowing who was guilty would result in anything he discovered.

It, thought Sundry. *The fellow said, "You're not letting a stranger drag it up." Who refers to the remains of a loved one or family member as* it?

Many a tale was told of people stumbling across water-lost bodies in horrible situations. How could it be other than horrible? There was even a ballad or two, conveyed to these shores from the old country long ago.

He thought he'd grasped his gauntlet lost,
But held her hand instead;
The seeming wrack of seaweed tossed
Was hair upon her head.

Her eyes were green as grasses grow,
Her lips still plum and full;
And as the waves went to and fro,
His hand hers seemed to pull

Oh, bide with me in ocean waves,
My kiss will grant you sleep.
And follow me to tidal caves,
Embrace me in the deep.

These tales and songs were etched deep, pressed firmly in the country heart, concocting a potent brew of horror and melancholy to which Sundry was not callous. The drowned maid was always comely, her lost voice mourned as grace irretrievable, her heart as true and broken. All this made her the more terrifying, were you to peer into the water and see her pale beauty in a shaft of watery light, her long tresses rising in the spring currents as upon an ocean breeze. She was the sharp blade that bid you, "Cut!" and the cliffside that whispered, "Leap!"

Dutten Pond mirrored the paling sky. Lazy ripples from the boat and the swifter eddies pulled by the sweep of the oars chattered the water, and Sundry started at the glimmers and winks that seemed to rise from below. He thought about what he had learned from Uncle Cedric, but truthfully there are few hard-and-fast rules in the realm of dowsing. Apple tree boughs are among the favored *divining rods*, but other fruit trees are sometimes used, as well as willow wands and copper rods. Uncle Cedric had tapped the side of his head, laughing, and said, "Go to a place in here that you haven't filled up."

Sundry had laughed, too. That was the larger portion, at any rate.

"Hold it loosely with the joined end pointing up," said Uncle Cedric.

With both hands, Sundry held the apple bough out past the bow of the boat, moving it from left to right and back again as they drifted. It seemed easy to search out that portion of his brain that he hadn't filled yet; the strangeness of his predicament, his lack of proper sleep, and the focus of his own shadow, cast by the lantern in the stern and slipping against the trees before him, conspired him into a peculiar state of awareness.

He wasn't sure that he wanted to find what they were looking for—or if he wanted to find it soon or late. Once he thought the apple bough dipped, and he shifted in his seat so that he could hover the branch over the same patch of water as they passed it. He heard a grunt from behind him, but he shook his head, realized that this small gesture might not be seen, and said, "No."

Mr. Normell slowed the boat, however, and Sundry scanned the immediate surface of the pond to be sure. Soon they were moving again. He forgot about the people on the shore and almost forgot the men in the boat with him. The air was cool and welcoming, the animate smell of the pond and the woods mingling bloom with decay. The sky paled in unseen degrees and the last star went out. Light made its way into the brush, articulating leaf from branch and pine from birch, but Sundry watched his apple wand, held loosely in his hands, and waited for something more than its natural weight to pull at it.

They reached an extremity of the pond, and Mr. Normell turned them about. Sundry took a deep breath, not knowing how long it had been since he'd taken the last one. Shifting in his seat, he cricked his neck and glanced back, when something caught his eye—not in the water but among the trees. He would have thought it was a great pinecone if the appropriate evergreen had been anywhere near that tangle of branches. It was, perhaps, a clump of maple leaves, not yet fully blown from the bud. But Sundry noticed other similar clusters among the birch and oak as well. And there *was* a pine bough, downshore, hanging over the pond and drooping with some extra load.

The boat was oared further out on its way back. The crowd at the landing had not moved. In the gaining light Sundry tried to imagine and then to perceive what depended from the trees in ranks along the pond banks. As the boat moved, the reaching branches turned before him like objects on a carousel, and one long arm of maple shifted in his perspective to stand out with its burden in the early-morning light.

A dead robin hung there by its legs, and in one brief and innocent moment Sundry wondered how it had trapped itself there. But the sight of the bird was like the key to a cipher, and he began to recognize crows and goldfinches, doves, and even a wily jay hanging in scores wherever Normell Acres and Droone land met the water.

Sundry was appalled. "There must be a hundred of them!" he said, and then he realized that there *were* a hundred of them, without exaggeration, and more, and that there would be a dead bird for every Droone and Normell watching and waiting by the shore.

He was a farmer by birth, and there are practical matters that lie between livestock and the larder, but few can despise senseless killing as much as a man who must sometimes do so to feed his family.

"I don't know what it is that you must have from this water," said Sundry to the other men in the boat, "but if I were you, I would doubt any need that drives you to this." *Perhaps*, he thought, *it is better to have it done with.* He looked from his boat fellows to the people on shore, watching, waiting, growing more visible. He wondered where Melanie was and could imagine a dozen misfortunes that a little girl could stumble upon, alone in the countryside. He only hoped that he had given her enough time to get away.

It was time to have done with it. He glanced once more at the birds hanging from the trees.

No wonder it's so quiet on this side of the water.

He looked back at Mr. Normell and said, curtly, "Take us out to the center of the pond."

49. An Elf from the Woods

Emery Swamp was not really suited to Robin Oig's great long oar or even the bulk of his haversack hanging from the back of Cram's saddle. The branches were never high enough, the paths straight or long or wide enough. Robin Oig himself was ill matched with the snagging creepers and tripping underbrush. Mosquitoes, roused from a pre-dawn slumber, found the sailor's great swatch of unprotected neck and ears an obliging feeding ground. Mr. Cook's fly ointment made little headway against such swarms. So the pastoral quiet of the moon-haunted swamp and the surrounding acres, usually counterpointed by the gentle frog or lonely night bird, was for a time broken by the invective of a vexed and land bound sailor. There were no mosquitoes at sea (he vowed) or (he trusted) at Fiddler's Green.

The lantern he carried was necessary to navigate these tracts, but it also drew more insects; its glow described a series of rooms from the stages of swamp and marsh, branches of grasping alder and willow forming walls and ceiling, spaces separating hummock from grove of spidery brush invoking doors and corridors, with mosquitoes filling everything in between.

Life on a farm breeds early risers, but that does not go far enough to explain how Abijah Cook came to be leading Robin Oig and two horses by way of a little-known shortcut long before dawn. *Accountability*, as Robin had expressed it, must answer.

From the time he was old enough to be told ghost stories, the vicinity of Dutten Pond had always meant mystery and possible danger to Ab. He had seen the occasional Normell and Droone when he went to market in China, and these strangers had seemed *normal* enough, but he had been impressed by their *apartness*. People dealt with them, behaved in a polite manner to them, but they did not "share the day" with Normells and Droones.

Different is what different does, or what is treated differently, or perhaps what imagines itself as different. The Normells and Droones had not disabused people of their *distinction*, and Ab had caught a suspicion of them, as someone might catch wind of a tale that did not quite vary as it passed from ear to ear. The stories sounded preposterous and felt like truth, and he was not anxious to approach their estates; but he worried that he and his father had not warned Mr. Moss clearly enough about the perils of doing so. He had wakened in the small hours of night to an apprehension that had not left him since the previous afternoon.

Robin Oig had experienced his own restlessness and had not been quiet falling out of the hayloft with his oar. Neither oar nor man was broken, however, and he banged his way past the stables and almost clipped Ab over the head with the blade of the sweep as he emerged from the barn. The farmer had decided not to allow another innocent to go blithely down to Dutten without the requisite warnings and possibly his own company to the very door of Normell Acres, and Robin Oig, for his part, was glad of the company and pleased enough to be shown the shortcut till he was in its midst.

"Are you sure they couldn't just pick us up and fly us there?" asked Robin while they walked a log bridge past a pool rippling with the retreat of a hundred frogs. "These mosquitoes?" he added.

Ab was no more happy to have come this way, but he felt most guilty about leading old Cram and their other horse, Bolt, through this ambush. He would have turned them around at that point if they weren't already halfway through the swamp. But stars reached them through the brush in increasingly frequent sparks and glimmers till entire constellations rose out of the places between branch and leaf and finally a quadrant of the speckled sky loomed over a long field and a ridge beyond.

Ab mounted Bolt when they reached the end of the swamp's watery grasp and after Robin had clambered atop Cram, they climbed the hill from which they could see the sheen of the sky reflected in Mud Pond and perhaps a light or two in China Village. Descending the farther slope, they left a dark trail behind them in the fields. Robin Oig rode pretty well for a sailor—that preposterous, quixotic oar perched upon one shoulder. Ab might have left the man at the top of the hill with a point of the finger and the requisite directions, but he felt his honor was at stake and so went forth.

They met no one on the road to China and didn't think they met anyone in the town itself, though they had the impression of a man—some drunk, perhaps—standing in the shadows of a storefront, watching their progress.

It was beyond the further limits of the village that Robin Oig began to hum and then to sing.

> *Returning robin trolls the sky aloft,*
> *Now welcome, summer, with its sun so soft,*
> *That casts winter's unkind weathers back,*
> *And drives away the long night's black.*

Ab knew the words, though to a different tune, but he was not long in picking up Robin's melody and joining him.

> *God's summer sun awakes the upper story,*
> *God's smallest wren sings out His glory,*
> *Now welcome, summer, with sun so soft,*
> *Delight the tar at sea and farmer at his croft.*

> *Each man and beast will have his reason well,*
> *Grand praise to God, and so Creator, tell,*
> *And whether plows the land or sails the sea,*
> *Men fill the air with song like robins in the tree.*

There were more verses, and they sang them all, and when they were done, they started over again, for they almost seemed to be singing daylight into being. The east paled, and the stars along its border weakened and winked. It must have been an hour before dawn, but a soft glow buffered the distant hills from the night, and the first birds of morning had joined the farmer and the sailor in their song.

They had long left the sleeping town, and were only just reaching (for the second time) *"Each throat and warble sing what can, / Each child of God sing out the Child of Man"* when they came to the place in the road below the hill that Sundry and Maven had climbed for a view and supper. Ab brought Bolt to a lumbering halt, and Cram trudged some yards farther before he realized that he had left his fellow horse behind.

"What is it?" wondered the sailor, who had lost his accompaniment.

The farmer didn't quite know. He pointed toward the fields northeast that bordered the treeless southern shore of Dutten Pond. The first blink looked like a firefly and not so far away, but Ab soon picked out several similar glimmerings, as from distant lanterns, that lined the eastern banks and at least one spark that skimmed the surface of the pond itself.

"What is it?" wondered the sailor again, but more specifically.

Lights glittered down at the geographic source of local gossip, and Ab was not as sure about going there as he had been while he and Robin had been harmonizing in the predawn. He had not expected that the Normells or the Droones would be up and pursuing their mysterious designs.

Robin, too, appeared uncertain. It was curious to see evidence of waking life—or at least so much of it—along the banks of a rural lake before sunup, and he had been impressed by the stories he'd heard about this place at the Cook kitchen table. "What do you suppose they're all up to?" he wondered.

"Odd, isn't it," said Ab. What the lights betokened, he couldn't guess, but he suspected there was *troll*craft in the works. He had heard tales of midnight rituals and of strange spirits roaming those shores.

It is human to particularize fear, to imagine that the finger of premonition or the evil eye is pointed at oneself. Robin and Ab might be standing half a mile from those lights, but they had the strong notion that they were anticipated, perhaps even watched from the shores of Dutten Pond. The silent portion of the night had arrived—that moment when the world and nature hold their breath for the sun, and though the lights were far away, it was eerie to see them and hear nothing.

All about the two men suddenly seemed watchful and expectant, and when they spoke, it was in near whispers.

"I wonder if Mr. Moss is down there," said Robin.

"Hard to say," said Ab. He was pretty sure they could wait till the day was well established before they went to find out.

Robin was pretty sure that he didn't know why he had to catch up with Mr. Moss in the first place. "You're sure he didn't change his mind?" he said, straining his eyes toward the pond.

"He might have bedded down in China, I suppose," said Ab. It did seem sensible to go back and inquire.

Robin thought it sensible to return to his original purpose and hike west with his great long oar, which would also entail hiking in the other direction. He was on the cusp of announcing this intention when he first saw the figure of a child cresting the next hill east and walking in their direction. It was a curious sight at that hour—a lone child walking in a pale blue dress and yellow coat before the dawn—and uncannily reminiscent of the song they had been singing but moments ago.

"What is that?" wondered Ab, loud enough for Robin Oig to hear.

Robin almost pronounced the vision a *child of God*, sung up like the coming day, but decided to wait till more evidence was gathered. The little girl did not hesitate when she saw them, but only hurried her approach. The rugged, hard-handed farmer and the giant sailor with the loom of an oversized oar propped over his shoulder, the both of them mounted on massive Percherons—these men might have been daunting to a small child but she seemed anxious to reach them.

A breeze gathered with the first glow of dawn, and her short brown hair wafted about her head. Her dress and coat were bleached to white in the strange illumination, and Robin held the lantern to one side to see her better. She was a pretty creature, and her eyes shone as if he and the farmer were just what she had been looking for. She almost ran up the short slope between them. She wore odd shoes for a little girl, and the collar of her dress, visible as her coat flew open with the wind of her motion, had the appearance of being on backward. Robin had heard of folk who wore things backward when they came in from twilight fields (he had, in a sense, been searching for just those sorts of folk), but he never guessed that he would really see one.

Ab had heard as much himself and had never *wanted* to see one.

The little girl stopped in front of Cram's broad nose and considered the horse with a thoughtful smile. She reached up and stroked the velvet muzzle, and Cram let out a low, appreciative snort; Bolt, a jealous one. Then she turned her attention to Robin Oig and, specifically, to the great long oar over his shoulder. She looked at the oar—looked it up and down—her mouth hanging open, her eyes pondering the device as if she had never imagined such a thing. Then she turned to Robin himself and smiled.

"What's that you've got there?" she asked.

50. The Dowse

"Don't ever doubt that it's your eye and not the bough that knows," Uncle Cedric had said, and that was the most important lesson of all. "We're animal creatures," the old man maintained. "Yes, we have souls, no doubt, and minds above a horse or a dog, but I think the old people long ago might have peered over a field and picked a likely water spot without a witch stick or an apple bough to guide them. There might be something to it, I suppose"—and this from a man who was famous in his parts for dowsing—"but I wonder if there's a memory or a recollection or a sense of smell I'm not aware of, or a sense of shape in the land that pulls my feet and twitches the stick."

Certain matters (as little Melanie Ring so wisely understood) may be hidden in plain sight, and Sundry knew that people often tend toward landmarks, even when they are not aware of doing so. To begin with, Sundry had to tell Mr. Normell three times to take him to the center of the pond, and then the man shouted to the shore for Charles's authority.

"What's this all about?" asked Mr. Droone in the boat.

"It's out there," said Sundry, nodding toward the middle of the pond.

"How do you know that?" asked the man, looking wary.

"I don't, really. It was a feeling I had last night. That's what *you* have, isn't it? Feelings?"

There seemed to be some agreement on shore, and Charles Normell shouted, "Take him out there."

When Sundry called back that he wanted to dowse the reflection of the elm on the other shore as seen from the Normells' landing, there was a visible excitement among the crowd, and anxious voices began to direct them to the spot. Mr. Normell rowed them back and forth while the people on the shore took turns correcting their course. Sundry situated himself at the bow with renewed purpose—that is, to have done with it—and left the memory of Melanie and dead birds behind to skim his thoughts over the cool veneer of water.

He did not find *it* directly. A person would have had difficulty rowing to such a place without guidance from land as Sundry had, but *some*one's impulse, if not an eye, had pulled that other boat toward a landmark in the broad clarity of the pond's surface and a shadowy place in the midst of the water that must have hinted, however accurately, at depth. Mr. Normell paused in mid-stroke, then set one oar as a drag to correct their drift.

Sundry moved the branch to one side and back again. His heart beat faster, and he took long breaths, experiencing a heavy sensation—a full, purposeful intuition of success even before the tip of the forked bough gave a tug, like the end of a pole when a fish takes the bait. "It is a relative matter," said Uncle Cedric. "Probe about, first to be sure you felt something and then to be sure of the exact place." Sundry felt the strain leave the bough, and then he had to lean out to locate the source of tension again, sweeping over that portion of the pond. The branch gave a distinct pull, and he eased it back. Mr. Normell dipped the oars to bring them closer. Sundry went up on his knees and waved the bough, feeling the strain pull and let go, pull and let go, as if something were jerking a line.

Then he remembered what *was* pulling at the bough, and he let it drop in the water. They were in the shadow, if not the reflection of the elm, but the sky in the unobscured surface of the pond was a striking blue. A robin laughed from the trees, and the sun was up.

"That's what you're looking for, I guess," said Sundry to his escorts. "Unless you people make a habit of dropping bodies in here."

"I wouldn't be joking, Mr. Moss," said the man in the stern.

"I wouldn't put it past you, so don't take it for granted that I *am*."

"You'll have to cast the net," said Mr. Normell.

"And let a stranger drag *it* up?" Sundry looked back at the man and was unpleasantly surprised (when he thought there had been more than enough unpleasant surprises of late) to see that Mr. Normell and Mr. Droone both held revolvers, the muzzles of which were generally trained on their conscripted dowser. He had the nasty impression that they meant to exchange bodies with the pond—that is, *his* with the one that was purportedly down there already.

"You will cast the net, Mr. Moss," said the man in the thwart. "You will pull what you find into the boat and leave it in the net at your feet. We will shoot you if you attempt either trick or levity, I promise."

Sundry turned himself about and planted his feet firmly on the nets. He folded his arms, and with a racing heart he set his somewhat oversquare jaw and said, "Then you had better shoot me now and get it over with— the idiot pair of you! I guess I won't bother to dig my own grave first!"

Mr. Normell blinked at Sundry and then at the gun in his hand. "We have no intention of harming you if you simply do what we say."

Sundry folded his arms. "*I* have no intention of *believing* you until you toss those guns."

"We will drag the pond ourselves then," stated Mr. Droone flatly.

"No, you won't, or you would have done it already. You wouldn't have needed me in the first place."

"What is the matter?" came a voice, startlingly close. Sundry and the two men had not observed the pair of boats coming out to join them, manned one by Droones and the other by Normells. Charles Normell sat in the bow of the nearest boat, and Sundry took note that the man in the stern carried a rifle. There was a similarly armed fellow in the second boat, seated behind Mrs. Droone. "What has happened?" said Charles.

"He refuses to bring it up?"

"You found it?"

"Yes, I found *her*," said Sundry.

"Then what's the trouble?"

"I'm not keen on being shot for my pains," said Sundry.

"This is Jeffrey's doing!" said Bridey Droone angrily.

"Yes," admitted Sundry, "it's too bad he didn't trick someone into coming here that you could walk all over."

"Mr. Moss," said Charles, "we have no intention of shooting anyone. It is each other," he added, "that we guard against."

"You've given me a lot of reason, of course, to accept your word."

"We can find someone else, Mr. Moss."

"I have the impression that the people on shore aren't going to like waiting for someone else." He nodded in that direction, but Bridey Droone and Charles Normell did not look back. "Whatever *it* is you want down there, I'm wondering if they'll have much more patience with the lot of you if you come back without it. Maybe you can bully them all at once, or maybe there's one or two of them who aren't cowards and will fight back."

"You are talking through your hat, Mr. Moss. You have no idea what is at stake here."

"I'm beginning to get the general idea," ventured Sundry. "There is no body, is there?"

"Whatever gave you that notion?" said Charles.

"And no one was dragging the pond last night, or you wouldn't need me to do it now. It was just a show to make your story plausible."

"You're putting yourself in the badger den, Mr. Moss," said Mrs. Droone. "If you like clever arguments, try this one. You can force us to shoot you now and search for someone else to drag for the body. You can jump overboard and try to escape, which I am sure you are considering, and similarly force our hands. Or you can do what we ask and take your chances. I myself, who *didn't* trick you into coming here, give you my word, however much you cherish it, that we will not shoot you if you only do as we request."

Sundry sat with his arms crossed and watched the woman as she spoke. When she was done and he had thought for a moment, he said, "I had a great aunt, Mrs. Droone, and when we were young and she meant to scold us or curb bad behavior, she'd always say, 'Do you want me to look right over the top of your head!' It sounded like an awful threat when we were kids, and we never quite dared find out what it meant."

"I never threaten, Mr. Moss," said the woman.

Sundry disliked her about as much as he disliked any of them but thought he might trust her a little further. The robin sounded in the elm, and he saw the splash of a fish or a frog beyond the Droones' boat and closer to shore. It was turning into another beautiful June day. The Waltons were probably in Halifax by now. Miss Morningside was in Ellsworth and separated from Sundry by more than miles. He turned to the men in the boat with him and relaxed his posture. He nodded slowly. "But you fellows might point those in another direction," he said.

51. The Knight on the Road

When Melanie Ring first saw the two figures standing in the gaining light, she thought they might be two knights, and indeed, one of them appeared to be carrying a lance over his shoulder, though otherwise they did not entirely resemble the few pictures she had ever seen of knights and squires and chargers.

It was not till she had considerably divided the distance between them that she realized what the one man was carrying, and then she knew him for the giant fellow with the great long oar at the Grand Trunk Station in Portland and the very man Mr. Moss had been telling her about—the sailor looking for Fiddler's Green. She was not even astonished to see him there, nor could she imagine how astonishing it was to see a little girl, neatly dressed, walking down the road with the promise of dawn behind her. To Melanie, the important thing was to find someone who might help rescue her father and Mr. Moss and Mr. Flyce, and if the sailor and his companion were no knights, they certainly looked large enough to lend a hand.

The men gaped at her as she approached them, and even the horses seemed at a loss for words. Melanie liked the big old fellow that the man with the oar was riding, and she reached up to stroke his soft nose. Then she turned to the man with the oar and quite astonished him (and rather delighted herself with her cleverness) by asking what he was carrying.

The man with the oar gaped and leaned down to see her more closely, then straightened in his saddle and closed his mouth, then looked at his companion, who gaped and did not close his mouth. The sailor turned back to Melanie and opened his mouth to speak but thought better of it. (Folk from Fiddler's Green will surely vanish if you tell them what the oar is.)

"What did you say?" asked the sailor.

"What's that you have there?" she asked again.

"It's a great long spoon," he said, and this was considered a standard reply to such a query.

Melanie laughed, which did her good but startled the two men. "Am I to follow you?" asked the man with the oar.

Melanie nodded. "Down there," she said, pointing to Dutten Pond.

"Down to Dutten?" said the other man.

"You have to help rescue my father and Mr. Moss," said the little girl. She wondered, in the next moment, if she had said too much.

"Mr. Moss?" said the sailor. "I have to rescue someone?" Clearly he had not understood that a *deed* was part of the transaction.

"Down to Dutten?" said the other man again.

"It's got to be quick," she said. "They've been kidnapped." She offered no more on this subject but turned and led the way.

"Kidnapped?" said the sailor. It all made an odd sort of sense if he had to rescue Mr. Moss. Hadn't he been following the man from the start? And who knew but what Mr. Moss might be from Fiddler's Green himself?

Robin Oig looked to Ab, and Ab, who was still gaping, said, "I don't know about rescuing someone from all those Droones and Normells."

"Sometimes you don't really *have* to do a deed," said Robin. "You just have to look like you're willing."

"Should we get help first?" said Ab.

"Should we get help?" Robin shouted after the girl.

"That would be fine!" she said, stopping for a moment in the road. "But *you'd* better come with me," she said to Robin.

"Go for help," said Robin, "but *I* have to follow her!"

Ab hesitated. "Take Cram, in case you have to get out of there."

Robin didn't know if he *was* getting out of there. He had begun to meld Dutten, in his mind, with Fiddler's Green. Robin watched Ab and Bolt charge down the western slope of the hill, and he realized that the sun was just at the rim of the earth and that the sky was light all the way to the pond. He could see a dab of activity on the water. He could see the little girl, some distance away, waving him on.

Robin gave Cram a jolt or two, shook the reins, and bounced off after the little elf ahead of him. She waited at the bottom of the next short slope, and he slowed only long enough to pull her up behind him.

52. Body of Lies

Cautiously Mr. Normell and Mr. Droone put their revolvers back in their coats, but Sundry was aware that other barrels were still pointed in his general direction. Mr. Normell rowed them back, a little beyond the place where the object of their search had betrayed its presence.

Deliberately, Sundry took up the net from the bottom of the boat, shook the weights out forward, and cast it over the water. The sinkers disappeared, and the further end of the net dissolved from sight. He had never used a net in this fashion, and he was sure he wasn't manning it the way a fisherman would, but he braced himself against the bow seat and dragged it by the lines as Mr. Normell rowed them through the shadow of the elm.

"That was a very clever thing," conceded Charles from his remove, "guessing where to find it."

It, thought Sundry, but he said nothing. On the fourth haul the net took a sudden snag, and they all sat a little straighter, craning their necks.

"Do I come forward?" asked Mr. Normell, confused in his excitement.

"No, no," said Sundry. "Back off, but slowly."

"Yes, back off!" demanded Charles. "Slowly, though!"

It was apparent to everyone that Sundry had something. The oars dipped and splashed, and with the ropes he drew the corners of the net in as the boat drifted back. Ripples circled from the boat, and the upper knots of the net made stirrings in the water. Sundry had an eerie sensation, not unlike the initial tug upon the apple branch that came several times, as if someone were indeed down there, tugging back at his grip.

> *. . . the waves went to and fro,*
> *His hand hers seemed to pull . . .*

He had been convinced minutes ago that there was no body down there, but the strange force yearning back to the water almost startled him into dropping the net as he had the apple bough. The beautiful drowned girl had disappeared from his imagination, and in her place was what small knowledge he had of bodies thus recovered. But the force against him became less erratic, smoother and more willing, and soon he was pulling something weighty, but consenting, to the surface. A pale flash below the surface of the pond renewed his qualms, till a metallic box, about a foot or so long and several inches deep, rose in the folds of the net.

Those with him held their breath, and even Sundry steeled himself for the next surprise, unpleasant or otherwise. He was considering his chances if he leaped overboard when the boat rocked a little, and he heard a double click just behind him. In the periphery of his vision, Sundry could see Mr. Normell standing just ahead of the thwart.

"You hadn't ought to make a fellow nervous like that," said Sundry. "He might drop something."

"Just pull it up," said the man.

"Jules," said Charles cautiously, "let him be."

Jules Normell glanced briefly at the other boat, torn between his own desperation for whatever was in that box and fear of his chief.

"Jules!" snapped Charles.

Sundry had the box out of the water, and with every ounce of balance, weight, and strength that he possessed he swung the net around and clubbed Jules in the head with his catch. It was not a very heavy blow, but Jules went down like a fallen tree, and with an alarming explosion the pistol discharged a bullet into the upper gunnel before it bounced from the man's hand and *plipped* into the water. Jules crashed into his Droone counterpart, whose own pistol was thus pinned against the stern.

There were shouts and curses, and Sundry, who had nearly thrown himself overboard with his effort, leaped to the back of the boat and scrambled for possession of the second revolver. The Droone man was struggling beneath Jules, whose arms and legs kicked and swung. A shot was fired from one of the other boats, and Sundry thought he was going to have to push Jules overboard to get at the pistol. Jules caught him in the side of the face with a flailing hand, and he was about to return the same when the butt end of a rifle connected with the back of Sundry's head.

Not unconscious, but momentarily dazed, Sundry went down. A fist or two or a foot or two struck him in several places. His head was pressed to the bottom of the boat, and while shouts and curses rang in his one ear, the wooden hull and the water beyond it did strange things to sound in his other. Amid orders to "leave the box alone" and to "hold him down," Sundry rose from his brief stupor.

"That was a very foolish thing to do, Mr. Moss," said Charles, who was still in his own boat, but clinging to the gunnel of Sundry's. There was some scrambling as Jules staggered back to the bow, and Mr. Droone stepped on Sundry's hand as he shifted to the place between the oars, one of which had to be retrieved from the water.

"If you think *that* was foolish, you should consider the alternatives," returned Sundry.

Charles actually chuckled, but it was not a congenial sound.

"One of those girls didn't kill the other, did she?" said Sundry. "They ran away, the both of them." It was strange and almost frightening how he could see the young women in white dresses by the old cellar hole that he and Maven had passed the day before.

Charles was quiet now. Sundry had his face pressed against the bottom of the boat, and he had to blow to keep the water out of his mouth and nose. Charles reached out and jerked him up. With surprising power, even from so big a man, Sundry was set down in the space between the thwart and the stern. Sundry spent the next moments taking in air while he glared at Charles Normell, with an occasional voluble glance at Mrs. Droone, who was passing a rifle and possibly *the* rifle butt back to one of the men in her boat.

Mrs. Droone stared back. Charles said nothing.

"But first," said Sundry when he had half caught his breath, "they had to concoct some cockeyed spell to keep you from finding them. Or at least they had to convince you they had. I guess there's more than a *pair* of idiots in this neck of the woods."

"Do be quiet, Mr. Moss," said Bridey Droone.

"And this Burnham you've been waiting for," said Sundry. "I expect he's joined your two missing women."

This was not a possibility that anyone else had considered, and Charles and Bridey looked at one another with renewed concern.

"I really do mean it, Mr. Moss," said the woman. "Be quiet."

Sundry fell to catching his breath and said no more, but only because his anger had risen above the point where words would suffice. At least they were being rowed ashore—in tandem, as it were, with Charles at the bow of his own boat grasping the gunnel of Sundry's by the stern as if he were pushing them all by the force of his own not so very insignificant will. Bridey Droone's boat ventured almost as close, and it was instructive to see that the man in the stern still had his rifle at the ready but that he seemed to have it trained on Charles Normell.

53. Cruxes and Cranks

Sundry wondered what people back on shore had made of the excitement out on the water. There did appear to be a little more hope in their faces as the boats drew near but, to Sundry, the tableau they made was silent and unsettling—the attention of the crowd, unwavering and direct. It was this lack of sound that seemed so strange; it put Sundry in mind of that other silence, and as the boats drew near the landing, he scanned the shoreline trees and their macabre decorations. "Not a lot of song on this side of the pond," he said to no one in particular.

"You wouldn't understand, of course, why we had to do that," said Charles.

"I can guess why you *thought* you had to do it," said Sundry, "but you are right, I wouldn't understand. Is that to keep everyone else from running away?" he said with a note of irony in his voice.

Charles made a sound like a chuckle. "You see, you can't guess *or* understand."

For the first time since the struggle, Sundry looked down at the box, which lay at his feet, tied up in thin rope in the manner of a Christmas package and tangled in the net. It looked like a large jewelry chest, but fashioned crudely out of silver with childlike figures of people and animals marked upon its side. *That could dent a fellow*, thought Sundry, and he looked, almost with sympathy, at Jules, who was sitting in the bow, rubbing his head.

Sundry wondered if there were two (or perhaps three) more dead birds in the box. The self-enclosed logic of such practices was not entirely beyond his experience or imagination. There were people he knew who brushed the forehead of a newborn child with a rabbit's foot and one old woman who led her chickens with a trail of corn around her house on the first day of spring to bring good luck. And hanging dead crows in the cornfield to frighten other crows was not exactly a practice to be counted among the mystical, but there was something about it reminiscent of totems and amulets.

Sundry imagined that the two women had run away and that they had conjured a spell to keep from being found, but the more he thought of it, the more it failed to answer for the fright and apprehension among these people.

Mrs. Droone watched him—watched him *think*—Sundry caught her at it when he lifted his gaze from the box at his feet. She did not look away, and she appeared angry rather than frightened. In such circumstances, of course, logic went only so far. Fear and self-involved anger do not follow rational paths but sprawl about, unheeding of anything more than immediate need.

"Move away, move away!" demanded Charles of the crowd on the shore. "We told you before, move away!" Even then the two clans hesitated, and for the first time they seemed to Sundry like one mob. They did divide, however, but not in such definite factions.

"He should get out first," said Bridey Droone when Sundry's boat had scraped against the shore.

"Yes, Mr. Moss," said Charles. "Take up the box, carefully, and carry it in the net up to the stump just north of the summerhouse." He might have been reading instructions on how to build a kite, for all the pleasant tone in his voice.

"Right on the line," said Sundry.

"The line?" said Charles.

"Between Droone and Normell."

"That's right, Mr. Moss," said Charles. "Right on the line."

"I think I *am* beginning to understand," said Sundry as he gathered up the net.

"I must admit that you have proven to be very sharp," said Charles, but he could not suppress a look of cunning.

"You'd like me to think so, wouldn't you," said Sundry. "As soon as a fellow thinks he's figured it out he quits figuring."

"We only want you to do as we ask. Your understanding is entirely beside the point."

Sundry hefted the box in the net and thought it weighed about twelve or fifteen pounds. He didn't think there were any dead birds in it. "Curiosity killed the cat," he said.

"Indeed," said Charles.

"And if I do what you ask, you think that you'll be able to protect yourselves again."

"Protect ourselves?"

The look of cunning had dropped from Charles's face, and Sundry would have liked to watch the man some more. Instead, he clambered out of the boat with the net slung carelessly over one shoulder. All eyes, he knew, were on the box. "From the rest of the world," said Sundry. "And perhaps even from each other. This spell by the two who ran away. Or the three. I had guessed that it was a blockade, so to speak—a way to keep you from finding them. But the reason you're all so afraid is that this spell keeps you from *seeing* them, not like a wall that obstructs your view, but by taking away your ability to see at all."

"What three?" said someone. "Who's the third?" Normells and Droones began to notice each other again, but with renewed suspicion.

"You may not trust one another," said Sundry, turning around when he came within a few steps of the summerhouse, "but the real reason you needed me to find this box is that you've lost the ability to do it yourselves." *Or believe that you have,* he thought. "There must be objects belonging to each of you in here, and each of your abilities are wrapped up in them— locks of hair, pieces of clothing, and jewelry." He could see what they had intended now, and—in a flash and so clearly that it startled him—see the collection of things in the box he had slung over his shoulder.

"There you have it, Mr. Moss," said Charles, who stood in the bow of his boat. "Now you understand how anxious we are."

"Aside from my own natural skepticism, *Mr.* Normell," said Sundry, whose natural skepticism was almost overwhelmed by something like a vision of these people lining up by the stump to retrieve each their own precious, humble object, "I can understand the end," he said, feeling dizzy, "but not justify the means."

"It is not yours to justify—"

"And I have a particular dislike for bullies, by themselves or as a mob." Sundry stood above the people on the shore, which seemed to give him a certain eminence beyond the physical—and perhaps it was more than simply where he stood. But Charles Normell was not accustomed to having his motives questioned or to being disobeyed, and the crowd, too, was both fascinated and frightened by Sundry's defiance.

"If you went suddenly blind," said Charles, "I daresay you would do most anything to retrieve your sight."

"I wouldn't kidnap people or kill songbirds, if that's what you mean. You've imagined yourselves as having some sort of . . . *power*, and that's hard to let go of, I guess. It helps that everyone else around these parts thinks you have it, too." Charles was moving his great bulk out of his boat now, and Mrs. Droone was signaling to one of her kinsmen, but Sundry continued to speak. "But among bullies," he said to the crowd, "power is prerogative, isn't it? And what *you're* not considering is that *these* two— Charles Normell and Bridey Droone—wielded most of it. Don't you see, if no one has it anymore, none of you have to be afraid of *them* anymore."

Charles was hurrying up the bank, and Sundry was mindful of the beating the man had given to one of his own family. But he also knew that fear is never a place of strength, and he took advantage of this discernment by swinging the box by the net in an arc and slinging it over the approaching man's head. Sundry was glad to be rid of it.

The shock of the crowd was obvious. The box landed some yards behind Charles, at Jeffrey's feet, and Sundry was sorry that it didn't burst open. Horrified, Charles stopped his advance; he looked as if he hardly dared turn around. Someone let out a frightened shout. Several people from both sides closed in on the box, and Bridey Droone ordered everyone to stand away from it. Charles himself hurried his bulk back down the bank, but the tall woman had wrestled a rifle from the man behind her and fired a shot in the air. Sundry walked as calmly as he was able toward the summerhouse.

"Someone had better stop him," said Bridey Droone with exacting calm, but no one appeared ready to leave the box. "If anything untoward does happen to what is in that box," shouted the woman, "we had *better* have him and everyone with him!" Sundry worried that she had lost her steely composure and that a bullet in his back was only a moment of panic away. Then the door to the summerhouse shot open, and Maven Flyce stepped out, his face as wide and astonished as Sundry had ever seen it.

Maven halted on the stoop long enough to shout, "He's alive! Mr. Ring is back from the dead!" and with his limbs flailing like a thresher, he tripped down the steps and windmilled past Sundry, screaming, "He's alive! He's alive!"

Sundry himself was startled by this entrance and people in the mob appeared wary and uncertain; they were people expecting the uncanny after all.

"Don't be fools! It's a trick!" shouted Bridey Droone.

Maven Flyce darted about the yard like a frightened animal. Sundry thought it an admirable hysteria. Apprehensively, the crowd watched the man run and several people shied from him when he hovered too close. Truthfully, they seemed more worried about Maven than what Maven was worried about. "Run, run!" he was shouting. "He's alive!"

"Nonsense!" snapped Charles. Bridey Droone raised her rifle, the business end of which wavered as she attempted to train it on the running man.

The door to the summerhouse shot open again, and there stood Burne Ring, like the back side of a hard life. His cheeks were hollow with a day's growth of beard and his eye sockets seemed to blear to the back of his head. His voice, when he spoke, was terrible with disuse. "What have you done with my child?"

If not for his herald, Burne's entrance might not have had the same effect upon the Droones and Normells, but Maven had provided the prime for the ailing man's shocking appearance. The crowd fled, and, with a shout of horror, Maven himself went off, though completely in the wrong direction. Mrs. Droone got a shot off with her rifle—aiming for Burne Ring—but she was struck by someone running by, and the bullet went wide. Burne stalked down the steps of the summerhouse, his arms out to facilitate his balance, his groans lost in the din of the panicked crowd.

Maven darted off alongside the very people he should have been escaping and Sundry realized that to rescue them all, he would have to change tactics.

Charles Normell's attention was divided between the doomful figure of Burne Ring and *the box* as he wrestled for it with one of the Droones. Stepping up to this struggle, Bridey managed two or three glancing blows to Charles's head with the sight end of her rifle before Sundry plowed into her, shoulder first, at a run. The woman, her rifle, and the box made separate splashes in the shallows of the pond. Charles roared angrily. Sundry leaned down, ostensibly to recover the box, and, as the larger man loomed toward him headfirst the young man's fist came up from the level of his boots and took the Normell chief on the end of the nose.

Charles Normell was more accustomed to meting out punishment than receiving it, and, with a look of Maven-like astonishment, he appeared to hover against gravity before his overbalanced weight carried him down like a rock. In an instant, Sundry had the box and was leaping over the man's inert form. Then a real rock almost struck Sundry's head. The crowd had returned, walking dead man or not, and several of them threw stones at the man who was running off with their second sight.

"Where is she?" Burne was moaning. "Where's my child?" A rock whizzed past his shoulder, and another bounced off a nearby tree and caught Sundry in the leg, then another hit him in the back of the neck and half knocked him down. Burne actually bent over to help Sundry up and Sundry thought, in a red-hazed muddle, that he could hear Maven shouting for help.

The ground seemed to shake with the falling of stones. A new shout went up. The shaking, the thumping, was not from stones striking the ground but from hooves, a furious snort, and angry cries from horse and man and elf child.

54. One Fell Sweep

By the accident of contradictory impulses, Cram performed like one of his heroic ancestors, charging and plunging, snorting angrily and whinnying while Robin Oig pulled up on the reins and Melanie Ring thrashed the horse's rear quarters with a switch she had snapped from a pine tree on their way down Dutten Lane.

Robin's oar pitched forward from his shoulder, and he gripped it beneath one arm as they plummeted down the slope toward the pond; wavering in the air, the blade of the oar reached six or eight feet in front of the horse's head like a lance of old. People in the crowd leaped away, but the sweep knocked down one stone thrower, who knocked down several of his companions. Robin could not know how terrifying he was, coming after days of tension and the last minute spent running away from Burne

Ring's convenient specter. To these people the large man on the large horse was simply more bewitchment, not the least for wielding such a strange weapon or for having a manifestly out-of-place little girl clutching the back of his shirt who shouted happy encouragement while waving a pine branch.

In one last effort to overcome their fears, the crowd came forward, clutching at the horse's harness and raising their stone-filled fists. With his impressive brawn, Robin Oig was able to pivot the oar out among them so that they were forced to duck their heads and fall back. The horse leaped forward, stamping and snorting. Releasing the reins, Robin took the oar with both hands. Swinging it over Cram's head, he drove back the mob further still. Without conscious thought or effort, he slipped from the horse's back, Melanie still clinging to his shoulders as he waded into the fiercest resistance. Cram kicked his forelegs to the other side in an effort to find a way out, which way soon revealed itself in all directions as the Normells and Droones dispersed.

Charles Normell, eyes wild with fear, was the last to attack the sailor. Robin poked the man in his broad stomach. Charles fell back, and Bridey Droone tripped over him in her retreat. Charles rolled down the shore, over rocks and tree roots, till he came to the shallows of the pond, where he scrambled into a boat and rowed himself out of harm's way.

Sundry Moss sat up, shaking his head from a rock-induced stupor. The box was in his lap and he was experiencing an uncomfortable realization of the fear and hope invested in that object. The crowd of Droones and Normells had disappeared into the surrounding trees, but he was oddly and awkwardly aware of them all. Before he knew what he was doing, he had a knife from his pocket and was cutting the thin ropes around the metal box. When the last of these had sprung away, he looked up at Robin Oig, who was trudging toward him, and was startled to see that the sailor had two heads.

Melanie Ring peered around the large man's neck—victorious and ex-ultant. "That was some business!" she declared. Then her face grew serious. Her father lay still, against a nearby tree. She slid down Robin's back and touched the ground running.

Sundry had wanted to open the box, for curiosity and other reasons, but he dropped it and scrambled to the wan and withered figure. He set-tled Burne more comfortably against the rough trunk of the tree, though he wondered if it made any difference, now. Still breathing hard from his own exertions, he laid an ear against the man's chest. He opened his mouth wide as he listened. There were cries from people in the woods. Sundry listened carefully for life in Burne Ring and could hear nothing. He pressed his head closer to the smoky clothes and felt nothing. He straightened up to study the man's gaunt face. He touched Burne's neck.

Melanie's shadow fell over them. "Daddy," she said.

Sundry's heart went out of him. The little girl had seemed so happy and exultant; she was so pretty and charming with her dress on backward and Tim Spark's old brogues swallowing up her tiny feet.

"Daddy."

Robin Oig's shadow fell over them. Cram, still skitterish, clumped up uncertainly. The little girl stood with her hands at her sides and her shoulders hunched, as if against a cold rain.

Sundry thought the wind in the trees sounded like a faraway voice.

"What was that?" said Robin Oig.

Sundry glanced up, but the trees were not moving.

"Not yet." Burne's eyes were open, but barely.

"Daddy," said Melanie, but her voice was not altered.

"Is that what you had in mind?" Burne asked Sundry. "Them thinking I was dead?"

Sundry wasn't sure how many more times he could do this. "That was better than anything I had thought of."

Burne Ring almost smiled.

"How you got such a show out of Maven Flyce, I'll never understand," admitted Sundry.

"It wasn't my doing," said Burne between breaths. "I was watching you down by the shore . . . and was about to come out to put the fear of God into them . . . when Maven woke up . . . and went to the front door. He stood there a moment before he saw me at the window."

"I wouldn't have credited him with a plan," said Sundry, shaking his head and thinking that he owed Maven an apology.

It was a beautiful June day, and birds sang from the other side of the pond. Cram nudged Melanie's shoulder, and she stroked his velvet muzzle. "Where *is* Mr. Flyce?" she asked.

"If he didn't get caught in the crossfire or the stampede, he's somewhere over the line," said Sundry, pointing north. He peered past Robin Oig's legs in hopes of seeing the fellow come through the trees. Then he turned his attention to the box.

Abijah Cook arrived about half an hour later with the local constable and half a dozen men on horseback. None of them looked very happy to be riding into Dutten, and their uncertainty was not mitigated by the odd group surrounding Burne Ring's seemingly lifeless body.

"Is he dead?" asked Ab.

"Not yet," said Sundry.

The sheriff got down from his horse and surveyed the clearing between the summerhouse and the pond. He might never have seen that water from this outlook before. He frowned at the man in the boat, then touched the silver box with the tip of his toe. "What's the box for?" he asked.

"Nothing, I guess," said Sundry, who was standing now, rubbing the back of his neck where the rock had stunned him. "It's empty."

The sheriff wanted to know what had happened but was taking his time forwarding the pertinent inquiries. He considered Robin, then looked at the device in the sailor's hand up and down. "*What* in the world have you got there?" he asked. It was an academic question.

55. The Last Time He Saw Several People

Robin Oig was puzzled when he realized that the little girl had not led him to Fiddler's Green. He was more puzzled still when Mr. Moss insisted on putting the disparate and mostly mundane objects from the silver box into the haversack, which hung from the back of Cram's saddle, and insisted that Robin say nothing about them to anyone. The sailor was glad enough to see Abijah Cook and the sheriff with his men but thought they had arrived a little after the fact. They all stood about and peered at the lake. The man in the boat didn't seem to be fishing.

Sundry went looking for Maven Flyce and found the man stalking the path from Droone Acres with great caution, Lillie and Topper calmly walking behind him. Topper had taken a liking to Maven; the gelding nudged Maven in the back and almost knocked him down. Lillie let out a snort of recognition when she caught sight or wind of Sundry.

"Is he gone?" asked Maven Flyce. He watched the woods and the path past Sundry with wide eyes, his cowlick almost with the personality of a dog's ear—cocked for the first signal of danger. "Did he disappear?"

"What?" asked Sundry.

"Is he gone?" said Maven. "Is Mr. Burne's ghost gone off somewhere?"

"You don't have to act frightened anymore, Maven. The sheriff is here."

"What?" said Maven.

"You don't have to pretend to be frightened anymore."

"Pretend?" said Maven.

"I thought you—" began Sundry, but he stopped himself and considered Maven's innocent expression. "Maven, I told you last night that Mr. Burne was still alive."

"Oh," said Maven and the look of fear altered to one of rudimentary amazement. "I forgot."

When quizzed, Maven described a chaotic scene among the Droones. He was astonished. Many of them were packing valuables into wagons and carts and readying themselves to leave. Maven had never seen anything like it. He thought some of them were raising new spells, and he had watched one woman running about in the woods with an armload of household objects. What would Horace say?

Sundry thought that the simplest way for all of them to get out of Dutten and get home was to tell the sheriff and his men no more than they absolutely must.

As it turned out, the men from China village were only too glad to call it a false alarm. There were still shouts in the woods toward Albion and flashes of life above them as Normells returned to their homes with their own plans for departure or survival. The sheriff and his men viewed it all with apprehensive posture and started several times at unexpected shouts from the woods. Behind the summerhouse, Sundry found the chaise and horse that Jeffrey Normell had hired in Vassalboro. When he came back to the shore, the sheriff was looking like a man who wants to leave and isn't very certain how to do it gracefully.

"Do we know what happened here?" asked the sheriff.

"There was a difference of opinion," Sundry admitted. "But I think it's straightened out now."

"You're not from around here, are you?" said the sheriff, as if this fact alone would explain how Sundry came to Dutten Pond. "Come back sometime, and tell me what it's all about," he said. He raised an abstaining hand and added, "Long after it's done."

It was a quiet journey out of Dutten, under escort of the sheriff and his men. Sundry had leisure to be surprised, in retrospect, to see Robin Oig and Abijah Cook and managed to get the most of their story; he would pursue Melanie's later. The man with the oar pondered mightily on what had occurred that morning but didn't seem to get very far with it. He looked from Sundry to the little girl and back again, so that it appeared as if he were shaking his head.

When they got Burne Ring into the open chaise, and Melanie climbed in after, Sundry took the driver's seat and brought the horse around. There was still a sense of peril on the road out of Dutten, and Sundry was glad to come out into the sunlight and onto the main road with the sheriff and his men behind them. On the road to China they passed the southern extremity of Dutten Pond, and the sheriff thought to ask who was out in the boat.

Sundry and his companions lost their escort when they reached the town. The sheriff repeated to Sundry his invitation to come tell him what had happened—in due time. Robin Oig had explained to the men from China what he was doing with a great long oar over his shoulder. The sheriff did not specifically invite Robin back. He and his men lingered on the porch of the local post office and watched the strangers ride out of town.

The nearest railway station was in Winslow, and the six travelers took the northwest road. Halfway there they came to a road pointing south and Abijah announced that he and his horses would be leaving them. "We told you Dutten was a chancy place," he said to Sundry, when he had been thanked profusely.

"I never doubted you," said Sundry, and the young farmer laughed.

"Good luck," said Abijah Cook to Robin Oig as they shook hands. "I bet you're halfway there."

"Do you think?" said the sailor. He watched Ab ride off on Cram, with Bolt on a lead behind. "His father saw a machine at the fair," said Robin. "It moved all by itself," he informed Sundry, though he didn't appear to completely understand what this meant.

"He can build a stone wall," said Sundry.

"I am amazed," said Maven.

Robin Oig decided to head north and west, no matter where Mr. Moss and the elf child were going. Looking at Melanie in broad daylight, Robin wasn't sure she *was* an elf child. Clearly he had reckoned wrongly when he hitched his quest to Sundry Moss.

So they parted company with the sailor outside Winslow.

"You'll want that stuff from the box," said Robin. "You can put it in one of those sacks in the carriage."

"Stuff?" said Maven. "My word! I didn't know there was any!"

"Not at all," replied Sundry. "Take it with you, please, and far away from here." Then Sundry thought, *He might find something in that haversack that he can trade for good directions.*

Robin looked unsure about it all. He frowned, looked at the ground, and kicked at a stone. "Hmmm," he said. "I might find something in it that I can trade for good directions."

Sundry himself frowned and nodded.

Another two miles down the road, they came to a crossroad where stood a weathered sign that said BENTON FALLS.

"That's north, I guess," said Robin, pointing to the right, and with very little ceremony, he took his oar and his haversack and went his separate way. The others watched him go. He walked like a man going somewhere, renewed in his purpose. Someone would ask him what he was doing with that great long oar and he would tell them about Fiddler's Green. The last they ever saw of him was the tip of the oar disappearing down the farther slope of a hill.

"What will he do with it all?" asked Melanie.

Sundry understood that she was speaking of the humble objects found in the silver box and also a few objects that were not so humble, including a gold watch with the initials *C. N.* engraved on its back. "I couldn't say," said Sundry. "If those things harbor all those people's second sight, he's going to be a very smart man."

"I am amazed!" said Maven.

As it happened, they had another parting in Winslow. Maven had taken a great shine to Topper and the admiration appeared to be mutual. It was the cowlicked fellow's honest sadness at leaving the gelding behind that settled Sundry on a plan he had been contemplating since they left China.

"You won't get off the train till you reach Portland?" Sundry made Maven promise.

"My word!" said Maven. "Who'd have thought it?"

"And you'll stay awake?"

"I got quite a nice nap in, back at the house," said the fellow.

"We're going to Brownville," said Burne Ring when the word "Portland" sunk into his head.

"You're going to take your daughter home, Mr. Ring," said Sundry.

"We don't have any home," said the father.

"The Sparks are *her* home," replied Sundry, and Burne did not argue.

"Home is where your hat is," declared Maven. Horace had said this once. Of course, Maven didn't wear a hat, and he tapped the top of his head when he said this as if he were just now realizing it.

Once they had their tickets, Sundry took his companions to a restaurant for a large breakfast, and Maven was even able to obtain (with Horace McQuinn–like efficiency) some small beer for Burne Ring's specific thirst. Melanie had never eaten in a restaurant before and she looked almost as surprised by it all as Maven. Burne ate little or nothing, but everyone else discovered a hearty appetite.

Sundry saw them onto the train. Melanie looked uncertain when she realized that he was not traveling with them back to Portland.

"I'm here," announced Maven.

By the time Sundry was back on the platform, looking in through the window, the little girl was asleep next to her father. Burne sat back, his head up, his eyes staring coldly into the middle distance. Sundry signaled to Maven that he must stay alert, and Maven, misunderstanding him, checked his cowlick, as if it might have disappeared. Then he smiled and nodded.

"Don't get off the train!" shouted Sundry.

Maven might have put the window down, but instead he put his face next to the glass and shouted in reply. "I'll be riding backward!" He pointed at his shoulder and then at the front of the train behind him.

Sundry nodded. When the train was gone, he went into the station and wired the Sparks that the Rings and Maven Flyce were coming home. He was amazed.

He was tired but would ride some more before finding a roadside inn, where he might bed down and sleep. He trotted Lillie out of town, leading Topper and taking them south toward Vassalboro.

The fields were green, the Kennebec was broad and blue. It was a beautiful June day. Riding the country lanes he was filled by the songs of birds.

BOOK FOUR
SMALL ENDS UNDONE

(June 14–15, 1897)

56. The Mantel Watch
(June 14, 1897)

Just north of Jackman Station, about twenty or thirty miles from the Canadian border, on a rainy afternoon following a rainy morning, Clarence Nesbit was sorting accounts in the parlor and wondering when the pigs would litter when he looked out the window and saw, coming through the weather atop Heald Hill, the figure of a man with a sack under one arm and a great length of something slung over his shoulder. The solitary walker was on a footpath, well away from the main road, and Clarence thought he must be a little damp around the edges, traipsing the rain and the June grass.

"Evie," he called to his wife. Evie had come up from the cellar just before lunch with two quarts of peach preserves and announced that she was going to bake some pies. Clarence loved peach pie about as much as anything you could carry with a table fork, and he deplored to interrupt her good work, but he called again. "Evie, come look at this."

Evie came into the parlor, wiping flour from her arms with a grain sack towel. It was not usual for Clarence to call to her like that, and she approached the desk where he sat with curiosity and a little dread that he had bad news about what they owed.

"Who is that?" asked Clarence. The figure descending Heald Hill was almost to the point where he would disappear behind the near rise.

Evie squinted through her glasses, then squinted over them. "What's that he's carrying?" she asked in reply.

Then the figure did disappear, though the upper length of whatever the man was carrying continued to bob in sight above him.

"It's not Charlie Pintner?" Clarence wondered aloud.

"Charlie never walked *that* pace," said Evie.

"It *is* raining."

"He never walked in the rain, either," she said. "Nor walked when he could ride, and he'd wait a week to get one."

"John Beamus?"

"Out here?"

"Grant Goodey?"

"Too broad."

They could see the fellow's head, and then his shoulders. He was a good deal closer now, and they thought they could make out what he was carrying. By the time he reached the front of the Nesbits' farmhouse, where the footpath crossed the track to the main road, Clarence was on the front stoop watching him.

"Kind of *pondy* out there, isn't it?" called Clarence. "You'll need that oar, and a boat and a bale besides, if you follow that path much farther. Goes right down to Coburn Pond and the old landing there." The fellow looked over his shoulder, and Clarence invited him in. "Come out of the rain, and put on a pair of dry socks, if you got them."

The man thought about this, then walked up to the house and laid the oar beside the front steps. The fellow's boots squelched on the hall carpet when he entered, and Evie stood at the pantry door, watching him as he pried them off.

"No, no," said Clarence when the man looked about for a place to hang his coat. "By the parlor fire."

"Much obliged," said the man; those were his first words since entering the farmhouse.

"Come in, come in," said Clarence. He led the way to the parlor and swung a chair around for the man to settle his large frame. The fellow politely hesitated, considering his damp backside, but Evie came in with an old flour sack to put beneath him.

"I put the kettle on," she said. "You're too early for peach pie; but I baked bread this morning, and it's still warm."

The man blinked and nodded. Evie frowned at her husband, but more from curiosity than outright disapproval.

"Clarence Nesbit," said the husband. "This is my wife, Evie."

The stranger shook Clarence's hand and said, "Robin Oig."

"You look like you're going somewhere with that oar," said Clarence.

"Fiddler's Green," said Robin.

Clarence straightened in his seat and did his best not to look astonished.

"Is that up by Moose River?" wondered Evie.

"No," said Clarence with a short laugh. "I don't think it's up Moose River."

"Fiddler's Green," she said.

"Yes, ma'am," said the sailor, for it was plain to them he represented that breed.

"Is that where you hail from then?"

The man took a deep breath and weighed his answer before issuing the following statement. "Fiddler's Green, ma'am, is a form of paradise, that is, heaven, that is, anyplace that won't starve you, burn your hide, or freeze parts that you might be needing in port. Fiddler's Green, they say, takes some wandering to find, and there's only one way of knowing it. Throw an oar over your shoulder, take that oar with you wherever you go, and wherever you go, you go as far from the sea as the sea will allow (when you leave the sea, you'll *find* the sea if you go far enough, if you take my meaning), and you roam with that oar till you come to a place where they ask to look at it, and they peer at it, and they consider it, and they ask you what it is. And then you've found it."

"Goodness' sakes!" she said. "What could *that* be?"

"Fiddler's Green," he said with conviction. He looked to Clarence.

Evie was a little wide-eyed.

Clarence nodded and waved a hand. He had heard of Fiddler's Green—there had been a song that someone sang, years before—but he had never met anyone who believed such a place existed, and certainly not anyone who was looking for it with an oar over his shoulder. "You're heading north then," said Clarence.

Robin Oig nodded. The guest had come from farm stock himself, they soon discovered, and he could talk great sense on the subject, so that they began to wonder, before he thanked them for tea and a sandwich and said he must be moving on, if they had heard him right after all.

But in the hall, once he'd got his boots on again (wincing a little as his dry socks squelched against the wet leather) and shouldered into his coat and lifted his sack, Mr. Oig looked out into the rain and looked relieved to see the oar leaning against the house. "I hope it was all right to leave it out there," he said.

"An oar means to get wet," said Clarence.

"It'll get wet today," said Evie. "I wish we could save it all up for August when it gets droughty."

"Don't you have a well?" asked Robin Oig.

"Well," said Clarence, "we do. But it doesn't last the summer." He pointed down past the eastern corner of the house.

"You want to dig over that way," said the sailor. He pointed in the other direction. "About six or eight yards this side of that oak tree."

"How do you know that?" asked Clarence.

"I couldn't tell you," he said. "It just sort of came to me. My oar has been leaning toward water these days."

Clarence and Evie exchanged glances.

The sailor thanked the Nesbits again, took up his haversack and his great long oar, and went out into the rain. He seemed to study the weather for a moment, squinting at the dark sky and the wet. He waved when he was up the track some yards, heading for the main road.

"Goodness' sakes!" said Evie.

"You never know, do you?" said Clarence.

"I certainly didn't when I got up this morning. This side of the oak tree!"

"What do you think?" said Clarence. He leaned out into the rain and looked west. "Should I try it?"

"What, dig a hole over by the oak tree?"

"He seemed pretty sure."

"Yes, his oar leans toward water."

"I never did hear of a sailor who could dowse," said Clarence.

"I never did hear such nonsense, but I suppose you won't sleep soundly till you've dug up those oak roots and made an ugly hole in the yard."

Clarence laughed. She knew him too well. "I don't suppose I will," he admitted. "It was you who brought it up."

Evie shook her head, made a noise, and went into the parlor to clean up after their unexpected guest. Clarence looked after the man, but he was gone; then he leaned out into the rain again and looked over at the oak tree.

"Clarence?"

"Yes."

"Clarence?"

"What is it?"

"Since when have you a gold watch?"

"Since when have you lost your mind?" he replied with a laugh.

"I mean it!"

"A gold watch." Clarence shut the front door and wandered into the parlor. His wife held something golden in the palm of her hand.

"It has your initials," she said.

"What?"

"*C. N.* Look!"

Clarence peered over her outstretched hand, then gingerly lifted the gold watch from her palm.

"It sure does appear, doesn't it," he said.

"Wasn't his name Robin?"

"Where did you find it?"

"On the mantel, big as life."

Clarence held it to his ear. "It ticks nicely."

"Do you suppose he left it?"

"Who else?"

"But did he mean to? Why would he leave a gold watch?"

Clarence held the timepiece to his ear again and shook his head. "I couldn't say. I'd better harness up the rig and go after him."

"In this weather?"

"What else?"

"I'll get your slicks. Your boots are in the pantry closet."

Evie was a little worried when Clarence didn't show before evening. She had liked their unexpected guest, though she thought him odd, but as the hours passed she began to wonder if *odd* wasn't somehow *sinister*. Several times she thought she heard something and went to the door, and finally she tried to keep her mind occupied and her hands busy by baking that peach pie.

Clarence came in when she wasn't looking or listening for him, and her heart jumped.

"Goodness' sakes, Clarence!" she shouted from the kitchen. "Where have you been?"

"Everywhere and all about," he called from the hall.

She met him in the pantry and didn't know whether to "get after him" or give him a kiss. "Did you find him?"

Clarence looked the smallest bit distressed. He shook his head and produced the gold watch from his pocket. She could hear it tick against the small noises of their house and the sound of rain upon the windows. "He wasn't so long ahead of me, I didn't think, but he wasn't on the road to Dennistown. I went back the other way and talked to some of the fellows down the mill. They got up a little search party and went out in all directions, but not a bit of him."

"Where did he get to?" she wondered.

"I couldn't say. It's troublesome to lose a fellow that size. Earl Capp and Beanie McKeevy even went to the swamp over to Moose River."

"And nothing."

"Nothing." Clarence shook his head. He held the watch to his ear.

"What'll you do with that?"

"Put it back on the mantel, I guess, and keep it wound against the day he comes back for it."

"Odd, it having your initials."

"It is odd. It gives me a queer feeling carrying it." She nodded, but he didn't think she understood. "It is odd," he said again. He shook his head and went into the parlor, dripping. He gave a couple of turns to the stem of the watch and set it back on the mantel. He checked his back end, and when he decided that he wasn't too wet, he settled himself onto the settee.

"Fiddler's Green," said Clarence to himself. "I hope he finds it."

"What's that?"

"I'll have some pie when it comes out of the oven."

57. Men with Little Motive
(June 15, 1897)

Mr. Christopher Eagleton had not intended to walk Spruce Street on his way to the residences of his two long-standing friends Mr. Matthew Ephram and Mr. Joseph Thump, but his feet had (seemingly of their own will) veered in the direction of Mister Walton's home and the scene of that recent event so famous in the annals of the Grand Society. Eagleton was in fact thinking about the day of the wedding and the ceremony itself, the letter that he had received that morning like a dowsing rod pulling him toward the habitation of its writer.

Eagleton was tall, and his legs were long; he walked at an admirable pace, his hands clasped behind him, his elbows out, his head erect. He walked with such a brisk step that whenever something warranted more leisurely attention, he usually found that he had walked past the object of his interest and must *back up*, as it were, to look at it more closely, and so it was that morning when he passed a thoughtful-looking, darkly mustached fellow in an elegant gray suit. The man stood with his back to the street, perusing a letter, which he held out nearly at arm's length.

It was the distance between the paper and the man's nose that first struck Eagleton as familiar; countless times he had seen Ephram reading the *Eastern Argus* at that exact remove. The gray suit and the handsome gray hat, worn at the most proper angle, also put Eagleton in mind of his friend, and the dark mustaches finished the resemblance so uncannily that Eagleton turned his head, keeping to his excellent velocity, as he passed this fellow and forthwith ran into something broad and solid.

"Good heavens!"

"I do beg your pardon!"

"Hmmm?"

"Gentlemen!"

"How careless of me!"

"Are you injured?"

"Hmmm?"

"Let me help you up!"

"Eagleton!"

"I beg your pardon?"

"Thump!"

"Hmmm?"

"Ephram! Thump!"

"How extraordinary!"

"Once again our paths coincide with uncommon exactness!"

"My word! I couldn't have said it better!"

"Oh, I'm sure you could!"

"Not at all!"

"Good heavens, Thump! Let me help you up!"

"Oh, yes! My letter. No. This is addressed to you, Eagleton."

"Thank you, Thump. I must have dropped it."

"I couldn't help but see that it was from our chairman himself."

"It is indeed," said Eagleton. Truthfully, he felt the smallest bit guilty in having received a letter from Mister Walton, as if that honor might have been better bestowed upon one of the other charter members. "I believe it was intended for all of us, certainly," he added.

"I was going to say the same about the letter he sent to me," admitted Ephram, who had been feeling a mix of emotions quite similar to those of Eagleton.

They engaged in this dialogue, all the while helping Thump to his feet and dusting him off, and did not observe the man who walked toward them on Spruce Street with two horses in tow.

"I have had similar communication from Mister Walton," Thump was saying, "similarly communicating to us all."

"How very communicative of him!" declared Eagleton.

"A more thoughtful and gracious chairman could not be had!" intoned Ephram.

"That's very good, Ephram."

"Thank you, Eagleton."

"They had extraordinary weather on their voyage."

"Did they?"

"Not unlike what we were experiencing, in fact."

"Extraordinary!"

Eagleton nodded. "Three very sunny days in a row."

"Mister Walton was quite precise as to the moment of their arrival," said Ephram. He referred to his letter, once he had separated it from Eagleton's. "*And* also the times of several salient events as they sailed."

"It will not surprise you to hear me say that it doesn't surprise me."

"It won't surprise you, then, that it doesn't."

"Not at all."

Thump made a sound that seemed to indicate some penetrating thought. It was a slight variation from his typical "hmmm," and Ephram and Eagleton were interested in its motive. Thump appeared to be considering his beard, and his fellow Moosepathians also peered into that remarkable brush, thinking that he had perhaps discovered something unusual there, when he looked up and said in his deep tones, "I, too, am not surprised. But I think I speak for us all when I say that a lack of astonishment in no way indicates that his perpetually gracious behavior is in any way or manner taken for granted."

"Bravo, Thump!"

"Ever in the fore!"

"It doesn't surprise me!"

"Not at all!"

By this critical juncture in their colloquy they had continued not to observe the man with the two horses, though he stood on the street but a few paces away from their earnest and enthusiastic group.

"The tides in Halifax are quite extreme," said Thump. "According to our chairman."

As one, and without any apparent destination in mind, the gentlemen of the club advanced west on Spruce Street, and the man with the two horses fell in just behind them. To the people they met, this fourth man appeared a member of their little group, as much for the pleasure he manifestly took in their company as for his physical proximity. When the party slowed before the Walton home on Spruce Street, the larger horse in the fourth man's keeping nudged Thump's shoulder with her muzzle.

"I beg your pardon," said Thump.

"I'm sure it was nothing," said Eagleton.

The fishmonger came down the street, his own lazy mare plodding the hard-packed way in half a doze. The horses greeted one another with small, friendly sounds and the monger touched his hat to the man holding the reins of the dark mare and the gelding. The three well-dressed gentlemen in top hats were very taken with the Federal style brick house behind the wrought-iron gate and up the walk. The fishmonger knew that no one had been at home there the last few days, and he rattled his little dray past and continued down the street.

He was a little way down a knoll in the street when he heard a voice come up from behind him.

"Mr. Moss!"

And another: "Good heavens!"

And a third: "Hmmm?"

From Mister Tobias Walton
Halifax, Nova Scotia,
June 9, 1897

Dear Sundry,

The Manitoba *made Halifax this morning, and Phileda and I wasted no time in reporting to the government offices for news of recent English steamers in hopes of locating Victor. No word of him has reached this city, however, though the* Gawain *is expected from Portsmouth (England) in the next day or so, and Phileda says with great confidence that "this is the boat." I think I will be more surprised than she if it isn't.*

Halifax is a wonderful place filled with a gracious and warm-hearted people. It has, perhaps, a touch more of the Old World about it than our own Portland and so evokes a little mystery for an American. Phileda and I walk the wharves, waiting for Victor's ship or word of him, listening to the jumble of languages and watching the variation of country and continent represented in the faces of sailors and merchants, and think ourselves in a good book. You will excuse my blush if I admit that it is a pretty good chapter while Phileda is on my arm.

Though the short voyage from home to here was necessarily dotted with thoughts of my nephew and who he must be and how he might fit into our lives, the trip was not without moments when all matters except those between Phileda and myself were forgotten. We have discovered how we can soak up one another's worries without really suffering ourselves from what we have taken on. Thus we shoulder one another's infirmities and troubles without half knowing it. An arch is stronger by far than a free-standing column. (And an old romantic who has spent several days with his romance waxes more poetic by far than he ought to.)

I hope you are not enjoying your independence from my company too much. Phileda and I are both convinced that your part in Victor's adaptation to our home and ways will be invaluable, as is your continued friendship.

Toby Walton

P.S. Please stay well and away from that "keg" business, whatever it was about. I have had a troubled mind about it.

Toby

58. Passport and Verification

"Well, God rest the man," said Mabel. "He did ask to be remembered to you."

Sundry had yet to take a seat at the kitchen table of the Faithful Mermaid. Standing at the counter with his arms folded before him, he had said very little since hearing that Burne Ring had died in the night. Sundry had ridden into Portland that morning, paid a visit (quite by chance) with the members of the club, and attended to several duties at the Walton home before walking to the Faithful Mermaid, his riding side being a little sore after some days of unaccustomed miles in the saddle. He hadn't really known the man and hadn't really liked him for some of the time that he had known him, but he was sad to hear that Burne Ring had passed away.

Melanie sat at the table with Tim, contemplating lunch. She had hardly left her father's side since they returned to Portland five days ago. Burne had taken sick again as they trained into Portland, and Mr. Flyce had carried the man to a carriage and paid the driver with the money Mr. Moss had given them. Mrs. Spark had hugged Melanie and cried when the little girl appeared at the back door with her dress on backward and Tim's old brogues on her feet. Thaddeus himself had looked uncertain about his emotions, blinking and nodding and saying, "Well, now, it's best you're back, isn't it. No doubt about it. You can't make room for someone without feeling something's missing when they're gone. No, it's best you're back, and no doubt."

When Burne Ring was upstairs again, looking frail and deathlike, Thaddeus stood by the bed for some time with Melanie, one large hand over her shoulders. When Mabel came in with a cloth and a bowl of cool water and a bottle of small beer, saying she would stay with the little girl, the burly taverner leaned down and kissed Melanie on the top of the head before he left the room.

"You're awfully good to us, Mrs. Spark," said Melanie.

"Hush, now," said the woman, who was still at the high end of her feelings. "It's what family does," she had said with her chin up.

For the first time in her short life Melanie Ring had a home and a family and people who would take care of her, yet, as she sat there in the kitchen of the Faithful Mermaid on the morning of Mr. Moss's return, the only family she had ever known was gone. She had never been left alone in the sickroom; Mr. and Mrs. Spark and Davey and the girls all had taken their turns sitting with her. Bobby was too young for such a duty, and Tim—younger still—stood at the periphery of Melanie's consciousness during those days, looking strange and confused.

Mr. and Mrs. Spark both had been there when Burne Ring's too-short candle had blown out. Melanie rose from her chair and leaned over her father, listening, and when Thaddeus suspected and then knew that Burne had died, he took the little girl's hand. Mrs. Spark breathed as if something heavy were on her chest, but no one cried, just then. There was something that Melanie almost said to them, but she held it back.

Standing in the kitchen that morning, Sundry Moss knew none of these details, but he could imagine most of them. "Horace and Maven aren't in the tavern, are they?" he asked Davey Spark when the taverner's son came into the kitchen with some empty mugs.

"Haven't seen them," said Davey.

"When you do," said Sundry, "would you tell Maven that his horse is over on Spruce Street?"

This intelligence merited an explanation, which explanation merited the whole tale of Dutten Pond as Sundry had lived it. The Sparks came in and out (mostly in) and caught what they could of the narrative in the course of their duties, and Mrs. Spark let a pie burn. They might have been an entire clan of Flyces for their honest amazement. Tim let out several exclamations, one or two of which his mother would have objected to under the spell of less intense curiosity.

"I could hardly credit it when Melanie told us," said Mabel.

"Maven didn't say a word," said Thaddeus.

"I'm not sure as he quite took it in," said Sundry.

"Ben Gun should hear it!" said Thaddeus.

Sundry almost laughed. He had yet to feel wary about the old penny dreadful writer. Mabel laid an overflowing plate on the table and ordered him to sit and eat. Thaddeus heard a call from the tavern, and he and Davey went out to tend the custom. The Spark girls were herded back to their chores, and Mabel turned her back on the table to see to tomorrow's stew.

Timothy had fallen to, but Melanie had yet to address her lunch. She was in one of Annabelle's old dresses, her lengthening hair in a blue bow. Sundry tried to see Mailon in the little girl's face and realized that she was returning his gaze.

"I don't think he had a very happy life," she said quietly. The thought was meant for his ears only, and if anyone else did hear, he or she did not respond.

Sundry held his gaze, a fork poised above his plate for some moments before he thought to set it down. "I think," he said, and he thought a little more before saying, "I think that everything he was ever happy about was rolled up and folded away in you." He picked up his fork again and considered his plate. He was still thinking.

Tim glanced from Sundry to Melanie and back again before his mother gave him a look signifying that he should tend to his own business. Her own ears were probably not shut, however.

"Some people do have trouble being happy, it seems," said Sundry, almost as if he were thinking out loud. "The rest of us had better be thankful. And it seems to me that you owe it to your father to be just as happy as you can." He punctuated this opinion with a squinted eye and a shake of his fork.

Sitting in the kitchen of the Faithful Mermaid with the Spark family about her and with the sturdy presence of Mr. Moss before her, Melanie Ring was not *un*happy and perhaps had felt guilty for it. Something in Mr. Moss's injunction lifted the burden of self-censure from her small shoulders, and the lightening of that weight prompted a lightening in her expression. She would say to someone else, years later and in troubled circumstance, "We owe it to one another to be happy when we can."

Or, as Mister Walton would once append to a similar thought, "Why else face trouble?"

Sundry himself felt a little lighter, and for some reason (and for the first time) he was able to recall dancing with Priscilla Morningside without also knowing a pang of overriding sadness.

"Your friends from the Moosepath League were by the other day," said Mabel, and she began to tell of Messrs. Ephram, Eagleton, and Thump's latest visit.

Sundry listened happily as he turned his attention to his meal.

"Do you want to go over to the Oaks?" asked Timothy. He and Melanie were out in front of the Faithful Mermaid, kicking a can back and forth on the sidewalk and stepping aside when anyone came walking by.

Melanie looked interested but uncertain. She squinted up at the third floor of the old tavern and located the window of the room where her father had died. He wasn't there anymore—or his body wasn't; someone had come and taken it away. There was to be a funeral on Wednesday, and several people, including Mr. Moss and the Sparks, had pitched in for the expenses. Before the arrangements were finalized, the Moosepath League would help defray costs, and even Burne Ring's old employer and master mason would show up with flowers for the hearse and a ten-dollar bill for the deceased man's only surviving child.

Melanie didn't know if she should be out in the street playing with Timothy. Perhaps she should be in her own room, alone and contemplating what it all meant. Then again, she recalled what Mr. Moss had said.

Timothy's mom came out, and it was strange to see the woman at the front of the tavern, standing on the sidewalk with her hands on her hips. "Melanie Ring!" she said. "You remember how you're dressed and how you're expected to act." She shook a finger, but there was nothing angry or even stern about her manner. Mabel Spark was simply adamant in her sense of propriety. "You can't climb trees in a dress. And no clambering around on wharves and roofs."

"Mom!" said Tim.

"Timothy Spark!" she returned, but only followed this declaration of her youngest child's name with a silent expression of precise warning. "Melanie?"

"Yes, Mrs. Spark," said the little girl.

Mabel heaved a large sigh. Before she went back inside, she took the little girl's face in her round, warm hands and kissed her on the forehead. Timothy looked more upset than Melanie did. He kicked the can against the wall of the tavern with a resounding clatter.

"You can go if you want," said Melanie. She looked resigned and shrugged philosophically.

"You want to see a secret?" he asked, looking around, as if desperate and nearby enemies might be keening their ears.

She nodded, and he made a gesture to indicate that she should follow him. She really did try to be a little more ladylike and not run so fast, but it was hard to fight the old habit of dodging pedestrians and skipping through the traffic on the streets. When she leaped over a sleeping dog, she glanced back to be sure that she wasn't being watched, then slowed her pace and made Timothy slow down so that she could keep up with him.

When they came to the shack behind the old molding mill at the end of Pleasant Street, she stared up after her friend as he scrambled onto the roof. "I'm not supposed to go up there," she said when he looked back at her.

Timothy signaled that she should wait for him, and she backed away from the building so that she could see him skittering the rooftops and leaping the tiny places between the tightly packed buildings of the working district. She lost sight of him after a moment and waited, feeling conspicuous by herself and in her girl's clothes.

She heard him before she saw him. She had taken to watching a crew that was building a brick wall across the way and was turned in the other direction when his unmistakable hop and jump came down the slope of the molding mill roof and banged on the tar paper shed. Melanie was astonished when she saw what he was carrying. Timothy held the boys' shirt and trousers, the socks and beaten brogues out to her, smiling as if he had counted coup against their bravest foe. He was out of breath.

She did not take them at first. She only stared at them and held her hands behind her back as if they might sting her. It was only when the happiness began to fade from Tim's face that she reached out and took the clothes.

"You can change into them in that old cellar hole beneath the soda factory," he said, but not quite as triumphantly as he might have suggested it a moment before.

She nodded. Perhaps the only thing more fun than running the roofs and wharves as a boy was running the roof and wharves as a girl in boys' clothes. Her face lit as doubt left her.

"I'll stand guard for you," he said, and he blushed a little.

Half an hour later they were racing above Danforth Street, climbing one of the taller roofs for one of their favorite views of the harbor, when she heard it again, though the name spoken by that voice was not entirely clear. Melanie stopped, and Tim's pace was arrested by the sound of her faltering steps. He turned around just above her on the roof and said, "What is it?"

"Did you hear that?" she asked.

"The whistle?" he said. There had been a toot from the harbor, but that had been some time and a roof or two ago.

She shook her head.

"What was it?" he asked.

"I don't know," she said, though in fact, at that very moment, she did. She knew that he couldn't have heard it and that it would have been wrong side to if he had. She shook her head again and laughed.

"We'll have to get you a hat," he said. "When your hair gets longer."

"Race you!" she shouted, and she laughed and she sped ahead of him up the roof as if there were clouds on her feet, and for the first time ever, she beat him to the top.

She didn't know where the voice had come from, but she did know to whom it belonged. It might have come from the air above or the street below. It might have come from inside her. All this would have seemed contradictory, or even paradoxical, if a six-year-old street waif, an orphan, and an only child with a brother and a family and a home could have understood such a thing.

It wasn't her poor dead mother, and it wasn't her father calling from his deathbed. It wasn't anyone else. Someday it might call out her real name, but whatever it said and however often it spoke, she would never have to look over her shoulder again.

It was a beautiful June day. The sadness caught up with her a little when she and Tim sat at the top of the roof and they began to count sails in the harbor. He seemed to know it and did most of the counting, and when he was done, he suggested nothing else but sat with her in the sun and the breeze. He said nothing and did not look at her when tears came down her cheeks.

Mr. Spark had always said that Tim was born with philosophy.

EPILOGUE
HARD BUSINESS
June 16, 1897

I can't understand it! It's been two weeks and nothing in the papers." Harold Trowbridge crouched his great shoulders over the scatter of journals on his desk, and when he raised his head and fixed his gaze on the young man at the door, he had the appearance of some powerful animal preparing to lunge. The window shades were pulled and the mahogany shelves and the black leather upholstery of the chairs commanded the room with their hues, the shade behind Trowbridge glowing with the afternoon sun so that the gray-haired man was almost in complete silhouette. "You tell me you went to Harbottle and engaged him to have the barrel delivered."

"Yes, Mr. Trowbridge." The young man did not blink.

"Yes. I know you did, as I went to talk with him yesterday."

The young man already knew this but said nothing.

"You paid him," said the older man.

"Harbottle? Yes."

"And he sent two men to deliver the keg of rum."

"I watched them carry it in the back door and come back out without it."

"What does that mean?" snapped Trowbridge.

"It means, yes, I saw them deliver it."

"Then say so! Don't be smart when you answer my questions."

"I beg your pardon, sir," said the young man. He looked anything but contrite.

Trowbridge knew he meant none of it, but the young bull always did what was asked of him. The problem here was understanding what went wrong or who was lying. "You called the police from that tavern you haunt."

"The Weary Sailor, yes." The younger man's expression was not easy to read in the relative gloom. "I saw the police at Walton's house myself."

"And they didn't know who you were when you called."

Apparently the young man had not been very impressed with the previous outburst regarding his answers; he only shrugged.

Trowbridge let out a low growl and shifted in his chair. "I can't understand it. Nothing in the papers. This Walton has more pull in high places than I would have credited. Not so much as a mention or a vague hint of anything untoward on Spruce Street that day. What's that man of his called?"

"His servant, there at the house? Sundry Moss."

Trowbridge grunted. "Maybe something can be done with him."

"Disgrace his servant?"

"To the devil with his servant! Pay the blackguard to disgrace his employer!" Trowbridge watched the young man's face—a broad countenance that may have been deemed likable to those who considered such things, a wide sly mouth with white teeth, beneath a nose that had been broken once or twice, and slate blue eyes. Those eyes looked doubtful, and the mouth took a skeptical twist.

"You don't think so," said Trowbridge. This might have been meant as a warning (or a threat) or might have been an honest query into the opinion of one servant about another.

"No one is going to pay me to disgrace *you*, Mr. Trowbridge," said the young man.

"Are you saying you could?" This was more obviously a warning (or a threat).

"I'm saying they couldn't pay me to try," feinted the man by the door.

"And who do you mean by 'they'?"

The young man did not blink. The mild expression never left his face. His voice was steady and certain. "Everyone else, I suppose."

Trowbridge leaned back and folded his hands over his stomach.

"I think they're in with the police," said the young man. "I think this *Moose*path League has been working to get control of the wharfside and are just the sort of men, high enough up, to monkey with the law and share the wealth."

"Controlling the wharfside," said Trowbridge.

"They *did* for Adam Tweed and if you can believe the papers, Walton himself pulled the trigger. Just last month everyone was talking of Mr. Thump and how he walked right into the Weary Sailor one morning, demanding to see Fuzz Hadley and how Thump warned Hadley off with Hadley's men standing about and this Thump sipping tea all the while."

Trowbridge had seen Mr. Thump and had difficulty picturing this. Only those down in the wharf district, or with connections down there, had even heard of this confrontation; among those in the know, only two people knew that it wasn't Mr. Thump at all, but his near twin Thaddeus Spark—and one of these was Mabel Spark.

"You did *some*thing wrong," pronounced the older man.

"*You* haven't paid me yet," returned the man at the door.

Trowbridge opened a lower drawer of his desk and pulled out a little strongbox. There was no lock or combination, but only a hasp that he flipped to open the lid. He dipped into the contents, came out with a few small bills, and tossed these on the desk.

"Much obliged," said the young man, and he snatched up the money.

"I will expect results the next time."

Counting the bills, the young man said, "Results are only as good as the plan ahead of them, Mr. Trowbridge."

"Get out of here," said Trowbridge.

The man at the door put the bills away, and from a back pocket he produced a brown cap, which he waved in salute. "Always a pleasure, sir," he said, and there was no reason to doubt him. Mike Peat prized the extra cash and enjoyed the perilous walk in the company and conversation of Harold Trowbridge. The *old man* was just that to Peat, but a force to be reckoned with nonetheless, and a physically powerful one with a short fuse and a full charge. Mike Peat felt a little stronger and a little happier every time he left that room unscathed, which was more often than not these days.

Trowbridge had already, and ostensibly, turned to other matters before Peat closed the door between them. The young man looked up and down the hall, then walked to the front of the house, glancing past doorways as he went, as if searching for some particular thing or person.

"Mr. Peat," came a voice. The old man's daughter stood halfway up the broad front stairs, looking indecisive.

"Miss Trowbridge," said the young man quietly.

Alice Trowbridge came a step or two down the stairs and chanced a look over the banister and into the hall. She was well past her majority, Peat knew, but not past her father's grip. Her features were plain—her nose a little too fine and her jaw not quite fine enough—but her complexion was flawless, and her nearly white-blond hair made for an abundant fall past her shoulders. Her figure, too, was plain enough, to Peat's way of thinking, but there was something precise in the way she dressed that sparked his interest and curiosity. "What did he say?" she asked him.

Peat walked around the foot of the stairs to put himself out of sight of Trowbridge's door. "He's a little put off that Walton's name hasn't shown up in the court news."

"Does he know what was in the keg?"

"How could he?" Peat said quietly. "Who's going to tell him? I don't think Ipse is going to take your father's money, then tell him he took someone else's to cross him. That was the clever thing, of course; anyone else would have paid him *not* to deliver it at all."

"He would have known if it hadn't been," she said. She was undoing the little drawstring purse that hung at the sash of her dress.

"Maybe." Peat nodded. "You must admire this Walton fellow. Or is it simply the pleasure of fouling your father's traps?"

"That's my business."

"You're not so afraid of the old man, are you."

"*You're* not afraid of him."

"Harold Trowbridge?" said Peat like the edge of a boast. "He scares me to death," he finished with all seriousness. "But as my dear mother always told me—" and here he put on the burr of the old country— "'A man afraid of heights had better find a mountain to climb.'"

"Here is your money," she said, and with a quick glance at the hall, she thrust several bills at him.

"Ach!" he said with a wave of his hand and his mother's cadence still in his throat. "I couldn't take it."

"What does that mean?" she hissed. "Mr. Peat, you had *better* take it!"

"Not for anything I enjoyed so much."

She thrust the bills at him again, but he turned her hand aside with an odd smile. She was ready to say something else; but a sound from the hall warned her, and she tucked the money in a pocket just as her father's large gray head came past the banister.

"What's going on here?" demanded the man. He was taller than Mike Peat and seemed to his daughter as tall as she, though she was three steps up the flight of stairs.

"I was just telling this . . . man here," said Alice quickly, "that he was to employ the service entrance."

Trowbridge looked from one to the other of them, suspicion coiling like a snake inside him.

"It seemed the shortest way," said Peat with a shrug.

"Get out," said Trowbridge, and when Mike Peat offered to walk around him to the back of the house to the service entrance, the older man threw open the front door and said, "Get out!" with just a little more anger and a little less volume.

Peat did his best to leave gracefully; but his stride had a hitch in it, and his back was stiff with the expectation of a blow or a kick. He caught a heel on one of the granite steps and almost tripped, recovering himself just a little as he made the gate and walked down the sidewalk. He had not left unscathed after all.

Trowbridge shut the door and fixed his attention on his daughter.

"Thank you," she said, which appeared to turn his immediate displeasure, if not his overriding suspicion. He watched her till she turned and went upstairs.

Alice did not hear him leave the hall, and she did not look around to see if he was still standing at the foot of the stairs. She had been careless, and he had very nearly caught her handing money to Michael Peat. For all his size, her father could walk like a cat. In her room she felt out of breath and dizzy. She had been careless. If he ever discovered how she had foiled his attempt to discredit the chairman of the Moosepath League, she might finally learn the limit of his anger. Several weeks ago she had been responsible for lighting the spark of her father's malice for the members of that club simply by an innocent and unmotivated comment about them (inspired by a laudatory newspaper item). It was his scorn and the vehemence of his reaction that inspired the plan she had been wanting to help her escape this house and its master.

She turned to the mirror above her vanity and considered herself there. What had Mr. Peat been looking at with such interest? She had no illusions about herself. Her father's craggy features and her mother's delicate, lovely face had not produced a beautiful child, but her father's consistent guile and her mother's slow, sad demise had produced a determined one.

She thought she could hear him walking below, and then, startlingly, the door to her room opened and he was standing there. Alice had just been thinking that he wasn't as smart or clever as he thought he was, and now, unexpectedly, she was seeing him as she had when she was a child. She sat very still in the vanity seat and waited for lingering, horrible moments before he spoke.

"Never talk to that man," he intoned. "Never talk to him or to any other business associate that comes into this house."

She blinked at him, and then, stupidly (and long after she should have), she realized that he required an answer. (She could never guess ahead of time whether an answer would mollify him or be judged an impertinence.)

"Yes," she said, but fearing this was not the correct response, she added, "No, I won't."

There was another lingering, horrible moment as he soaked up her uncertainty and fear. He left, and she thought she heard his footsteps in the hall. His unheralded presence at her door, however, was proof enough of how little she could trust to what she *thought* she heard.

She opened the drawer of her vanity, where she kept her mother's picture, and gazed at the pretty face where it lay among the combs and ribbons. She could not remember her mother ever looking like that, only the sickly, frightened expression that watched from the pillow till it grew so sickly that it need be frightened no more.

Alice paled to think of what she planned to do. She gazed at her mother's face so that her anger would chase away fear, though with anger another fear visited her—the fear that, in her anger and in her cleverness, she was more like her father than she cared to admit.

I will turn it to good use, she promised herself, but then there was an unwelcome qualification. *If only to my own good use.* She wondered what the Moosepath League would think to have themselves put to *her* purposes.

Alice went to the window and looked out over Newbury Street. Mr. Peat was long gone. He always went south, toward the waterfront. He could get away from her father, and yet he came back whenever he was called. She wondered why he had turned away the money she owed him for crossing her father.

A solitary walker on the sidewalk caught her eye, and she leaned a little to see past the trunk of the oak. It was her grandfather, the old rake. He hadn't come home last night, and her father would be furious, not the least because Grandfather would simply yawn in the face of his son's fierce objections. She didn't know how the elderly man dared.

Her grandfather disappeared from sight as he wandered up the walk to the front door. She could hear him enter, and she listened for her father's voice, which should momentarily issue from the study. "He's not as smart as he thinks he is," she said to herself. "And he's no more clever than I." She had been working her plans right under his nose, and he hadn't suspected a thing—she hoped.

Something in the window caught her eye, and her sight foreshortened upon a reflection in a single pane. The day darkened briefly beneath a broad cloud, and the ghost of her face, caught in that single pane against the oak before her window, looked in at her and seemed, for a moment, to expunge everything that wasn't of her mother.

Author's Note

Robin Oig, Robin Orge, and even Robin Oar—the name varies, but older denizens of several Maine communities still recall the tales that *their* parents and grandparents told about a quiet, resolute man who marched through their villages and unorganized townships in the latter days of the nineteenth century. By some accounts he was little more than an eccentric and possibly sea-addled sailor, by others a perceptive visitor who found long lost objects and even dowsed a new well for the town of Anson using an oar of seemingly mythic proportions. The further north and west one goes, the stranger and wilder these tales become, till Robin begins to sound like an old world wizard or a mystical Paul Bunyan.

The trail of tales ends abruptly at Jackman Station and its correlation with the history of the League might never have come to light if not for Ms. Judith Stoone of Rock Creek, Ohio. It was while interviewing an old woodsman from Jackman (about the 1914 Moosepathian dust-up with the Engine Gang), that Ms. Stoone first came to suspect the connection between the vanishing sailor (mentioned only in passing) and the man accidentally involved with Sundry Moss, Melanie Ring, and the strange events on Dutten Pond in the summer of 1897. It was fortunate for those who care about the Moosepath's history that a year-long bout with hepatitis did not close the curtain on this insight, and after a period of convalescence, Ms. Stoone finished the legwork for her well-considered monograph, *Oig, Orge, and Oar: What Disappeared from Dutten Pond?*

Sundry Moss, who never did write anything like a journal or a memoir (though there are many of his letters extant), did in latter days tell people that he often wondered what befell the big fellow with the great long oar. It was some years later that an early chronicler of the Moosepath League, Henry Dare, fell into a chance meeting with none other than Maven Flyce and asked the man what he remembered of Robin Oig. "I was so surprised!" was all Maven could summon for answer.

The Nesbit well, some yards from the ancient oak at the old farm in Jackman Station, is still used by the present-day owners. Even in the worst

drought, it has never dried up. The house has only been sold with the stip-
ulation that the gold pocket watch will not leave the parlor mantelpiece,
except for winding, cleaning, or repair. To this day, no one has come to
claim it.

The tale of the Droones and Normells has engendered a lot of puzzle-
ment and even skepticism, but one can hardly recall the behavior of cults
in the twentieth century and be surprised at what might occur among two
close-knit clans in a small nineteenth-century community. There were in
fact some fairly obscure groups that sprang up in Maine (and indeed all
over the country), often centered around clan and kin. Peculiar communities and eccentric groups that isolated themselves from their communities
were often the result of hardscrabble lives in confluence with Victorian
mysticism. Sundry Moss's oft-heard statement that he "never met a story
[he] couldn't add something to," should not put the reader off. This was
one tale he never varied.

A look through the present day directories of Albion and China will
turn up no Droones or Normells. In the past hundred years and more, the
presence of these families and the very foundations of their houses have
been allowed to fade and fall into memory and forest.

The events of June 3 through June 15, 1897 are known (among members
and historians of the Moosepath League) as "the Adventure of Fiddler's
Green," and also "the Adventure of the Midstream Horse" (which, by my
best guess, might refer to Melanie Ring). These days, members of the
Grand Society enjoy remembering it as "the Adventure of the Gentleman's Gentleman."

The first rumbling of the club's next extraordinary experience would
begin (if not actually be heard for what it was) when an agent for Colonel
Cobb's Wild West Show appeared at the Waltons' front door with free
passes as an appreciation for Mister Walton's and Sundry Moss's rescue,
during the previous July, of Maude the bear. The first anniversary of the
meeting of Messrs. Ephram, Eagleton, and Thump with Mister Walton
would prove itself memorable, not the least for their introduction to Al-
bus Crowstairs, the man who (in Sundry Moss's plain manner of speak)
"blew up things." It was this meeting, as well as their run-in with Alice
Trowbridge, that would eventually lead to the Moosepath League's hair-
raising involvement with the Dirigo Tontine (late summer 1897) and so to
the Original Moosepathian Hunting and Fishing Expedition (fall 1897).

But it was the Trowbridge affair that came next, as the disappearance of Alice Trowbridge and a long-awaited telegram from Mister and Mrs. Walton propelled the gentlemen of the club into what has been called "the Missing Mission of the Moosepath League"—but sometimes spoken of, in Moosepathian circles, as "the Adventure of the Wild Westerners" and "the Adventure of the Cloistered Conspiracy."

Someday it may be told.

The writing of a book can be a solitary thing, but I often come blinking out of my study to discover that kind thoughts and encouragement have arrived by post and by e-mail from "Friends of the Moosepath League." Ideally, Mister Walton, Sundry Moss, and the charter members would be here to read them. From all of us to booksellers and readers, book clubs and libraries—thank you. The Moosepath League can be found at www. moosepath.com. I can be reached at vanreid@midcoast.com.

Continued appreciation goes out to my agent, Barbara Hogenson, and to her assistant, Nicole Verity, who field practical matters, dumb questions, and authorial angst with unwavering graciousness and poise.

And much gratitude goes out to Carolyn Carlson, senior editor at the Penguin Group, who has shepherded the exploits of the Moosepath League into print; and also to all the folks at the Penguin Group who have copy edited, designed, and otherwise worked over this book and its five predecessors. Thanks to assistant editor Audra Epstein. Best of luck and many thanks to Lucia Watson.

It's been more than a year—at this writing—since I worked at the Maine Coast Book Shop in Damariscotta, but it continues to be "bookstore central" for me and I would like to thank everyone there, including Susan and Barnaby Porter, Penny and Ewing Walker, Frank Slack, Joanne Cotton, Bobbi Brewer, Lauri Campbell, Tyler Dobson, and Sue Richards for their continued friendship and support. Extra appreciation goes to Kathleen Creamer, Trudy Price (whose marvelous memoir of life on a Maine Dairy Farm, *The Cows Are Out*, is due to be published in the fall of 2003) and those wonderful Waldoborians Jane and Mark Biscoe. I'll be right over for some of that *Hires* root beer!

Thanks to the bookstores, libraries, and organizations that have hosted me this summer and fall (in chronological order)—Machias High School, the Lincoln County Historical Society, the Maine Writers' Conference at Westbrook College, the Kennebunk Free Library, Oxford Books 'n'

Things, Sherman's Bookstore in Boothbay Harbor, Books Etc. in Falmouth, Bookland of Brunswick, Bridgton Books, Devaney, Doak and Garrett in Farmington, the Rockland Public Library, the Falmouth Library, the Owl and the Turtle in Camden, and Nonesuch Books in South Portland.

Continued thanks to author James L. Nelson and his family for friendship and nautical advice and to author Nicholas Dean for the same. As always, thanks to David and Susan Morse.

My gratitude to my family grows in near geometric progression as I grow older—to my parents, to my brother and sisters, and to my terrific nephews and nieces. Thanks to my wonderful in-laws.

But most of all, my gratitude goes to my wife, Margaret Hunter. Without her love and support, not to mention her keen eye for a grammatical misstep and a gifted ear for what is *true*, these volumes would not exist. This is fitting, for they were, first and foremost, written for her. Also under "most of all" are our children, Hunter and Mary, who cannot yet know (but hopefully will someday realize) how, with their mother's sterling example, they inspire me with their generosity and goodness, their curiosity and their laughter, and therefore inspire those very traits as manifested in the hearts and deeds of Mister Walton, Sundry Moss, and the honorable members of *the Moosepath League*.

Dear Reader:

The Saga of the Moosepath League series will continue with more adventures. Please see www.moosepath.com for information on future titles.